a picture worth a THOUSAND WORDS

NICOLE LANE

OMNIFIC PUBLISHING

LOS ANGELES

Omnific Publishing
2355 Westwood Blvd., Suite 506
Los Angeles, CA 90064
www.omnificpublishing.com

First Omnific eBook edition, July 2023
First Omnific trade paperback edition, July 2023
The characters and events in this book are fictitious.
Any similarity to real persons, living or dead,
is coincidental and not intended by the author.

Library of Congress Cataloguing-in-Publication Data
Lane, Nicole.

A Picture Worth a Thousand Words / Nicole Lane – 1st ed.
ISBN: 978-1-623422-76-9

1. Contemporary Romance — Fiction. 2. Hollywood — Fiction.
3. Movie Star — Fiction. 4. Television — Fiction. I. Title
10 9 8 7 6 5 4 3 2 1

Cover and Interior Design by Sweet n' Spicy Designs

Dedication

For Ettie Elese Young

Acknowledgments

As ever and always, thank you to Nicole Jordan.

Thank you to Lori-Anne Cohen, Angela Lopez, and Jamie Grimes for your support and kindness, and your patience when listening to me talk through plotlines.

Chapter 1

Kline Scott

"**B**ullshit! This is bullshit!" Kline cried, slamming down his phone, upsetting everything on the table. Orange juice sloshed over the rim of his glass as he cursed again. "Where do they get this shit, Roland?"

His agent was dabbing madly. His own juice had splashed out over his pants. "These are silk, Kline. These stain. And don't worry about it. It's your name and it's a big bit. True or not."

"I'm not worried about the true or not," Kline growled, "but they've got my kid in it. Why do they think it's all right to do that? It's mine and Nina's mess, not his. This is bullshit." He picked up his phone, swiped to take another look then put it face down on the table again.

"They think it's all right because it sells. Your adoring public can't get enough of this stuff. The only thing fans love more than idolizing their stars on the rise is having a front row seat when that star begins the downwards spiral. People want to know that you're just as miserable as they are. It makes them feel like they understand you."

"I don't care. I don't want my son's picture plastered all over everywhere. I just barely got Nina to agree to stop using him for her mommy-blog fodder. They can say and print what they like about me or his mother, but not him. Do whatever you have to do, Roland, but get the point across. Jack is off limits."

"I'll work on it." Roland gave his inseam one last wipe then rolled his eyes and tossed the crumpled napkin on the plate. "I wouldn't worry about it too much. I mean, Knight opened so well you're already generating Oscar buzz—you're top of the world. You of all people know that means you'll be popping up in the press over and over again. You've got to stay seen. You've got to give the world a storyline they want to read. And speaking of that, how's Kara? Kara is a good storyline. At least until Lone Star opens, she's a great storyline. People love you as a couple."

Kline sighed. "And again, Kara and I were never a couple. And no, we aren't seeing each other. At all. Ever."

"That's not what is says in the blinds, Kline, and you need a date for the Oscars. You're presenting this year, but you're going to be a nominee next year. Use this red carpet as a practice run with someone else who needs the publicity just as much as you do. Kara's a hot property. You might want to reconsider," Roland said, checking his watch. "I have that meeting with Stew in a half hour, so I gotta hit the bricks. Don't forget you have that interview today."

"Isn't that what my assistant is for? Talking alarm clock and calendar? I'm taking Jack to the Oscars," Kline retorted. "Tell Stew I said hello."

"Great idea, Einstein. That'll keep him off Getty. Take a date. Jesus, Kline, go out on a date. You need to be seen. We need to get you into the right relationship. You've shot up in Q factor in the last twelve months, and a lot of that had to do with interest in you and Kara. You single only gets so much press. Anybody can be single."

"I thought staying single was playing the game and I had fucked up my career when I married Nina."

"Early in your career, yeah." Roland dabbed at his trousers again. "You were just getting started, and I think it took years off your trajectory. You needed to be out showing people you were desired, so they'd find you desirable. You're on the rise now, but you've got that messy divorce and custody thing–it takes some of the shine off. You need to be seen with someone who is either America's sweetheart or on the rise to that. J Law's off the market."

Kline sighed and pinched the bridge of his nose. The worst

part of acting was how his real life had to bend into the shadow of his celebrity persona. "What about someone like Selena Gomez?"

"Not a bad idea. Yeah, we could probably get you Selena adjacent."

"Adjacent?" Kline's eyebrows rose up his high forehead.

"You're an underwear model turned romcom actor with one action-slash-period piece out and his first serious film coming out. Reach for the stars, but realize you're not quite competition for a Hemsworth. Yet. Yet. We'll get you there, box office gods willing."

"Get out, Roland. Before I come to my senses and fire your worthless ass."

Roland laughed and patted Kline's shoulder, rising. "I just wish I'd had you before you married Nina. You're one of the best looking men in Hollywood. Maybe the world. And you're a good actor. We just need to push to get you more positive press and that'll take you the rest of the way up the marquee. Trust me. You're getting buzz this year. This year? It's going to be the year of Kline Scott. Guarantee. People's Sexiest Man Alive. Just stick with the program, okay? I'll get to work on Selena-adjacent."

"I can find my own dates."

"Can you?" Roland made a show of looking around. "I'll see you Tuesday. When does Nina get Jack again?"

"Next month. Two weeks. She's taking him on a cruise. What the hell a six year old is going to do on a cruise is beyond me, but she's insisted."

"I'll try and schedule most of your press while he's gone," Roland said, heading for the door.

"Maybe when he gets back, I'll take him home for a little while. I need a vacation."

"No you don't. You need to be seen, you need network, and you need to get laid."

"Out," this time Kline was laughing. "Now. Get out."

Roland chuckled as he disappeared out the front door, leaving Kline alone at the kitchen table. He looked down at his phone again. That argument with Nina had been a bad move. Especially in public. He couldn't help it, though. She always knew how to dig the knife in deeper and get him so turned around he didn't know if he was coming or going. He had gotten better at shutting her down, at ignoring her entirely, at telling her no and meaning it. He'd finally been able to walk away from her and file for divorce. The only thing that kept her in his life was the fact that she had given birth to his son. If he had his way, he'd never see her again.

It also hadn't helped that he'd unloaded on the photographer who had been shutterbugging nearby. There'd be a lawsuit from that dust up soon enough. He'd whipped the camera off the photographers neck, ripped out the film and then smashed it to bits under his Nike's. No one was hurt, but by the time the law-sharks got it the photographer would be in a neck brace and rolling in a wheel chair.

Kline watched Roland leave, then padded up the stairs and into his son's room. Jack lay sleeping in a wad of tangled sheets, mouth open, arm slung over a favorite race car. "Hey, buddy," Kline said quietly, giving Jack's bottom a light swat. "Rise and shine. Time to get up."

"Ugh," the boy groaned. "I don't wanna."

Kline smiled and leaned over close to his son's ear, "C'mon, the sun's out and it's a gorgeous day. Up you go."

Jack opened his eyes and squinted at his father. "Do you have to work today?"

"Not until this afternoon. I thought you and I could spend the day together. Want to go watch your uncle Thad shoot his show? I need to go into LA for a while."

"Yeah! They've got the Craft table!" Jack was up like a shot. "Is Kim coming?"

"Kim's off today," Kline shook his head. "Delia will come with us."

As though summoned, the part-time nanny appeared and said her good mornings, starting to help Jack pick out his clothes for the day. Kline considered her. Cute and young, but probably a bad look to start dating the nanny, not even the full-time nanny at that.

"We're going to go over to Television City," he told her as she shooed Jack out to brush his teeth. "Chelsea Handler's doing a special taping out here on the lot, so you can hang out with him there, or at Thad's taping. Whichever one he wants."

"Cool. I'll keep us low key."

Kline thanked her and went off to his wing of the house, passing his own movie and television posters as he walked through the main hallway, a glassed in feature running through the center of the mansion that allowed him to see into the landscaping of the interior courtyard on either side. Now and then, he stopped to marvel at the fact that his house had wings to it. Hell, even the courtyard was bigger than the council flat he'd grown up in.

Roland's words from earlier came back to him. Underwear model. Sitcom actor. Romcom actor. Finally, maybe a serious actor. He'd come up the ranks in housing just the same. From a council estate in Leeds, to a bedsit in London, to a model apartment in Manhattan, to roommates in LA, to his first home with Nina, to this. And this was a ridiculous, sprawling, modern affair that was way too big for one man and his part-time son.

Sometimes he thought that LA real estate agents were working with the studios to keep actors in ridiculous digs. The price he was paying for the view he had? He wasn't going to be able to stop working until he was dead. But, as Roland always told him, it was part of the game.

He showered, thinking through the list of women he knew who might fit the bill for a publicity romance. He half wished things had taken off with Kara. That would just be easier. But they were like oil and water, and she didn't like kids. It had to be someone who liked kids because when Kline had his time with Jack, he really tried to keep close.

It wasn't exactly kosher for him to be dragging the kid along to tapings, but no one had told him not to either.

He shaved, patted on some cologne, dressed and shook out his hair. Everyone else in Hollywood was wearing their hair close cropped this year. Even Brad Pitt was sporting a buzz cut. After wrapping Knight, Kline had kept the longish style he'd had in the film. Styled right, letting his glossy brown hair curl under enough mousse to sink a ship, he thought he had a Jim Morrison vibe going on.

Chelsea's team would still work him over for the TV cameras, but he would go in looking like the street version of his movie poster anyway.

Delia had Jack kitted out and fed by the time Kline made it back to the middle of the house, where a hotel lobby-like living room connected the east and western sides of his home. "Ready?" He asked. They were, so the three of them trooped down to the garage and picked the SUV to drive out to the studio lot.

Kline waved at the handful of fans hanging around the driveway gate, then asked for musical preferences from the backseat. Jack picked the Encanto soundtrack, and Kline sighed, but cued it up on Spotify. They were going to have work on his musical taste if Kline was going to survive many more car rides. Maybe his tastes would improve with age?

In a half hour, they were turning into the gates at Television City, checking into the closed lot parking and heading toward the sound stage where Thad's show was shooting. Usually, one or more of Thad's all-girl brood were running around on set, along with the kids who played his on-screen family, and Jack provided a welcome playmate.

The backstage area was madness and they found Thad with his stage wife, running lines before going out to shoot them. The affable Australian was starring in one of a long line of sitcoms based around the everyday, normal life of a celebrity.

This was the third spin-off of the first sitcom he'd done, and where Kline had met him. Knock Three Times had been an ensemble cast of barely legals trying to get their big break at an arts school, that spun off half the cast into Higher Ed, which was exactly what it sounded like if you liked puns about weed and college life, and finally that had spun off Thad and Kelsey Karter, as Thad's long-suffering wife, into Simon Says, a show about an actor who has finally made it.

Thad had a fake wife, fake kids, a fake house, and of course an array of fake in-laws and neighbors who had free run of his home and provided much hilarity at any given moment. What gave Kline the biggest laugh was how backwards the show had it.

Thad didn't live in suburbia, and his current wife, number three, was not his high school sweetheart, but a supermodel who didn't even know where the kitchen was, much less how to use anything in it. The only thing close to the truth was the houseful of kids, but Thad's sitcom counterpart only had four. He actually had six. Kline couldn't fathom playing Thad's part of bumbling, amiable, dumbass day in and day out for years, but then, that's what acting was. You pretend you understand, even when you don't.

Two of Thad's children came running up to Jack with squeals of delight, and before Kline could even greet them, the three were off to Thad's trailer to play. Thad already had one baby girl when Kline had met him, with twins on the way. They'd started calling him The Impregnator before the first season of Knock was over.

"Was that Evangeline?" Kline asked, as Thad walked over. "She's a tree!"

"Yeah," Thad nodded after the cooling trail of children. "Not even thirteen and I've got little bastards calling the house for her all the time. And old bastards. Not as bad as Eugenie yet," he said naming his eldest daughter, "but getting there."

Kline shook his head. "Impressive. So, what's up today?"

"Taping starts at noon. We're redoing some scenes so no live audience. Laugh track. I hate that shit."

"Yeah, when it's canned, the viewers think you knew it wasn't funny, but you filmed it anyway."

"That, and I don't like not getting an immediate response.

It's difficult to tell what's working and what isn't."

"How's the hot new show runner working out?" They had joked that the show runner job on Simon Says was like the Defense Against Dark Arts job at Hogwarts. No one stayed for more than a year, and they usually left cursed.

Thad's blue eyes widened, and he shook his head with disbelief. "Really well. She's got a lot of good ideas and she keeps telling me off. I like her a lot. She's honestly really good. I was skeptical."

"I remember. Too young. Too inexperienced. Too fucking hot. A sure sign that the network just wanted a reason to cancel you. But if she's telling you off? I like her already. Is she single?"

"So single. I'd introduce you but," he said looking around. "I don't see her. Eh, she's around here somewhere. Lying in wait to pounce on some poor unsuspecting producer, no doubt."

"Rick could do with some pouncing on," Kline said, naming another of their friends who had come up with them through Knock, but who had splintered off from acting into production. "Why don't you set her up with him?"

"Rick loathes set ups and sabotages them more often than not."

"Only if he knows it's a setup," Kline pointed out. "When's the last time you saw him, anyway?"

"We had dinner last week. He's just gotten back from the UK, actually. He's working on some deal for BBC America, and he had meetings over there to sort out the details for transferring rights or something," Thad said, with a shrug. "I'm sure he'll be calling you to try and get you to do some PR for it. It's to do with Knights. Is that why you're here?"

"Yeah. I've got an interview taping here in a bit. Yeah, tell him to call me. I'll help him out, however. So how's Monique?"

"She's great. Somewhere in Milan, I think. She's doing a shoot for Dior. Or Gucci. Or something." Thad flapped his fingers.

"You don't know?"

"Don't know. Don't care."

"Well, that sounds promising. Things not going well?"

Thad shrugged. "Some fucked up shit has been going on. She said some shit to Carra about her weight, and we got into it. Not everyone's born looking like an El Greco. Carra got on this insane diet–it's already hard enough out here without having a living breathing model in the house telling her how to restrict calories."

Kline smiled sympathetically. Thad was always under fire for weight himself. The likeable Aussie was tall and built like a redwood, but every beer showed up under his chin or hung over his belt five minutes after he was finished drinking it. And Thad could drink more beer than anyone Kline had ever seen. At twenty, the two of them had been the bane of their wardrobe department. One who had to battle like a gladiator to keep five pounds off, and Kline, who was double fisting carbs trying to put some weight on.

"Wait until she hits thirty," Kline said, patting his own middle. "It all goes to hell for everyone. I'm on a diet."

"You?" Thad's guileless blue eyes widened.

"Yeah. Six pack was starting to look like a keg. It all goes straight here now."

"Well, I have a feeling we'll have at least two more marriages between us before she hits thirty," Thad said with a sigh. "I hope they're both hers, though."

"Let's see," a voice said from behind. Kline turned to see an above average looking young woman in black jeans and a grey turtleneck walking toward them with pages in her hand. "She's twenty-four, so that's six years from now. If you divorce her before Christmas, you can probably get in at least three wives and six more kids before she hits thirty. Here are the changes to the laundry room scene."

"Ouch. Ah, thanks, you're a star," Thad said laughing. "Hand delivered from on high?"

"You're the star, baby," she replied, "and I'm still trying to figure that one out."

"Ha. Ha. Ha." Thad grunted, then noticed Kline looking at him with raised eyebrows, "Oh, right, Rhiannon–show runner–this is my old friend, Kline."

"Hello," she said, offering a hand. "Rhiannon Charles."

"Kline Scott," he replied, shaking it. "Good to meet you."

"And you," she said, offering a genuine smile. "I enjoy your films."

"Gracias," Kline grinned, flashing the sparkling smile that made him a star. "Can't believe you're having to babysit this lout. How are you holding up?"

"He's easy enough," Rhiannon laughed.

"So his reputation is intact," Kline nodded. "That's good to know."

"Well, he has good PR reps."

"I am standing right here," Thad said.

Rhiannon looked over her glasses at him. "Yes, we know."

Kline mouthed, "Rick" to Thad over her head. "Just his type."

"Just who's type?" Rhiannon asked. She pointed to the mirror behind Thad's head and flicked her auburn hair over her shoulder. "I read lips."

"Backwards? Shit!" Kline laughed in appreciation. "I'm single--you want to be my type?"

"That depends."

"On what?"

"How nicely you ask," she said, crossing her arms.

"Oh, darling," Kline chuckled, a purr sliding into his voice. "I'll ask as nicely as you need. Like to go have a drink sometime?"

Rhiannon smiled. "Oh, you are smooth, aren't you?"

"Unless you like it rough."

She cocked an eyebrow. "I don't give that kind of information to men I've just met. But you might get a chance to find out," she said, producing a card. "Give me a call and we'll see."

Thad was rolling his eyes. "Leave my boss alone, Scott," he sighed. "Anyway, I thought you wanted me to introduce her to

Rick?"

"That was before I met her," Kline smiled crookedly, not taking his eyes from Rhiannon's.

"Don't you have an interview to get to?" Thad reminded.

"Fuck!" Kline looked at his watch. "Shit. Yes. Jack's with Vangie," he reminded. "Delia's around here somewhere."

"I'll keep an eye out. If he goes missing, I'll just give you one of mine."

"Fair," Kline said. He pointed a finger at Rhiannon. "I'll be calling you."

"I know," she said, turning to Thad. "I'll have the other pages for you shortly."

"There are more? How long are we in the laundry room?"

"The other pages are for the bedroom scene. That's the last reshoot."

"Oh. Right. Thanks."

She nodded, then excused herself and walked away.

"Hotcha," Kline breathed. He was gathering himself to head to the studio where Chelsea was taping. "I need to come back to serial television. There be hotties here."

"There be," Thad agreed with the same pirate accent Kline had put on, starting to walk with him. "But aren't you seeing that Kara Viceroy? Speaking of hot?"

"Speaking of bitch, more like." Kline laughed. "No. I took her out once or twice while we were on location, but that's it."

"Did you tap that?"

Kline nodded. "She shags like a corpse."

Thad grimaced. "Shame."

"Yeah. Waste of time," Kline said, shaking his head. "Then again, that's pretty much in line with my track record."

They came to door by which Kline would leave and Thad said, "Well, if you score that one, your record should improve considerably. And if you do, make sure you tell me about it. I'm dying to know."

"If that works out well, you'll never know. I'm no fool."

He and Thad hugged, then he started out the door, turning on the animal of charisma as he walked. He needed to get into character as himself, well, the movie version of himself. Himself was Scott Kline, a tall, skinny, spotty boy with questionable teeth, who had fallen into modeling after a scout approached him after a school track meet.

Having no body fat at all meant more than just being cold all the time. It meant that on camera, with good lighting, even the barest of workout routines showed up like he'd trained to be a superhero. He did a few test shoots, got a makeover, changed his clothes and was walking for John Galliano that spring.

He slouched into his runway strut just for fun. No paparazzi were around on the lot to catch him in the act.

His then-agent had asked him to change the order of his name. "To sound more mysterious. You're selling a mystery. There's nothing enigmatic about Scott." Since half his mates called him by his surname anyway, it hadn't mattered much to him. Then, it had been an unexpected benefit to be able to put on Kline Scott like a garment from his runway rack and relax back into Scott Kline when he was finished with work.

When he moved to New York after signing with Ford, he had taken on Kline Scott full time, only wearing Scott Kline like pajamas or a towel out of the shower. It was his chance to be more than the gangly kid with too-short sleeves and trouser legs, from the poor family, who got lucky. He could be whatever he wanted. And, his agent had been right. Kline was a mystery.

Kline was also a charming son of a bitch, who used his American dental plan smile to light up the eyes of every woman he met. Young, old, fat, thin, plain, stunning didn't matter. He flirted with everyone. Kline Scott wasn't just a lady killer. He resurrected them, too.

Scott Kline had been hopeful and earnest. Kline Scott was certain and confident, and he was deep into that persona by the time he was seated in Chelsea's guest chair, laughing at her jokes about his romcom history, then getting serious when she asked him about his foray into action. "It's a big difference," he said, leaning forward toward her, then taking the audience into his confidence with a shy smile added, "I was nervous. I was a little afraid I wouldn't stack up. There are so many good movies out there, and so many great leading men."

"Do you think you'll do any more romantic comedy?"

"I hope so! I love making people laugh. Romcoms are a lot of fun."

"Did you worry about being typecast? You've been the prince of romance for a while now."

"I'd worry about being typecast if I didn't like the type," he said with a grin. "But getting typecast as a charming, funny guy who gets the girl? What's to complain about that?"

The audience laughed and applauded, as Chelsea rolled her eyes and groaned before going back to her questions. Kline was getting a little pissed. She was supposed to be talking about Knight and Lone Star, or what he had planned next, not bringing up his old films. He'd told Roland he only wanted to do press about his future, not his past, so when Ellen brought up Knock Three Times and brought up photos from his runway days, he was ready to get up and walk off her set. When she brought up Kara Viceroy and the wrench that had thrown in his personal life, he nearly lost his temper.

Instead of saying what he wished, he remembered to breathe through his nose, and said, "You know, one of the things I learned from doing so many romcoms is that the way to get the girl is to show respect, kindness, and keep your mouth shut about what goes on in private. And you know me, Chels. I like to get the girl."

The audience cooed and clapped again.

"Oh, I do know that, Kline," Chelsea said back through a tight smile and suddenly Kline remembered having abruptly walked off mid-sentence of a conversation with Chelsea to chase another girl at a party years ago. He almost laughed. Grudges were bad for business, though. He collected himself even as he felt a blush rising on his cheeks.

"What I've learned from moving into action is that the less said, the better." And he turned his last fifteen seconds into an elevator pitch for Knight. He tied it up with a bow just as Chelsea was getting the signal to throw to wrap it up, and he sat back to make eye contact with various audience members, waving up into the cheering crowd as he did. He couldn't see shit, but everyone up there was going to believe he had looked right at them.

He congratulated himself on keeping his head, his seat, and getting the promotion pitch in, finished out his segment, then winked at Chelsea as he walked off stage. After signing a few autographs, he picked up an apple from the craft table, then started back over to the Simon Says set to look for Delia and Jack.

He found his son giggling madly as Evangeline, Carraway and Shaunsie performed a staged rendition of an old Spice Girls song in front of Thad's trailer. Jack had been conscripted to play Scary Spice and was growling and laughing as directed. Carraway had decided that the sisters were going to be a pop band, and she worked her siblings relentlessly. Jack got hugs and praise, where the other girls got sharp orders and clipped commands.

Kline stood watching for a moment, head tilted. The girls had sharp moves and decent voices. A little more adult than they should have been, but then so were all the other girls in LA. He waved to Delia, who was standing back watching, and she pushed away from a trailer wall and started toward them. "Hey, Jacks. Time to go, bud."

He looked a bit disappointed, but nodded, "Okay, Dad."

"Uncle Kline!" Shaunsie squealed, breaking from the ranks to run and hug him.

He gave her a squeeze and smiled down at her. Carraway's twin, she showed her wish for individuality by keeping her hair cut short and wearing glasses, but she still had her Scandinavian mother's good looks. "How are you, sweetie?" he said, nodding towards the others. "That routine was great."

"We still need to practice," Carraway insisted, giving Shaunsie a stern look.

"It's fab, doll," Kline winked at her. "You're brilliant. Couple of years, good management, and a band behind you and you'll be bigger than your old man ever was."

Carraway beamed at that and stroked her hair, batting her lashes. That one was going to be trouble. "Go on," she pretended to blush.

"We'll see you later, Jacky," Evangeline said, squeezing the boy before ruffing his hair.

"Be good."

He screwed up his face when Carraway kissed his cheek noisily, then wiped off the girl-cooties quickly. "Gross, Carra," he whined. "Don't put your dog lips on me!"

"Now, Jack, be nice," Kline said, pulling open the door.

"Sorry," he mumbled to Carraway's hurt expression before turning to go. "See ya." He was off and running with Delia in hot pursuit, and Kline said goodbye to the girls before following after them.

He was still scowling in the car on the way home and Kline tried not to laugh. "It washes off," he said, eyeing Jack through the rearview mirror. Delia sat beside him, earbuds in, nose almost pressed against her phone to give the father and son a semblance of privacy.

"It's gross when they do that."

Kline sighed. "Believe it or not, Jacks, you're going to be wishing girls would kiss you when you get a bit older."

Jack put out his tongue. "I'm not going to be like you all, blablablaaaaa," Jack intoned, wrapping his arms around himself in a mock hug, making mawkish kiss faces in the air. "No way!"

Kline snorted out a laugh. "Blablablaaaa?" He howled, laughing. "Bright boy, that blablablaaaaa is one of the best things in life. Just you wait."

"Well, it's gross when she does it. She's always wanting me to pretend I'm in love with her or something. She's weird. I like Vangie and Shaun, but not her."

"Yeah, Car's a bit ah-old for her age." He glanced over at Jack's crossed arms again. "So, what do you want to do now?"

"Let's go get burgers then go to Gameworks. I want to do the new gyroscope."

"Burgers?" Kline squinted. "How about if we go to Staci's? You can get a burger and I'll get a salad. I've got to drop a few pounds. No carbs for Da."

Jack wrinkled his nose. "You're weird too. I'm never growing up. Grownups can't eat anything good."

"Yeah, we can. I just have to watch it a bit. You just work on that not growing up thing. I like that idea."

Jack rolled his eyes and looked out the window, watching people on the street as they passed. They arrived at the restaurant and sat down at a quiet table near the front, Delia seated nearby but not with the family. The last thing he needed was to be photographed with the nanny. When the waitress arrived, she immediately recognized Kline and began flirting with him while taking the order. After she walked away, Jack scowled after her. "See? Girls are weird."

"Yeah," Kline conceded with a laugh. He and Jack chatted over lunch about the upcoming cruise. The boy was excited about it, but was also wondering what there would be to do. Kline was detailing what prospects Jack had when a familiar laugh caught his attention and he looked to his left. "Hold up," he said quietly. "Jack, I'll be right back."

He stood up quickly, tossing his napkin on the chair and strode over to a nearby booth. "Jill?" he asked, leaning around the back of one seat, interrupting the groups' conversation.

"Kline?!" A wide, beaming smile greeted him from the inside seat. "Hi!"

He grinned back, noticing without reacting to the displeasure creeping up the face of the man seated next to her. "What are you doing in LA, love? And how are you? You look splendid!"

She laughed and shrugged, "Business. I'm great and thanks--so do you. But you always look good. Oh, Kline, these are Michael and Royce Anderson, and Phil Rozando. Guys, this is Kline Scott."

"I know," Michael said. He was the fussy looking one. Kline ignored him completely.

"How long's it been?" he asked, thinking back to the last time he'd seen her. He had dropped her off at her door and then gone straight to the airport, heading for LA. He could still remember how she'd looked at him, waving goodbye.

"Eleven years," she said easily. She was still smiling, though, eyes twinkling at him. "Do you want to join us?"

"Oh… no, I'm here with my son," he jerked his thumb toward his table. "I have a son. I…did you know that?"

"Of course. Everyone knows everything about you." Jill leaned forward and waved at the boy who was staring and kicking the rungs of his chair. "Kline junior, called Jack. Right?"

"Right," Kline said, nodding. "Well, I should be getting back to him. How long are you in town?"

"We're discussing that," Royce said, with a smile to Jill. "Trying to talk her into staying longer. I think we can really make her a movie star."

"They want me to be a star," Jill stage-whispered to Kline. "Something about my own series, or movies. It's all very big and bright."

Kline could feel the smile freezing on his face even as it slipped from his eyes. It was like there was no one else in the room. "I never called you," he said haltingly. "I meant to. I just…"

"Silly, that was years ago." She waved off the words. "It was good to see you again. You do look great. Your son is beautiful--looks just like you."

"Is he working?" Royce asked Kline, "Because that kid could work."

The question broke the spell a bit and Kline looked at the man. He recognized the smarminess of studio executive on the guy and shook his head. "No, and he has no interest in it, either. I wouldn't put him through that, anyway," he said, straightening as he turned to Jill. "I'd love to see you again while you're here. Where are you staying?"

"I'm renting a house in the Valley. Is that right? I have no idea what anything is here. Uh--what's my address?"

Royce flicked out one of his business cards and scribbled on the back of it, then flicked it at Kline with a toothy grin. "She's staying here. That's my info on the other side if you decide you want to talk about your kid. I'm casting for a Spielberg flick--he'd be great."

"He doesn't act," Kline said, taking the card. "Jill, maybe we can get together?"

She shrugged, her own smile was wavering. "I'm so busy! We'll have to see. You've got my info."

He smiled, pocketing the card. "I'll be in touch. It was really great to see you."

"You, too," she said, nodding. "Take care."

"Gentlemen," Kline said, barely glancing at them before turning away and walking back to the table where Jack sat wearing a frown of displeasure.

"What?" Kline asked.

"Who are they?"

"There's a lady over there named Jill. She's an old friend of mine from when I lived in New York--before you were born. I had to go say hello."

Jack looked down, pushing a French fry around his plate for a few minutes before saying, "Can we go to Gameworks now?"

Kline sat stunned for a moment, then nodded. "Absolutely. Come on." He waved at the server and put on his sunshades. Within seconds he had his and Delia's tabs to sign, and then he and Jack started off with Delia a few paces behind.

"Can we call Kim to come, too?"

"It's Kim's day off, Tiger," Kline said, starting for the front door. "But we'll have fun. Delia will be with us."

"Okay," Jack said, though he sounded far less enthused about that idea than he had been about the rest of their plans.

"She's not as fun."

"But I'm fun, right?"

"I guess."

Kline frowned, looking back at Delia, who shrugged. The valet brought his car around, pausing before the stand so that Delia could get into the back with Jack behind the blackout windows, then pulled it all the way up to the awning where photographers were waiting to snap Kline getting behind the driver's seat.

At Gameworks, they played together until someone sent out word that Kline Scott was there, then fans started to arrive, along with photographers, ruining Jack's fun. Since that last dust up, the photogs were getting aggressive to see if they could get a rise out of Kline for better pictures.

This time, he played it cool and sent Delia and Jack out the back door with a store manager, while he took fifteen minutes to sign autographs and pose for selfies. By the time he got out to the car, Jack was sitting with folded arms and a look on his face that mirrored what Kline was feeling inside. "Sorry, Tiger,' he said. "Your old man is popular."

"I want a burger."

"What?"

"I want a burger."

"You just ate!"

"He didn't eat much," Delia said from the back. Regardless of how tuned out she appeared to be, the nanny was always ears-on for whatever Jack needed, and he had learned to listen to both Delia and Kim when they made a suggestion.

"Fine. What is it with you and burgers, kid?"

"I want In and Out."

"Fine."

The drive-thru was easier to navigate than the restaurant had been, though driving home with the meaty smell of burgers was making Kline's lean-meat-and-veg only stomach growl with hunger. When they got home, he saw everyone inside, then changed into his workout gear and hit the home gym, carrying the two business cards he'd collected with him.

While running on the treadmill, he considered each one, weighing what he thought might be an easy score against a hard conversation. Jill looked good, he thought. More refined. She had always been fairy tale pretty before, big eyed and wispy, but baby-faced. When they'd met, she was barely legal and still casting as a tween, struggling to break out of those child actor roles into more serious work.

She was sheltered by an omnipresent stage mother, but precocious for all the professional work she'd done. She had three major roles on Broadway and two touring companies under her belt by the time they met. Still, he hadn't even broken a sweat stealing her away from the friend of his she was dating.

She was cute with this confusing, quirky sex appeal that was muddled up between the prettiness and the razor-sharp wit. But she'd also been a foot in the door with lifelong connections most people only dreamed about. In truth, he had started cultivating the relationship more for his career than anything else. Those first few months of dating, he'd seen her as little more than a cute girl with a hot resume, which he supposed was the exact problem she was having with casting agents.

When he had realized what he had on the hook, it was like pulling a rip cord to his soul. A whole parachute of unexpected emotions and repercussions exploded out of a kiss and before he knew it, he was half in love and mostly living in a brand new studio apartment Jill had scooped up on her eighteenth birthday to emancipate herself from the overbearing mother, and provide the privacy she wanted to keep fucking Kline's brains out between their auditions and parties with his model-slash-actor-slash-waiter buddies.

That's all he did for a summer--audition and fuck. And not just Jill. He was young, he was attractive, he was in the city that never slept, and he was making the most of it. She would find out and cry, he would apologize and remind her that they weren't really together and that they were way too young to limit themselves to each other, then they would start the next round of the same.

He preferred her studio to his model apartment, and he couldn't complain at all about her company in the double bed they shared. He'd been the first to get into both Jill and the bed, and he'd gotten both her performance and his pillow into the exact shape to fit his wants. Then, he'd gotten the call that he'd been cast for Knock, and he'd left without much of a goodbye at all. He hadn't even told her he was leaving.

She was, what, twenty-nine, thirty, now? She didn't look like a child anymore. He had logged onto the internet after his workout and pulled up pictures. This was what fairy tale princesses grew up to be, he thought, biting his lip. Photos of her collecting a Tony award made him sit up a little straighter. He didn't pay much attention to those. He cared about SAGs, Golden Globes, Emmys, and Oscars.

Three Tonys. She'd won three. That was the easiest information to find on her, along with a couple of articles about her charity appearances. Otherwise, she only turned up on stage.

The most recent photos were of her as a presenter at the awards show, her lithe, dancer's body in a simple and trim slip dress of steel gray satin, making her eyes look like thunderclouds. She was remarkable. "From sunbeam to ice queen," he whispered to himself. He thought she'd had her nose done. Something was different, something other than just losing the baby fat in her face. Something had taken that prettiness to the next level.

Whatever it was, it was good work. He couldn't figure it out. He'd had his teeth and nose done before getting Knock and still wondered how long he would have struggled without having had that done.

Tapping the business cards he'd carried with him, he shut down the internet and picked up the landline to dial a number. It was archaic, but more personal. While hackers concentrated on cell phones, he could feel pretty confident that his landline calls were secure. He was too wiped for the hard conversation. "Rhiannon?" He said, when the call was answered, "It's Kline Scott. I wanted to see about setting up a time for that drink."

"Wow. You called the very same day," she said, after a pause. "You must really be thirsty."

"Something like that," he smiled into the phone, then breathed, "So--you interested?"

"Of course. I don't give my number to just anyone. Those business cards aren't cheap."

Kline laughed. "I think I understand why Thad's show's doing so much better now."

"Nah, his wife's out of town," Rhiannon said, without missing a beat. "So, are you free tomorrow night?"

"I can be. How about I pick you up around nine? Wear your dancing shoes."

"Okay, we should be done shooting by seven, so that sounds good," she said, before giving him her address.

"See you then. Can't wait." He let the purr back into his voice before hanging up. He stared at the other card for a long time and then pinned it up on the cork board by the phone. He couldn't make that call just then.

He poured himself a drink then wandered into the den to watch Jack play games for a while, cheering him on before heading upstairs for a bath, still thinking about Jill. Seeing her had been a shock.

He was remembering how that whole time in his life felt. It was loud and colorful, and full of bright young people with big dreams, who were all working their asses off to achieve a moment, and playing their asses off when things didn't pan out. Jill was one of those things that didn't pan out, and they'd broken up a bit before he got the audition for Knock. She'd come home to find him in their bed with another girl–dick move on his part–and kicked him out.

Of course, not having her and then seeing her out with another one of their friends made him want her more. "Fuck," he pushed his hands through his hair. Jack was right, he was weird. So, a few weeks later, knowing that Knock was locked in, with his airline ticket already packed in his bag, he had taken Jill out, wined and dined her, then to a hotel for privacy–another guy had already moved into the model apartment like a shark's tooth filling in a gap.

He poured everything he was feeling but didn't know how to say into her body, then walked her back to her studio the next morning. He had kissed her on the lips and said, "I love you. I will always love you." Then, leaving her wearing a smile like sunshine, was on his flight to LA two hours later. He had never worked up the nerve to tell her he was going because he was half-afraid she'd ask him to stay, and he was terrified he might.

He had loved her, in his way. He knew that then and he knew it now. Seeing her brought it all rushing back and he wondered if they could have survived the early years of his acting career.

They likely would have ended up like he and Nina had, and that was the last thing that Kline wanted for Jill. Of course, he realized it was probable that she might still hate him after all these years and that show of politeness may have been just that. She was an actress, and a damn good one, as he remembered it.

He suddenly wondered if the number and address tacked on the board in the kitchen was really hers, but he couldn't bring himself to test it and find out.

"Hey, Dad?" Jack called through the bathroom door. "Delia says to say I'm going to bed now."

"Ah--okay. I'll be in to tuck you in soon. I'm in the tub."

"Okay," Jack called. "Night."

"Night," Kline said, rubbing his eyes with damp fingers. He climbed out of the tub and toweled off, taking a moment to stare at his reflection in the mirror. Thirty-three had crept up on him and he could see it in the lines of his face. He'd aged better than some, but it was still becoming obvious that he couldn't compete with the younger set. As long as he kept his box office up, he could pull out at least another ten years of leading man roles, maybe even fifteen. It was bread on the table, at any rate. He sighed, looking himself over again before tying on his robe.

He went into Jack's room and tickled him for a while, then tucked him in securely with hugs and kisses before telling him to sleep. He backed out of the room, finding himself wondering what Jack would have looked like with a different mother. Would he have had Jill's dark blonde hair? Her stormy blue eyes? Would his nose have turned up like hers?

It was the nose! She'd had the tip of her nose refined. That mystery solved, he went back down to his gym where he spent a good hour working on his abs and chest. If his face showed his age, his body wasn't going to.

When he was satisfied and felt the stress had been alleviated some, he took a quick pass in the sauna and rinsed in the club shower built into the gym before going into his room. He settled into bed with the stack of scripts his agent had sent over and picked through the pile until he found one that grabbed his interest.

He fell asleep reading and didn't wake up until the sounds of Kim and Jack playing in the backyard made their way through the open sliding glass door of his balcony and into his dreams. He squinted at the clock to find it was after noon, so he struggled out of bed, showered again, dressed himself and went to say hello before leaving for a round of meetings with Roland and his publicity team.

With the Oscar buzz generating for Knight and with Lone Star's imminent premier, his team wanted to shift gears to build more around his social media audience. Roland was still set on the romance angle, and to Kline's dismay his team agreed. Clara, his social media manager, talked him through what the timeline might look like. For peak engagement, they would want him going IG official with a woman by February the following year–in time to do a little dance for the Academy, who would start voting after the BAFTAs. In fact, she had mused, going official at the BAFTAs was a great idea.

Clara had put out feelers to Selena's team at Roland's request, but she was concerned about the internet drama that had plagued the actress since her Justin Bieber days, so she wasn't entirely on board with that, and offered up a number of other names instead. Kline waved off all of them.

"I keep telling you people I can find my own dates," Kline grumbled.

"Let us help you help yourself," Roland laughed and Clara grimaced.

Finally, she shrugged. "I don't know any other way to say this: You need to be in a relationship. It needs to be with someone whose profile matches yours, so the public is interested. It needs to follow a storyline so the public will engage with it, be excited by it, and want to see more of you. Right now? Your reputation is kind of…well, the people who don't see you as a fuckboi see you as a dud. If you want an Oscar, let us rehab your persona. Give us eighteen months of your life and we'll give you the prestige you need to live like Leo and his revolving door of teenagers, if you want."

Kline had been properly offended by that but threw up his hands. "I have a date tonight with a woman who is a show runner. Is that high profile enough?"

"What's the show?" Clara asked, perking up.

"Simon Says."

She deflated just as suddenly. "Ugh. A sitcom? No. Absolutely not. Wait—isn't that the one that spun off from your last sitcom?"

"Yeah."

Her face shifted through several thoughts before she said. "Okay. Maybe. Would she be up for it? Pretending to be in love for a year?"

"Why pretend?" Kline turned on his charm, falling flat at Roland's disapproving frown.

Clara coughed and blushed. "Feel her out. If she's interested and that's the route you want to go, we'll give it a try. It's better than some no-name or a fan."

He left the meeting angry and frustrated, but also excited because his team really thought they could campaign him into that Oscar win. He'd once given up a woman he loved with his whole heart to pursue this career, what was a year and a half? He didn't have a biological clock ticking. And, if he played his cards right, maybe he could just date whom he wanted. He was sure he could make a relationship work without his team orchestrating it. Hell, people had year long romances and then broke up all the time. He knew that better than anyone. Fuckboi.

Sighing, he pushed it out of his mind for the moment. He was home again by five, in time for dinner with his son, then he went upstairs to work out before getting dressed for his date, where he started to think about it again. He wondered if Rhiannon would be into the idea? She was a writer. She could collab with his team to build a storyline. That thought satisfied his mind enough that he could concentrate on getting night club ready.

Showered, shaved, and dressed to kill, Kline strode downstairs to say goodbye to his son. He and the live-in nanny were playing Mario Kart in the living room, and barely looked up as he kissed Jack's head, and started out the door in a blaze of black silk and custom cologne.

He arrived at the address Rhiannon had given him, a tidy bungalow in Malibu, and walked up to the door with his smile firmly in place. He'd been looking forward to this all afternoon and anticipating what he hoped would be a nice evening with someone who was industry without being an actress. It was just a little before nine when he rang the bell, and he heard heels clicking on hardwood before Rhiannon opened the door and greeted him with a smile. "Hi."

"Oh, look at you," he grinned, handing over the bottle of wine he'd picked up on the way. She was decked out in a black strappy dress that hugged, flattered, and generally did all sorts of things to her figure that he found himself interested in doing right along with it. Her thick, auburn hair was pulled up, but wisps of layers hung low, framing her face. The glasses had been dismissed and he grinned at her, "Green eyes--gorgeous. I love green eyes."

"I love them, too, but brown is good," she said, noting his own. She looked at the bottle, then raised her eyes to him. "Is this for now? I thought you were taking me dancing?"

"I am. This is a lovely parting gift for my hostess. We'll part with it for now. Sound good to you?"

"Definitely," she said, tilting her head slightly. "Come in while I put this away and get my bag."

He followed her inside, looking around. "Nice place. Did you just move in?"

"The boxes give it away?"

"I'm observant, you see. Do you have a good view?"

"A beautiful view. I can walk out my back door and be on the beach. Quite a change from the fifth floor walkup in Manhattan. I'm not sure if I like being this close to the water yet, but I spend so much time at work, it doesn't really matter. The breeze is nice."

"You're from New York?"

"No, I'm from Boston. I went to college up there, then moved down to New York for work."

Harvard, he thought. Then probably writing for late night, and taking the pipeline into sitcoms. That was the career path. He said, "I lived in Greenwich when I first moved to the States. Loved it there."

Rhiannon nodded appreciatively. "I spent a lot of time there. It's a great place." She put the bottle in the rack on the counter and picked up a small black bag. "Are you all set?"

Kline smiled and offered his arm, "Absolutely."

He whisked her off in his Mercedes. She was responding to his charm just like he hoped she would. Industry-not-actress meant she would be savvy enough to understand how his career either robbed him of, or blessed him with free time, but removed enough that he could still turn on Kline Scott for her and watch the fireworks light up behind her eyes. She was bewitched, bemused, and blushing by the time they'd gotten past the first traffic signal. He had her number all right, and prospects for his evening were looking good, especially considering the way she shivered when he brushed his knuckles up her bare side arm.

The valet at Blue, LA's latest hot spot, ushered them to a private entrance where a host greeted them and whisked them off to the VIP room. She was appropriately impressed. Industry-not-actress meant she had heard of these places, but wasn't high enough up the food chain to actually be allowed in, or recognizable enough to enjoy the star treatment. It was a lazy way to date, like regifting PR he'd received to family and friends for Christmas and birthdays, but it worked. His mother had loved the Hermes bag he'd gotten at the last BAFTAs. What was he going to do with a bag?

Now, he focused on the woman by his side. She was a perfect height for whispering in her ear, sharing bits and bobs of information about other actors in the room, making her laugh. When he put his arm around her waist, his hand fit nicely on the luscious curve of her hip. Catching a glimpse of their reflections in a mirror, he thought they would look great on a red carpet together. This could work, he thought. And maybe she didn't have to know.

Acting with a partner was like dancing. If you were any good at leading, you could make a novice look great. And Kline was nothing if not great at leading. Besides, she was funny. He liked that.

They mingled with other VIPs, had drinks, then he spun her out on the dance floor like they were the only couple in the place, where he stole kisses until she was just giving them to him. Then, her eyes shining like she was getting drunk on his attention alone, Rhiannon reluctantly excused herself to go to the ladies' room and Kline escorted her off the floor then went to the bar to refresh their drinks.

He had just cleared the bar when two dancers wobbled off the floor into his path, forcing him to step back into another body. When he spun around to survey his damage he was jostled again and fully sloshed one of the drinks he held onto the dress of the woman in front of him. She groaned and threw up her hands, starting to say something, then seemed to realize who he was, and then he realized who she was, and both started talking at the same time. Him, calling for napkins, her saying, "I'm fine. I'm fine. Just wet. Don't worry about it."

Kline stared and stammered, then apologized again before smiling crookedly and teasing adolescently, "I can still get you wet after all these years." Oh god. He hadn't. He cringed as the words left his mouth.

Jill blinked at him, those blue eyes cool and narrowed. She tilted her head and made a sound that might have been a laugh. "But now it takes you two drinks to do it. You've obviously lost your touch."

"I'm just rusty. Give me a little more time and I'll have you eating out of my hand." He tried a rakish grin, realizing how utterly boorish he sounded, but he couldn't seem to stop himself.

"Been there. Done that," Jill said lightly. He was radiating nerves instead of charm and he struggled to get a grip on himself, but she hadn't walked away.

He fixed his face and let his eyes soften as he stepped forward, "Listen, Jill, can we talk sometime? Seeing you yesterday-- It brought back all sorts of things. I'd really love to see you. Spend some time catching up. Could we do that?"

She tucked a strand of hair behind her ear, clearly considering. He pressed, using his nerves as leverage, switching gears from horn dog to puppy dog, "Please? I have so much to say, but none of it is fit for–this." He paused and waved his drink-filled hands around to indicate the club, sloshing more.

"I'm in town for a while," she admitted. "I might be convinced to listen to you apologize over brunch. With mimosas. Lots of mimosas."

He smiled, realizing she was leaning into her own nerves and ad-libbing into the scene he'd set. He wasn't talking to Jilly any more than she was talking to Scott Kline. She was in character as Jill Parker, Broadway star, having a chance encounter with her former lover, the movie star Kline Scott. "So, brunch? Sunday?"

Suddenly she laughed, dropping out of the role. "Are you trying to make a date with me while you're on a date? Are you actually doing that?"

And he was a flustered kid again. "Maybe? Can you blame me?"

Her laugh was magical, and she shook her head letting the mirth fade into the music pumping out of the speakers. "Call me later and ask properly. Then we'll see."

"When I call you later," he let his voice drop so that she had to lean in to hear him, "what will I see?"

Before she could answer, a proprietary arm linked through his as Rhiannon appeared beside him. "Miss me?" she asked, some salt in her voice before fixing her competition with a dark smile. "I'm Rhi—Oh! Jill?"

"Rhiannon? Oh my goodness!" Jill took a full step backwards, away from the pair.

"What are you doing in LA? I thought you were allergic to sunlight and scene."

Jill's smile narrowed somewhat as she read the situation. "I am. Absolutely. Which is why I'm out at night and also why I was leaving. My god, this place is awful. Are you out here full-time now?"

"I am. I've been out here a little over a year."

"You're kidding," Jill said. "What are you doing?"

"Show runner for a multi-cam sitcom."

"Oh, fab! I had no idea!"

"I guess you've been too busy to notice anything outside of your little world."

Kline watched between the two of them, wondering if he was going to need to step in to mediate the conversation, but Jill seemed to shake something off and laughed. "Oh, you know. Let's see, last year I opened Devil's Party and that was eight shows a week, and I did a special run on the West End with Phantom for four weeks. Now, I'm out here to take my role to the big screen. I'm going Hollywood. What's the sitcom you're writing for?"

"I'm the show runner for Simon Says." Rhiannon supplied, bearing down on the title. "They brought me in to save the show."

"That's some heady stuff! You're a sitcom superhero!"

Kline stood back and watched as his present and past dates nattered on with one another in a strange kind of pissing contest, completely forgetting he existed as they stepped away from the dance floor closer to the wall to hear each other better. He shrugged and tossed back what was left of his drink, drank Rhiannon's, then signed a couple of autographs for the girls who had gathered around him. Apparently, it was after two and they were letting in a few from the street.

A quarter-hour later, he watched Rhiannon excuse herself from the conversation after getting Jill's phone number. There was a stiff hug and a European kissing of cheeks, and Rhiannon turned off toward Kline. Jill caught his eye and smiled a bit wistfully, then shrugged with her eyebrows and waved before turning back into the crowd to disappear.

When Rhiannon reached him, he was tactfully trying to decline what appeared to be a rather lascivious invitation from one of the scantily clad women at the bar. It was entertaining to watch her response. Once more, she walked up and linked her arm through his, forcing the bleached blonde tanning bed refugee to move slightly away. "Sorry, honey, no threesomes for Kline tonight. Check back with us on Friday, though, you might get lucky."

The girl's lips peeled away from her teeth in an unflattering sneer and she huffed, then changed tactics abruptly with a purr to Kline as she slipped him a card. "Call me."

She sauntered off and Kline laughed. "No threesomes? Damn."

"Not on the first date," Rhiannon scolded. "What kind of a girl do you think I am?"

"The kind that's just my type."

She laughed. "I would have thought I wasn't nearly tall enough--or blonde enough."

"Do I really seem that shallow?"

"Not in person."

He laughed and wrapped an arm around her shoulders, willing himself not to look for Jill. Bird in hand, he repeated to himself. Bird in hand. "So? More dancing? Drinks? Go elsewhere? You're far too lovely to waste on an evening you aren't enjoying."

"Hm, well, there is this really great bottle of wine back at my place," Rhiannon said, thoughtfully, "and it is nearly last call."

"Are you inviting me back to your place?" His eyes danced as his lips curved up.

"You have to drive me home," she answered, "I may as well let you have a drink when you do."

"Fair enough," he said, guiding her through the crowd towards the door.

The air was cool outside, and he felt the shiver that ran up her spine as they waited for the valet to bring the car. "Cold?" he said, peeling his jacket off as she nodded and placing it around her shoulders. "That should help."

"Thanks," she said, gathering it around her. She melted into the fabric with a sigh, so Kline leaned over and pressed his lips to hers, fingers sliding up the side of her face to stroke a stray lock of her hair. He pulled back after a moment then said, "If I forget to say it later, this has been a great night."

Rhiannon smiled. Her eyes were twinkling like she was holding back a joke. Thad had said she was quick with the zingers. "It has," she agreed. "I'm really glad you called."

He nodded, turning in his seat and putting the car in gear. "So am I. This is the first proper date I've had in ages. I'd forgotten how good dates could be."

"Sometimes you get lucky, I guess. Take a chance and see how it goes," she said. "That's the best way."

"My dates are generally set ups. Roland, my manager, is always sending me off with some starlet or another. Generally vapid, wasteful, horrid things full of plastic. You are a breath of fresh air. How is it that Baddie Thaddie hasn't tried to tie you to his side?"

"I keep telling him no."

"Brilliant," Kline laughed. "He's accepting that?"

"In spurts."

"He really was aghast that you gave me your number."

"Oh, he's always aghast when it isn't his idea."

"That's one of his six expressions. Aghast. He's got aghast, horny, post-coital, surprised, in love--which is rather like horny-- and ill, which is rather like post-coital. I know them all well."

"Six years on a series together will do that to you, I guess. Were you friends before?"

"Nah. People always think so because we both have ac- cents–they always think he's a Brit, but that's where we met. Orig- inally there was only one Brit written in, but they liked us both equally, so they split out the character into two."

Kline veered onto the freeway, speech slowing until he was safely in the right hand lane. "He does fucking good accent work. And, he's a good guy and we struck it off."

"Yeah, I suppose he's all right. It's good that there's no an- imosity between you. A lot of people don't survive sitcoms with friendships intact."

"Well, the truth of it is, Thad and I are mates. The rest of the cast didn't fare so well. The rest of us are only on speaking terms if there's anybody watching."

"There's always someone watching, Kline."

"Then I guess we're always on speaking terms," he shrugged amiably.

"You met your ex-wife on the show, didn't you?"

"Yeah. She was a special guest for a three-epi arc. I had her knocked up by the end of the second ep. Thad was furious, as he was making moves on her and calling her his future ex-wife. He was close, just no cigar."

"Do you two always compete for women?"

"We used to, when he was between wives, you know? We were always trying to prove ourselves. I'd only been in LA for a year. The show was a huge success, and we were treated like princes. It's easy to get caught up."

Rhiannon nodded. "I hope old habits don't die hard."

"They do for some. For him, when he's married, he's married. For me, once Jack was born, things were different. I couldn't just fuck around anymore. I mean, I had a great childhood. My parents were great. Really in love. I wanted my kid to have that. It's important. But it didn't work out, you know? Nina had other priorities and I don't think she ever really forgave me for putting her out of work for a year. But Jack's the best thing in my life, so I don't regret it. Shit," he laughed, "like you wanted to hear all that."

Rhiannon was smiling. "Actually, I think that was the most genuine, unaffected thing you've said tonight, and it was great." She turned in her seat so she was facing him. "Priorities are important and kids are the top, or they should be, no matter what. What I was getting at was that I hope that you didn't ask me out to get one over on Thad, but now that you've said all of that, I don't believe that you did."

He glanced over and shook his head seriously, "No, it had nothing to do with Thad. I just fancied you. Still do. Hope you don't mind?"

"Not at all."

They rode in silence for a bit then he asked, "So how do you know Jill Parker?"

"Jill? We met back in New York. Spent time in some of the same social circles. We lived in the same building when I was in film school at NYU after I finished my undergrad in Boston, down the hall from one another, actually." Rhiannon said.

"Good friends?" he asked.

She laughed, "Did that look like good friends to you? I mean, I guess? We were friends-ish? Friends adjacent. We weren't close. I'm not sure Jill's close to anyone. At first, we hung out a little more. She told me I needed to rub off some of the Boston if I was going to fit in, but she was doing a show too and dating a producer, so I didn't see her a whole lot. I'd say we were friendly? But maybe not friends. Acquaintances. Why? How do you know her?"

"I lived in New York when I first came to the States. I think I said that already. I give so many interviews I forget what I've said to people and what I haven't. I should keep notes."

"You did tell me that, but that doesn't tell me how you know her. The Village is a big place."

"We met through some friends. A girl I knew. Uh, and she dated one of my friends."

"Not Thad?"

"No, didn't know him yet, remember? No, she was hanging out with my friend, Gus. He's a designer now. He was at F.I.T. then."

"August Hall?"

"Yeah! Gus. That's the one."

"Oh, I know him. He goes by August now. He's a riot."

"You know him?"

"Sure, Jill introduced us at a party. He's very sarcastic. I liked him instantly."

"I had no idea he was still around there."

"He's not. He's out here."

Kline's eyes flew open wide. "What? Really?"

"Yeah, he's doing costume design for Lucasfilm."

"Really?"

Rhiannon nodded as they pulled up in front of her house. "I haven't seen him since I've been here, of course, but he left New York about three years ago."

"That long?"

"Yes, it has to be. He left while I was an intern with Colbert," Rhiannon said, as he was getting out of the car to come around and open her door for her. As she was getting out, she added. "Aren't the two of you still friends?"

"Colbert, huh? You worked for him? I kind of burned a lot of bridges when I left," Kline said uneasily. "And, I stole a couple of girls out from under Gus back in the day. I don't think there's any love lost between us."

Rhiannon looked like she might ask more questions, so Kline repeated, "You worked for Colbert?"

"I did an internship on his show."

"He absolutely hates me!" Kline laughed.

"Why? I never worked directly with him, but I've only heard great things."

"Nina. She's part of his social circle somehow. She got him in the divorce and god knows what she's told him," Kline said, Clara's earlier declaration of "fuckboi" ringing in his ears.

Rhiannon clucked her tongue against her teeth, punching in the code to her door's lock pad. "That happens sometimes. Still want that drink?"

"I'd love it," he said with a smile, following her inside. She led him into the kitchen, handed him the bottle and the opener, then went for glasses as he uncorked the wine. "You said you lived in the same building with Jill. Did she still live in the old Lemmon building?"

"No," Rhiannon shook her head, holding out a glass to be poured. "She moved out of there when her mother died. Got a nice one-bedroom on the edge of Greenwich. She had the front unit, so she had a mini-balcony and a lot of windows. I had a middle unit that was dark as the grave."

"Her mother died? Shit." Kline said. "That woman was a bitch. I always thought she was too mean to die. When'd she die?"

"Before I moved there. She'd been on her own for a couple of years I think."

"She was much better off then, I'm sure," Kline said, pouring them each a glass.

"Seemed so," Rhiannon said, taking a sip. She put the glass on the counter and looked up at him. "You and Jill were pretty close, huh?"

"We were all tight in that group. We were young and trying to get started in the business. Well, Jill was already in, but she was trying to transition from child actor to adult roles. That can be worse. That's back in the day when I was just modeling. It's just-

-strange, suddenly seeing people from the past. Feels a bit like a school reunion. It's funny how it brings back exactly how awkward and how much of an arse I was."

"I suppose it does," Rhiannon agreed. "Funny that we know the same people and yet we never met before yesterday."

He nodded and swirled his wine before drinking it. "What about you?" he asked. "I've been on about me and people I know. But it's you I'm interested in. What should I know about you?"

She gave him a sly smile over the rim of her glass. "You should know that I'm debating about whether or not it would be wise to sleep with you on the first date."

"Oh?" He shifted to change his body language, his whole demeanor telegraphing interest and he leaned onto the counter. "Who's winning so far?"

She hummed. "There's this concern, you see. Even the most self-assured, brazen of us have this concern. If I sleep with you on the first date because I really want to, will you call me again? And if I don't sleep with you, even though I really want to, will you call me again? To do or not to do, that is the question and it's a toughy."

"I'm going to call you again either way," Kline smiled slowly. "Just decide if you want me to call you in the morning from a few miles away, or from your shower."

Rhiannon laughed, a warm throaty sound, and leaned across the counter. "Kiss me and then I'll give you my answer."

Instead of meeting her halfway, Kline put down his glass and walked around the counter behind her. He pressed his body up against hers, wrapping one arm around her waist, sliding his other hand up into her hair to pull out the clip that held it. When it was free, he took a handful and gently used it to guide her head back against his shoulder, then he pressed his lips against hers, fingers spidering down her throat as he kissed her.

She slid her hand up along his arm until her fingers were brushing his collar and tangling in his hair, drawing him closer as the kiss deepened. Kline turned her slowly in his arms and began trailing his lips down her chin and along the expanse of her throat. "Have you decided?" he breathed against her neck, raising gooseflesh on her skin.

Rhiannon turned her head and nipped at his ear. "The bedroom's down the hall."

Without another word he picked her up by the waist and she wrapped her legs around him as he carried her in the direction she'd indicated. He pushed the door open easily, and deposited her on the bed, his lips on hers, hips pressing into hers. He took the time to kiss as much of her body as he could reach before pushing up her skirt and peeling her out of her g-string. Then he buried his face between her legs and took his lazy time exploring with fingers and tongue until she was begging him for more. It was a pride thing. No one was going to say Kline Scott was bad in bed.

Rhiannon strained to meet him when he finally brought his body in line with hers. She knew what she was doing, and she knew what she wanted him to do, which was a nice surprise. It made the coupling much less first time, and much more let's do that one more time. So, he did.

She was still thrumming when he rolled away and slipped off to her bathroom. He used the toilet, flushed and washed his hands, then he walked back in to her appreciative smile. "Someone works out."

"Part of the job," he grinned, winking at her. "You okay?"

"I dunno, am I?" she teased, arching an eyebrow with the question.

"You're delicious, darling. But I want to make sure you're not riddled with regret."

"No regrets here," she said, shaking her head as she raised the sheet and peeked under it. "None here, either."

Kline laughed. "I should go home." He rubbed his face. "I try to be there when Jack wakes up if I'm not there when he goes to sleep."

"Ah. Well, so much for calling me from my shower in the

morning," she said, gathering the sheet around her and sitting up.

"I can call you from my shower. I just can't let him wake up without me there. Not without telling him first. He'd be hurt."

Rhiannon shook her head, "No, of course, I understand. I was just teasing. I do that a lot." She laughed. "You should definitely be there."

He nodded and raked a hand through his sex-tousled hair. "Right. I'll call you then? We could have dinner on Wednesday."

"Absolutely. You know where to find me," she said, sliding from the bed and wrapping the sheet around her more securely. "You might want to put some clothes on before you go, though. Otherwise, you could get arrested."

"Easier to strip search me this way." He pulled her close and kissed her. "Wednesday night. I'll pick you up around eight. If I don't call before then, it's because I don't have a moment free, but I'll see you Wednesday."

Kline drove home, humming along with the radio, feeling as relaxed and content as he had in weeks. Rhiannon had been an unexpected pleasure in a random day, and he was already looking forward to seeing her again. It was nearing six in the morning when he pulled onto his street. There were already (or still) a handful of girls at his front gate, so he turned left and went in the back way, parking in the garage for a change, then entered the house through the kitchen.

He grabbed a banana from the fruit dish and lingered there munching on it. His eyes fell on the corkboard by the phone and followed the thumbtacks down to the card at the bottom. Jill. Why was Jill in LA? She'd always been ambitious, but only for stage acting. She hated television and film, calling celluloid actors unprofessional and undisciplined. In theater, you had to know your lines, your blocking, and your audience. You couldn't afford retakes and cue cards. It made her crazy when a popular tv or film star took the boards expecting someone else to feed them lines.

She had emailed him a few times after he'd left New York. He'd answered maybe twice. She'd been tentative, and tried to be positive about his move, but was obviously hurt. He'd been cav-alier, ignored her hints that she could come to visit, and glossed over her heartbreak with generic talk of how perfect life was in LA, and how busy.

Word had come from August that she was despondent. Kline cared. He truly did, but at the time he couldn't force himself to act on it. He figured that he couldn't afford to be tied down. He knew that his marketability had to do with his single status. "Love isn't enough," he'd written in his last email. She'd finally worked up the nerve to ask about his former declarations and he'd been as poetic as possible in blowing it off. He cringed now at some of the things he'd said.

Kline plucked the card off the board and sat down, flicking it between his fingers. The first time she'd broken up with him he'd shown up at her door with an armful of flowers, begging for a second chance.

"I love you," he'd told her. "And I want to be with you. I can't promise perfection. I can't even promise decency when it comes to me. But I'm offering to be there for you in the bad and the good. I want you." And he'd meant it. He had loved her. He just also loved attention, women, and he had a dream to chase.

So there had been more bad than good, but the good was perfection. She put up with the infidelities for whatever reason. Maybe she liked the kiss and kick as much as he did. Given her mother, maybe she was only comfortable with love when she had to beg for it. He shuddered hearing his therapist's voice in his head.

He hadn't been able to figure out how to end things when he was preparing to go to LA. He knew she loved New York and would hate it there. He knew he'd never be able to do long dis-tance. So, he'd done the passive-aggressive thing, slept with her best friend and let her come home to find it. She'd broken up with him. But then he couldn't stand that she'd started to date August, and he'd seduced her back. She'd thought it was a new beginning.

He tossed the card down and rubbed his face. He'd always felt bad about it, but it had been out of sight, out of mind. Now it was living in LA with him. And looking better than ever. Fairy tale pretty had grown up into quiet, classic beauty, but her eyes still telegraphed everything she felt. It was part of what made her such a great actress.

He mused a little longer, then got up. He'd been what he'd been, and he couldn't change it. All he could do was move ahead and learn from the mistakes.

Before hitting the shower, he shot his assistant a voice text with some delivery instructions. A box of Cubans to be sent to Thad James with the attached note, "I owe you one." Two dozen lilies to be sent to Rhiannon Charles with the attached note, "Not as beautiful as you. See you Wednesday." And a bouquet of daisies to go to Jill Parker's rental, the note reading, "Are they still your favorites? I'll call you soon." That done, he washed up, and went to bed.

Rhiannon Charles

"Aw, who died?" Thad asked, frowning at the arrangement of lilies on Rhiannon's desk.

"Celibacy. May it rest in peace," she replied, finishing the sentence she was typing before looking up at him.

"On the first date?" he said, dropping into the chair in front of her. "I'm surprised."

"Yeah, so was he," she sighed, saving the file she was working on. "What do you want, Thad?"

"I have come for the pages, darling. You promised me the rewrites by two," he said, tapping his watch.

"Liar. I'll send Josie out with them when they're ready. What do you actually want?"

"I wanted to find out how things went with Kline last night."

"Ah. Ulterior motive," she said, pulling a small sheaf of papers from a folder on her desk. "Things went fine. As you can see, he sent me flowers."

"Are you seeing him again?"

"Wednesday," she said. "Dinner. Now, if you want to know any more details, you will have to ask him."

"I did," he replied, wrinkling his nose. "He told me to fuck off."

"Well, I would tell you the same thing, but I like my job."

"I wouldn't fire you if I deserved it."

Rhiannon raised her eyebrows and stared at him for a long moment. "You can't fire me, you moron."

"Alright, I'm going," he said, unfolding himself from the chair and heading for the door. He paused and looked back at her. "I would have sent you roses."

"You should anyway. Ratings are up," she replied, now focused on the computer again.

Thad blinked at her, a small smile tugging at the corner of his mouth, "Touché. So, about that date…"

"Not in this lifetime."

The smile disappeared in a sigh of exasperation as he pulled the door closed and walked away.

Rhiannon couldn't help but laugh. Thad was a fair match for wit, and he didn't hold it against her when she was a little rough with the teasing. It really was part of her personality. Her mother called it a defense mechanism and was sure that her bright, beautiful daughter was going to die alone because she kept scaring all the men away.

It was true that some men didn't know how to take her, and some were even threatened by her, especially when she made it very clear that she wasn't some moony-eyed female just waiting for a man to come along and make her life worth living. She gave as good as she got, and sometimes better, and for the most part, she ended up on her own because men either couldn't keep up with her, or didn't want to try.

There had been a few contenders. One had lasted the better part of year, in fact. They'd lived together in that flat in Greenwich while she was interning. He wanted to be an actor, but he was terrible at it. No presence. Rhiannon tried to be supportive and instead ended up his harshest critic. She was honest, but not brutal. Everyone else was too nice to him. They all led him to believe that he was better than he was, and he was setting himself up for disaster.

When his classes didn't go well, he blamed her. When he didn't land the parts he auditioned for, which was most of the time, he blamed her. He had come home drunk after a particularly bad audition and threatened to crack her skull open. She went to stay with some friends and never went back, except to collect her things while he was in class.

After that, she went through a dry spell. More self-imposed than anything. There was interest. Always. She just didn't reciprocate. She focused on the work and dallied with a few casual acquaintances. A fling with a professor at NYU. A stage manager at the late-night show. A hot bartender from that club down the street.

Rhiannon looked at the creamy white fluted flowers that Kline had sent her and puzzled over them. What did lilies mean? They weren't really romantic if you weren't in a church, and even then. Tigers and Callas were pretty and exotic, but white Easter lilies were a bit funereal. It was a lovely gesture, of course. She hadn't expected flowers. In fact, she half expected him to ghost her. Rhiannon who? That was his reputation after all.

She'd lain in bed after Kline left, thinking through the evening, analyzing it more than she knew she should. It was a habit, and completely unavoidable considering that the man in question had been inhabiting her fantasies for almost a decade. It was all still a bit too surreal to have the poster on her wall come to life in her bed. The date had gone well, she thought, aside from the sex, which was pretty hot. They seemed to click. He seemed to really like her. But he pretended to be in love for a living, so what could she really go by?

And he did get up and leave pretty fast after bedding her. She knew he had a son, and his kid should be a priority. She firmly believed that. It just seemed odd that Kline hadn't been too worried about getting home before they did the deed. All the talk was about being together in the morning. She'd had men make excuses and run on her before, once they'd scored.

Rhiannon sighed. She was going to have to be careful with this one. He was dangerous. It would be easy for him to get close and do some damage. Better to be casual and not expect too much. Better to wait on his next move and see how things played out. If he didn't cancel Wednesday, that would be a good sign.

She pushed her glasses up on the bridge of her nose and turned back to her work, finishing the last page and printing it off before heading into the staff meeting to go over plans for May sweeps.

She'd been laser-focused for hours when her phone rang twice before she answered, and Kline said hello.

"Wow--somehow I expected not to hear from you 'til Wednesday," she said after he'd spoken.

"Yeah well. What can I say? You're intoxicating and I couldn't wait."

"Aw, I'll bet you say that to all the girls," she said, though she could hear him smiling.

"Just the smart, pretty ones."

"Know a lot of those, do you?"

"Lots of pretty. Lots of smart. Very few pretty and smart at the same time. So," he grinned, "I had a great time last night. We're still on for Wednesday, right?"

"Absolutely. I never turn down a free meal," she said, then laughed. "I'm awful. I really need to stop talking. Just ignore me."

"That would make for a very one-sided and boring conversation. Please, continue."

"Glutton for punishment. Wow, I learn something new about you every day!" she said, the smile still in place. "Thank you for the flowers."

"My pleasure. I've got some Callas growing in my back garden. I love them. I thought you might."

"Callas are very pretty, but so are the Easters you sent. Lovely blooms," Rhiannon said. "I've been getting a lot of attention today. Condolences mostly."

"Easters?" His voice went up an octave. "Fuck! Easters? Aw, Rhiannon, I'm sorry. They were--heh--I can only imagine what you thought that meant," he started to laugh.

"Thad asked me who died," she said, seriously.

"Oh no," he said, shaking his head at the mistake. "What did you say?"

"Celibacy. You should have seen his face."

Kline laughed again. "I didn't tell him shit. He asked."

"He said he did."

"You two seem close?"

She chuckled, "He calls me his work wife, which is confusing because he has an actual work wife."

"He has all kinds of wives. Work, ex, current, next. All kinds."

They chatted until she heard a voice in his background. "It's my PA," he said, apologizing. "I have to go. I've got an appointment with the stylist and I'm meeting her down on Rodeo."

"Playing dress up?"

"Shopping for the Lone Star press tour. I'm trying to get edgier."

"Wear a kilt."

"So you can look under it?"

"Maybe." She grinned. "Definitely."

"Definitely. No, though. No kilts. I will call you later and make arrangements for you to see everything you want, though. Good?"

She laughed, "Good."

Rhiannon got back to work. Kline aside, she felt like she had a lot to prove. She had come into Simon Says in its fourth season. The show had won an Emmy in its first season as a spinoff from Higher Ed, but egos and tempers between the show runner and head writer meant a revolving door until both were out. She had walked into a mess that wasn't sure whether it was a sitcom or a sitdram, with a schizophrenic storyline and a leading man who had basically become a handsome Homer Simpson.

The cast was phenomenal, and the writing team was strong. All they really needed was a direction and for the powers that be to stop fighting like jealous gods, and give them room to be great. And thank god for that because when Rhiannon had stepped into the role it was widely known that the executive producer had hired her to put the last nail in the coffin.

By all accounts she was too young, too inexperienced, and too much of a New York late-night writer to be a good fit for the job. Even she agreed with that, but she wasn't about to pass up a chance at the title and the salary. So, she'd put her serious glasses on and gotten down to business digging out the threads of what had made the show great in its debut, and finding ways to knit that back into the current story arcs. It was like darning an old sock, and frankly, the sock was toast when she got to it.

Comedy writing was hard. Situational comedy writing was even harder without falling into the trap of reducing your characters to the bare bones of what made the audience laugh. That's what the writers had done to Thad, and it was heartbreaking to watch old episodes and see him throwing everything he had into the character of Simon Saenz, when all Simon was saying was, "D'oh."

The actor had been nothing if not dejected in his role when he'd met Rhiannon for the first time, and by the end of their first handshake, she had decided she was going to give him a reason to feel good about his job if it killed her. He was genuine and nice, something that was rare in any industry, much less entertainment, and he had welcomed her to the team like she was as big a name as he was, regardless of her actual inexperience. She wasn't going to let Thad down, regardless of whatever else happened.

The first episode of the season was hers and she'd written Simon a rollicking take on the audition process that established actors faced after a certain age. It was the old, "get me a young

George Clooney" thing and was funny for the fact that "Simon" was still young and could still be gotten. The overall gag was that the teenaged boyfriend of his oldest daughter ended up getting the role. It gave Thad a chance to show off some chops as a man facing down his mortality with good humor and grace, and it set up the rest of the season as Simon started chasing down more mature roles.

With that direction established, and a fresh outlook for the worn-out jokes about Simon's ego and looks, the writing team took up the theme and spun gold out of the simple thread. Now the marketing team was preparing their package for the Emmys, and it actually felt like they had a shot. They fully expected that the nominations came down, Simon Says would be on the cards for both outstanding writing and leading actor in a comedy. Season five was secure, and so was Rhiannon's reputation as she started to network slowly into the LA scene.

The differences between New York and LA were night and day, even the parties were polar opposites. She figured it had to do with people in LA never having to worry about getting cold or rained on. Everything was love, light, and namaste. Even the knives you had to pull out of your back every now and then were dripping with false friendliness. She often found herself missing the in-your-face values of Boston, or the cold disdain of Manhattan.

A few weeks into the scene with a handful of those parties under her belt, Rhiannon had gone out with a writer from another show, an entertainment attorney, a realtor who was trying to break into acting, and off-and-on was still seeing a guy who directed music videos and short film. She wondered about him, then remembered he was off in Europe directing some indie thing he hoped was his big break.

He wasn't serious because of his schedule, but maybe if he was rooted in one place, he could have potential. Distantly, she wondered about Kline's schedule. If he started picking up more films, he'd be all over the world on location soon enough. Not that she could see herself settling down with a movie star, and no doubt that's what he was.

"Playtime's over," she growled at herself, finding she'd fallen into a daydream of what life might be like on his arm. "Work."

But, as soon as work was done for the day, she was cataloging the personal maintenance that needed to happen before her next date and making appointments to get everything ready for his close-ups. Just thinking about what that man had done with his tongue sent a jolt through her pelvis. Whatever she had to do to make that easier for him, she was going to do!

Jill Parker

"Daisies?" August laughed when Jill walked back into the kitchen of her Hollywood Hills rental with the flowers that had just been delivered. "Who sent those?"

"I ran into Kline Scott at lunch yesterday," she said noncommittally. "Royce gave him my information. Then he spent the rest of the afternoon telling me how great it would be for my career if I could be seen around town with him."

August slowed, looking at her as she put the arrangement down on the counter, then he plucked the card out of the holder and read it, eyes narrowing. "Well, that's presumptuous."

"That's just Kline. He's Kline."

"When he calls are you going to see him?"

Jill sighed and pushed her hair back. "It's been ages, August. A decade since the last time I had any real contact with him. I'm kind of over him."

"You never get over your first love."

"I'm not going to argue with you. Besides, the odds of him calling are about as high as the odds of my staying in LA past this film. Decreasing by the minute."

Dropping the card beside the flowers, August swiveled on his barstool to watch Jill go over to the window and let down the blinds, so she performed the act more than just doing it, giving him something to watch. She wasn't really unhappy with LA. In fact, she was being fussier than normal because she liked it more than she'd wanted. True, she hated the clubs and the oily suits, but she was loving the house she was in, loving the pool with the landscaped grotto, and absolutely, albeit silently, adoring the beach.

"You're getting tan," August teased. "You can be an ice princess and a beach bunny at the same time."

"I'm a pool princess! Where's Lola? Don't you have something to do with her today?" Jill growled playfully, naming August's girlfriend. "Can't you go harass her? I'm sure she misses you."

"Lola is filming today. You are the only person I have to harass at all. Lucky!"

Jill went back to what she'd been doing before the doorbell rang; sorting invitations. August had been helping her paw through the stack and had been instructing her on who was a Who and who was a Huh? "How's this one?" she asked, holding up a card. "It's to Denver Dawson's Oscar's after party."

"Please," he rolled his eyes. "Denver Dawson is trying to get anyone to her do. No. You'll go to the Vanity Fair party."

"I don't think I'm invited to that."

"Of course you are, darling. You have Tonys. If you don't have a paper invite, you'll be my date."

"Lola's gonna love that," Jill laughed, then hummed. "I'm presenting at the Grammy's next month. Dateless."

"Take me. I'll dress you."

She hummed again, non-commitally. Mentally sorting through her plus-one options as she went through the stack of envelopes. The divorce was going to be her headline, given that the final court date was literally days before the Grammy's. Presenting was going to be a necessary nightmare to endure. Let the internet talk about her fashion instead of her failed marriage. If she could snag an interesting date, they would talk about that.

When she'd finished sorting, she had more envelopes left than options. She wondered about Kline. In the past, he was always up for anything that shone a spotlight his way.

She felt August's eyes on her and sighed when he asked, "So are you going to see him?"

"I've already seen him. What else is there? He looks the same."

"Botox," August said, with a smirk.

"I don't think so."

He frowned. "You're right. Maybe not yet. Give him a few more years out here and he'll be having it all done."

"We all will," she said dismissively. After a beat she looked him in the eye. "If he calls, do you want to go with me to see him?"

"Oooh. Could I? I would kill to see the look on his face."

She chuckled. "So would I, actually." Jill leaned back in her seat and sighed. "August, it's been so long. So why, when I saw him, did I immediately feel like it only happened a month ago? Or a day ago?" In a softer voice she added, "And why did my stomach flip?"

"Unfinished business," August replied, with a shrug as he fingered the raised lettering on one of the envelopes.

"But it is finished. He finished it. Kaput. Buh-bye, Jill. Finished. And I'm a thirty-year-old woman now." She shuddered dramatically at the last statement. "Twenty-nine year old woman. I'm in the middle of a divorce. Everything is different."

"But you didn't get any answers. Even after all this time, you want to know why. Why did he just go without a word? Why did he not love you the way you loved him? Why did he have to break your heart? You never stopped loving him, Jill. You just compartmentalized the feelings and moved on. Seeing him again brought it all back."

"Oh, he left without a word because he's a coward. He didn't love me like I loved him because--well, he just didn't. You can't make people love you. Why'd he have to break my heart? There just wasn't any other way out of it for him." She sighed again, rolling her eyes at herself. "It's this divorce. I'm just completely unstable. Completely. Yes, come to the Grammy's with me. Dress me. Make me over into your vision of my greatness."

August laughed. "What a fantastic invitation. Lucky for you, I'm too desperate to get my hands on your closet to turn you down. For now? Why don't you let me take you to lunch and then we'll do some shopping? Your wardrobe is not LA. You look like an uptight ghoul. I'll have you smiling and looking like you belong here in no time."

"Mm shopping. Lunch. You. Okay," Jill winked at him. "Let me change clothes."

She trotted out of the room just as her phone began to ring. "Get that will you?" She called, "It's Royce. He's calling to tell me what we're doing tonight. Just write it down or something. Or just forget it. I don't want to know!"

August was laughing as he picked up the phone, "Hello?" he asked mirthfully.

She did a quick sweep through her closet, frowning. He was right. She was not outfitted for LA. Everything she had looked like Upper East Side and everything she'd seen since stepping onto the plane at Newark had been more surf than chic. August could help her build a small capsule wardrobe that would last until she could get back home.

If she went back home. Just the word home didn't feel right anymore.

Finally, she chose a pair of champagne-colored, silk palazzo trousers and tucked a salmon-colored chemise into the high waist. Back in New York, she would have completed the look with pearls and nude Manolo's, but she wasn't in New York, so she picked up some gold hoops and wedge-heeled sandals instead. It was fine, she decided in the full-length mirror, then pulled her hair up in a ponytail that felt too casual until she wound it around into a bun. Again, she thought, fine. Adequate. Would do for the moment.

August was pressing the end button on the phone and setting it on the counter when she walked back in. "And good riddance."

Jill walked in, giving him a twirl to critique. "Was it Royce?"

August rolled his eyes, "No. Unfortunately. You look lovely. Maybe studs instead of the hoops?"

"You don't think that's too stiff looking? I'm going for relaxed, not chic. Who was on the call then?" she asked, pausing for a moment before adding. "Oh, was it Rhiannon?"

"Rhiannon? That's a name I haven't heard in a while. Mm, I think chic is always preferable."

"So, not her," Jill said, raising her eyebrows, starting to take out the hoops. "Who called?"

"Kline Scott. You know, the movie star?" August followed her back to her bedroom where he started sifting through her jewelry. "Here. Wear these." He handed over a pair of diamond studs.

That made her laugh. "You were awful to him, weren't you?"

"I was," August smirked. "And it felt good."

"Oh! Oh! August, I totally forgot! Guess who I saw Kline with?"

"Kara Viceroy. His costar on his last film."

Jill shook her head, fastening August's preferred earrings. "No. I'll give you a hint." Her eyes twinkled and she thought for a moment then said, "Which handsome action star was out dancing with a winsome wordsmith? Rumor has it that this tea party transplant once shared building space with another of the mega-star's old flames."

August's eyes went wide. "He's dating Rhiannon? Our Rhiannon? How did that happen? I thought she had some taste."

"Hey! I resemble that remark! I think they're sleeping together. I'm not sure if they are dating? She was very territorial." Jill laughed. "She came out of the ladies looking like she was going to take my head off for talking to her man."

"Rowr. Well, she isn't a shrinking violet or a shady queen like you. She'll say it to your face. Very up front, that one."

"Shady queen?"

"Mean girl? You like that better?"

"Hey!"

"All I'm saying is that you're passive-aggressive and she's aggressive. And now we'll get to see which of those Kline likes more." His eyes glittered with mischief as he said it.

"Tsk! Don't be mean!"

"But you dumped me for him," August sniffed. "Twice."

"You were too good for me," Jill said, swatting his shoulder. "Shopping. Come on and I'll tell you all about last night."

"Oh god, that's who he was with when you saw him out? Does she know about the two of you?"

"Only if he told her. You know I don't kiss and tell. I never named names when it came to him."

August shook his head. "It will never last. Might be good to see him get a taste of his own medicine, actually."

"His wife left him, August. That's strong medicine right there. Don't wish ill on him. Bad juju."

"Juju my ass."

Jill transferred the contents of her purse from the black Chanel she'd worn the day before, into a cream-colored Celine that matched her sandals, and pushed her Jackie O style sunglasses up on top of her head. "Are you driving, or are we taking a car?"

"I'm driving, Darling. This isn't New York."

New York or not, once they were inside the shops the atmosphere was universal. They started at Chanel and worked their way through Hermes and Louis Vuitton with August acting as the most expensive stylist in the world. Even with her budget for spending, Jill was starting to feel lightheaded by the time they came to Prada. She wasn't even sure she liked what he was piling up for her, but he'd been in LA for five years, so she supposed he knew what he was doing. At the very least, he knew what looked good on her.

They were laughing together in a fitting room when August walked out ahead of her so she could come consider herself in the three-way mirror.

"I don't know why you need to see it. Look at it in the mirror of my eyes, darling," he said, drawling out the soapy words.

"Let me be the window to your soul!"

All she could do was laugh and then laugh harder when she saw herself in the dress he'd chosen. Instinctively, she put her hand up to hide her naked breastbone, then froze, meeting a different set of eyes in the reflection of the middle mirror. Kline's usually heavy-lidded bedroom eyes were wide, his head tilted with a strange smile on his face.

"Oh... Kline. Hello."

As soon as she spoke, he seemed to force his face to rearrange into something friendlier, less hungry. "Hello again. Fancy meeting you here."

August stepped out in front of her, all his Bonhomme gone. "Well, look what the wind blew in. You really are everywhere, aren't you, It Boy?"

"Gus," Kline smiled tightly. "That's a nice dress," he said to Jill, admiring the daring frock. "Are you looking for something for the Grammys? I heard you were presenting."

"She's wearing an original for the Grammys," August answered. "A little something I've cooked up."

"I was threatening to go back to New York," Jill said, trying to inject levity. "So August brought me shopping. He's trying to convince me that LA has all there is to offer."

Kline nodded. "The best shops. The best restaurants. Great weather. Golden opportunity on every corner. You can't ask for more."

"Hm. I miss New York. Things feel different there," Jill said, smoothing the dress she was wearing, keeping her sternum covered. "Less fake."

"More tension," Kline offered.

"More fabric," Jill mused. "This dress isn't going to work."

"Well, there's plenty of other boutiques, darling," August said, cheerily, "and if you don't find anything you like here, we'll just go to my studio."

"In New York, Gregor just sends things over to the apartment." She sulked slightly.

"We'll move Gregor out here then," August laughed.

"I'm not letting you go back now that I've got you again."

She rolled her eyes to Kline and looked him up and down. She couldn't help but smile. He was still just so handsome. "Get an Armani. You've got the shoulders for it."

He nodded. "That's usually what I end up wearing. I'm thinking that I might go for something with a bit more edge to it, though. Maybe a kilt? Haven't decided."

"I hear powder blue is making a comeback," August said, before turning to Jill again. "Let's get you out of this dress. We'll be late for the showing at Dior."

"Not a kilt," Jill said, shaking her head around August's shoulder as he started to maneuver her. "Trying too hard."

August was moving her back toward the fitting room and she shrugged apologetically before smiling. "Go for Armani. But leave your tie undone and don't do up your top button. Do just-been-done Rat Pack edge. No one else is doing it this year. You'll look delicious and the media will eat you up."

He smiled. "Sounds just the thing. You always did know what looks good on me."

"I like men. I know what looks good on men."

"What's Gus going to be wearing?" he asked.

Jill laughed, hoping she sounded insouciant and not desperate to get him flirting. "Me."

"Of course." Kline nodded. "Lucky guy."

"Lucky me. If you'll excuse me, I have to go be undressed so he can dress me up again. I've moved into the second stage of my career, you know. August's Barbie."

"That's sounds like a full-time job," he said, grinning. "It was great seeing you again. I'll look for you at the awards."

"It's muse, not Barbie," August called, "now get your injection-molded-self back in here!"

"Are you going to be at the Grammys?"

"I did an audiobook. Got to grind to get that EGOT," he said.

August's disembodied voice said, "Got to have talent to get the O and the T."

"I've got one E more than you'll ever have!"

"Have fun losing the G," August called. "Angela Bassett is up in your category."

Jill laughed, covering her mouth with both hands before saying, "I have to go." She waved at Kline, then turned back into the dressing room. As she did, she could hear Kline speaking to someone. "Let's go. I want to wear Armani," he said. "Rat Pack chic. Vintage cuff links and all."

August said nothing, but his mood had clearly soured, so when she was dressed again Jill asked, "Is Lola joining us for dinner?" August had invited himself along with Jill to meet with her Los Angeles management, suggesting he might be able to help steer her. She hadn't wanted to hurt his feelings, and it was always good to have his company, so she'd agreed he could come along.

"I hadn't thought so."

"It might be nice," Jill suggested gently, patting his chest. "I don't know anyone out here and I'd love to have a girlfriend. It would be nice to have another girl at the table anyway. You could call her while I'm at the spa."

"Oh, am I getting shut out of the luxury experience?"

"You want to sit through my makeup and blow out? God bless you. We're meeting Royce at Giorgio Baldi. I'm sure Lola would love to join us, right? See and be seen? On your arm? Her boyfriend?"

August grumbled but assented. "When you change for dinner, put on the Louis Vuitton strapless. It looks stunning on you, and it won't be terrible with the jewelry you have on."

"Oh, high praise," she chided him softly. So much ego to balance in such a small man.

They took a pass through Gucci before August left her inside the Jose Eber salon with an admonishment not to do anything drastic. He jabbed a finger in her direction and said to the assistant who'd come in as he was leaving, repeating, "Nothing drastic."

Jill apologized after he'd gone and sighed. "He's my Hollywood Svengali. He's afraid I'll ruin his creation if left to my own devices. And I might! So, nothing drastic. I just need a little more movement, maybe a little light, and then a look for the restaurant tonight."

"Of course! It's so nice to have you in. I saw you in Walter Tango Foxtrot a couple of years ago. You were sensational."

Jill beamed at the recognition. "Thank you! I had so much fun doing that. I loved that show!"

"Your big number in the second act—oh my god. Chills. Every time. I have the soundtrack." The girl sang a little, "In the sunset of your smile, I watch your love fading fast, behind the clouds in your eyes, and I reach for you at last."

"Beautiful! Lovely! So nice!" Jill enthused. It was off-key and poorly enunciated, like a pop artist might sing it, but that was for a casting director or a Simon Cowell type to tell the girl, not her. A few minutes and several screechy bars later as the girl sang through Jill's shampoo, Jill was wishing she'd just said, "It's a no for me, Dog," and been done with it.

Jose finally appeared, horrified and apologetic, whisking her off to his chair in a private setting to get to work. Jill explained, "I can't really change much because the studio expects the same Jill Parker they hired, but I feel so muted and so obviously from out of town. I'm going to be here a while and I'm making the rounds, so I need to just freshen it all up without changing it."

"Of course," he agreed. "Nothing needs changed anyway! You're perfect, Darling."

He continued to gas up her ego as he did a quick snip and trimmed some movement into her mid-back, blunt cut and painted in some face-framing highlights. In no time, with a round brush and blow dryer, he had taken her from chilly perfection to eternal spring. Then, she was off to the makeup chair for a beachy glow-up.

When August came back for her, she had changed into the new dress he'd suggested, and was feeling more confident than she had since she'd gotten off the plane at LAX. Air kisses and hugs sent her on her way, and out into August's car, waiting at the valet.

"Lola's meeting us," he said. "I didn't have time to drive back and get her, but I did have time to do just a little more shopping." He passed over a bag from Cartier before easing the car out onto the street.

"What's this?"

"Just a little gift to update your look for the night."

Jill pulled two boxes from the branded bag and found a lovely gold necklace with her initial, and small, tasteful gold hoops. "Oh, Gus! Thank you!"

"It's nothing. In the back? There's a bag from Gucci. I couldn't fathom the idea of you wearing those wedges with that dress."

In the time it took to get to the valet at Palisades restaurant, Jill had changed into the nude stilettos August had chosen for her and updated her jewelry to his taste. "These look all right?" she asked, as she exited the car.

"They look amazing."

She took his arm and let him lead the way up to the hostess stand just in time for Royce to appear and announce their reservation. "Somewhere visible," he told the hostess to be sure. "We want to be on the fence."

"Of course!"

They were two courses in, with Lola joining them before appetizers, when Jill stood up to excuse herself to the ladies' room. She had just passed inside the restaurant when she realized she was looking at Kline again, and she laughed. He rose as she came close to his table.

"Trying to tell me something?" He made a show of asking the night air.

She felt herself smiling crookedly, "You again? Do I need a restraining order?"

"You're in my town, love," he said, with a shrug. "Stands to reason we'd end up in the same places."

"True, but I thought the world was bigger than this."

"Who're you here with?"

"Gus–August. I keep forgetting. He hates Gus now. Ah, his girlfriend, Lola, and my manager."

"Here to be seen?"

"It's like an endless parade of me. The paparazzi are going to be tired of me before they catch on to who I am."

"I can't imagine that." He clucked his tongue then said, "I also can't help thinking I keep running into you for a reason."

"The reason being we're both out and about trying to be seen, and there are only a handful of really good spots for that?"

He chuckled. "Not just that. I didn't even want to come out tonight after the shopping, and yet, here I am and here you are--"

"And? It's a coincidence." She was feeling as breathless as his proximity had always made her when they were teens, and she was hoping it didn't show too much. 'Act, Jill,' she told herself. 'Do the acting.'

"I'd like to see you on purpose," he said. "Seriously. I'd like for us to sit down and talk about…things."

She hesitated. As much as she wanted him to ask to see her, she wasn't sure she could survive another go. Besides, Kline didn't like anything that came easily. "I don't know that we really have anything to talk about, Kline. I mean, it's been years."

He sighed, running a hand through his hair in a familiar gesture that told her he was nervous. "A lot of years to catch up on. I have missed you, Jill."

She bit back the response that flew to her lips and pressed them together instead. She decided to tell the truth. "Things are complicated right now, Kline. I don't know that I'm up to it. It took a long time for me to…be okay with things. Now there are other things going on and I have to focus on them. But it's not that I don't want to see you. It's good to see you. And that you're doing well."

He released the breath he'd been holding and nodded slowly. "I understand," he said, waiting a beat before quirking the corner of his mouth and giving a slight snort. "I guess I should be thankful that you don't hate me. I'm glad to see you're doing well, and hopefully, we'll run into each other again. Soon."

"I don't hate you," Jill said softly, reaching out to touch his hand, brushing her fingers over his before dropping her arm back to her side. "I never did. And at the rate we're going, I'm sure we will run into each other again."

"I look forward to it," he said, offering a smile. They locked eyes and there was a long pause before they both started speaking, making excuses to get back to their tables. Kline wished her well, leaning in to kiss her cheek, before walking away.

Chapter 2

Kline Scott

"Find a friend?" Roland asked, rising to meet Kline as he walked back to the table they would share. "Mmhmm. Jill Parker. We knew each other in New York."

"The Jill Parker? Devil's Party Jill Parker?"

"The same."

Roland laughed. "Jesus Christ! Now that is what I call a friend! She'd be a perfect date for you. High profile. High Q status. Super hot commodity, especially for that play. You know she's down to the skin in that? Fuck yeah! Lots of media attention right now. She's the wounded darling, you know. What kind of mental midget cheats on that? Guess it just goes to the saying, show me a man fucking a hot woman and I'll show you a man tired of fucking that hot woman"

Kline blinked. "I'm sorry? What?"

"Yeah," Roland took a drink and laughed again. "Apparently she'd been married to this producer for a few years, and nobody knew about it until she filed for divorce. He's sleeping with a celebutante. I forget which one. Maybe a Hilton? Interchangeable if you ask me."

Kline took a sip of his water, "Hm. I had no idea." He glanced over his shoulder but couldn't see past the wall that separated the rooms. "That must be what she meant about things being complicated," he said, under his breath.

"What was that?" Roland asked.

"Nothing," Kline said, shaking his head. "I was just talking to myself. Memories, you know?"

"You should ask her out. It would be great dish for her reps, too. Talk about trumping a Hilton sister! You're much higher profile."

"I just tried. She shot me down. Anyway, I'm seeing someone," Kline said casually.

"No, you aren't. Kara's in Spain."

"I'm not seeing Kara. I'm seeing a writer." He tried out the line like he meant it. He could be seeing Rhiannon. She was nice, great in bed, and seemed really into him. Roland was on his last nerve about setting him up, and the idea of being set up with someone who had just shot him down, no matter how nicely, was not a great feeling.

"What? Who?"

"Rhiannon. The writer. I told you and Clara about her," he added to Roland's blank look.

"If you have to add clarifiers, then why bother? Anyway, what's her last name?"

Kline floundered for a moment. He thought she had a first name for a last name, but he couldn't call it to mind. So, he said, "Roland, you really can be a reprehensible twat."

"What's your point? You pay me to look out for your best interests, remember? I'm telling you, right now, you need to be seen with someone high profile. A knockout. Someone who will send the media into a frenzy. An Academy Award, your very career, hangs in the balance."

"I'm seeing someone, and Jill's not interested. I kind of fucked her over back in the day."

Roland dabbed at his mouth with a napkin. "I'm not talking about love here, Kline. Or even like. This is business."

"Roland..."

"I'll get with her people. You'll have lunch here next week. Public--the paparazzi will love it."

"No," Kline said, raising his hand for emphasis. "Just stop this. I let you set me up for a lot of things, but not this woman. Not this time. Just leave her out of your grand schemes." He sighed, tossing his napkin on the table and settling back in his chair. "Besides, what part of 'I'm seeing someone' doesn't register?"

"All of it. I say who. I say when. I say how long."

"The line is how much."

"Whatever. I'm not Julia Roberts. Hell, she's not even Julia Roberts anymore. Jill Parker would be a great PR vehicle. And you know you want to drive that. Who wouldn't want to drive that!"

"That was over a long time ago. I'm not interested, and neither is she. Just, please, Roland--let this one go. I don't want to use her for publicity, and I don't want to mess up what I've got going, okay?"

"We'll see."

They sat and ate, talking of mundane business until Kline saw that Jill and her party were standing to leave. Her manager went first, and then August lagged until his girlfriend practically dragged him along ahead of Jill, who wagged her fingers at Kline. She seemed to reconsider following the rest and walked over to his table instead.

"Hi," she said to Roland, "I'm Jill."

"Roland Davies," he introduced shaking her hand as he did. "Kline's manager."

"Right," she nodded, then looked to Kline. "I don't think you have my cell phone number–just the landline to the house. Would you like to have it?" She pushed back a lock of hair.

Kline couldn't hide his surprise at her appearance and her offer, but he recovered quickly. "Of course. Yeah, I only have the house number."

"I could put it in your phone," she said sheepishly.

Before she could finish her sentence, Roland had grabbed Kline's phone and was putting it in her hand. "There you go. Drop your digits, Honey. He'll call you."

Half her mouth quirked up. "You're from New York, aren't you?"

"You bet I am."

"I like him," she said to Kline.

"Glad someone does," he said, shooting a warning look to Roland as she entered her number in his contacts.

"Most of the managers out here come off smarmy and fake," she said, handing his phone back to him. "At least he doesn't seem fake."

"Oh, he's for real."

She turned her most winning smile on Roland and laughed, "If you didn't belong to Kline, I'd hire you."

"You got management issues? I could hook you up."

"Not issues. No. I just have a very oily manager. He gets me dirty." Kline watched as she bit her lower lip. So fetching. She had turned on the charm and Roland was practically barking like a seal.

"I can take care of that." Roland produced a card. "Call me. We'll talk."

She took his card, then leaned and kissed Kline's cheek. "August doesn't answer my cell phone," she whispered in his ear.

Intoxicated by her warm breath in his ear, a sexy smile stretched across his lips. "Thanks, I'll definitely call you."

"He'll definitely call you before the week is out," Roland added. "Maybe before you get back to your table."

Jill laughed bemusedly and excused herself. "I was just leaving, so he'll have to turn back time to do that."

"If I could turn back time, I'd have called you a lot sooner," Kline said, rising to his feet to give her an actual hug. "A lot sooner."

August, clearing his throat just feet away drew Kline's attention up from where he had whispered the words into Jill's ear.

"Are you coming, Darling?" August asked, the testy voice coming from a placid face. "The valet's got the car already."

Roland popped up from his seat like a prairie dog and pounced, offering his hand to August. "Roland Davies! Pleased to meet you. Listen, I was just asking Miss Parker if I could get fifteen minutes of her time. Kline will be glad to drive her home if you have to run."

Kline looked down at Jill who was wearing an expression of bewilderment that had to match his own, but he recovered quickly and said, "Yeah, I will see Jill home safely if you need to get on your way." Over August's shoulder, a tall, wispy young woman was watching with a face that actually matched August's voice. "Is that your date waiting for you?"

"I'll be fine, Gus. August." Jill said.

"I guess you just want me to bring your shopping round to you tomorrow?" His eyes narrowed and Jill sighed.

"No, silly. I'll come over and pick everything up. You're my Svengali, not my servant. I, I am your humble servant." Kline watched as the warmth in her tone and her glittering good humor worked the tension from August's shoulders until he rolled his eyes and smiled.

"Fine. But call first. I don't get up before noon."

"Noon?" Roland was back in action with a stream of words, navigating August toward the front door using the handshake he'd never disengaged as a lever. "Man, that's a nice life! How do you do that? What's your line of business?"

"Wow," Jill said, as Kline pulled out a chair for her to sit. "He's good. Is that how he negotiates your deals?"

"The studio never sees him coming. You don't have to stay if you don't want. I can call you a car?"

"Do you want me to go?" She looked stricken.

"No! Not at all. No. I'm—I meant what I said. I'd have called you a long time ago."

She relaxed into those words and thanked a waiter who brought her a water and asked for her order. "Just the water, thank you."

They had a moment of awkward silence before Roland returned. "That was August Hall. He did the costumes on that art piece Susan Sarandon did two years ago. You know him, Kline?"

"Yeah. He, Jilly, and I came up together."

"And Jill Parker," Roland turned his toothy smile to her. "Thanks for letting us steal you."

"I've been in LA for three weeks," she said, "and I haven't sat down at a table with anyone who wasn't August, his girlfriend, or my team. How could I resist?"

Kline sat back and watched Roland work his brand of charm. He was brash and rough around the edges, and a couple of times he thought his manager's words might snag on Jill's delicate sensibilities, but she just chuckled and leaned forward into Roland's monologue. Kline realized Roland was pitching her and he groaned. "I'll be right back," he said, going for the toilet.

He did his business, washed his hands, washed them again, then ran his damp fingers through his hair, trying to get the front to fall the way he wanted. It was making too much of an m shape and he felt like badly drawn anime, so he flipped it to a messy side part, scrunched up the curl, then headed back to the table.

When he returned, Jill had pulled her chair closer to Roland. She was sitting with her legs crossed, a dangerous-looking shoe dangling from the tip of her toes as she leaned in to see something on Roland's phone, and when she spoke, Roland looked up surprised. She shrugged and laughed, then scooted her chair back to its place and started talking again, laying her hands palm up on the table.

"I want to retire," she was saying. "Five years and retirement. Six tops. But that's where I want to be financially before I retire. I can't do that in New York. I can't do that in television. So I'm hoping the deal with Devil's Party opens the doors I need. I don't feel like Michael and Royce are on board with that vision.

"It seems like they're either only willing, or maybe only able to get me into smaller auditions, but I'm not just some ingenue. I have three Tony awards. I open successful shows on Broadway. I have multiplatinum records. It's just a matter of getting me in front of the right people. I'm bankable."

Kline sat down as Roland hummed.

"Nice," he said. "You take yourself seriously as a commodity. I like that."

"I know what I'm worth. I've got the experience and the

drive. and I know how to work press. I can bring box office. I know what I want and I'm not afraid of working to get it. But I need to work smarter, not harder if I want to get out."

"Why do you want to retire so early?" Roland asked, leaning back, cutting into the steak he was eating.

"I've been working since I was born. I have not known a time in my life that there wasn't a project, show, or event scheduled in for me. I'm tired. I could retire now, but I would still need to work now and then. I want to make enough money in the next few years that I never have to work again. I can just let my investments work for me."

Roland eyed her seriously. "I handle a few big names," he said. "They do what I tell them because I can get them what they want. Are you willing to work like that? Like Kline. I called Kline up tonight and said, 'You need to be seen,' and told him to be here in an hour. Here he is. Are you willing to do that?"

Jill glanced over at Kline who shrugged. He was bored, but did crack a smile at her answer.

"Until I make what I want, yes. After that, hell no."

"I can get you where you want to be. I think I can get you more. I'm sure I can. How airtight is your contract with your management?"

"Not at all beyond Devil's Party, and a couple of small obligations. I signed a limited representation deal with them. I'll have my attorney call you."

Roland grinned and cut another big bite of steak, and Jill looked at her watch, "That was twenty-five minutes, not fifteen."

"Ready to go?" Kline asked. He was.

"Wait, wait, wait," Roland waved a hand. "Since I got you both here."

"Roland, don't," Kline begged.

"I've been asking Kline how you might feel about a little shared PR? Nothing serious. Just being seen out together. He's got an awards season coming up and having his name in the press is a good thing, but even better if the name comes under a picture of him with Hollywood's hottest new commodity?"

"A showmance?" Jill asked, laughing. She looked at Kline and he felt himself wilting.

"Not even that. Just be seen around. Let Kline show you the city's hot spots. Just be out where you can be photographed."

Jill demurred. "I told Kline that I'm in a complicated situation right now."

"The divorce?"

She looked surprised, but rallied quickly. "Yes. I'm expected in court next month to finalize everything. It's complicated because my husband and I are both well-known, but no one knew we were married. To the public eye, we kept very separate lives. The city rags feel betrayed and Gary, my husband, hired Clark & Checks for PR and they've pretty well eaten me alive there in the last few months leading up to the big event. I'm lucky it's contained to the Manhattan society and that no one is interested in my ex nationwide. It's part of why I'm here in LA. I needed to be able to breathe."

"So you understand the power of good and bad press," Roland said, nodding.

Kline felt Jill's eyes on him, so he opened his own. He had shut them halfway through that conversation and tried to pretend it wasn't happening. The last thing he wanted was for her to shut him down in public over a fake romance. "Are you okay with this?" she asked.

The question surprised him. "Rol and I have been talking about Selena Gomez–trying to get something moving there."

"Oh," Jill said.

"But, Sweetheart, you're three of her!" Roland said.

She looked back to Roland. "Like I said, I've been working my whole life. I fully understand the difference between my public and private persona. I kept a marriage hidden from the public for years, among other things, while theater gossip linked me to everyone except my husband."

"And you didn't mind those links?"

"I can't control what people think," Jill said. 'I know what my job is. My job, as Jill Parker, is to disappear. My job is to become someone else. Sometimes, my job is to pretend to be a different version of myself."

"You hear that, Kline? That's a smart woman talking. Listen, I think both of you will do what it takes to get where you want to be. Why don't you talk about it on your drive home? I gotta get out of here anyway." He shoveled the last bit of steak into his mouth and wiped his lips, standing. "I already got the check," he said around the chewing. "You two have fun."

As soon as he was gone, all the warmth lighting Jill's tone faded out into ice. "Is that why you wanted to talk to me?" She asked. "So you could use me for a fake relationship?"

"No!" Kline hissed, leaning closer, careful to keep his voice down and his face pleasant, just like she was. "No. I had no idea he was going to spring that."

"But you were going to spring it, when?"

"I wasn't. I've already told him no about you."

She hesitated. "You did?"

"Yes. I told him I'd really fucked you over before and I didn't want to try to use you for publicity."

"You did really fuck me over," she agreed with him.

"I know. And I'm sorry. And I would never ask you to do that. I wouldn't use you like that."

"Why not? You did before."

Kline winced at the truth in the words. "Can we get out of here? I'll drive you home."

"Fine," Jill said, rising, tidily pushing her chair back in.

"Fine," he agreed. Out of habit repeated every time he had a woman as company, he put a hand in the small of her back to guide her out, nodding at a few people who waved as they passed, surprised by the bank of flashbulbs that met them on the way to the valet. Fucking Roland, Kline thought. He had to have alerted the swarm of photographers who were calling Kline's name, trying to get a reaction from him.

Jill gave a hard shiver beside him, but by the time he looked down to gauge her level of discomfort, she had pulled a bland smile over her face and found her light and an angle to lean into to make the most of the candid photos being snapped just feet away from her face. When Kline's car came around, he helped her into the passenger side, using his body to shield her from any upskirt photography, then he flicked off the pack of paparazzi as he slung himself into the driver seat.

She was full-on gaping at him as they drove away. "Is it always like this for you?" she asked, stunned.

"More often than not, these days. I got into a scrap with one of them a little while ago and now they're all trying to get me to react." He shifted gears and asked, "What's your address again?"

Out of the corner of his eye, he watched her thumb through her phone. She gave him the address, which he set in his nav system, and she dropped the phone back into her bag. "I need to learn this, I guess."

Shifting again, Kline grunted his agreement. After a few moments of silence he said, "I was young and stupid, you know? Back then. I wasn't trying to use you for connections—not blatantly anyway. I thought it was nice to get to know someone who had them, and that maybe it would work out for me that way, but I wasn't trying to trick you."

She sighed. "Water under the bridge. I've been married. You've been married. You have a child. I have a…"

"Gus. You have a Gus," Kline told her, grinning as she pinched the bridge of her nose. "What's that all about anyway?"

"I adore Gus, you know that. I think he's still a little in love with me. I try to keep him at arms-length because, well, I'm a little afraid he would subsume me."

"He'd lock you in a tower like Rapunzel."

"That's the last thing I need. But I do love him to pieces and he's my only friend out here."

"What about me? I'm out here."

She fixed him with a narrow gaze that made him glad he had

to keep his eyes on the road so he could avoid looking directly at her. "Are you my friend?"

"I'm not your enemy," he said. "I'd like to be friends, at least."

"At least?"

He glanced over and grinned his most winning smile. "I mean, you look great, Jill."

"You're disgusting," she laughed, shaking her head. Then she said with a reluctant sigh. "You look good, too."

"I say two people as good-looking as us have to be at least friends. Otherwise, it's like Zeus and Hera clashing."

"Zeus and Hera?"

"Ares and Aphrodite?"

"Heracles and Deanira more like."

"I don't know that one," Kline frowned.

"Brush up on your Sophocles," she said lightly. "Friends. We can be friends."

"At least?"

"Don't push your luck, Kline." She was laughing, though, and laughing was good. Pushing her hair behind her ear she said, "I wouldn't mind being seen out with you. It can't hurt my image to be seen with the hottest man in Hollywood. If it's something that you want to do–if you think it would be a boost for you–I don't mind."

"Honestly, I didn't come up with that. I swear. It was all Roland."

"Roland seems like he's good at his job."

"He's very good at his job, and that's the only reason I didn't drown him in his soup tonight."

"Then why don't you take me to lunch or something, some-where there are lots of photographers, and we'll see what hap-pens?"

He was pulling up in her drive then, and once he'd put the car in park, shifted to look at her full-on. She was almost too much to look at, and he wondered how the screen was going to take her face. He'd seen her on stage and she used every inch of her body in her acting, how was she going to reign all that in for the closeups on that perfect face? "I like that idea."

"Maybe when I get back from New York?"

"Definitely." He reached over and pushed one of the fresh layers in her hair back over her bare shoulder, feeling her shiver with the touch. "Do you want to invite me in?"

"Definitely," she breathed, but then smiled wickedly. "But I'm not going to. If you come in, you'll ask for a drink. I'll give you one, and you'll ask me to come sit by you. I'll do it, then you'll kiss me. When you kiss me, I'll forget I was ever angry enough with you to be just-friends and nothing else. And then I'll wake up in the morning in a bed full of regrets–and you'll be long gone!"

"I live just down the way," Kline teased, jerking his thumb over his shoulder. "So, technically, I'd just be down the way."

"Go home, Kline."

"I will, Jill." He was matching her smile, until she bit her lower lip and let out a breath, opening the car door at the same time.

"Stop being so charming."

"Stop being someone I want to charm."

She laughed and shut the door, leaning into the window as he rolled it down. "Lunch. After I'm home from New York."

"Perfect. And Jill?"

"Yes?"

"Thank you. I'm sorry for…everything."

"Make it up to me."

"I will!"

"I–" She interrupted herself biting her lip.

"What?"

"I did ask Gus to be my date to the Grammys, but maybe…"

"Maybe that's a good place to launch our love for the life-times?"

"Maybe I can keep Lola as a friend if I'm not taking her boyfriend on dates."

"I'm going Rat Pack chic. You come Grace Kelly glam and we'll steal the show."

"Okay," she almost whispered. Then, she shook herself and turned up the walk to her front door. He watched her go, those long, lean muscles sculpted by years of ballet and whatever else she did made her look taller than she was, so did those shoes. Distantly, he wondered how long before he could get those legs wrapped around him again? Friends was a start.

Rhiannon Charles

Rhiannon kicked the last intern out of her office at half past four and locked the door behind him. She was never going to finish the scene she was working on if the interruptions didn't stop. She poured a cup of coffee and settled in her chair, reading over what she'd written as she stirred in the cream and sugar. When she put the spoon on her desk, she glanced down and noticed the card with Jill's information printed on it. In the shuffle, she'd forgotten to call her. After a moment's consideration, she plucked the card from the corner of her blotter and picked up the phone to dial out. The number rang three times and Rhiannon was preparing a message to leave when a familiar voice picked up.

"Hello?"

"Jill?"

"Rhiannon! Hello! How are you?"

"Good. Good. How are you? Still hating LA?"

"Meh. Yes and no. I'm working on getting new management, so hopefully, my stay will be lucrative at least."

"So, you are planning on staying?"

"Yes. There's nothing for me in New York. If I'm going to make a move, it has to be now."

"I hear you. I wasn't too thrilled at the prospect of living out here, but I'm adjusting."

"Adjusting like crazy I'd say. Spending quality time with Kline Scott?"

Was she fishing? Rhiannon wasn't sure, even less sure what to say. "Yeah, well, that's a very recent development. Too soon to tell what to make of it."

"Oh?"

"Yeah. Actually, you ran into us on our first date. I'm going over to his place for the first time this weekend. He's been to mine, but I've never been there. His son is out of town."

Jill made a noncommittal noise then said with something that sounded like relief, "Well, I'm sure you'll have a nice time. He's a good guy. We ran into each other again and I sat down with him and his manager for a little while. Roland is hysterical!"

Rhiannon paused, considering whether she should mention that the conversation on their first date had mostly been about her, but she decided against it. That wasn't a discussion for the phone. "Seems so," she said, fingering the spoon on her desk. "Anyway, I called to see if you were free tonight. I thought maybe we could get together. Maybe dinner?"

The surprise in Jill's voice was only matched by gratitude. "Really? I would love that! Oh, Rhi, that's a great idea. Can we do something normal and not celebrity-ish? I've only been out with my managers and August, and they just want to go to all the hotspots."

"I could cook. I'm not much of a celebrity, so my idea of dinner is pretty low-key."

Jill sighed happily, "Oh that sounds great. That sounds so great. Should I bring anything?"

"Just you and your appetite. Italian okay?"

"Sure. I'm low carb right now, but I can cheat for a night. Just give me a time and address. I need to hire a car."

Rhiannon rattled off the address and her cell number, in case there were any difficulties finding the place. "I'm right on the beach. See you about seven? I'll need to stop at the market on the way home."

"I'll see you then."

Rhiannon laughed as she hung up, remembering her first

days in LA. She'd come out to a full job, though, with built-in company, and a room full of writers who wanted to suck up to their new boss. From what she recalled, August was a lot of fun for snarky conversation at a party, but he wasn't exactly warm. And there was no such thing as a warm manager.

Thinking about Jill's carb issues, she went ahead and made zucchini noodles along with fresh pasta and sauce. Thad was always on some kind of diet, as were the rest of the cast, so she'd heard everything. If Jill was going up on the big screen, cheating her diet would be as stressful as losing her hair.

It was just after seven when she arrived, a bottle of wine and a gorgeous charcuterie board in hand.

Rhiannon opened the door, smiling brightly. "Jill Parker! Come in. Come in!" she said, swinging the door wide.

Jill stepped inside and accepted a sideways hug and air kiss. "Thank you so much for having me over. Honestly. I could cry."

"Please don't," Rhiannon said, seriously. "What's this?"

"I couldn't come empty-handed, so I stopped off at Erewhon," Jill said with a frown. "Did I say that right? August said that's the place to go."

"Aw, thanks. Alcohol goes with everything," Rhiannon tugged the hem of her gray hoodie down over her hips, glancing at Jill's trim, jersey sheath and Chanel flats. She looked like an off-duty ballerina. Accepting the bottle, she smirked slightly, reading the label. "Huh."

"What? You don't like this vintage?"

"Oh, yes, I do. It's lovely. Just had some last weekend, in fact," Rhiannon said, with a bit of a laugh. "Kline brought the same exact wine."

Jill huffed a laugh. "Well, let's hope it means we both have good taste."

"It was good," Rhiannon nodded, still smirking. "Just how well did you know him?"

"I knew him for years. We met right when he moved to the city. I was just finishing a run in Les Mis as Cosette, and looking for my next job. I'd gone to see my boyfriend--I was dating August then--at the Fashion Institute, and Kline was up there with some of his friends. They all knew each other. He just became part of the group."

"Hm," Rhiannon said, leading the way into the kitchen. She put the bottle on the counter and went to the stove to stir the bubbling pot. "I made a quick marinara for some fresh pasta I picked up, and some zoodles for you. Figured we'd have that and a salad and you don't have to cheat. Sound good?"

"Sounds beautiful. Thank you! That's so considerate. Do you need help with the salad?"

"Everything's on the counter. It just needs to be maimed and thrown together in a bowl," Rhiannon said, tilting her head toward the small collection of vegetables. "Feel free to take out your aggressions."

"Oooh! I get to chop!" Jill took up a knife and went to work, chopping the vegetables like a pro. "I dated a chef," she said, when Rhiannon looked over. "Well, not a chef. He worked in a little tavern on the East Side, but I learned a few things from him."

"I'll say," Rhiannon said, with a smile. "Don't make it too pretty or I won't want to eat it."

Jill laughed and began scooping bits of lettuce into a bowl. The two women worked quietly for a few minutes before Rhiannon took up the conversation again, "So, you said you're getting new management? Who? Not that Michael guy."

"No, Michael and Royce just weren't cutting it. I'm in talks with Roland, actually. I have some things to work out, but it shouldn't take too much."

"Kline's manager?"

"Yeah. He's good."

"Well, looks like the social circle is tightening up again. Just like old times, huh?"

"Hardly! No. It's business. I just need someone who will work for me, not work on me."

"Still, you'll probably see more of Kline, too. It's hard for

Roland to be in two places at once."

Jill shrugged, an elegant gesture, "Sometimes, I'm sure I will. But then, I've been running into Kline all over the place since I got here, so that wouldn't be anything new. We talked about having lunch when I come back from New York–I'm up there next month–but it's more Roland would like his star to be seen with someone who isn't Kara Viceroy. It wouldn't hurt me to be seen with him, you know? Business. It is funny seeing him again. It's surreal."

Rhiannon chuckled, "Yeah, seeing him has the same effect on me."

Jill tilted her head and smiled wryly, "I doubt that. You're sleeping with him, right?"

She was fishing for answers. Jill could never just come right out and ask something. Rhiannon fought a scowl and said, "Right. It's still a bit surreal. I'm actually surprised by the whole thing, and you know how difficult it is to surprise me."

"Why are you surprised?"

"Why do you think?"

"Because it's Kline? Yeah," Jill nodded, dicing a carrot quickly, "But you're smart, funny, beautiful, and you're likely to let him have the spotlight." She looked up then and grinned. "Just don't outshine him."

"I couldn't compete with him, so I won't even try," Rhiannon sighed, pulling down plates. She went to the table and laid out the placemats and silverware. "What was he like when you dated him?" Two could play her fishing game.

"I never said I dated him," Jill said, shaking her head, "but back in the day he was alternately cocky, sweet, flighty, sincere, and always a good friend and good listener. But he was pretty young and ridiculously good-looking. All the girls wanted him then like they do now. He took full advantage of it."

"So, you didn't date him?"

"Define date? Kline wasn't one for big commitments back then. We all sort of went out in that group. It was very incestuous.

I'm sure he's all grown up now, though."

Rhiannon looked at her for a long moment, then went to the stove and began dishing food onto plates. "You two must have been close. You have the same memories. Well, you tell the same story, anyway."

"In a way, we grew up together. He was in New York alone, like August. Geri, Alex, Mel and Jimmy, who rounded out our little group, were in varying stages of horrible dysfunction at home. I was the only one of us who was working, but I was also the youngest of the group and my mother was evil to the core. In a lot of ways, we were all each other had.

"Actually," she paused and smiled. "Kline did really help me find a way out from under my mother. I mean–you met me after I'd fired her as my manager. Kline talked me through the finer points of how he found his management back then, too. He was with Ford. It gave me the courage to pretend I had some courage and go talk to Gersh. It was the beginning of my freedom!" She threw her arms open wide, then remembered she was holding a knife and reigned it in. "Sorry. If you ask August, he'd probably tell the same stories, too."

"Yes, and how is August?" Rhiannon said, taking the plates to the table.

"He's doing well. Loves his job. Loves using me as a Barbie doll. Has a gorgeous girlfriend. He's living the life."

"August could live the life in Wichita."

Jill guffawed at that, "Oh no he couldn't! No one would 'get' him there. It's very important to August that he be 'gotten'. Poor dear."

Rhiannon laughed. "True. So, what are your plans for the weekend?"

"Nothing major. This is my last truly free week before I have to start behaving like someone in a movie. I'm in New York the first week of February–I have some legal stuff going on, and it's nearly settled. Then it's back here for the Grammys–I'm presenting–and then pre-production for the film starts. I haven't met my leading man, yet. He's off in Canada or something, shooting another film. Honestly, I'm just looking forward to sleeping this weekend."

"Oh. Amen to that. I don't know when I'll get to sleep. I'm about six hours short for the week already," Rhiannon said, grabbing up the bottle and uncorking it. "Those early morning calls are murder. You know how I hate the sun."

They giggled over Rhiannon's set gossip until they sat down for dinner, where the subject changed to what Jill knew of all Rhiannon's old companions in the city. For someone who rarely went out to mingle, she knew all the gossip. Halfway through the meal, Rhiannon's phone rang. She went to answer and was pleasantly surprised to hear Kline on the other end of the line.

"'Lo there, Beautiful," he cried over a din of background noise. "I wanted to say hello. I was thinking of you."

"Hello," she said, her smile growing wider. "You sound like you're trapped at a party."

"Trapped is the word."

"Don't you ever stay home?"

"I'm staying home tomorrow and Sunday night," he grinned. She could hear it in his voice. "And I can hardly wait."

"That makes two of us," she said, biting her lip. "I've even cleared my schedule in the afternoon so I can be there sooner."

He didn't say anything for a moment then purred, "How about if we start Saturday tonight? I can get out of here in about an hour."

"Oooh, that's tempting."

"So, say yes, and I'll make it forty-five minutes."

Rhiannon sighed. "I can't. Not in an hour, anyway."

"How long?"

"I'm actually in the middle of dinner with a friend. I-- two hours?"

"Two hours is great."

"Alright. I'll see you in two," she said, the smile returning.

Jill was watching her with a slight smile, keeping her expression carefully blank. "Something come up?"

"Yep, but I'm not running you off," Rhiannon said, seriously. "Not entirely. No rush. I can be a little late."

Jill laughed and started to fold her napkin. "Honey, booty calls. I think you should rush. I know I would."

"No, I made plans with you and I'm enjoying it. I'll get to him when I get there."

"I should be getting home anyway. I need to get some things together for New York. Make sure all my paperwork is in order. You know."

Rhiannon watched Jill get up and go to her purse. "I have to call for the car," she said, "but as soon as he's back here, I'll be on my way."

Before Jill could unzip her bag, her phone started ringing from within. She plucked it out, looked at the caller ID and snorted before swiping her caller into voice mail. Then she dialed for her car.

"Bill collector?" Rhiannon asked, standing to clear the table.

"Absolutely," Jill grinned.

"Kline?"

"Why would Kline call me?"

You've been running into him all over the place since you got here and you're going to be sharing management maybe? You're being so cagey about him. Are you going to level with me? If there was nothing between you, then it wouldn't be a big deal if an old friend was ringing you up. On the other hand, if there is more to it than either of you are saying, that would explain why you're being so evasive."

Jill's eyes went wide. "I'm sorry?"

"I said you're being evasive. What's going on, Jill?"

"I-- I'm going through a divorce," Jill said after a moment. "My life is very complicated right now. Gary—you remember Gary? We were married. We kept it very quiet to avoid scrutiny, but now we're getting a divorce so obviously the press found out and it's made life hell. I'm here because I just couldn't handle being under the microscope anymore. If I seem strange, uptight, evasive, or any other negative adjective, that's why. Because I am uptight, on edge, and absolutely not myself. Kline has nothing to do with it.

"I'm sorry I seem evasive. I knew Kline ten years ago. I'm ten years removed from the man he is today, you know? Of course, I had a big crush on him." She smiled miserably. "He didn't feel the same way about me, as I did about him. He saw me as a foot in the door to the industry. It's embarrassing. I'm embarrassed. Every time I see him, I'm embarrassed. All I can think about is how many times I threw myself at him and he didn't even try to catch me. You know? And now his manager wants to set us up as a publicity couple, and Kline is keen, which is just another reminder that I was never going to be what he wanted, but I am someone who is useful. It's embarrassing.

"But he's a wonderful person, or I'd never have tried to catch his eye. I'm sure he really enjoys you and your company!"

Rhiannon blinked at her, momentarily stunned by the outpouring of information. Jill always seemed like an open book, but she was really just giving you the Cliff's Notes most of the time. You had to get really lucky to get to read the actual novel.

"I didn't know you and Gary were married," was all Rhiannon could say. Jill and Gary had always had an odd relationship, but they'd seemed happy. At least, on the surface. They spent a lot of time apart because she was always in a show, and he was always traveling for work. Rhiannon had heard the rumors about the Hilton sister, but she thought it was just gossip rag bunk.

"More embarrassment for me," Jill said with another strange smile. She was trying not to cry. She let out a breath and said, "I've been in therapy forever. I'm finally at a point where I see that I was trying to recreate the kind of love that felt normal for me, instead of the kind of love I wanted, blah blah blah. Now it's over, and now maybe I can work on getting to what's good for me."

"Oh, Jill, I'm sorry," she said. "When did this happen?"

"The unraveling? About six months ago. He told me he

wanted out. He'd met someone. So, I filed and that was that. Then his slut gave Page Six her own blind item and Bam! It was everywhere. Things with Devil's Party going to the big screen were all happening around the same time, so it just made sense for me to come out here, and August is out here--he's my family. He's what I've got. So here I am. And you don't need to worry about my old social circle reforming. At all. That's not going to happen."

"Oh, god. I thought that fling was just a rumor."

"No. He really did it."

"What an asshole," Rhiannon said, going to Jill and hugging her. "I'm so sorry that you're having to go through this, but he never deserved you, anyway. You're destined for better. Just think of all the delights freedom can afford."

Jill forced a smile and nodded. "I keep telling myself that. Anyway, I'm sorry that I've been so--odd." A knock came at the door. "That's the car. I have to get going."

Rhiannon walked her to the door. "Call if you need anything, Jill. I mean it. Even if you just need to be somewhere other than the rental. I have a whole big beach out the back and you're more than welcome to it."

"I'll remember. Thanks for dinner. It was great."

"Sure. We have to work out our schedule to make time for more normalcy."

"Definitely."

They hugged again at the door and Jill was gone.

Rhiannon went back into the kitchen and cleaned up, wrapping the remaining pasta and sauce up to take with her. She and Kline could make a meal of it and spare the need to call out or cook something. After putting the dishes away, she went into the bedroom and grabbed the bag she'd packed to double-check the contents and add a few things to it to allow for the extra night she was spending with him.

She took a shower, her mind wandering beneath the spray. The evening's conversation was echoing in her head, and she was trying to shake the nagging feeling that Jill was keeping more than a pending divorce and some embarrassing memories from her. Rhiannon felt bad for her friend (friend?) and was sorry that she was going through such a tough time. Of course, if Gary was the jerk, he'd shown himself to be, then Jill was much better off now.

The thing that was eating at Rhiannon was the fact that she was sure that Kline and Jill had been more than friends back in New York. What she couldn't understand was why neither of them would just say so. Even if things had gone badly between them, there was no reason to conceal the relationship in the first place. She could understand why Kline might have glossed it over, considering they were on a date when the issue came up, but Jill was her friend. Or was she?

Rhiannon got out of the shower, dressed, and dried her hair, then grabbed her bag and the food and headed out to her rented convertible to make the drive to Kline's place.

She drove into the Hollywood hills filled with a mixture of excitement, anticipation, and trepidation. The realization that she was going to his house had begun to seep in slowly. It wasn't the fancy house that gave her pause.

She'd already been to Thad's gated Malibu mansion and attended two rather large beach parties at one of the producer's houses since her arrival in LA. But this was *Kline's house*. She found the hidden driveway and made her way down the street, past a few rather expansive properties, all tucked securely behind sturdy gates, privacy walls, and shrubberies.

There were three stray girls at the front of Kline's drive, and they hurried to the edge of the street, camera flashes popping as Rhiannon made the turn. There was a moment of abject disappointment when they realized she wasn't Kline, then excitement when her car rolled up to the speaker box and pressed the number Kline had given her. Kline's voice came over the system, Rhiannon announced herself, and the gates started to roll open as Kline welcomed her inside.

"Are there fans out there?" he asked.

"Yep," Rhiannon chuckled. "Blinding me with their cameras."

"Tell them to come over to the box. I'll talk to them if they won't try to run in the gate behind you."

Rhiannon laughed but rolled down her passenger window and called to the girls, who were squealing at the sound of Kline's voice. "Come on over," she yelled to them. "Kline will say hello. Just don't come inside."

She pulled through the gates as the girls ran to the box, one in tears, and she could hear Kline's boisterous greetings as she drove away. It was another half mile up to the actual house. He had quite a bit of land, as was normal for that development. There were only seven houses built there.

She pulled up to the circular drive-in front of the house, and Kline was waiting at the front door, waving at her and talking into the silver box near the doorbell. He said goodbye to his fans as Rhiannon got out of the car, then hurried down the front steps to help her with her bag.

"You didn't have any trouble finding the place, did you?" he asked, taking the bag and slipping an arm around her.

"Not at all. I was a master spy before I got this writing gig," she said, her hand coming to rest on his hip. "Of course, all I needed to do was follow the screams."

"Yeah, they're a mess, aren't they? There are usually at least two of them out there. I don't mind unless they go after Jack. I mainly use the back drive when he's with me."

"The back drive?"

"Yeah, I'll show it to you when you go," he said, as they walked up the steps to the double doors and into the main foyer of the house.

"Some spy I am."

Once Kline shut the front door, he dropped her bag and turned her in his arms, then leaned in for a long kiss that ended with his contented sigh. "I have been thinking about you all day. That party was miserable. Couldn't wait to get out."

She smiled, leaning up to kiss his chin. "Now you're free and

I'm here. No more stress for the rest of the weekend."

He laughed, then scooped her up in his arms and trotted through the house. "Foyer," he said as they hurried through, "Living room. Stairs." He hit the stairs without as much spring, but didn't seem to be struggling, then he cleared the landing of a loft that turned out to be his master bedroom, deposited her on the bed and said, "Bedroom."

"Oh, I'm getting the grand tour, hm? I want to see everything," she teased, leaning up to grasp his belt loops and pull him down on top of her.

"I'll show you the bath in an hour," he growled in her ear, nipping.

"An hour?" She brushed her lips up the side of his square jaw. His skin, fresh from a shave, was flawless. She nuzzled into his neck as he did the same, and drank in the warm scent of his cologne, sinking into the mass of pillows behind her with the fragrance profile of leather and oakmoss, and something sweet filling her senses like good whisky in a low-lit room.

Then, his lips were on hers, full and soft, his tongue teasing between her teeth as he wrapped his arms fully around her and drew her close. He kissed her slowly, deeply, taking his time like he was enjoying something delectable, with no mad rush to get her out of her clothes, just a concentrated desire to have her in his space, like he was breathing her in, or maybe stealing her soul.

She heard herself sigh and then groan as he finally shifted away far enough to move his lips down her throat, figuring out her clothes as he went, teasing up goosebumps on every inch of her skin as he bared it to his fingertips and tongue. Rhiannon was lost, drunk on the sensation Kline created with the barest touch, his mouth on her sex kindling a fire in her core that he stirred with long fingers until she thought she would burn alive.

When she came, it was an explosion that wracked her whole body, but it wasn't enough. "Come here," she growled barely stopping herself from pulling him up from between her thighs by the hair. "Come here!"

Kline's dark eyes were dancing when he came back up to meet her, easily sliding his cock up inside her, a flicker of what looked like almost painful pleasure closing his eyes as he started to move. Rhiannon wrapped herself around him, grinding her hips up to meet every thrust. Something about him made her feel wild, and she let go of the thought as soon as she had it, to focus in on his body with the intent to make him feel just as desperate for more as she did.

It was a little less than an hour, but they were no less ardent when they wrestled their way into the standing double shower on the far side of the master bath. Both made plenty of contact with the icy black marble countertops before they made it under the steaming jets.

After a playful cleaning up, Kline toweled Rhiannon off and led her back into the bedroom where they slept tangled together for the rest of the night.

She was stirred the next morning by the aroma of coffee brewing and opened her eyes to find Kline's side of the bed empty. Sitting up, she stretched and looked around the room. Her clothes had been retrieved from the floor and draped over the arm of one of the rounded black chairs. Past the railing on the low wall, she could see a spectacular view outside the massive windows.

She got out of bed and went for her clothes, but noticed Kline's shirt on the other chair and slipped it on instead. It smelled like him, and she smiled at thoughts of removing it from his body the night before. The tails of the shirt covered her backside, so she eschewed other garments to pad down the stairs and seek Kline out.

She found him humming over a bowl of eggs that he was whisking, and saw several ingredients all lined up and ready to go into whatever it was he was cooking. "Hey, morning," he said, grinning at her. "Feel up for breakfast?"

"I'm starving," Rhiannon grinned back. "What are we having?"

"Well, I'm on Atkins right now, so lots of protein. I'm doing an Italian frittata. If you want some fresh fruit, I've got some. Actually, I'm sure I've got some of everything. Jack doesn't keep my diet. Neither does Kim."

"Kim?"

"Jack's nanny. She's the full-time live-in. Delia's the part-time weekender."

"Ah, I'd forgotten," Rhiannon nodded, then glanced around. "Is she here?"

"Not in the house, no. She has the guest house, but actually she's taken a vacation while Jack's away. Cozumel, I think."

"Sounds fun. Can I help with anything?"

"Absolutely! You can sit right down there and talk to me. Tell me everything about you. I've been hitting the circuit telling everyone all about me, and I'm sick of me. Tell me about you."

Rhiannon laughed, but launched dutifully into her autobiography, answering questions he asked, and expounding when prompted. She found that he was very easy to talk to, but wasn't sure if he was the greatest listener. Still, he acted full of interest, and after a half-hour of her going on about her childhood and college days, he had produced a lovely looking dish, and was doling it out on cobalt blue stoneware.

Before handing one over to her, he added some fruit and a side of toast she hadn't seen cooking. Then he pointed her to the variety of jams on the long table.

He joined her with his plate, then brought over the carafe of coffee, "I'm not giving that up," he'd said almost violently. And a carafe of juice for her.

"So, you're really doing Atkins? That's so old fashioned."

"Yeah. I need to drop at least five pounds and I know it works."

Rhiannon blinked at him. "From where?"

"My gut," he shrugged. "When I get my leathers on, I have a roll. I'm wearing them when I go on Colbert, so I'm doing a bit of a crash. Extra workout, less food, major protein. No alcohol. It's killing me at parties! How are you supposed to go to those things sober?"

Rhiannon laughed at the expression on his face. From what she could tell, he was as fit as he could be, down to the tightly cut muscles of his stomach. If there was fat there, she had yet to see it, and she'd inspected rather closely. She shook her head. "It must be hard to have to be so body conscious all the time."

"It's life," he shrugged. "Everyone has to do something uncomfortable for their job. Some people sit at computers and get carpel tunnel. Some people sit and smell my feet doing pedicures. I just have to watch what I eat and sweat a bit. Mine pays more, so I can't gripe about it."

"Well, if this acting thing doesn't pan out, you've got a great future as a chef. This food is amazing," she said, giving him a wink.

He chuckled. "I worked as a cook in New York. Did I tell you that? My dad worked in a restaurant in Leeds, and I grew up in the kitchen there. When I moved to the States, it was getting a gig as a waiter or a cook. I picked cook. So, I'd work the night shift and then hit the auditions during the day."

"Were you now?" She chuckled, thinking back to Jill's vegetable-chopping skills. "All this and he can cook, too. Hm."

They talked for a while longer, until both had finished their meals, then Rhiannon helped him clean up the few dishes.

"You don't have to do that," he said, as she began drying plates.

"Well, you cooked. It's the least I can do," she said, with a shrug, "Besides, if I help, it means that it will be that much sooner that I can have you back in bed."

"Oh, bed!" Kline grinned, then made a dramatic face, "Ah--not being twenty years old anymore, I might need a little more recovery time. You want to watch a movie? Go get in the pool? Hot tub?"

Reading the look of humor in her eyes, Kline snorted, "Fuck it all, I'm getting Viagra. I swear to god, I'm getting a prescription."

Rhiannon laughed and began unbuttoning the shirt she wore, "Well, until you do, I'll just have to come up with other forms of inspiration." She stopped at the second to the last button and allowed the shirt to hang open slightly. "The hot tub sounds like fun. Where is it?"

"Right out that door," Kline pointed, eyeing her appreciatively.

She dropped the shirt and padded outside, with a glance back over her shoulder. "Coming?"

"On my way."

Kline stripped down before he stepped out the door, then met her on the edge of the tub for a deep kiss. They eased into the warm water and Kline turned on the jets, then spent the next several minutes doing everything he could short of pulling her onto his lap to make her purr, stretch, and be otherwise delighted.

The joke about Viagra was forgotten as they made love in the swirling water, and after, when Kline lifted her from the tub and carried her, arms and legs wrapped around him, into the house. Eventually, after a brief tour of the leather couch in the living room, they made their way back up to the bedroom and lazed the day away, alternately making love, talking and snoozing until the sun went down.

She woke before he did and availed herself of the huge bathtub in the master bath. While she was soaking, she noticed a stack of scripts within arm's reach, so she plucked one up and thumbed through it. She'd gone through about four when the water started to chill, so she let the tub drain and sat down on the loveseat across from the vanity and finished perusing the others.

Kline had made a name for himself playing an insecure, but romantic hottie on a Friends-like sitcom. He'd distinguished himself from his castmates, Thad included, by starring in two back-to-back romantic comedies, then opened up his personal Hollywood world by taking the lead in an action flick. Currently he was wanted for every role that required a hunky leading man. None of the scripts were particularly interesting, Rhiannon thought. He was a better actor than anyone had seen so far, but nothing in that stack would show it off.

She wandered back into the bedroom around 3 in the morning and settled in with him. Both slept soundly into Sunday morning, when she woke to the smells of another home-cooked breakfast. She padded down the stairs in his bathrobe and smiled to find him yawning over the stove. "Tired?" she asked.

"Just completely relaxed," he answered. "You rest well?"

"I did."

"Good." He explained the morning's breakfast and they talked a little before she asked, "You're doing Colbert, right?"

"Mmhmm. Press for Lone Star starts in New York. Colbert, then the Today Show. Then Live with Kelly. I have to be up at the ass-crack of dawn for those, but it's a feature segment interview. Good press for the film and I can talk about Knight."

"I'll set my alarm so I can watch Hoda Kotb fawn all over you."

"Is she the Today show? Thank god! I thought I was getting saddled with Savannah Guthrie. She drives me up a tree. I thought about doing some crazy indie film just so when she interviews me, I can say shit like, 'I took the role because I've always wanted to murder someone--this was the closest thing to it.'"

"Oh, I meant Savannah Guthrie," Rhiannon said, wrinkling her nose.

"Ugh."

"Maybe she'll be out sick, " she said, with a shrug. She paused for a moment then added, "You should do an indie film, anyway."

He mirrored her shrug. "I think about it. But there's no money in it, you know? Don't tell anyone, but I'm all about the money."

"There could be money in it. You're an a-list star, Kline. What's more important, though, is that you've got real talent," Rhiannon said, seriously. "You're making millions a picture, but none of the films has set you apart or allowed you to really show people what you've got. There's plenty of money to be had in rehashing old, tired storylines, but what about something darker? You can't remake Hugh Grant movies for the rest of your life. It would kill your career. Action movies are fine, but they're fluff. Schwarzenegger could hardly speak English properly, but he blew a lot of shit up and people loved him for it. He doesn't try to stretch because he can't and you've never seen him up for an Oscar, have you?"

Kline's posture had changed, and he was pulling back slightly, "I could be governor! I could be governor of California!"

"You could be anything you want if you play your cards right, but you have to play the cards right. You know, Roland's not going to be around when your credibility dries up after you've made too many forgettable films, because he won't be able to sponge off your spotlight," she said, matter-of-factly. "Market more than your face, Kline. Seriously. Do a thriller or a gritty crime drama. Play against type. You've got the chops. Don't you have any producer friends who might help get you into something edgier?"

Now his mask was slipping, and true discomfort was showing through. He got up to clear the table and start the dishes. "Yeah," he said. "I do."

She frowned and fingered the napkin on the table, "I'm sorry if I upset you. That wasn't what I was trying to do. It's just that I've followed your career and I've seen what kind of amazing talent you have and it's obvious to me that you've got so much more to offer."

"No, I'm not upset," he shook his head, clearly upset. "That's really flattering. I just don't want to talk about work if you don't mind. I've got two weeks ahead when I don't get to talk about anything but work. Starting tomorrow. Is that all right?"

"Of course," she said, somewhat sheepishly. "Forget I said anything. I have a tendency to engage my mouth before my brain, in case that hasn't been made perfectly clear by now."

"I like both your mouth and your brain," Kline smiled sincerely. "Want to go put them in the hot tub again?"

"Hm, actually, how about a dip in the pool? More room," she said, winking.

"I'll beat you to it!"

They raced out the door and spent the rest of the day much

as they had the day before. Kline had an early flight in the morning, though, so he put a stop to all activities before ten and they tucked themselves into bed for the night. He saw Rhiannon off just after five in the morning, sending her out the private, back drive. "I want to see you again. I've got a lot of press coming up, so some days I won't be good for much, but I'd love to see you."

"Of course! I want to see you, too."

"Good," he said, leaning in to kiss her. "Because I think I'm falling for you."

Rhiannon drew back to look at him, surprised. He was smiling. "Seriously," he said. "I think you're just exactly what I've been looking for. I'm glad I found you."

"Technically, I think Thad pointed me out to you."

"So, I owe him a finder's fee."

That made her laugh, and he kissed her again. Several seconds later, she pulled away. "If I don't leave now, I might not ever leave."

"Would that be so bad?"

She growled at him and rolled her shoulders. "You have work and I have work."

"Then I guess I'll let you leave. But only if you promise to come back."

"I promise."

A few more kisses and then Rhiannon finally made it into her car. Things went faster with celebrities, she told herself. When they weren't at work, they had nothing but time on their hands, so rather than seeing someone once or twice a week for a couple of hours at a time, they could hole up for weekends or weeks and fast track through all the first-crush-rush of serotonin and get right down to love.

Or breakups, she reminded herself. They broke up just as quickly as they got started.

"Fast flames flame out fast," is what her mother always said. But something about Kline felt different. She could actually make a difference for him. She could do for his career what she'd done for

Simon Says and take him from just another pretty face to a serious star with a career to rival the most respected actors.

And as she rose in the ranks of her career, they could be such a power couple. She fantasized about that all the way home, and into a hot shower, through to a light lunch and then finally into her own bed where she was asleep before her head hit the pillow.

Jill Parker

In preparation for Divorce Week, as she was calling it, Jill had met with Roland again to sign all the paperwork necessary to give her career over into his capable hands, including ironclad NDAs for her own comfort. They sat down over drinks at a private club, and she explained the whole of her situation to him. From marriage to divorce and everything in between. It felt good to say it all out loud to a stranger. A semi-stranger. "I need to know I have PR at the ready," she told him earnestly. "This is the first time in my life that I've been painted as the bad guy in the press, and my current team just hasn't been able to handle it. Bad or good, I know a good PR handler can turn it into money."

Roland had smiled at her savvy but fretted a bit at her obvious worry. "You need to think positive," he told her. "No matter what, I'm going to be making sure you get the best press out of this possible. I only win," he insisted. "You only win with me. You call me as soon as your court case is finished and tell me everything. I don't want to get caught with our pants down. I've already got some ideas."

She'd gone into court expecting the waiting media. What she had not been expecting was to be greeted by an interview Gary had given. There, in black and white, were his reasons for the secrecy of their marriage, the insanity of the union, and the problems that caused the split.

He called her depressive, fragile, and needy. He said she was dangerously reclusive, which was the reason for the secrecy. She was terrified of the press getting even an inch of her personal space. He called her frigid, and he cited her miscarriages as the last straws, saying how hard it had been to convince her to even try for a family. He wanted more children, and he went so far as to suggest that she might not have had miscarriages at all.

She'd read the article in the limo over to the courthouse and was in shock by the time she finished it. Even more shocking was the sight of Gary with his new girlfriend--his very pregnant new girlfriend--walking into court together. It wasn't even the same girl he'd thrown her over for. This was a newly minted celebutante who had barely just made her debut, an oil heiress from Alaska of all places, whose family had bought their way into society only a few years before.

The judge was fair if uninterested, and aggravated by the press, and it didn't take long to finalize the dissolution of the marriage. The pre-nup stood. Jill got everything she'd taken into the marriage plus a cool five million for his philandering. He got what he'd taken into the marriage, plus her reputation. It was done.

A bailiff ushered her into a private side room so she could avoid the melee, and in a daze, she dialed Roland and mechanically related the entire scene. "You got a car there?" he asked.

"I just need to call for one," she told him.

"Don't do it. I've got just the thing. You wait right where you are until I call you, then you go on out to the front steps. I'll send one of my people for you. I got this under control."

Jill agreed before hanging up. She sat in the room too stunned to even have a cohesive thought until her phone rang again a half hour later. It was Roland instructing her to go on out. "I want you to walk out alone. We're going for maximum drama here, okay, sweetheart? I promise you, that once you walk out that door the press is going to forget you were ever even married."

"I'm trusting you."

"Then start that pap stroll, baby. Chin up, head held high.

Down, but not out."

Jill almost laughed, but couldn't quite, so she just hung up and did as instructed.

Straggling press snapped her picture as she walked out of the courthouse to the stairs. She'd donned her Chanel sunglasses and tightened the belt of her trench coat. She'd chosen to wear seamed hose with a Cuban heel and smart black stilettos. Now she was hoping her divorce costume held up in print, or at least to the heat.

As she walked, ignoring the questions the few reporters left were throwing at her, a limo pulled up and the back door flew open, just as a swarm of paparazzi appeared out of nowhere.

Stunned by the surge of them, for a moment she didn't recognize the man running toward her, but then Kline came loping up the stairs two at a time like something out of a movie. He wore a look of determination on his face as he made a beeline for her. Jill put one hand against the nearby pillar for support. It was criminal how good he looked in his leather jacket, with a simple black V-neck and charcoal-colored trousers. It was even more criminal how happy she was to see him.

"Oh my god," she breathed, stepping forward to his outstretched arm. He pulled her into his arms, kissing the top of her head, using his body to shield her from the press until they were safely inside the limo. He gave the driver further directions before turning to Jill, "Are you alright? They didn't hound you too badly, did they?"

She shook her head, not trusting her voice for a moment, then tried a smile and said, "When Roland said he was sending one of his people, I expected--I don't know. A suit? A mobster? Not you. What are you doing in New York?"

"Colbert tomorrow. I've got a little press run for Lone Star. I just arrived a little bit ago, so it all worked out. I guess he figured you needed a friendly face, and I was already in a limo, so…" he said, giving her a bit of a smile, "here I am."

"Here you are," she echoed softly. "Thank you. Did he tell

you..."

Kline nodded and reached for one of her hands. "Yeah. And I came for you."

"I'm glad you did."

"I read the article," Kline added, offering a sympathetic and searching look.

"I am mortified. Yes, well, leave it to Gary to make this even more sordid than it already was," she sniffed. "I'm just glad that it's over now. I'm finally free of him and have no reason to have any contact with him after today. I can't believe I loved him. I can't believe I thought he loved me."

Kline nodded. "I made the same mistake. Learned the hard way." He was quiet for a moment. "Listen, why don't I take you out somewhere? I'm free until tomorrow. I'm pretty sure I could cheer you up. Roland would probably like that. Can't have his newest client sad."

"Sure. Do you mind if we stop off at my place first? I'd like to change. Actually, I'm feeling stifled and am fighting the urge to tear off my buttons and scream while throwing my shoes at men who look like Gary."

"I think I'd like to see that actually," Kline said, waggling his eyebrows at her.

Jill laughed. "Let me think about that interview a little longer and you'll be a witness."

"So, where's your place?" Kline asked, flicking on the intercom to the driver. She gave directions and they started off down a different street.

At her building, the elderly doorman welcomed her with a huge smile, and she leaned to kiss his cheek, asking after his family before taking the lift to her apartment. Kline followed her inside and smiled, looking around. It was perfectly New York, Architectural Digest chic. A far cry from the comfortable nest she'd made herself in the apartment they'd shared before.

Catching him looking she said, "I didn't decorate it. Gary said I had garbage taste and had a designer do it. Come on in and make yourself at home. Can I bring you a drink?"

"Just mineral water, please. I'm off the sauce for the moment."

"Atkins again?"

He nodded, patting the flat of his stomach. "Television adds five pounds, you know."

"Ten," Jill said passingly. "I'm on it, too. I'll be right back."

She returned a few minutes later wearing faded jeans and a white ribbed tank top under a cozy blue hoodie. She handed him a highball glass full of mineral water and kept one for herself. "Thanks again for coming to get me. It was--it was pretty bad."

Kline listened as she told him the whole story, blinking back tears at the description of Gary's girlfriend before taking a deep breath. "I should be glad though. When I lost the babies, both times people told me that it was nature's way of saying something wasn't right. I'll say. Oh god, I'm a mess. I'm so sorry. I shouldn't have said all that."

"Come here," Kline offered, opening his arms.

It was too easy to cross the floor to him and let him gather her into his lap, the warmth of him exactly as calming as she remembered. Jill laid her head on his shoulder and let him cradle her close. "First of all," he said, his voice a pleasant rumble, "you don't need to apologize to me for anything. Especially not for telling me about this. If nothing else, we're friends, baby. You can tell me anything. And…that must have been horrible for you. But the positive side of it is that you don't have to share custody of a child with that low life. You'll find someone who's worthy of you and have a family when the time is right. Well, you'll find someone who's close to being worthy of you. I'm not sure that perfect match actually exists." He kissed the top of her head.

She laughed and closed her eyes. "Well, I've been an absolute failure as a daughter and wife, or so I've been told. I'm just hoping that my success as an actor is enough to balance it all out. I'm not quite human, you know. Gary said. Bastard. I'm not a robot!"

Kline chuckled. "Your mother was a bitch, and he's obviously an idiot and he's only managed to make himself look worse. Whatever he was hoping to accomplish by saying all of that dreck, all he's done is make people more sympathetic to your situation. But to further guarantee that everyone knows that you are not sitting at home crying over that loser, let's go out and have some fun. We'll celebrate your freedom."

Jill tilted her head back until she could look him in the face. "That means changing clothes again, doesn't it?"

"Indeed, it does," Kline grinned. "Why don't you let me choose something?"

"You just want an excuse to paw through my panties."

"Oh," he frowned, "I have to have an excuse? You know what looks good on me. I know what looks good on you."

Before he could put his lips to hers, because he had that look about him, Jill rolled her eyes and rose up from his lap. Kline had always done most of his comforting with his body. Whenever she was upset, after listening and validating, he always went right to kissing before he could run out of words. She wasn't sure she could withstand one of Kline's kisses right then. She wasn't sure she wanted to, which meant she should avoid the temptation. "You'd better not say I look best in nothing. Come on back."

She opened the door to her closet and urged him inside watching him sift through hangers and open drawers in her bureau. "I think we should talk about Rhiannon," she said as he held up a red dress then put it back.

"Rhiannon? Why?"

"Because you're seeing her?"

He looked genuinely confused so she said, "Because I don't know if you're seeing her seriously? Because you being here, going through my closet feels…familiar and honestly, every time I see you, my stomach does the same backflip it did the first night I met you. Because I was just sitting in your lap? So, if you and Rhiannon are serious, I need to know."

His brow furrowed at the sudden turn in the conversation. She watched him deciding how much to say. "It's new.

We're sleeping together. She's a great girl, but I haven't made any commitments. We're not exclusive. It's casual. We literally just met hours before I ran into you. We haven't talked at all about anything serious. Right now, it's just sex, but she is great."

Jill gave a nod. "She is great, and she's my friend. Well, we're friendly."

"Are you okay with that? With me seeing her, I mean?"

She nodded again. "Yeah. I haven't told her about us. Our past, I mean."

"You've seen her since you've been in LA? Apart from Blue, I mean?"

"Yes. We had dinner on Friday night."

"Ah. You were the friend she mentioned," Kline said, puzzling for a moment before asking. "Is that why you hung up on my call?"

Jill smiled and nodded once more. "You'd just talked to her. So, yeah. It wasn't a good time."

He blushed and managed to look sheepish. "I feel a bit caught out."

"You should," Jill said, with a shrug. "She thought it might be you, anyway. I just didn't want to get into it. It's too awkward."

"She's not my girlfriend," Kline said. "We just met, really. But she's a great girl and I appreciate that you handled it that way."

"Nice way to put it," Jill chuckled. "So, is that what I'm wearing?" She nodded at the hanger in his hand.

"I think so, yes. Feel up to dancing? Haven't been to a decent club in ages."

"You're making me go to a club? I hate clubs."

"Roland thinks you need to be out and seen having fun."

"Damn him," she muttered. "All right. Dancing it is."

Kline waited while Jill changed again and praised her mightily when she reappeared, resplendent in red, with sexy strappy heels and dramatic, artful makeup. "You're gorgeous as ever, darling," he said, offering an arm.

"Hmm," she dismissed. "So, take me downtown. We can

stop off for dinner first. Eric always has a table for me at Le Bernardin."

"Good enough."

She rang down to the door and had them call a car, so one was waiting by the time they made it to the ground floor. Jill walked ahead, Kline hanging back a ways to watch her hips sway. She put a little extra swish into her step for him, smiling over her shoulder at the expression on his face. "Come on, Pokey. Quit staring and get in the car."

He slipped into the seat beside her, their hips touching, but neither of them shifting to break the contact. Something in the air had changed, Jill thought. Kline gave the driver the address and they were off to Le Bernardin where both of them were welcomed in like family. Rich, famous family, but still, the smarm was at a minimum. A who's who of New York celebrity was seated around the restaurant and Jill offered hellos and hand squeezes as they were led to their table.

"This is your town now, isn't it?" Kline asked, smiling.

"In some corners it is. But Gary got half of it in the divorce. Maybe more. LA is yours, though. They love you there." She offered him a warm look and then blushed a little, "I've seen all of your movies. They're right to love you."

He winked at her and pulled her chair out to seat her before settling in the chair opposite. "You'll take LA over before you know it. I'll have to come to you for work."

"Ooh," she purred playfully, flirting. "I'll have to employ the casting couch then."

"And I would work twice as hard to make sure you knew just how badly I wanted you--I mean, to 'work' with you," he said, with a hint of a smile.

She groaned at him and hid behind her menu for a while. She never knew where she was with him. She was constantly off balance. She wasn't even sure he honestly found her attractive. Their last encounter flashed through her mind, and she blushed with humiliation at how he'd left her. But he was here now and being kind and charming. She knew what to do with kind and charming.

Their dinner was interrupted by a few visitors, people stopping by to offer their support or condolences to Jill over the recent ugliness. She held her head up high and accepted the sympathies, introduced people to Kline, and generally behaved like a good hostess at a very small dinner party, all the while mortified at how many people knew her private business.

A couple walked away, and she deflated slightly. "I'm exhausted," she whispered. "It's worse than working the circuit. But at least I can pretend it's a play, right?"

"That's what actors do. We pretend."

"You're pretending to absolutely adore your costar in Knight right now, aren't you? Kara Viceroy? Why do you despise her so much?"

"Is it that obvious?"

"To me. You're acting like you did when we were going out with Philip and Jean all the time, and you hated Jean."

"Yes, well, it doesn't make for positive buzz when the costars hate one another, does it? Roland thinks it's good PR for us to be cozy. I'm pretty sure she's frigid, or a lesbian, but as long as I don't actually have to make the rounds with her, I can pretend to like her."

Jill gave a slow, bemused smile. "She slept with you once or twice, then cut you off?"

"Shut up," Kline winced.

She giggled and pointed at him, "I still know you, Kline."

"She's vapid and cruel, so I had good reason," he said, defensively. "But never mind. We'll just leave it at that."

"Mmhmm. Okay." Jill leaned forward a little. "So… how serious are things with you and Rhi?"

Kline sighed and settled back in his seat. "Again?"

"It's an interrogation tactic to circle back to the same question and ask it in a different way."

"You don't trust my answers?"

"Not as far as I could throw you."

He laughed and rubbed his chin. "It's hard to say. I like her. We get on well, but what can you tell from a relationship that's only a week old?"

Jill considered him for a long moment, then toyed with her salad before glancing up through her lashes. "It's important. If you're serious about someone who might be my only friend in LA…I just wanted to know before I…before we go dancing. So, I know how close I can get. You know?"

He raised an eyebrow and a slow smile tugged at the corners of his mouth. "You can get as close as you like, beautiful. I will certainly have no complaints. What happens in New York, stays in New York."

"I like to dance close," she said softly.

"I remember."

She licked her lips and looked down, trying to blink herself back into focus. Kline glazed her brain like a donut. She couldn't think straight for the sticky sweet sugar rush of his proximity. "She's my friend," she reminded herself out loud.

"Technically," Kline said, tapping her nose with his index finger. It was a familiar gesture. "You got here first."

"Technically."

"Also, she said you were *friend adjacent*, not friends, so…"

"What?"

"Yeah. I asked her about how you knew each other. She said you were, and I quote, friend-ish."

Jill felt her lip curl slightly. She flew through a thousand thoughts, cataloging the people she trusted and considered friends, and wondered if there was an app just for platonic relationships like the dating apps before saying, "Well, I feel less conflicted."

He kissed her cheek. "So, dancing?"

"Do you mind if I choose the place?"

"Of course not. This is your town. I'll take you wherever you want to go."

"Do you still have a little goth in you somewhere?"

"I am wearing all black."

She reached down beside her and plucked a tiny bag from her only slightly larger purse and pushed it across the table. "You need some eyeliner."

He smiled, plucked the bag from the table, and pushed his chair back. "Right. Back in a mo, love."

"Wait," she said, halting him mid-step with a half-smile. "Wait. I'll put it on you."

He sat back down. "All right?" he said uncertainly.

"Trust me. I know what looks good on you."

"I know what looks best on me."

The line broke the spell just a little and Jill laughed. "If you say me, I'm sending you home for being ridiculous."

"Then I'll keep my trap shut."

The rest of dinner was spent in a strained excitement until they were back out in the limo. Jill gave directions to the driver, then put up the privacy window. "Now," she breathed, tilting her head as she looked him over. "Liner."

She pulled the eyeliner from her purse, then slid over to straddle Kline's lap to his surprise. He couldn't breathe, much less speak as she leaned over him. "Look up," she whispered. It was all she could manage, and that move had been quite a lot. She wanted him to feel as undone as she did whenever he showed up. Or at least make him feel like maybe he was missing out on something by missing out on her. "Look up," she said again when he didn't release her gaze.

That time he did, and she kohled his lower lashes and the inside of his lower lid, then smudged with the other end of the pencil. She took it between her teeth, then ran her fingers through his hair, tousling it up before sliding from his thighs and back into her seat. She put away the liner, then handed him a mirror and said huskily. "Now you're perfect."

"You prefer the rock star version," he said, giving her a wicked smile. "I may need to keep you with me all the time. You make me look incredible."

She laughed a little. The rest of the ride was silent, until they stopped outside a building and Jill let down the privacy guard. "Go into the parking garage," she told their driver, "and go up to five. We'll get out there. You're welcome to wait or come back at four. As long as you're here by four."

He nodded and followed her instructions. When they reached the fifth floor of the garage, the driver opened the door for them, and Jill swung out, legs first. "I'm going to change clothes," she said to Kline over her shoulder. "I'll meet you by the bar."

"What?" He followed, completely off balance, looking back at the car like it was a last bastion of safety. "What are you changing into?"

"Clothes I have here." She smiled, winked, and disappeared through the door with a word to the bald, tattooed bouncer.

Kline followed her in. The throbbing bass hit him first, then the tangible pulse of bodies as he made his way to the bar. The club was dark and blue lit, full of beautiful men and women in various dress. He'd expected more of an S&M environment from first glance, but it seemed innocuous on second look. Just a lot of people around his age, some maybe older, some maybe younger, who were clubbing to the music that had been popular back in his early twenties. It was strangely comfortable and just strange.

Jill met him in the bar, changed into a wisp of a black slip dress over fishnet stockings and platform heels. She'd done a bit more to smoke out her eyes and felt beautifully dangerous. It was another costume, maybe another character, maybe someone from Cabaret, she didn't know, but she was sure she couldn't face the rest of the night as herself. She didn't want to be Jill. She wanted to be someone who could seduce Kline Scott. "Do you like it?" She asked. "I'm a part owner."

"It's--you are?" he asked, his glass paused in midair.

"Uh-huh," she said, nodding. "I bought into it with Teddy to keep it going and he gave me a piece of the business."

Kline shook his head in amazement. "You're just full of surprises, aren't you?"

She cut off her instinct to demur and let a Kit Kat Girl come forward to purr instead. "Mmm. I have a few."

Kline swallowed hard under her heavy-lidded gaze. "It's great. It looks harder core."

Jill let the Kit Kat Girl laugh. It was throatier than her own. "Parts of it are. We have the whole floor. But what I don't know won't hurt me."

"What you don't know?"

Truthfully, she said, "I've never gone back further than the second room. I stay in the front."

"So, this is an S&M club?" Kline asked, looking around a bit nervously.

"People play in the back rooms, Kline, it's not as though there are live sex shows in the gallery. Why? Is it a problem? Are you afraid someone's going to see you?"

He considered a moment, then shook his head. "No. It's fine. Would you like to go back past the second room?"

"Would you?"

She had called his bluff and his cheeks pinked. From what she remembered, Kline was better than an average lover, but he had simple tastes. He redirected. "Would you like to dance?"

Jill nodded so they moved out on the floor. If anyone recognized either of them, there was no indication of it. They were simply anonymous members in a crowd of like-minded people, none of whom wanted to be recognized on the street.

An old Nine Inch Nails song started to throb out of the walls and Kline pulled her up close by the waist, just like he used to do when she'd been so shy about him it was almost impossible to breathe, must less make a move. He still had that effect on her. Wanting to touch him, being afraid he would reject her because— look at him.

They danced together as one song segued into the next, heat and sweat rising on their skin as they moved. He seemed to be remembering her, maybe waking up to her. Whatever it was, it was stoking something inside of her so that when he leaned down to finally kiss her, she was ready. Instead of her lips, though, he opened his mouth against her neck, flicking his tongue over that spot that always made her forget to breathe.

She started and he chuckled. "What did you expect?" he asked against her ear. "You can't show me that throat and not expect me to want a taste."

He tangled his fingers in her hair and then kissed her until she was dizzy. Somewhere in the back of her mind she scolded herself for thinking she was up to Kline Scott plus a decade of experience and growth in his own seduction game. Just barely she could hear herself say, "There are rooms…"

He slowed for a moment and took her face in both his hands, and she knew she had miscalculated. "Jill," he said seriously, looking her in the eyes, "I want you. I want to be with you right now, but I don't think this is the right time. If I'm with you right now, then we just have a repeat of our past. You understand?"

He swallowed hard as her eyes filled with tears, but she nodded and blinked them away. He didn't let her turn her face, though, and he kissed her lips softly. "I don't want to hurt you again. And I don't want to take advantage of you. You've had a really shitty day. When this happens…and I want this to happen…I want to know it's a good day." He brushed away a stray tear with his thumb. "Okay?"

"Okay," she agreed.

"Good. Let me take you home before I lose all that resolve and drag you off into one of those back rooms by the hair. I'll go see if the car is still here."

"I can get home myself," she said. "You can take that car and go wherever you need. I'm okay here."

He looked at her for a long moment, obviously concerned, "Are you sure?"

She nodded, completely herself again, the Kit Kat character melting away with the heat of Jill's embarrassment. She wished she could melt away into the floor. "It's my club. I'm not ready to go home, but you're right, things were getting out of hand. I'm sorry."

Kline leaned to kiss her forehead, then pulled her into his arms and swayed with her for a few minutes before releasing her, the sweat that had felt like a sexy sheen on her arms before, now just feeling clammy as he murmured. "No apologies. "I'll call you tomorrow."

"Don't say it if you're not going to," she asked of him.

"Baby, I will. I've got Colbert at two. I'll call you before then. No repeats of last time."

"Okay. Thanks for tonight. I'm sorry I…ugh." She hugged him tightly and said close to his ear before releasing him and hurrying away toward a door on the far wall, "I've missed you."

"I've missed you, too," he called after her. "I think I just realized how much."

Chapter 3

Kline Scott

Kline watched Jill walk away, disappearing behind a door and he wondered at the wisdom of leaving her alone there, deciding that she was more in her element than he'd realized. It was like old times again. Like no time had passed. It was all he could do not to follow her, but he managed. He meant what he said. He didn't want her sleeping with him because she'd had a bad day and he was there. He wanted to know she was sleeping with him because she wanted him.

Likely the limo ride would have been more discomfort than either of them could have managed if they'd taken it together. With a sigh, he made for the exit and found the chauffeur leaning against the car, chatting with another driver. As he approached, the man hurried around to open the door for him. Once inside he told the driver to take him to the Bowery and instructed him to return to the club to wait for Jill after dropping him off. Kline checked in with the night clerk, glad of the quiet, deserted lobby, and made his way up to his suite.

After a shower he checked the clock. He wasn't ready to go to sleep yet, and he was had all kinds of nerves about Colbert. He wanted something to take his mind off of that, and maybe boost his ego a little, and realized it was still early enough in LA for him to ring Rhiannon. "Hello there," he said when she answered. "You're not going to believe the day I had."

"I saw you on DeuxMoi," she said, and he could hear her shifting around in her bed. "How's Jill?"

"I was on DeuxMoi?" he asked, and then, "You read that?"

Rhiannon laughed. "Yes. How's Jill?"

"She's all right, I guess. The court thing was brutal for her." He went on to explain how Roland had called him, explained the situation and sent Kline to collect his newest client. "So, I took her to dinner and then went to a club. Now I'm back at my hotel. I'm knackered."

"I'm sure you are. You should get some sleep. Big interview tomorrow. Stephen can be tough."

"I suppose." He didn't want to think about that. "What did you do today? Anything good? Find a dress?"

Another rustle. "I was in meetings all day. We're putting together our plan for our Emmy package, and everyone's arguing," she said, holding the phone away to yawn. "It's months away, but marketing plans in years. I did some shopping for the Oscars–if that's still on–but I haven't found anything I like yet."

"Absolutely it's still on! Maybe we can shop together? So, I'll see you when I get back?"

"Hopefully."

"You sound a little distant. Did I interrupt something?"

"No. I'm in bed. Still recovering from the weekend," she said, with the first audible smile since he'd said hello.

"Ah. Good. You had me worried."

"Nothing to worry about unless you've got a guilty conscience."

"Ha-ha! No. I have no conscience," he tried to sound chipper, but couldn't shake the feeling something was wrong. "I'll call soon. Goodnight."

"Okay, have a good interview," Rhiannon said, then added, "tell Jill I said hello. 'Night," before hanging up.

Kline hung up the phone and rubbed his forehead. Neither he nor Rhiannon had made any promises to one another, but they'd certainly spent enough time that she might expect explanations should he decide to be with anyone else. He hated figuring out relationships. He liked the part when he was sure he'd gotten the girl, but the rest of it? Nothing but the anxiety of trying to get her, and then trying to keep her.

His alarm went off at ten and he got up, had another shower, then dialed Jill's number. She answered on the third ring, sleep clouding her voice. "Morning, princess," he said. "I wanted to make sure you made it home in one piece."

"I'm home," she drowsed. "One piece."

"Good. Listen, why don't you come down to Stephen's studio? Meet me. We'll go get something to eat when my interview is over. Roland would love it."

Jill yawned and sighed, and he could hear her rolling over and caught himself wondering what she was wearing. His favorite mornings had been the ones when he woke up to find her sound asleep wearing his boxers, splayed out on her stomach so that the leg of his shorts cut up across her bum, giving him a slice of cheeky cheesecake. He felt his groin tighten. No, his favorite mornings had been the ones where he woke up to her half passed out across him, naked and rumpled from the night before. Suddenly, he wondered if anyone was there waking up with her. "Mm okay," she sighed. "It's at two, right?"

"Two, yeah. You'll be there?"

"Sure," was the dreamy reply. "I'll be there."

"Great, see you at two," he said, offering a smile she could hear before saying goodbye. She mumbled to him and he could picture her in his mind. He laughed as the line clunked and went dead.

He grabbed his suitcase and set about getting dressed for his appearance. It had taken Roland a month to get him on Colbert's schedule and he was sure that his recent box office success was the only reason it had come about. He'd been the butt of many a Colbert joke in the past, so everyone knew Stephen didn't like him much. When the guy with the reputation of being the nicest in late night is barely civil to you, people talk.

Still, not even Colbert could ignore how Knight had blasted into theaters. People were comparing it to Top Gun: Maverick for the business it was doing. It would be interesting to see how the interview went, all things considered.

After a very light breakfast, he called for the car and headed to the studio. There was guest prep and makeup to go through well before the taping began, so he arrived a little before noon. One of the production assistants ushered him into the dressing room and told him that Stephen would be meeting with him in the Green Room prior to airtime.

He was scrolling through his phone when a tap came on the door, followed by Jill walking in. She was wearing a simple black wraparound sweater and a pair of slim black trousers over high-heeled boots. Her hair was pulled back into an elegant twist, and she wore minimal makeup. Kline smiled. "You are one of the few women I know who looks even more beautiful dressed down than up. Come on in."

She grinned at him and walked over to sit by him on the couch. "So, are you ready for Stephen?"

"As I'll ever be. He loathes me."

"It's because you're so pretty."

"Yes, I'm sure that's true. Well, you know what they say, those who can't act make jokes about those who can."

"Is that what they say?" She giggled, leaning to kiss his cheek. "Listen, about last night…thank you. I wasn't thinking straight."

He smiled. "I knew you were going through a lot. I didn't want that to be the reason…you know?"

"I know. Honestly? That wouldn't have been the reason, but– I got caught up in the moment. It felt familiar. Good. You know? But that was a long time ago."

Kline cleared his throat, ignoring the last bit. "Yeah. It means something to me, too." He hesitated for a moment, then said, "Er, Rhiannon phoned. She saw a bit about us yesterday on DeuxMoi last night. I think she's upset."

"She reads that?"

"That's what I said!"

Jill closed her eyes for a moment and nodded. "I shouldn't be here, should I? It is serious, isn't it? Or at least she thinks it is."

He shook his head. "I'll talk it out with her when I get home. She and I haven't made any commitments and you and I haven't done anything wrong. It just isn't something that can be discussed over the phone. I want you to stay. Please?"

In spite of looking like she wanted to bolt immediately, Jill shrugged. "You were there for me yesterday. I can be here for you today. But tell me something, because if I don't ask, I'll wonder until I find out and I don't want to find out the hard way. Are you going to try to make a go of things with her? Are you going to make commitments?"

Kline pressed his lips together and considered his answer before meeting her eyes. "I don't know. I honestly don't know. I one thousand percent don't know."

"Okay," Jill nodded quietly. "Well, let me know when you do."

He reached out and gave her hand a squeeze, then withdrew when the door opened, and Stephen Colbert walked into the room to begin the prep interview. The man greeted his guest and offered a smile to Jill before leaning to kiss her cheek.

"Hey, sweetie," she grinned to him, "I haven't seen you in a while."

"You won't come on! My booker's been trying to get you for weeks."

"I'm in LA now. Just here finishing up the divorce. You've not met Kline, have you? He and I go way back. We used to run around together a lot in the lean days."

Colbert was surprisingly pleasant and welcoming to Kline as he said they had met, which put Kline at more at ease than he had been since arriving. Jill stayed for a minute longer, then excused herself to get some tea while the men prepared for the taping. She watched the show from the wings and was tucked into a dark corner with a great view when Kline was introduced. He stepped from between the draping curtains to uproarious applause and several screams, flashing his winning smile and waving to his adoring public, before shaking Stephen's hand and settling into the first chair in the line.

The interview started well enough, but then Stephen asked Kline if he had any reaction to the new photos.

"What photos?" Kline asked.

Colbert laughed derisively and mimicked back, "What photos? You know," he went on in regular Colbert voice, "the latest pictures of you and your mystery girl ramping up to triple X. Nice tattoo by the way!"

The audience laughed, and Kline felt his jaw tighten. Stephen pulled up a couple of the pictures, black bars censoring everything but his identity, and Kline did a double take. "I hadn't seen those yet," he forced out, sounding much more amused than he thought possible. He pointed at a shot of his ass that would surely be pixelated out later. "I see they got my best side."

The bubble of tension burst as the audience laughed with him and stole some of Colbert's thunder. Kline felt like his soul left his body, finishing out the interview in a state of shock, gracefully dodging more probing questions with relative the muscle memory of media-training, managing not to punch the host in his smug face. They finished the interview with some parting comments about Knight and the upcoming Oscars where he was presenting.

"I'd say we'd be getting to see more of you soon, but… Now, we can only see less of you!" Stephen shook Kline's hand and sent him off, still the shining It Boy to the crowd that clapped until well after they'd cut to commercial.

Jill met him backstage as pale as he was. "Are you alright?" she asked. "Can I do anything?"

"He fucking ambushed me," he said, under his breath, still walking down the corridor towards the dressing rooms. "I have to call Roland. Christ, I have to call Rhiannon."

He started patting himself down, "Where the fuck is my phone?"

"My driver is waiting. Come on, I'll get you out of here."

"Where is my goddamned phone?" He roared, and Jill grabbed his arm.

"Be quiet! Here, use mine!" She pulled up Rhiannon's number from the last conversation they'd had. "Here."

Kline snatched the phone away from her as though she were a thing, not a person, punching the dial button and pacing. "Rhi?" he asked, when the call connected. "Have you seen the pictures? Are you okay?"

"I've seen them. Everyone's seen them," she said, fighting to keep her voice calm.

"I'm so sorry-- I didn't know. I was taping Colbert and he brought them up. I called as soon as I could. Are you okay?"

"Colbert brought them up? On the show?" she said, her voice rising.

"Yeah," he said, "he ambushed me with them."

"What did you say?"

He paused. "Fuck if I know. I have no idea. I was doing good not to pass out."

Rhiannon heard a voice in the background and Kline snorted. "Apparently I said, 'at least they got my good side' as Stephen was showing my ass."

"I can't talk to you about this right now," she said, quietly. "I have to call my parents before someone else does."

"Right," he said, "Call me later."

"On Jill's phone?" she snapped, saying just before hanging up. "Sure thing."

"Shit," Kline said, handing the phone back to Jill without looking at her. "Jim," he said to the driver, "take me to the airport. Now. I don't need to go back to the hotel, just take me straight to the airport."

Jill stared now, "What about your--"

"This is more important," he cut her off, holding up a hand.

She huffed slightly. "You won't be able to leave right away. Go back to the hotel and get your things and call to make flight arrangements."

Kline took a deep breath and let it out slowly, then nodded. "You're right," he looked at her. "I'm sorry. It's just--I keep making things worse without even trying and I can't take care of this over the phone."

"Of course, you can't," Jill said reasonably, looking out the side window to avoid eye contact.

"Where are we going?" the driver asked.

"The Bowery," Kline said, "Or do you want to go home first, Jill?"

"The Bowery, Jim. Take him to his hotel."

They arrived at the hotel to find a small throng of photographers waiting outside. "Drive around, Jim," Kline said. "We'll go in the back way."

The driver did as he was told, and Kline and Jill took the security entrance to the service elevator and went up to his suite. When he walked in, he heard his cell phone ringing and went to retrieve it from the bed where he'd left it. "Hello?"

"Kline? Where are you?" Roland asked.

"I'm at my hotel. I'm packing."

"I need to tell you something."

"I found out. Colbert had everything all ready for me when I arrived."

"Stop packing," Roland said. "You run home and it looks like you've done something wrong. You keep your happy ass in the city, and you do the Today show and Kelly tomorrow. You go on and you charm that Guthrie bitch out of her panties. Let me handle damage control."

"You can't handle this, Roland," Kline said, seriously. "Not all of it. Rhiannon's terribly upset and I need to help sort this out."

"So, call her and explain, Kline. You didn't do this. Those fuckers at the STAR did it. It's not your fault. Stay in New York and do your interview."

"I can't! This is my life, Roland! We're talking about my personal life!"

"We're talking about your career! You want to risk everything you've worked for over a girl you met an hour ago?" Roland growled. "If she's for you, then she'll understand. Otherwise, you've blown your wad for nothing. Now listen to me. You go on that show, and you smile like a trooper. You do it for your career and you do it so it's died down before Jack gets home. You come back to LA now and blow off an interview, and you've just assured yourself of another two weeks of media blitz. You understand?"

Kline gripped the phone and closed his eyes, his son's name working wonders in bringing rationality back into focus. He knew that Roland was right. If he went home now, it would only exacerbate the situation. Best to stay and finish the press as though nothing was out of the norm and work on mending things with Rhiannon when he got home. "Yeah," he said, finally. "Alright. Just fix it, Roland."

"Done. Consider it done."

They hung up and Kline let out a sigh before turning to Jill. She was watching him with her carefully blank expression, but her eyes spoke volumes. "So, it's that serious, huh?" she asked softly. "Very serious."

He stared at her, then ran his hands through his hair. "She's upset, Jill. There are naked pictures of her all over the internet. She's just been exposed to the world because of me."

Jill licked her lips, then bit the bottom one, completely unsure of what to do or say. "Okay," she said, furrowing her brow. "I should--go? Do you want me to go?"

Kline sighed. "I think it would be better. The media will be on full alert now. Even more than they already were. You have enough to deal with without getting mixed up in my mess."

She nodded slowly, eyes welling again. "Okay. Well… good luck."

"I'll call you when this blows over, okay?"

She nodded, but then turned back at the door. "Actually, no. I don't know if that is okay. Can I be honest?" He didn't say anything, so she went on, "I still have feelings. For you. I didn't realize it until I saw you again, but–wow. It's all really fresh. I…I don't think I can do this. I realized it last night. Last night, mistake or not, I would try to make that happen again because I really wanted it. So, maybe it's best not to see you. And honestly again, I don't think you'd ever put me ahead of your work like you're willing to do for Rhi, so, you should go with that. I'm just going to disappear. Again. Well, from personal things with you."

"Jill--"

"No," she said, turning for the door. "I think it's best for everyone. I know it's best for me. I can't go through this with you again. It was too difficult getting over it the first time."

"Jill, I wanted last night, too," Kline said quickly. "And I don't know what's going to happen here but don't check out on me right now. Today is too crazy for you to check out on me."

She leaned against the door, hand on the brass knob and shook her head. "I can't trust myself with you," she said. "You're my weakness. You always have been."

Kline set his jaw. He was not about to make the same mistake twice. He'd make a different mistake this time.

He strode across the floor and took her by the shoulders. "I need you, Jill. I can't make any kinds of promises because I don't want to break them, but I found you again, and whatever capacity I stay in your life, I want to stay in your life. If you walk out that door, don't walk out forever."

"Make me want to stay," she said, her voice thick with emotion.

"Fuck," Kline cursed helplessly, then pushed her hard up against the door and pressed his lips into hers. She made a small noise, then wound her arms around his neck and pulled him closer until his body was crushing hers against the uneven surface.

It all flooded back. Every curve, every plane, every tender spot. She was longer and leaner, and she had picked up some skill, but he was twenty years old again, with his hands full of fairytale, loved and in love to his surprise. And she wanted him.

He still couldn't believe she wanted him. He was still surprised, still delighted, still couldn't help wondering why because he was always just Scott Kline around her. And there was the problem. She knew him too well.

She knew him so well that before they could fall back into the bed, she managed to stop herself. And he knew her well enough to see the Herculean effort it took. "Tomorrow," she said raggedly, ducking out from under his arms and grabbing her sweater up to her naked chest, putting distance between them. "Tomorrow. If we still feel this way tomorrow, then… I've waited this long. I can wait."

Kline groaned and sat back on the bed with his head in hands, nodding. "Right. Yes. Right."

Jill disappeared into the bathroom and came back out mostly repaired, keeping space between them, both of them knowing the brush of fingertips would ignite the flame again. "I'll meet you at the Today show tomorrow and be moral support. And I'll leave now so I'm not immoral support."

She was trying to joke so he gave her a crooked smile. "Where were you last fucking week?" he asked.

"Don't ask me that. I know what that means and that's cruel."

"I'm sorry."

She had the door open that time. "I'll see you tomorrow and we'll…see."

"Jill?"

"Yes?" She paused, but she didn't look back at him.

"Thank you. For being you. For never hating me because I bloody well deserve to be hated."

"I couldn't if I tried, and believe me, I have tried."

She walked out and let the door shut behind her before she could throw herself at him again. It was exactly like old times. She half expected to find August lurking around the corner, waiting to console her.

Rhiannon Charles

Rhiannon sat up in bed and flicked on the television for the Today show. After an hour's worth of teasers for Kline, commercials finally bled into his introduction. Megastar of romcom and action film, notorious slightly-bad boy, currently starring in the romantic action-drama Knight and excited about the upcoming premiere of his first major dramatic turn in Lone Star.

Samantha Guthrie welcomed him effusively, seeming a little starstruck. Kline smiled disarmingly to her and complimented her, which sent her into a blushing giggle. She was composed soon enough and had launched into her interview, asking about his film, showing a clip, then gave a vulpine grin after the screen faded back to the two of them.

"Well, the latest rumor is that you are dating three women. Your costar in Knights, Kara Viceroy, a writer for your best friend, Thad James's sitcom, and one of New York's very own, Tony award-winning actress, Jill Parker. How do you weigh in on that?"

Kline laughed merrily and rubbed his thighs. "Well, I'm sorry to say that I am not, nor have I ever been the object of Ms. Viceroy's affections. I certainly wouldn't have minded!" The studio audience laughed with him. "We worked very closely together--the film nearly got an R-rating, you know--but outside of that, we were really just friends. We didn't have a lot of choice on whom we went out with, so we spent a lot of time in the same company. She's got a boyfriend, though."

"And your writer friend?"

"She is a lovely girl I know from back home in LA. I'm not sure how those photos came to be, but if you can look past my stunning date, you'll see that they were taken at my home—likely with a long-range lens. It's an absolute violation of privacy and I'm sorry she got dragged into the media madness that is my world. She deserves much better than that." He paused for Guthrie's validation, then leaned in. "Not that I won't be suing the bollocks off the photographer. Can I say bollocks?" He asked someone slightly off-camera, looking innocent and adorable.

"I think so," Savannah nodded eagerly. "Now I noticed that

you brought the lovely Jill Parker to the studio with you. Is there something going on there?"

Again, Kline looked slightly off-camera, focused on something and smiled genuinely as his face lit up. "Jilly and I are very old friends, who look out for each other," he said, still focused away from the interview. "She knew me back in the underwear modeling days."

"So, you're not officially seeing anyone?"

Kline glanced back to Savannah and shrugged. "I could take you for drinks," he offered. "See where the night takes us."

Rhiannon snapped off the remote and jerked back down into bed, nestling into the covers miserably angry. He certainly seemed to be taking the photos well. Her parents had been as understanding as possible, but her mother had called to say that her grandmother was thinking of disowning her. She was just humiliated, and Kline was calling her a stunning date. For all she knew he was sleeping with Kara Viceroy, Jill Parker, and half of Hollywood.

She dragged herself out of bed, showered, and dressed for work. Thad had told her she should take a few days off if she wanted to, but she couldn't face knocking around the house aimlessly, doing her own head in. She needed to work. Everyone was going to keep staring, and so be it.

She couldn't believe how angry and upset she was. Aside from the humiliation and utter embarrassment of having her sex life splashed all over the pages of who knew how many papers, the Martha's Vineyard crowd was going to have a field day with that, she was discovering that there was so much more to Kline and Jill than just 'old friends', despite their assurances to the contrary. Rhiannon knew that she didn't have any right to make demands on Kline, and he'd made her no promises, but the last thing she wanted to do was be in the midst of a sordid triangle with him and one of her friends.

If he or Jill had just told her the truth upfront, then none of this would have happened. Especially not their cozy weekend live sex show. The fact that neither Kline nor Jill, who she thought was a friend, had been straight with her about the whole thing was most upsetting of all. At the moment, she wasn't sure she would be able to face either one of them again. She wasn't sure she wanted to.

Tears sprang to her eyes again and she had to sit down, grabbing for tissues to dab them away. Her first lesson in love in Hollywood had been a harsh one. She'd never wanted to be the star of a scandal. She hadn't even given the media a thought. Looking back, that had been naive, given who she'd agreed to go out with. Why had she thought that dating Kline would be a good idea? He wasn't a person. He was a fantasy. Every girl's dream come true. Her teen dream had turned into a nightmare. Of course, he had come out of all of this as the conquering lothario. Never mind what effect it was having on her life.

She'd warned herself not to get too close. Not to care too much. Not to be too eager or hopeful with him. But she had done all of those things. Instead of pressing the issue with him about Jill, after her dinner with her friend had yielded similar secretiveness, she had gone over to his house and ignored the warnings because she wanted to believe him. She wanted to believe that he was feeling similarly for her.

Then he'd taken a call from Roland and left her house like his tail was on fire to take the next flight to New York, and right away he and Jill were together. He explained it away by saying Roland had sent him to rescue Jill from the courthouse. That may have been true, but who does that? If they weren't close, why would Roland send an 'old friend' to pick Jill up and not some muscle-bound handler?

Even if she could dismiss that as PR spin, it didn't change the fact that he was with Jill at Colbert, and when he called her afterwards about the photos, and apparently, she was with him at the Today show as well.

Rhiannon growled through the tears and tried to blink them away. She was usually a rational person. She was careful. She thought things through. She never let anyone too close without extreme caution. Now this. She had been reduced to a seething, jealous, teary, quivering mess over this man. She didn't know which particular piece of the puzzle upset her more.

Eventually, she pulled herself together, tossed the sopping tissues in the waste basket by her bed, and went to splash cold water on her face. She reapplied her makeup, slipped on a pair of dark glasses, and picked up her bag, intent on going to the studio and getting some work done. When she opened her door, she was met with a light show of flashing bulbs and people calling her name. She froze for a moment, caught completely by surprise until something clicked in her head, and she slammed the door closed again. She threw the bolt closed and wrestled her phone out of her pocket to call the police.

After that she dialed the studio and talked with one of the secretaries, then she dialed Thad.

"Rhiannon? What is it? Are you alright?" he asked, immediately concerned. He'd been surprisingly caring and supportive through this whole mess, but it still amazed Rhiannon to hear the timbre in his voice.

"They found me," she said, with a sigh. "There's a troupe of them on my doorstep. They know my name."

He sighed. "Right. I was afraid that would happen after the Today show this morning. Bloody Savannah Guthrie." He was quiet for a moment, then said, "Alright. Have you phoned the police?"

"Yes. They're on their way."

"Good. First problem solved. Second problem--I'll send two rather large blokes to come escort you to work. You do still want to come to work, don't you?"

Rhiannon tucked her hair behind her ear and gripped the phone a little tighter, "I can't stay here, Thad. I'll just go crazy. Especially now."

"You'll be safer at the studio, anyway. We'll sort the rest of it when you get here."

She sighed, slightly relieved. "Thanks, Thad. I really appreciate it."

"No worries, love. See you in a bit," he said, before ringing off.

True to his word, Thad had two men at her house in no time. She recognized them as his own personal assistants, who went out with him to the bigger events, and she relaxed finally. These guys knew their stuff. She watched through the peephole as they muscled their way to the door, the press easing back away from them, then nearly laughed when one of them pulled out a pop-up screen that reminded her of what she used to block sunlight off the dashboard of her car. Once it was in place, the other knocked and they ushered Rhiannon through the now mewling throng and into the backseat of a limo. Once they were inside, one in the front seat, one in the back with her, the bald one grinned hugely, "I'm Chuck," he introduced, offering a beefy hand to shake. "That's Doug. Our driver is Ned."

Rhiannon said hello and thanked them. "No problem!" Chuck hooted, "I love getting the best of those monkeys."

They made a quick trip to the studio where Chuck saw her inside and handed her off to Thad. "There you are," Thad smiled. "And all in one piece. Hey Chuck, be back by six, yeah? She'll need an escort home."

Thad followed Rhiannon into her office and shut the door behind them. "You okay? You look like you've been crying."

"I'm wearing sunglasses," Rhiannon half sniffed, half laughed. "How can you tell?"

"Well for one, you're wearing sunglasses. How are you?"

"Oh, I'm fine," she rolled her eyes as she took off the shades. "I'm humiliated, betrayed, and violated, but I'm fine."

"Humiliated and violated I get," Thad said, kicking back into a chair. "How betrayed?"

While she couldn't believe she was entrusting herself to Thad, of all people, as a confidante, Rhiannon didn't know anyone else to talk to, so she spilled out all her upset over Jill and Kline, angrier at herself than anything else.

When she finished, Thad gave her a wry look. "They used to date," he said. "I don't know how much of this is actually my business, but what the hell, huh? Kline dumped her rather nastily when he moved out here. He had the sitcom, you know? They were together and he moved without telling her he was moving. Too yellow to say anything. He told me about it, and he wanted to fix it, but it was done.

"I know they emailed each other a few times, but he just put the kibosh on it. He jonesed on her for a long time, especially when he'd get drunk, but he was living the life out here, and by the time he was ready to make real amends, he'd knocked up Nina. That was that. So, there's your sordid history and that's why he doesn't talk about it. Makes him look like an arse. And what chick likes to talk about something like that?"

Rhiannon's eyes had gone slightly round. "Oh… Oh, well she has told me about it. Just never told me who."

"Yeah. Well, there you go. So, I wouldn't worry about those two. And Roland's all about appearances. He probably sent Kline in so that Jill could be seen trumping her ex. Kline's a much bigger fish. Makes Jill look better. And him sweeping in on his white horse to rescue her--well, that's good press for Knight. It's business, baby. It's this business."

She rubbed her forehead and sighed. "I hate it."

"Then sell your house and move to North Dakota, because it isn't going to change. This is Hollyweird."

"He asked me to the Oscars--to be his date when he's presenting," she said a bit sullenly.

"Good. Go with him. Be beautiful."

"Are you kidding? There's no way I'm going now!"

"Why not? You get out there on his arm on the red carpet and you are automatically legitimized in the eyes of the media. You're not just some sex romp in the pages of Star. You get out there and be seen as his partner and you'll find out that you have a better leg to stand on. You have the power. You take the control.

"Don't let some anonymous coward with a zoom lens steal your power. So, you got caught having sex. Everyone does it." Thad shrugged dismissively, "You were doing it with the guy the whole world wants to have. You've got street cred you don't even know about. It happened. It's over. Now you've got a choice. Do you let someone else profit from it, or are you going to stand up, own it, and make it work for you? It's got legs, but you have to be the one to tell it where to walk."

Rhiannon stared at him and his earnest blue eyes. "When did you become my life coach?"

"Look, early on in my grown-up career, back when I was coming up in Sydney, photos surfaced of me in a photoshoot I did in my late teens when I was trying to break out of the kiddie tv mold. It was for good money, and I needed money. I had to make a choice, so I decided to just come out and say, 'Hell yeah, I did it. And I got paid, too.' The other guy, yeah guy," he muttered at her expression, "went underground over it. He was twice the actor I am. I just got on top of the problem and made everyone see what I wanted them to see.

"He got steamrolled by it. I don't want to see you get steamrolled by this, because you've got more talent in your little finger than that photographer's got in his whole body, or those gossip sites have got in their entire catalogs. You nailed Kline Scott," Thad said, "and you looked damn good doing it. Tell 'em how great it was. Don't let them make you ashamed."

After she sat there in stunned silence, Thad asked, "So he's called you?"

"Yeah. I didn't answer his calls this morning. I pretty much hung up on him last night."

"You know, it hurts him, too. He's a human being, Rhi. And he's got a kid he'd sell his own soul to protect. This hurts his kid. He'll do everything he can to protect both of you from this. But you've got to trust that he means well."

There was a knock at the door and Rhiannon said to come in. "Hello," a handsome, dark-haired man said, poking his head inside. "I was told Thad was in here."

"Rick!" Thad yelped jumping to his feet.

"Thad!" Rick mimicked the excitement with a laugh.

The men hugged and Thad chattered for a moment, then turned, "Rhiannon, this is Rick Sanders--producer extraordinaire. Rick, this is Rhiannon Charles, brilliant writer and shagger of Kline Scott. Get used to that," he said as an aside to Rhiannon, "it's going to be your title for years."

"Only if you keep bringing it up," she said, through clenched teeth before smiling and extending a hand to Rick. "Good to meet you. Please ignore him."

"Oh, no need to tell me to," Rick chuckled, shaking her hand. "I've been ignoring him for years."

"Ha Ha," Thad said, giving Rhiannon a nudge. "Just see if I name my next daughter after you."

"Your next daughter? Isn't six enough?" she said, glancing down, "In fact, don't stand so close to me. You're freakishly fertile."

Thad cackled. "Want to go for a hot tub, honey?"

Rhiannon punched him in the arm and he made a face. "She's feisty, Rick. But she's got a great rack. Want to see?"

"Thad!" Rhiannon yowled.

"Ignore him," Rick suggested amiably. "He goes away if ignored. But then you know this--that was your advice. Listen, you don't mind if I steal him away for a while, do you?"

"No," Rhiannon rolled her eyes, "please, take him."

Before walking out the door, Thad looked back seriously, "Think about what I said, Rhi. Okay?"

"Okay."

She spent the afternoon doing nothing but thinking. Thinking, looking at the papers, and trying to work on the upcoming script. Close to four she heard voices outside her door, then a knock. "Come in," she called.

Kline opened the door and walked inside, shutting it behind him. His eyes were dark and worried, though he was trying to smile. "Hey-- I came in straight from the airport. I wanted to see you. Are you okay?"

"Let's see, I had a mob of reporters greet me at my door this morning. My grandmother is considering disowning me. And we are apparently the lead subject of about a hundred websites a second. I'm peachy. How was New York?"

"Grimy," he said, jamming his hands into the pockets of his jeans, looking uncomfortable. "Full of unwelcome surprises. Far away from you."

"You did have Jill with you, though. It couldn't have been all bad. That was really cute on the Today show. I thought Savannah was going to swallow her tongue."

Kline's eyes narrowed slightly. He looked tired and rough around the edges, but Rhiannon didn't feel like coddling him. "I had Jill with me because she was fighting off her own bad press," he said, "and dealing with some very heavy things. And while the company was nice, yeah, Rhiannon, it was all bad. I don't know how you found out, but I was sitting in front of a live studio audience with a man who seemed ready to tear my guts out with his teeth. I couldn't get away from it and collect my thoughts. I had to think of something right there--in front of an audience full of strangers. I'm sorry if my answers came across as 'cute' for you. I'm downplaying this shit as much as possible.

"You want to know what repercussions have hit me so far? Since your rich grandmother might write you out of her will and all. My ex-wife's attorney rang. She's filing for primary custody to get my son out of the horrible rotating door of women I have. Are we even now? Since I fucking ruined your life by having you at my place and having some stranger take pictures of me in my own home? Since it's apparently my fault?"

"I never said it was your fault. I just don't know what you expect me to say. You asked me if I'm okay and no, I'm not okay. But what can be done about it? Nothing. I'm sorry that this is causing problems for you with your ex-wife," she said, honestly, "but I'm only one of the women in this equation. If I'd known that there was anything between you and Jill, this wouldn't be happening."

"What do you mean 'anything between' me and Jill? What's that got to do with this?"

She shook her head. "I don't want to play games, Kline. If you and Jill are working on making history repeat itself, leave me out of it, okay? I know you haven't made me any promises, and I don't have any real right to be jealous, but dammit, I am. I really like you and I tried to force that itch of worry away because I wanted to believe you felt something for me."

He looked genuinely shocked and hurt. "I'm not playing games. And I'm not here because I'm trying to make history repeat itself. Believe me, if that's what I wanted, I'd still be in New York. Jill and I do have history, yes. Do I still find her attractive? Yes. Could there be something there? I don't know. Maybe. But I just spent some really amazing time with you and I'm not going to just brush you off. I made it clear that I have some feelings for you, and I want to see where those go. I think we could have something.

"I left her there in her shit to come back to you. Are you okay with that?"

She considered him for a long moment, searching his face for sincerity. The anger and jealousy seemed to fade a bit as he spoke, and she felt herself letting go of the tight grip she'd been trying to keep on herself all day. "Yes, I'm okay with that," she said, quietly. "I'm sorry if I've been harsh, but I've been beside myself and I didn't know what to think."

He shrugged helplessly. "I'm sorry."

"It's not your fault," Rhiannon sighed, shaking her head. "You didn't make the man take the pictures, or the papers print them.

He tried a smile, but it faltered. "So anyway, I came by to see if you were okay and if you needed a ride. Thad told me your place was surrounded by press. You want to come to mine with me? I've called home and had my housekeeper shut the blinds, so we can go in the back way, and no one will see us."

She nodded, then stood up and walked around her desk so that she was standing in front of him. "I did miss you. Even seeing you on TV isn't nearly good enough compared to the real thing," she said, offering him a smile.

He folded her up in his arms and let out a sigh, then kissed the top of her head. "Come on. Let's go home."

Rhiannon woke early to the aromas she was getting used to at Kline's place. He'd taken her home with him and sent his assistant to collect some things for her. Wednesday melted into Thursday, when he took her to work, then went off to do his interview circuit for the day, only to retrieve her, and take her back to his place again.

Now, Friday morning, Kline was on the phone when she wandered down into his kitchen. "I know," he was saying. "And we talked about it before, but I just don't– Roland, listen, I– No, I hear what you're saying. I understand. Does she even want to do that? Oh. Okay. Yes, I understand that. Yeah, I get it. I got it. Yeah. Fine. See you then."

He hung up and sighed, slumping against his countertop until he spotted Rhiannon, then he stood up and plastered on a smile. "There's my girl!"

"Roland?"

"Yeah. The Grammys are this weekend. I have an invite and Jill is presenting. Roland wants us there together. She signed with him, and he wants to show us out together to take advantage of our respective Q levels or something." He waved a hand.

"So, you're going with her?"

"We'll meet up on the carpet and we'll sit together," he said.

"Why didn't you ask me?" Rhiannon crossed her arms before she thought about it.

"I didn't think you'd want to go. I didn't think you'd want to be on a red carpet so soon after the photos. If I show up with Jill, it takes the heat off you and you can get back to your normal life. It puts water on the fire."

The picture furor was still raging, and more and more was

coming out about her in the tabloid press. An old boyfriend had stepped up to give out information, and while he was very kind in his estimation of her, knowing he'd taken money to talk about her was painful. Her family was scandalized, and her mother had lost a social chair position because of it, which was low stakes in the real world, but in her parents' social circle was a hard hit.

If Kline was upset, he played his hand close to his chest and dealt with it while she was at work. She knew he'd met with attorneys all day Thursday, but he didn't say anything about it. When she asked, he changed the subject.

"Thad said the best thing to do was to be seen out with you, so I'm legitimized and not just some random slut."

Kline drew back from the slur like a vampire to garlic. "He said that?""

"Well, the part about being legitimized. I told him about you asking me to the Oscars." The look on his face brought blood rushing to her head. "You forgot."

"No," he said quickly. "I just hadn't thought about it again."

"So, from a PR perspective, if you show up on the red carpet at the Grammys with Jill, and then the Oscars with me, what does that do?"

"I–I don't know. I'd need to talk to Roland about it."

"Did you already tell Roland you asked me?"

"It hadn't come up."

"Oh, for fuck's sake, Kline! I was joking! Does that man really control everything you do?"

"Roland serves a very specific purpose in my life, and yeah, I trust him, so I do most of the things he tells me to do. Don't you do what your boss tells you?"

"But he's not your boss! He works for you! You tell him how high to jump!"

"I hired him to be my manager," Kline said seriously. "I hired him to tell me what to do. I hired him to help me set goals for my career, and then help me achieve them. He's not my assistant–he's my manager."

"And what's he telling you to do about me?" Rhiannon demanded.

"Keep you out of the spotlight! Let the frenzy die down and use Jill to shield you since you seem to mean so much to me!"

"Oh, he's not just telling you to dump me?"

"He does actually care about me, Rhi, as a human being. He's not going to tell me to drop someone I care about. But he is going to tell me what I need to do to keep both my personal and public life on track in a way that supports my career."

"I cannot believe how much faith you put into him."

"Then leave." He said it with a finality, sweeping his hand toward the door. "If you hate my job so much and hate what I have to do to perform it, then leave. You wouldn't be the first woman who went out with me because of who I am and what I do, then dipped the moment she saw the hard part of my job."

Rhiannon felt a vein starting to throb in her temple. "I didn't go out with you because of who you are."

"No? If I'd been just one of Thad's friends off the street, we'd have had the same first date?"

Rhiannon thought back to her own words that night, how she wanted him, but was afraid of his celebrity, even as she wanted him because of the fantasy role his celebrity had played in her mind. "Fuck," she said, hugging her middle. "I don't want to fight."

"I don't either. Look, Rhi, my job is my job. My personal life is something else entirely. I keep my personal life separated–like with Jack. If you want to make a go of things with me, you have to understand my job. I'm not going to show up at your work and tell you how to run your show. You can't try to tell me how to run the show that is my public persona. And, if you do get dragged into that, you have to trust me to get you out of it."

She frowned but nodded. "So, you're going to the Grammys with Jill."

"Probably."

"And the Oscars?"

"I think we need to wait and see how that shakes out. The

photos have kind of changed the balance of things. But you can trust me to figure it out. Okay?" He asked the question and opened his arms, and how could she resist?

Rhiannon walked into his embrace and let him stroke her back. This was totally against her better judgment, but he seemed sincere, and the truth was, she was catching feelings for the man she was going to sleep with and waking up to. Worst case scenario, she decided, she came out of this with photos she could show her grandchildren to prove Granny had been cool once.

After a few moments had passed he kissed her forehead and asked, "Feel like facing the outside world today?"

"Sure. Where are we going so I know how much camouflage to put on?" she said, pouring herself some juice.

"I was thinking about a sushi place in east LA. It's kind of a hole in the wall. No one will know us there and we can just be ourselves. Kind of hide in plain sight without having to worry about cameras."

She considered for a moment, then nodded. "Okay. I've never been there, though. Do I need to dress up?"

"No," he shook his head. "Jeans work. Just remember, in case we run into cameras, always wear something you won't mind seeing all over the internet."

"Right," she said, sipping her juice. The photographers hadn't let up since the naked pictures had hit, and she was being faced with cameras pretty much anywhere she went. It was all taking some time to get used to. She wasn't sure she'd ever get used to it. "I think I'd be glad to be photographed wearing any clothes at all. I'll go get a shower."

Kline was dressed by the time she got out, wearing faded jeans with a loose navy cable knit sweater. He smiled and took himself downstairs to wait. When Rhiannon appeared in her own jeans and a fitted black button down, he whistled. "You're gorgeous, baby."

"Thanks."

"Do you want to wear a different shirt?"

"What?"

"It's photos. You always have to be thinking about photos. Button-fronts gape sometimes and give you paunch when you're sitting. Not you-you, but everyone-you. I could–"

"I like this shirt just fine," Rhiannon interrupted his offer. "I'm good."

"Fab!" His smile was a little too bright, but she ignored it.

"We're going to take the convertible," he told her, "so you might want to pull your hair back until we get there."

"The convertible? I'm going to hide in the floorboard until we get there."

"Just 'til we get out of the driveway," he teased.

There were fans and photographers waiting at the front gate when they pulled out, so Rhiannon ducked down and Kline shouted hellos and waved before peeling out down the lane. She was immediately glad he'd chosen the car. The weather was gorgeous and the drive with his playlist was more fun than she'd had in a while.

Unfortunately, someone had tipped off the paps while they were eating, and they walked out of the little restaurant to a crowd of fans and photographers. Kline gripped her hand and whispered, "Just smile. All you have to do is smile."

He did his best to shield her face from the cameras with one hand as he ushered her into his car, but the droptop offered no such privacy and before he could get the key in the ignition of the classic Mustang, a woman had walked up to the driver's side and asked for an autograph.

Rhiannon saw his jaw twitch, but he signed a handful of autograph books, a napkin, a shirt and one woman's upper arm before waving off the rest. "Sorry! I have to go!"

"Thank you," Upper-arm woman waved, "I'm going to have it tattooed. You're my favorite."

"Well thank you, Love," Kline grinned. "Tattoo's a bit much though, isn't it? It's not even my best writing."

She giggled, "That's okay. I'm doing your autograph," she pointed to the space above it, close to her shoulder, "and I'm doing the logo from *Nonstop*. That was my favorite movie of yours."

"Oh! I've got the *Nonstop* logo on my back," Kline said, reaching to pat over his left shoulder. "It's pretty cool."

"I know. I saw it."

"We all saw it," one of the other women giggled, "and more."

Kline raised an eyebrow realizing they were talking about the photographs. "Then you all know I'm a healthy boy," he winked. "So, you don't mind if we get out of here now? Maybe you'll even give us a little assist?"

Rhiannon wasn't sure what he had meant, but then watched in awe as the fans managed to wrangle the photographers, who had never stopped taking pictures, away from the car so that Kline could ease it away from the curb and drive off.

When they were safely away, she asked incredulously, "That woman is getting your signature permanently inked into her arm?"

"At least she wasn't trying to get my DNA," Kline shrugged, steering them onto the highway where there would be no hope of conversation with the top down. "No tearing out of my hair or ripping off of my clothes. She can ink whatever she wants into herself."

"That was so surreal. It was like I wasn't even here. They didn't even notice me."

That's pretty normal," Kline nodded, raising his voice. "And low key, actually. The women won't ever acknowledge you. They're either threatened, or jealous, or both. Guys will notice you and try to get your attention. For the women the game is to get me to forget you're there. For the guys it's to get you to forget about me."

"You really live this way, don't you?"

He laughed. "Welcome to my world! Since we've been caught out, let's go see more of it. Let's go shopping for that Oscars gown!"

The next few hours flew by in Rhiannon's head like a shopping montage from a romantic comedy. Kline took her up and down Rodeo Drive, in and out of stores, selecting and discarding dresses in every store. She tried on no fewer than five everywhere they went. She couldn't decide whether she was loving it or hating it, but Kline was in heaven and the small crowd of photographers who were trying to follow along were bested by store security every time.

He was also trying on tuxes at every stop, modeling and posing. While they were bouncing from store to store, he was loading up on boxes.

"What are you buying?" She asked him as he sent another clerk off to his car to stow the purchases away.

"Just a few things. Maybe a few pressies for you."

"But--"

"I saw some things I liked for you. You'll love them. Come on."

They made their last stop at Gucci, where Kline finally picked out a black dress to die for. It was the third she'd tried on there, and when the sales attendant straightened the hem, Rhiannon knew this had to be the one. It was feminine and gothic without being frilly, and she felt like she could own the style rather than be swallowed by it. A soft crinkled, gauzy satin hugged her body in a sheer line. The deep V-neck was open to the middle of her chest, but laced up with a thin, satin ribbon. The sleeves fit close to her arms, but not uncomfortably so, and belled out over her hands. She was a dark fairy. "I love it," she told the clerk.

"It's Tom Ford. It's one of my favorites. Pretty sheer, but you can put a sheath under it, or be daring."

"Everyone's seen everything already," Rhiannon scowled. She stepped out and Kline whistled.

"Nice," he nodded. "Very nice. What do the others look like?"

"They're okay. I like this one."

"It looks great on you. I'm just not sure it's right for the red carpet."

"Why not?"

"It's very--casual. I mean, I know it's floor length, and it's a gorgeous cut, but it's more opening night than awards night. We'll get it. You can wear that to the Lone Star premier. That will photograph well from the front, but the back is sort of boring. We'll be getting snapped from all views."

Rhiannon started to say something about his plans for the premier and his thoughts on the dress, but decided not to make a scene in front of the store. She closed her mouth and turned back into the dressing room. When she walked back out again it was in a simple black one shoulder dress made of jersey, with a white lining. Backless, it had a soft drape that showed the lining, matching the two side slits that vented out when she walked. Kline's eyes went wide and he smiled. "Now that's the one," he said. "That is perfect. Andie," he said to their shopper, "We'll need shoes and the right undergarments to go with it. And a bag. That's perfect going and coming and from the side. Perfect."

She started to protest, but clamped her mouth shut again and walked back to put on her own clothes. The sales attendant smiled. "He knows his events," she said sympathetically. "And he knows what looks right. It is smashing on you."

"Thanks," Rhiannon said. With the girl out of the room, she dressed quickly and considered herself in the mirror. She never gave much thought to her looks. She knew she was good looking. She knew she was built well. Beyond that, she was comfortable unless duty called, and then she dressed to the nines. Actually, Jill had been instrumental in showing her the ins and outs of high fashion. The dress Kline liked was Jill's style.

There was a flurry around the cash register as they rang up the purchases, then Kline whisked her out to the car and back up into his mostly glass fortress where he sat her down and brought out the boxes. He had completely re-wardrobed her. Casual, evening, formal, underwear, shoes, accessories. There were easily several thousands of dollars' worth of merchandise all in her size. "Kline…"

"What? I wanted to," he was smiling hugely. "I mean, you're

going to be out and about and seen with me everywhere, and you didn't seem sure of what to wear for that, so now you're set. No worries about ending up on Go Fug Yourself." He was beaming. She was feeling steam start to rise.

"I don't worry about things like that," she said, seriously.

"No one ever does, until it happens, then it's a horror."

She stared at him, not sure which version of his persona she was actually dealing with here. He'd been on glamour patrol nearly all afternoon and didn't appear to be coming down from it any time soon. "A horror for me," she asked, "or for you?"

Kline tilted his head. "What do you mean?"

"I mean are you worried I'm going to make you look bad?"

"No! I'm just used to this. I know how it works. I thought… Well you're a girl, I thought you'd like new clothes."

"I do like new clothes, Kline, and I appreciate that you're trying to do something nice for me," she said, nudging one of the boxes with her foot. "It's just that most of this isn't anything I would have chosen for myself. You didn't just buy me some new clothes. You're dressing me the way you want."

"I bought you the latest styles from the hottest couturiers," Kline said, unbelieving. "Why wouldn't you want to wear that?"

"I'm not a label queen for one thing," she said, flatly. "For another, I wear what I like, not just what's fashionable. Do you not like the way I dress?"

"I think you look fine. I know how this works, though, and they will pick you apart. It's better to just wear the uniform and be done with it. You really want pictures of you with circles and arrows showing all your fashion fouls? I'd think that would be more upsetting than skin! I know it is for me."

Rhiannon huffed, "Not for me. I don't care what people think about what I wear, but I definitely don't want my naked body splashed all over the place. Considering that's already happened, they're out of ammunition."

"You'd be surprised," Kline grumbled, flicking on the television. "Fine. I'll take it all back. But at least keep the underwear."

"I like some of the clothes," she said, pulling out a sweater from one of the bags. "You just outdid yourself. It's too much."

Kline changed the channel trying to find the basketball game, but stopped when he heard his name. "Speaking of busy, Jane," the entertainment anchor was saying, "Kline Scott is certainly burning the midnight oil."

Voiced over camera footage of him walking in Central Park with Jill, their fingers twined as she looked up at him with an expression all too easy to read, the anchor said, "Scott was in New York for a few days spending time with an old flame, three-time Tony winner, Jill Parker. They were spotted at some trendy eateries, and she accompanied him to all his interviews." A pixilated version of some of the sex romp photos came up, "She didn't even seem to mind that he'd just been with Rhiannon Charles, a writer for the sitcom 'Simon Says.'"

Footage of Kline kissing Jill's forehead followed with the words, "Parker is in LA now, getting ready to start filming 'Devil's Party' one of her Tony-winning roles. She'll play a jilted lover who remakes herself in the image of an old boyfriend's ideal, only to leave him hanging. Literally."

"Well Kline Scott better watch out!" The co-anchor grinned, filling the screen. "If she dyes her hair red and starts running around naked, he's had it!"

Kline didn't even get the chance to turn around before Rhiannon was walking past him and out of the room, towards the kitchen.

"Rhi? Rhiannon!" he said, getting up to follow her.

"They really need to come up with some new material," she said, searching around the island for her purse. "I'm really getting tired of being the punchline."

"Rhiannon… We just have to ride it out."

"Oh?" She raised an eyebrow, "What else have you been 'riding out', Kline? Are you going to tell me I didn't just see what I saw? You two look beautiful together."

"Fuck all," Kline muttered, running his hands through his

hair. "You saw what you saw. You didn't see the before or after though. They don't show that. Listen, I told you. If I'd wanted a fuck, I could have had it any time. Jill made that abundantly clear. I didn't take her up on it, though, because of you. Because I wanted to be back here and make a go of what I have with you. Okay?"

She gaped at him, plucking her cell phone from her purse. "So, a nice romantic stroll in Central Park, holding hands and canoodling, was your way of reinforcing the lack of interest? Right. You must think I'm stupid. Really. But then, why wouldn't you? Everyone else does."

"We weren't having a romantic stroll! She was having a romantic stroll," Kline insisted, "but what you missed was me telling her no. Are you not getting that? If I wanted to be with her, I would be. I want to be here with you! Do you get that?!"

"Yes, you keep telling me that, and you also keep telling me that nothing happened between you and Jill, yet it's been one surprise after the next. Is there anything else that I should know about? Anymore charming anecdotes from New York?"

He sighed, "Look, there is nothing going on between me and Jill, okay? I took her out to a club the first night, to get her mind off the divorce thing. She came on to me pretty aggressively and I told her no. That's it. That's that. She was hinting and suggesting the next day, but I still said no."

Rhiannon's expression took on a shade of skepticism. "You mean that Jill was the aggressor in all of this?"

"Yes, that's what I've been trying to tell you."

"That's not like her, Kline."

"I blamed it on the emotional upheaval, myself," Kline said. "She was never the aggressor when we were together before. But it's been a long time. And she was hurting. And I was there, and I was safe, and I think she just wanted to get her mind off things. I do love Jill, Rhi. I probably always will. She's the first girl who ever meant anything to me. But that was years ago. It isn't the same." He shrugged and sat down on a barstool. "I don't know how many more ways to say it. I want to be with you. I want to see where this is going."

She sighed and shook her head, unsure of what to say. She wasn't used to this sort of drama in her life. The lack of control of the situation was disarming, but for reasons she couldn't' quite figure out, she wasn't ready to just cut her losses and walk away. "I'm not used to things like this, Kline," she said, after a moment. "This is all completely off the map for me and I'm not sure what to make of it."

"I don't know what else to tell you," he said miserably. "Other than I don't want you to go. Please stay."

Another moment's consideration, then she closed her cell phone and dropped it in her bag. "Alright. I'll stay. We'll see how this goes."

He opened his arms to her, and she stepped into them. When they came up for air, it was only because Rhiannon's phone was ringing. Both of them were giggling as Kline peeled himself off the kitchen floor to grab it for her. She was still laughing when she said hello, still fumbling to get a grip on the thing.

"Hey, Rhi. It's Jill. You sound happy! I was calling to check on you."

"Oh. Hi," Rhiannon said, leaning up to stop Kline from kissing her throat. "I'm doing alright. How are you? You sound cheery, yourself."

"I'm good. I just got back from New York and had a fitting with August, who is dressing me for the Grammys. It's not one of his dresses, but he's tailoring to suit. Can't leave well enough alone, that man. He's nodding. He has pins in his mouth."

Rhiannon looked at the time. It was nearly midnight and Gus was up tailoring? "Sounds great. I'm sure you'll be stunning," Rhiannon said, "as always."

"I'll be practically nude if he keeps hemming," Jill snorted. "He's rolling his eyes at me now. Oh, and he's waving at you."

"I'm waving back," Rhiannon said. "The dress sounds fantastic and I'm sure I would love it."

Kline mouthed "Jill?" to Rhiannon and she nodded. "So

how was New York?"

"Oh," Jill's tone flattened measurably, "it was rough. Rough."

"I'm sure it was. The press has been kind, though. I just saw the footage of your stroll in Central Park. You appeared to be holding up well."

"Stroll in Central Pa-- Oh! With Kline? Footage, huh? You know, I think Kline being there made all the difference. They weren't going to eat me alive because he's a much bigger name than Gary. Kowtow to the name, you know? He really rescued me."

"Yeah," Rhiannon said, quietly. "Well, I'm glad you survived, anyway. Listen, I've gotta go. You kinda caught me in the middle of something."

"Oh sure. I'm sorry--before you go, do you want to get together for lunch?"

"Um, sure, when?"

"Are you free tomorrow? I've got the Grammys Sunday, so that's no good or I'd suggest brunch."

"No. Maybe next week? I'll check my schedule on Monday and give you a call."

"Okay," Jill said unsurely, reading something strange in Rhiannon's voice. "Well, I'll let you get back to what you were doing."

"Right. See ya," Rhi said, as cheerily as she could manage before ending the call.

Kline put the phone back up on the counter, then helped Rhiannon to her feet. "You okay?"

"I don't know. You told Jill about us--well, I'd told her about us, too. But you told her, and she still tried to get together with you?"

He sighed. "Yeah. I know it's upsetting, but I don't think she was trying to hurt you. I don't think she was thinking clearly. The divorce really shook her up."

"Maybe. But she and I have known each other for a long time, and it just doesn't seem like she would do something like that. She was encouraging me to be with you."

"I don't know what to say," Kline shrugged.

"Maybe nothing. I'm going to go take a shower."

As she passed through the center of the house, she caught sight of Kline through the glass hallway. He had picked up his phone and looked to be headed for the deck. Was he calling Jill?

Rhiannon stood under the shower, scrubbing her body and trying to scrub her mind. She wasn't sure she could believe what Kline said to her, but she was also sure that Jill had never been honest about her level of interest in the actor. She knew her own mind, though, and her own level of interest, and she was damned if she was going to let Jill Parker snake this man out from under her.

When Kline finally made it back to his bedroom, he found Rhiannon in the closet, hanging things up.

"I thought we were returning that stuff?"

She shrugged, tucking away a pair of jeans. Jill didn't have any clothes in his closet. "It's growing on me. I just don't have any room in my closet for it."

He smiled. "Those things look good in there."

"You think?"

"Absolutely. You know, Jack's going to like you a lot. He's home on Friday."

"Yeah? I can't wait to meet him."

"I've told him about you."

She smiled, hanging the last of the blouses up before walking back towards the bed. "Well, as long as he doesn't read the papers, we'll be just fine."

"No," Kline said, shaking his head. "Never. Even Nina wouldn't let that happen. It's one of the few things she and I still agree on."

Rhiannon nodded, bending to retrieve a bag from the floor. "How are things going with the custody suit?"

"So far it's going alright. I don't think she's going to get what she wants. I'm mostly letting the lawyers handle the details," he said, clearing his throat. "Speaking of lawyers, mine thinks that our case against the photographers and at least the outlet they sold through is pretty solid. He's expecting the lion's share of a settlement."

She hummed. "I'm not after any money. I want the pictures destroyed and off the internet. Can't we get some kind of prohibitive injunction to stop websites from displaying them?"

"That's rather impossible, love," he said, lying back on the bed. "Besides, the terms of the settlement have already been decided. All that's left now is for us to win the case."

"What good will taking a lot of money from them do? The damage is done. The pictures are public. It won't change anything."

"It will make them think twice about trading in that sort of information."

Rhiannon sighed. "No, it won't. It will just make them try harder to nail someone else and make their money back."

"As long as it isn't us."

She shook her head and turned back to the closet. She just didn't feel like arguing anymore today. "What time is Jack coming home on Friday?"

"Nina's arranged to have him back by 4, so by the time you get home from work, he'll be here," Kline said, getting up to head for the bathroom. When he came back out, he was wearing track pants, and which meant that he was going into the gym to work out. After that, he'd spend ten minutes in the sauna, followed by a long, hot shower. She'd been sleeping over for less than the sum total of a week and already knew his routine.

She put the last of the clothes away and climbed into the bed with her laptop to work on some more revisions to one of the scripts until Kline came in and pounced on her, still dripping and warm from the shower.

She woke up early the next morning and left Kline sleeping while she grabbed a shower and got ready for work. With only the briefest consideration of the new wardrobe hanging in his closet, she opted for the clothes she'd brought from her place. Her standard uniform of comfortable, well-fitted jeans, a baby tee, and a light zipped sweater suited her just fine.

There was fresh juice in the fridge, and she poured a glass and took one of the low-carb, whole grain muffins from the counter. One bite had her scowling, and she tossed the rest in the garbage. She would stop at McDonald's on the way.

Leaving through the back way, she avoided the throng of reporters and fans out front, and headed off to the sanctuary of the studio. Work was good. Work would help her focus.

She arrived to the usual chaos, as sets were being rearranged and interns and stagehands were scurrying everywhere. She smiled when Thad appeared, bellowing something about the lighting and she detoured into her office and closed the door.

The day was filled with last minute script changes, meetings, and taping in the afternoon. Rhiannon was there until well after six and arrived back at Kline's to find that he'd made dinner for them. "A peace offering," he said, putting the pasta laden plates on the table. "I'm even eating."

They'd passed the evening in pleasant conversation and settled in front of the television for a while, Kline making an effort to avoid any tabloid shows and mention of him and Jill. Rhiannon found that she was profoundly grateful and when he took her to bed a short time later. She showed him in a variety of ways until they were both spent and sleeping comfortably together.

He left the house in the early afternoon on Sunday, going to meet his glam team at a hotel close to the Crypto.Com Arena, inviting her to join him. She had declined, opting for a quiet night in. "But I'll watch the red carpet and cheer you on."

That was a mistake. Watching the red carpet had meant watching him sweep a glammed out Jill past the photo call area, to land together at all the talk-spots set up along the entrance to the arena. She looked ethereal in a Gucci dress that August had tailored to her trim figure, and whoever had done her makeup had played up those big guileless eyes so that she might have stepped out of the pages of a storybook. If storybook characters wore Jimmy Choos.

She and Kline had an easy rapport and moved like a single

body from one station to the next with complimenting answers to every question they were asked, always stopping just short of saying they were officially an item, letting the entertainment journalists and audiences read whatever they liked into their matching, adoring grins.

When they'd finished the gamut, Rhiannon was spared the sight of them until Jill took the stage to present the award for Best Score Soundtrack for Video Games and Other Interactive Media, and the cameras panned to catch Kline letting out a siren of a wolf whistle when she walked out from behind the curtain. Jill made a joke about that being the soundtrack of her life when she lived in Manhattan and thanked Kline for making her feel so at home, and the crowd laughed.

In the next segment, Kline was spotlit for his nomination for Best Spoken Word Album, and Jill was there hugging his arm, and there again, leaning her head on his shoulder when he lost to Tom Hiddleston.

Rhiannon was torturing herself on Reddit threads already popping up about the couple when she heard the chime that let her know someone had opened the back door. It was a full three minutes before Kline appeared, his shirt already half unbuttoned. "I lost," he said, pouting.

"I saw."

"Hiddleston? Really? He's got a nice voice, but he was reading a biography of Winston Churchill. I read a spy novel, and actually had to give characterization! I can't believe he beat me."

Kline threw himself down in a chair across the room and started taking off his shoes, ranting over the injustice of being trumped by Loki. "I'm just jealous," he finally sighed. "I want his career."

"Well, it looked like Jill gave you plenty of comfort," Rhiannon said, hoping he could read the ice in her voice.

If he did, he didn't care. He paused and mused. "It was nice to have a friend there. You know, I've taken dates to the shows before, but that's different than a working partner." He was off on another tangent about how easy it was to work the lines with another actor. He didn't have to worry about her missing cues or getting flashbulb paralysis.

"I'm going to have a shower, then bed. Do you want to join?"

She waved her hands over the sheets, "I'm already in bed. You can clean up without me."

"You don't want to come help me soothe my ego?"

"No," she said flatly to his burst of laughter.

"Fine! But I will be extra grumpy tomorrow."

He wasn't, though. In fact, Rhiannon rose to find him already in his gym, running on the treadmill and panting to Roland via Bluetooth earbuds about his next voice gig. He wanted a video game because that seemed like the easiest Grammy grab. When he saw her, he waved and mimed *five-more-minutes* at her, then joined her for a green juice in the kitchen before driving her to work, talking non stop about how he planned to EGOT.

The rest of the week wasn't perfect, but it also wasn't so bad. Jill's name wasn't mentioned in her presence, and Kline made every effort to be available when Rhiannon was home. Roland was ever present, however, either in person or on the phone, and Kline was being called out almost every night to be 'seen.' Rhiannon went with him a couple of times, but she just couldn't keep it up and not drag her ass at work the next day. By Thursday, she was drained and weary of the whole mess.

The press was so used to Rhiannon being at Kline's, there were only two stray paparazzi hanging around her neighborhood. She was so used to them being at Kline's, too, that she just ignored them, pulled her mail from the box, then went inside and bolted the door. Kline had gone to pick up Jack from the airport, so she'd gone home for a night. Best to let them settle in, both she and Kline agreed. She fixed a cup of coffee, then started going through her mail, pulling out her subscriptions to US Weekly and People with a sudden morbid interest in whether or not she was in them. Laughing darkly to herself, she remembered when she'd enjoyed the mindless entertainment of reading about the stars. She hadn't dared look at DeuxMoi for days.

The covers of both magazines caught her cold, though. She'd been expecting to see her pixilated parts, not Kline and Jill smiling brightly. "Is It Love?" US Weekly asked across a still shot of the couple walking in Central Park. The sidebar of People had another picture from the same scene, this time of Kline kissing Jill's forehead. "Love Story: A Knight rescues his princess. But what happens next?"

Rhiannon couldn't help herself. She flipped through the magazine until she found the article. On a page and a quarter, there was a blown up shot of the picture from the cover. Inset were three more. One was a picture of the couple from years back. They were hugged up to each other, heads close, eyes sparkling, Kline in smudged eye liner mugging for the camera, Jill gazing up at him. The next was from the steps of the courthouse and showed Jill folded into Kline's arms, her face hidden in his shoulder. Finally, a picture of them backstage at Colbert, Jill looking tired, but smiling with Kline's arm around her shoulders.

"Parker and Scott canoodling their way through Central Park," read the first caption, followed by, "Young love: Parker and Scott shared digs for two years before he moved to LA to star in Knock Three Times," "Knight to the rescue. Scott consoles Parker after a bitter divorce hearing," and "'He's her strength,' said a source close to Parker. 'There's just this undeniable something between them. The chemistry is overwhelming.'"

Biting her lips together, Rhiannon started to read. The first part of the article was filler, giving Kline's and Jill's ages, industry backgrounds and whatnot before getting to the meat. "The couple met at a party thrown by costume designer, August Hall. Parker, just eighteen at the time, was dating the host. Scott, a cosmopolitan twenty, was dating a model. But they met and something clicked. In spite of her notoriously controlling stage mother's protests, Parker started seeing Scott right away. By the end of that year, they were living together, very much in love." Rhiannon blanched and skimmed down to a quote that caught her attention as her heart started to pound. "They looked very comfortable. Very much in love. He was incredibly tender with her, and she was just completely his."

"So what went wrong?" The article asked. "'Kline got the role on Knock Three Times and he felt like he couldn't turn it down. But Jill had a thriving career on Broadway,' a source close to Scott said, 'He didn't feel like he could ask her to go and give up her career. His intention had always been to get established, then work out the distance, but they both started seeing other people and things just melted away.' Not to say that the feelings were completely gone.

"Parker was very quietly wed to Broadway producer Gary Grissom three years ago. While their marriage was kept a close secret, their divorce played out with the very public display of Grissom's infidelities. After facing down both Grissom and his pregnant mistress (society celebutante, Carlie Ship), Scott hurried to her side in a show of support. They spent the next few days in close quarters, only emerging to make Scott's appearances on the Stephen Colbert and Today shows.

"Where Scott had been there for her after a public humiliation, Parker stood by her man with an impressive show of solidarity when he was faced with the pictorial scandal of what may go down in history as the rowdiest romp this side of Pamela and Tommy Lee."

Rhiannon flipped the page quickly, tearing it as she did. "So, what's next for the reunited lovebirds? Love scenes for one. Scott has just signed on to play opposite Parker in Devil's Party after the news that Theo James dropped out of the role due to scheduling conflicts. Parker is reprising her Tony-winning turn as a spurned lover gone insane. There were some hot scenes on the boards, but sources say we can expect things to heat up even more so on the silver screen. Maybe those pictures will only be a fleeting memory."

An old candid picture of the couple kissing was followed

by another that showed Kline's lips meeting hers as he leaned into a limo. "Then and now," the captions read. "Left, Parker and Scott at her nineteenth birthday party. Right, Parker dropping Scott at the airport last week."

"But what about the other ladies in Scott's life? Kara Viceroy, his costar in Knight, has admitted to a short affair, but her reps say they haven't seen one another since wrapping the film. She has been in Milan working on a new title due out in December and seeing current costar Colin Farrell. Rhiannon Charles, a writer on the popular, Emmy winning series, Simon Says, is another story."

This was followed by one of her pixilated poses and a shot of her with Kline from the sushi place in LA. She was unhappily surprised at how slouchy she looked. The outfit had looked very nice on her, but somehow, the way it photographed it just looked wrong. Her hair looked like a birds nest. She sighed and kept reading.

"Scott told Savannah Guthrie that Charles was the woman he was seeing back home, and that Parker was just a good friend, but sources close to Scott say otherwise. 'He's trying to do the right thing by Rhiannon. You know, sticking around until the photo thing blows over. He likes her and thinks she's a great girl, but there's just no denying the chemistry between him and Jill. He and Rhiannon haven't known each other long, so they both knew it was just a fling. He and Jill have a history that will take them a long way.'

"Scott's history is coming into play, though. His ex-wife, Nina Scott, has filed for primary custody of the couple's son Kline, Jr., citing Scott's 'revolving door' lifestyle as reason. It may be a tough battle ahead, but a friend of Scott's said, 'He'll get through it. And Jill will be there for him. She always is.'"

Rhiannon was finding it hard to breathe, much less keep reading, but she looked down to the bottom of the page where three colored boxes showed pictures of Kara Viceroy, her, and Nina Taylor. Each one had a little biography. Hers read, "Rhiannon Emerson Charles of the wealthy Boston Charles family is described by friends as a loving, free-spirited girl. 'She was devastated about the pictures," her friend said. 'because of what it would mean to her family. She's very natural and doesn't mind showing her body, but her family is very much old-school. But things happen. She and Kline are still friends.' Thad James, star of Simon Says, refused to comment."

Rhiannon stared at the magazine, her eyes skimming the copy again, before settling on the schmoozy pictures of the two. She didn't know how to feel first. Part of her mind was trying to remind her that magazines like this always went for the juiciest story, even if they had to make most of it up, but she couldn't look at the pictures and believe that there was nothing to it. The anonymous sources had spoken and once again, she was being set up for a bad fall. She didn't want to fight with Kline anymore, but she knew if she brought it up, he'd explain it away, and somehow, she'd believe him because she wanted it to be true. Doubting him was bad. Doubting herself was worse.

The only thing she knew for sure was that she couldn't keep doing it. Whatever it was between him and Jill, no matter how much they both denied it, it was a stronger force than she was. Kline said he wanted to see where things would go with her, and she'd agreed, but it was obvious that it was going nowhere. Her cell phone began buzzing in her pocket, startling her, and she dug for it to answer without checking the name, "Hello?"

"Hey Rhi!" Jill's voice chirped over the line.

"Hi," Rhiannon said, rubbing her forehead.

"How are you?" She remembered that she was supposed to call Jill back on Monday about getting together for lunch during the week, but it never happened. "I've been busy. Thad's a slave driver."

"You should fire him," Jill laughed. "Hot actors can't be too hard to come by."

"Yeah, they're a dime a dozen in this town," Rhiannon said, trying to match her humor. "But since his name's on the door, there's not much I can do."

"I guess you were busy all week for lunch, huh? Are you

free tomorrow?"

"No, tomorrow's bad, too, I'm afraid. I have to go into the studio in the morning, and Kline's son is home, so we're going to have dinner together and make the big introductions before he's off to do a Canadian press junket."

"Oh–that's big, meeting the kiddo."

"Yeah. You know. We're not just faking things for our photo sets."

There was a long pause. "Okay. Well… Rollie said Kline was taking you to the Oscars. I'm going with August, so maybe I'll see you there? Or at least at the Vanity Fair party after."

"I have no doubt," Rhiannon said, "I'm sure I'll see you there."

Jill sighed. "Well, you keep Kline on one side of the room, and I'll keep August on the other. Can't have them combusting in front of everyone."

Rhiannon gave a snort. "Sure. I'll try. But it's his show, you know? I'm just his largest accessory."

"He's just presenting. When you're up for your Emmy, he can be your jewelry. That's just how it works. You sound--busy? Should I just wait for you to call back?"

"Actually, I am on my way out. I'm sorry that I've been so unavailable, but life got hectic all of the sudden. You know how it is."

Jill's tone changed again, this time to something cool and breezily distant. "Of course. I won't bother you again. Have a good weekend."

"You, too," Rhiannon said, just as breezily, "bye."

Jill Parker

Jill put the phone down with a dark expression, then wandered down to August's workshop. He'd finished her dress a day before and was now putting the finishing touches on a small clutch. "Hey," she said, entering. "Rhiannon hates me now."

He looked up from his work confused and tilted his head. "What?"

She recounted the conversation and slumped into a chair. "All I can think is that it's something to do with Kline. I haven't seen her to do anything offensive."

"Well, the press has been on and on about the two of you since New York, love," August pointed out. "That may have something to do with it. And the Grammys. You were quite a pair. I doubt he's handled things well since returning."

Was it just three weeks ago, they had been walking through Central Park together after Kline's Today Show appearance?

"So," Jill had asked him. "So now what?"

He had given her hand a squeeze and swung it along with his. It was cold and his hair was damp with snow, curling up tightly, making him look more angelic than rakish. "So now I go back to LA in a few hours and face the music there. When are you back?"

"Saturday night, for the Grammys."

Kline nodded and stared straight ahead as they walked. He squeezed her hand again. "I'll be glad when you get there."

"Is this just a New York thing? What's happening with us?"

"I don't want to think so. Jill," he slowed his pace and looked down at her, as conflicted as he'd ever felt in his life. "I can't just give Rhiannon the brush off. I don't want to really, but I especially can't in light of all this. I've asked her to go to the Oscars as my date and those are weeks away. I need to keep things even until then at least.

"After that we can talk--she and I. By then the photos will have blown over. I haven't made any promises to her, but I think the ground was laid for them anyway, and I owe her an explanation. I'm not cheating on her, but I haven't been very open about our past together. If I'd met her a day later it wouldn't be an issue, but it is an issue. I really like her. She's brilliant. I don't want to hurt her. I don't want to hurt you. I need some time to work things out. Okay?"

"That's fair." They walked further in silence before Jill asked, "So I won't see you at all after the Grammys? Or what?"

"You know," Kline said after they'd gone a little further, "I don't even want to think about not seeing you for even a day." He stopped and leaned to kiss her forehead. "But we're just going to have to see how things work out."

"Okay," she'd said. She knew what that meant. She still wasn't enough to hold his interest.

He smiled and stroked her cheek. "Come on. Let's go get a hot dog before I have to leave."

She had watched him eat a hot dog, even let him kiss her with hot dog breath, then watched him climb into the back of a cab before she'd gone back to her apartment and packed a few things she'd left behind before. Then, deep in a misery of her own making had called her travel agent and asked to change her flight.

She wasn't going to hear from Kline again and she knew it. Unless it was business, it was done and dusted. That jagged piece of her heart that had been stuck like shrapnel in the pit of her stomach for so many years dislodged, and she sobbed like her world was ending. When she'd managed to stop crying, she realized that in a way, her world had ended. At least, that part of it had.

A few hours later, she had been in the backseat of a town car, huge sunglasses over her swollen eyes, then it was first class back to LA and a car straight out to Beverly Hills.

August had answered his door, talking on the phone, telling his caller he'd have to hang up. "What are you doing here?" He asked, as soon as she'd crossed his threshold. "You're supposed to be in New York until Saturday."

"I couldn't stay," she said, walking inside as he stepped away. "It was pretty miserable."

"Yes. I've seen the entertainment news. You and Kline looked nice and cozy."

Jill snorted. "I almost slept with him. We're talking so close I'm not sure that it counts that we didn't." She threw her purse down on his couch and turned to face him. "I have slept with two men in my entire lifetime. It's been almost a year since the last time Gary and I slept together. What is wrong with me?" She held out her arms so he could inspect her. "What about me is so horrible and vile that no one wants me?"

"I wouldn't say no one wants you. You just tend to have bad taste in men," August said, looking her over and then pulling her in for a hug. "You have exquisite taste in everything else, I guess you had to be bad at something."

She had sniffed, but found there were no tears left to cry, so she just sighed, letting August lead her around to sit down, where he sat beside her and pulled her close again, stroking her hair. "You're very bad for getting naked with Kline," he scolded gently, kissing her forehead. "He might get you dirty."

"Or he might not. I don't know which is worse."

"So what happened?"

Jill let out a shuddering breath. "He's seeing Rhiannon. He's got feelings for her. She's wonderful and perfect--and I can attest to that. I'm just...not. August? He was going to drop everything to come back here to her. Put off work. He'd never do that for me. Gary, who didn't even want to live together because he was so serious about keeping us a secret, is parading his pregnant girl-friend around town. And here I am. Whining to you again." She sat up and looked around. "Is Lola here? Am I interrupting some-thing? I didn't even think about that."

"No. She's gone off on a shoot. I don't think she'll be com-ing back," he said, dismissively. "How can you say that you aren't perfect? I've always thought you were perfect. Kline's an idiot. A sneaky idiot. And Gary is in serious need of some therapy. He left you because you started taking control of your life and didn't yield to his whims at every turn. He's still smarting from the fact that you scored Devil's Party without his help. Don't think it's something wrong with you, darling. It's them."

"Well, there're a lot of 'thems' out there, August." She low-ered her lashes. "I need to fall in love with someone who wants me."

August was quiet for a long moment, watching her with his dark green eyes, weighing his next words carefully. "Well, there's always me."

"Oh, Duckie," she smiled wistfully. "You've got Lola."

He sighed. "No, I don't. Lola is gone. She was a poor substitute, anyway."

"Lola's gone? When? What happened?"

"I sent her packing." August shrugged with a strangely cute laugh. "She--oh, hell. She's not you. Look, Jill, I've spent a decade waiting for a real opportunity with you. Kline snatched you right out of my hands twice, and then Gary. I know you've had some romantic interest in me now and then, because we have dated. You just like the bad ones. Now if you're interested in rewriting history, rewrite it with me. Take a chance on me, if you're not too afraid of loving someone who will actually love you back for once."

Jill stared at him, caught completely by surprise, even though she had always known in the back of her mind that he felt this way. At least, he had felt this when they were younger. The fact that it was still true had her blushing. "Oh, August. I-I don't know what to say."

He shrugged. "I'm not asking for the world, Jill. Just a chance. I know you've been through a lot and that you're still hurting from the emotional roller coaster you've been on for the last several months. I'm prepared for the highs and lows, and I'd like to take care of you. If you'll let me."

"You just want to see me naked," she tried to tease.

"I've seen you naked, love. But if that's part of the deal, then I'm all the more interested." He opened his arms. "Come here."

She hesitated. "August, I don't know. You're the one person in the world I can trust. What if…if it doesn't work? Then I lose you."

"No. You won't lose me. If we make a fair go of it and it doesn't work out, then we'll say we tried and move on. I know you won't do anything deliberately to hurt me and you know that you can trust me not to hurt you," he said, seriously. "As long as we are open and honest, as we've always been, I can't see an end to us."

She had made a decision in that moment. She was going to try doing things that didn't feel exactly right because what did feel right was always wrong. This didn't feel exactly right, so maybe it was. "Okay," she whispered against his mouth. "But I get to see you naked too. Moles and all."

"Moles? I don't have any moles, darling. I had those lasered off ages ago."

"Too bad," she teased quietly, nestling into his arms. "I brought my sharpie. I could do connect the dots."

"You could write a book on me if you want, I wouldn't care," he said, kissing her hair and holding her close.

Jill had leaned back and looked at him, tilting her head. "You're insane for doing this, you know? I'm damaged. I'm neurotic. I'm needy."

"I know and I know and I know," he nodded slowly, pulling her back to him for a real kiss, gentle at first, then more demanding. It wasn't their first kiss by any means, but he was relishing it like it was. "Come on," he said, standing after a while, holding out a hand. "We're going upstairs. I'm damned if I'm missing this chance again. And if Kline Scott so much as comes on the television before I've got you in my bed, I'm putting a hit out on him."

"Kline who?" she said, as he led her towards the stairs.

"Oh, beautiful girl," he had purred, pulling her to him for another kiss.

They had spent the next week getting acquainted with each other in ways August said he had only dreamed of, and Jill enjoyed it all very much. He was fully present and that alone was different from anything else she'd ever experienced. He wasn't trying to catch sight of himself in the mirror or looking at his watch. He didn't even wear a watch, and he never took his eyes off of her.

He had driven her to meetings with Roland and sat in while they planned and had gone with her to a handful of auditions and meetings. One of the casting directors she met had asked if he was her PA. The one thing they hadn't done was talk about Kline.

Now, today, his face was clouded by the name, but Jill couldn't stop herself saying, "But there's nothing going on! For heaven's sake, he picked her over me, didn't he?! Why's she miffed at me? I haven't even heard a peep out of him since New York."

"You could ask her about it, Jill. You've been friendly for ages. Wasn't there any indication that she might be upset before?"

"We didn't talk about it before," Jill sulked, crossing her arms. "She asked about my past with him, and I didn't say anything. If they had something, I didn't want to butt in." She groaned and leaned her head on the back of the chair. "I'm moving to Nebraska. I'm changing my name, moving to Nebraska and growing-- what do they grow there? I'll have a cow farm or something."

"I couldn't live in Nebraska," August said, getting up from his table to walk over and kiss her. "And neither could you. Talk to her, darling. Find out what the problem is."

"No. I've called her twice. She can call me if it's important to her. If not, who cares?"

"You do."

"Oh, go sew something!" She snarled playfully.

He laughed and went back to his work. Jill watched him for a few minutes before going in to the kitchen to make some tea. A knock on the door called her back into the living room and she opened to find Roland on the doorstep. "Hello, beautiful. How are you this evening?"

"Roland! Come in. I'm well thanks. How are you?"

"Wonderful, and I have great news!"

She walked him to the kitchen and settled him in with a scotch and soda, then sat down with him. "What's the news?"

"We signed a leading man for Devil's Party, and it assures you box office gold."

"Oh? Oh! I was so sad about Theo. He's a doll. Who did they get? Did they get Timothee?"

"Better."

"Better?"

"We got Kline Scott."

Jill blanched, then blinked, then stammered. "K-Kline? They signed Kline?"

He nodded, pulling a thick padded envelope from his case. "The press is eating it up. They love the two of you together."

Jill took the envelope and opened it to slide a stack of magazines and clippings onto the counter. Cover stories and bylines about her and Kline, their past, present, and probable future typed up in black and white and four-color gloss. "What is all of this?"

"The first round of publicity. We're already stirring interest and we haven't even gone into preproduction yet."

"Stirring interest in what, Roland?"

"In you and Kline. You're the new uber couple. Now we just have to get the two of you out there a little more."

"No, we aren't. He's dating Rhiannon and I'm -- August! August! You need to come out here!" She turned back to Roland and fretted, "August isn't going to like this. We're talking about moving in together. I can't pretend to be dating Kline."

"You want to retire in five years? This is your ticket, Jill," Roland said, seriously. "Whether you and Kline are really together off camera or not, you are darlings of the press. You play this close and carefully and you'll have everything you want."

August came in, wiping glitter from his fingers. "What's the matter?" he asked, seeing Jill's face.

"August." Roland grinned.

"Roland. What's wrong, Jill?"

She explained her five-year plan to him quickly, him nodding as he'd heard it before, then she went into Roland's plan to get her there. August was stunned and shook his head. "That's never going to work."

"Already is," Roland grinned, he pushed four magazines over to August. "We've already planted articles in these, and we've got more ready to go. The interest is building, and Clara's already had brands reaching out for partnerships. This is the shortcut to your plan."

August frowned as he read over the article in US magazine, then slid it across the table to Jill. "I think I've found the problem you and Rhi might be having," he said, pointing to the page. He turned to Roland, "You can't expect this ruse to carry them through the production of the film. She and I are attending the Oscars together next week and we're practically living together. No one's going to believe that they're a couple."

Roland chuckled, "No, August. No one is going to believe you are a couple. The press wrote you off as gay years ago. They'll see her as your beard or best friend. She's the Grace to your Will, but not your lover."

August narrowed his eyes sharply. "Kline has a girlfriend, as well. If he and Jill are never seen out together, how do you expect to convince the public that they're anything but old friends?"

"It's called a photo op. I'm already arranging them," Roland said, turning to Jill, who was skimming through the article. "That's one of the reasons I came over. You and Kline need to share a little time on the carpet at the Oscars and then at the parties afterwards. The more face time, the better. I know he's got plans to take his civilian, but no one's going to care about seeing her. I thought maybe August could–"

"No," August said firmly.

Jill's mouth rounded into a little 'o', and she shook her head. "Roland—"

"I'm not asking you to nail him in front of the cameras. I'm not asking you to marry him, or even go home with him. But you are friends, right? Say hello. Give him a hug. Share a glass of champagne at an after party. Just be near one another. August can be there, too. No one will think anything of it. The camera sees what it wants to see, and what it wants to see is you and Kline."

She looked doubtful. "Have you talked to Kline about all of this?"

"Yes, and he's fine with it. He understands how important it is, just as I know you do," Roland said. "Right?"

Jill glanced to August, who shrugged. "It's a photo op. I'll be right there. You're my beard," he added with dull impishness, "I can't get too far."

"I guess," Jill said slowly. "But Rhiannon--"

"Kline will explain it all to her. I'm sure he already has."

She sighed, then nodded. "Alright, but just for the photo op," she said, seriously to Roland. "Don't push this too hard, okay? Kline and I–just don't push this too hard."

"Me, push?" He held up his hands innocently and they all laughed. "All right. I'm off then. What are you wearing to the show? Something that will get attention?"

"Absolutely," she nodded. "August made it."

"Oh, then it's sure to be a stunner," he said, sliding from the seat and gathering his things. He leaned to kiss Jill's cheek and gave a nod to August. "I'll see you there. Five years," he said, holding up his fingers. "Give me five years and I'll give you the rest of your life. Three and a half if we play our cards right."

They said goodbye and watched him leave before August turned back to look across the counter at Jill. "You're sure you want to do things this way?"

She looked at the stack on the table and frowned, pushing it away. She was not going to read that. "I don't see that I've got much choice now. We did talk about this before New York. I did tell Roland I was game, and I was then. Now, it's different. Still, if I go forward and say all those things are a hoax, how much worse do I look? I'm trapped. Are you going to be okay with it?" Her brow creased with worry. "There are going to be scenes in that movie that are--fairly full on."

August smiled. "I'll just make sure I'm on the set. Constantly."

She laughed, "You really want to watch that?"

"No. I just want to make sure he stops when he's supposed to," August said, dryly. "And I want to remind him that I'm the one you're coming home with."

Jill crossed the floor and slid up next to him with a warm

kiss. "I'll make it abundantly clear."

"Mm. Good. Do that again."

She smiled and slipped her arms around his neck, kissing him with more heat. There was a niggling doubt about what she'd just agreed to, but for the moment, she forced it away with the feeling of August's hands sliding along her hips.

Chapter 4

Kline Scott

Kline's calendar was packed. He had missed the SAG awards for a three-day Lone Star promo junket across Canada and had come home to prep for the Oscars. No, he wasn't nominated this year. Yes, he was only presenting. But the closest anyone else from Knock had come to getting an invitation to that show was when one of the recurring extras had been a seat-filler one year. Just getting onto the stage to present was a massive win.

Knight was still doing well after its December release and Lone Star was getting buzzy after some important screener reviews had come out. For all intents and purposes, Kline was on top of the world. His job for the next nine months was to convince the Academy that he deserved a nomination for his work, then he would be working to convince them that he deserved to win. That meant showing up and showing out at every opportunity.

It also meant showing up and showing out with the right people, so he had agreed with the plan Roland and Clara laid out for him. One pap stroll a week with Jill, which only made sense now that they had announced him as her leading man, and romance on every red carpet. What he did behind closed doors was his business, but what he presented to the public was very much the business he paid his team to direct.

He hit the circuit again, doing every late night and daytime talk show on either coast, smiling, charming, and avoiding talking about the naked paparazzi photos as much as possible. The frenzy over those pictures had died down as interest in new photos of him with Jill surfaced, but he was still being asked about the sexy redhead in every interview.

"You know," he told Jimmy Fallon, "people like you and I have chosen this very public life, and I get why there is interest. My friend, and we are still very good friends, isn't a public figure, so I feel very protective of her and responsible for how this all shakes out. Her only mistake was finding me irresistible," he said, looking out over the audience with an impish grin. "And how many of you can blame her for that?"

No one could blame her for that, he thought, or for the fact that she'd asked him to put off meeting Jack just yet. She'd said she thought it was too fast, that maybe she should meet Nina first, and that Thad had told her to slow down. He'd said shacking up and shagging Kline rotten was one thing, but meeting the kid was something else entirely. He'd said the same to Kline.

"Take it from me, chief among sinners of bringing home a new mom before the ink's dry on my divorce papers. Anyway, you don't want Jack caught in a position of having to hide shit from Nina."

Kline had agreed with a little relief. He really did like Rhiannon. Loved her company. Couldn't get enough of the sex. But she kept bringing up his script pile and trying to convince him to take on different roles, *better* roles as she called them, as though she hated what he was doing now. A little of that was good for keeping his ego in check, but more than a little and he started to itch.

"And does your new leading lady mind that you're such good friends with, heh heh, such a good friend" Fallon asked, mugging to the camera.

"Jilly and I have known each other for so long, a few photos of good old-fashioned fun are the least she's had to forgive me for! You know we're working together in Devil's Party next, which has a lot of nudity." He acknowledged a wolf whistle with a wink. "We're calling those photos research into my character."

Fallon droned on until the segment was up and Kline shook his hand to leave the set. He wore his smile until he was behind the curtain, then let his face drop into the scowl he was feeling. He snatched off the mic he wore and thrust it aside to an aide, then strode back to where his PA was waiting. "Let's get out of here," he half-snarled. He was fucking tired of answering questions about those pictures. And fucking tired of being on.

He had to turn the smile back on to sign a few autographs, but once he was in his car, he was done. He'd had enough. He started the car, then sat there for a while, feeling trapped. He could go home, but he didn't want to do that. He wanted to be out around people–that's where his energy came from–but he didn't want to be out as Kline Scott, Movie Star. He couldn't think of a single place he could go and just be himself without having to worry that someone was going to take a picture of him looking less than delighted with his life. He didn't want to become another "Sad Ben Affleck" meme.

After thinking about it for a while, he rang Thad, and got through the usual niceties before asking, "You doing anything right now?"

"Nah. Just looking over tomorrow's shit. What's up?"

"You mind if I come over? I just need to–not be a movie star for a little while."

"Yeah, man, come on over. Come be Uncle Kline. You got Jack with you?"

"He's with Nina. I just finished Fallon."

"Oh." All of Thad's understanding was conveyed in one syllable. "Yeah, come on over. I'll get some beers out and we can play darts."

It was exactly what he needed, Kline thought. He could hang out with someone who knew him before the big fame, if not someone who knew him before he got his teeth fixed. He drove onto Thad's Malibu beach house property and found his friend on the back patio with the promised beers and a couple of pizzas. "I know you're on a diet," Thad said, "but if you want to feel like yourself, there's nothing better than carb loading to get you there."

"You mean if you want me to hate myself," Kline laughed, but he opened a box and groaned, taking a slice.

"Eat it like a hate-fuck. I give myself a cheat a month, and this is my cheat. Fucking large pizza and a six pack. Takes me a week to unbloat, but every time I look in the mirror, I think about how good it was. No regrets."

"No regrets," Kline echoed the sentiment though he stopped at one slice.

They made small talk and then played darts against the lattice Thad had put up for the game, then sat down to be an audience for Carra's latest talent show before Kline made his excuses. He was feeling better, but at the same time Thad's home and easy rapport with his children made him feel like he was never going to have what he wanted.

Before he left, what was really bothering him finally worked its way out. He turned to Thad and said, "I want to be bigger than Tom Cruise. I want to be bigger than Brad Pitt. And I want the wife and kids at home. I want to go out and be a star, and come home and be…"

"A different kind of star?"

"I want a wife who adores me and kids who adore me–like your kids do you. Jack just sees me as his idiot old man. He's not proud of anything I do. Hell, he's not even interested. He prefers the nanny to me, and he prefers Nina to the nanny, and I don't know if that's because of Nina, or me. He used to idolize me."

Thad laughed. "Hang on. Vangie!" He called back into the house. It was a few moments of grousing with the teen until she appeared, clearly unhappy. "Kline here seems to think you kids adore me like a star. You want to tell him how you really feel?"

She just huffed and turned around, skulking away before Thad could even get out the first laugh. "It's the age, man. He's growing up. You could be Tom Cruise and he'll eventually think you're just his idiot old man. It's all lighting and angles, Kline. You should know that better than anybody. And I clearly don't have the wife thing worked out. Just relax. No one has what they want. You just have to learn to want what you have and work with that."

Kline grimaced. "I'm not happy with the status quo. I want more."

"Then call your therapist. I'm sure he'll tell you that what you need is more therapy, and the question is always going to be when will you know you have enough? The answer is never because you don't know what success looks like beyond some casting director or box office numbers telling you how amazing you are, and human beings aren't always amazing, and having a bad day, or losing a part, or having a bad box office doesn't make you a failure. I'm telling you that you need to take time to enjoy the shit you've got right in front of you, rather than worrying about the people who are ahead of you. Do that, and you'll be fine."

"But how do I do that?" Kline asked seriously, throwing up his hands.

"You have a good time tonight?"

"Yeah."

"That's a start. You called me to hang out because you know you don't have to be on over here. You drank some beer, ate some greasy pizza, played some darts, played with my kids, and in the moment–until you got antsy–it was great. Baby steps to the Zen of just enjoying life. Maybe take up surfing. It gets you out of your head. You can't pay attention to your ego because you have to focus on your form."

"Spoken like a Gold Coast native."

"Shrimp's on the barbie, mate."

Kline laughed and hugged his friend. "Thanks, Thad."

"Anytime."

He did feel better driving home, and he thought about calling Rhiannon, but that meant crawling back into at least part of his movie star character, so he dialed Jill instead. She answered with a yawn and let him talk for ten minutes before saying, "Do you know what time it is?"

"Midnight?"

"I'm in New York. It's three."

"Oh! I didn't know you were there. What are you there for?"

"I did a charity event."

"Maybe I should do more charity?"

"Maybe you should do charity at all."

"Salty."

There was a smile in her voice when she retorted, "Sleepy, but I'm glad you feel like you can call me and pour out your midlife crisis."

"Hey! I'm hardly midlife. It's just an existential crisis. Jill?"

"Yes?"

"Are you happy with where you are in life?"

"Are you really asking me that? I just got a divorce I didn't want, from a marriage that I didn't really have, and am now in the middle of a relationship with a man who is trying to shave me into the image he has of me in his head because I'm too afraid to either be alone, or try to meet someone I haven't already known for twenty years."

"Gus wants to change you?"

"Gus has an idea of me and he's trying to get my outsides to match his vision of the insides. He keeps telling me how much he loves me, but I don't think it's me. I think it's this idealized version of someone he thinks I should be. I'm a character for him. I don't want to talk about this with you, though. Go on and tell me more about how miserable you are because you're a star and no one understands you."

"When you say it that way—"

"Because that's what it sounds like. Listen, I didn't choose performing. My mother chose it for me and by the time I was old enough to separate my talent from my training and my profession from my personality and question whether this was the life I wanted, I was an under-educated, over-exposed Broadway veteran with no other options but to stick to the stage or branch out into screen. But I have asked myself that question now and the answer is no. I don't want this life, but it's the life I have. So, I'm going to exploit it and bleed every dime out of it I can, so that in a few years I can tell it to fuck off and go live in Mexico or something."

"Gus would never live in Mexico."

"I said or something."

"Baby's stuck in LA forever," Kline teased.

"You know what I mean. I don't want to act anymore. I don't want to perform. I want to sit in the audience and enjoy someone else, then I want to go home and read a book."

"How long are you in New York?"

"I come home tomorrow."

"Too bad. If you were there longer, I'd come up and meet you."

"And what? Poke at me until I gave you the attention you craved, filled up your need void, and then disappear again? What's in it for me?"

"You are into charity and you like filling my need void?"

She laughed so hard at that he started laughing with her. "It's like you know me," she said finally, still giggling.

"I do know you."

"I know you, too, Kline. Call Roland and tell him you want more. Pick up another project. Fill the void with work, not people. And then call me and tell me to do the same thing."

"Are you breaking up with Gus?"

"No," she sighed into the phone, and Kline wondered if she was twirling hair around her finger. "I do love him. I really like him. He's easy and comfortable, and I don't have to do the getting-to-know you part of a new relationship. And he loves me. That's enough, right?"

"You tell me? You're the one doling out advice."

"I need to go to sleep, Kline. So do you."

"Fine. I guess I'll see you on the red carpet?"

"I'll come stand beside you and make you look like a million bucks."

"I can't wait."

"Goodbye, Kline," she said, but he could still hear her smiling.

"Goodnight, Jill."

Rhiannon Charles

Rhiannon arrived a little after ten on the Sunday morning of the Oscars, feeling tired and anxious. She'd been considering backing out on the date, fearing another round of public humiliation, but convinced herself that she should go, if for no other reason than to support her show. If Kline could play the PR game, so could she, and being seen with him might draw audiences to Simon Says.

She would face the scrutiny of the press with her head held high, and the focus on her would likely be momentary, given the buzz that was surrounding Kline and Jill. The 'will they or won't they?' phenomenon had already begun. When she parked in the back and walked in through the kitchen, she found Kline sitting at the dining table with Roland, discussing a game plan for the evening. Both men looked up when she walked in, and Kline got to his feet to kiss her hello. "You just missed Jack," he said, with some disappointment. "Kim just took him off for his playdate."

Rhiannon frowned, feigning disappointment of her own. Given the obvious course their relationship was taking, she thought it better if she didn't get too involved with his son and was becoming adept at just missing him. It was too hard on kids to have people come in and out of their lives like that. "I'm sorry I missed him," she said. "Traffic was bad."

"Always bad on award nights," Roland said. "Hey listen, I'm going to head out. Good luck tonight, Tiger. If we're lucky, you'll go viral!"

Kline laughed and saw him out before hurrying back to kiss Rhiannon. "Ready to go be pampered?"

"Oh sure," she smiled. "You're worse than a girl, you know?"

"I know. But look at me--it's worth it."

"Can't argue with that," she said, "so where is the spa?"

"Not far. We'll take the limo so we can relax."

Rhiannon nodded as he took her hand and led her out to the waiting car, and he chatted away as they drove to a secluded hacienda style building on the outskirts of Beverly Hills. They pulled up to the front and were escorted inside where they were whisked into a private room to undress and were soon being massaged, oiled, buffed, and toned.

It was after two when they got back to Kline's, and they hurried into the shower. "We've got to leave by five," he told her. "My stylist is coming at three, so I just need to be clean. I asked her to bring someone to do you up, too."

Rhiannon didn't argue, she simply nodded and submitted to the schedule he had planned out for them. He got out of the shower first, wrapping a towel around his waist. "I'm getting dressed downstairs. I've laid out your accessories and your dress is hanging on the closet door," he said, toweling his hair.

"Okay. It shouldn't take me long to get dressed," she said, rinsing off the last of the soap.

Kline chuckled. "I've heard that story before. Just call down when you're ready for the stylist, okay?" He leaned in and kissed her quickly, then he was gone.

Rhiannon narrowed her eyes at the dress hanging on the door. It was nice enough, but in the last week she'd decided she'd rather dip herself in poison than put it on. Instead, she went for the dress she'd preferred from the start. She slipped into a black satin thong, then shimmied into the dress, lacing it up over her naked breasts with a smile. It was sheer enough that her body was visible, but not so much as to be sleazy. In her clothes, she called the stylist up. By the time she walked downstairs, she was a spectacular sight.

Kline was talking on his cell and turned when he heard her on the stairs, smiling then dropping his jaw. "I have to go," he said to whomever was on the line, hanging up without taking his eyes from Rhiannon. "Oh god. You look amazing. Just--amazing. But aren't you going to wear the other dress? I thought we agreed..."

"The other one's fine, but I feel more myself in this one,"

she said, with a crimson smile. She knew she looked good. Better than he had considered when she was trying dresses on, and with the dramatic makeup, she knew the look was perfect. "Is that a problem?"

He frowned slightly. "I guess not if you're comfortable. You do look really good. Just…flashbulbs can…it's very…theatrical. Greta did a brilliant job. You look lovely."

Rhiannon's eyes narrowed slightly as he frowned, and she lifted her chin a little letting him talk himself into the praise. "Well, I guess you're dressed? Just need to tie your tie. Want some help?"

"Nah. I'm going like this. Everyone else will be very sleek. I'm going Rat Pack."

"You mean fresh off a bender. That's a look now?" she said, checking the small black clutch she was carrying.

"It's something different," Kline said, somewhat defensively. "Are you ready?"

"More than. We'd better go, or we'll be more than fashionably late."

They got into the limo where Kline was restless and fidgety. "I'm nervous," he said. "I can't flub my lines. I have to be perfect. And what if Keenan roasts my nudes? Or what if he doesn't roast me at all?"

"I don't think you have anything to worry about. The press loves you," Rhiannon said. His nudes? Who cared about his nudes? Everyone loved looking at his ass.

"Yeah," he sighed, wringing his hands. He pulled a little compact out of the inner pocket of his jacket and opened it up to the mirror, fussing with his hair.

What was she doing here? "Oh, Thad said to tell you to break a leg," she said, crossing her own legs. No sooner did she say it than her phone beeped, and she looked on the display to see Thad's name. "Speak of the *devil*," she said, emphasizing the last word as she answered the phone.

"Oi. Are you two on your way?"

"In the limo now. Should be reaching the lineup very soon."

"Everything okay?" he asked. Oddly enough, he had been the one to talk things out with her a bit the day before, when she confessed her upset and the reasons why.

She took a deep breath and let it out slowly. "For the moment."

"You'll be fine. Can't wait to see this smashing frock you're wearing."

"You'll know me when you see me," she teased.

Kline shifted next to her, looking a bit antsy, so she told Thad that she had to go and ended the call. "He said good luck again."

"He called me this morning."

"That's my third call today. I think he's worried you'll forget I'm with you and wander off in an ego haze."

"What?"

"You know, get so caught up in yourself that you forget I'm here."

He frowned at her, lines appearing between his eyebrows, showing the makeup placement there. "Fuck him. That's really bitchy to say. This is a big deal for me."

They were quiet for a time, as they drove through Beverly Hills, passing other limos as they went. When they reached the auditorium, they were lined up in a long row of cars that queued around the block. He was really nervous. She could see it in the white of his knuckles. The slow parade moved steadily forward, and Rhiannon reached over to take Kline's hand. "You're going to be great. Don't worry."

He kissed her hand with a bit of distraction. "Thanks. I'm really glad you're here with me."

"Even in this dress?" she teased.

"Yes. Even in this dress," he said, nodding. "You do look fantastic."

"I always look better when I'm comfortable," she said, with an elegant shrug. "So, they'll be interviewing you on the carpet and after, right?"

"Likely. It's to be expected."

She nodded. "Well, is there any topic I should know about? Anything to avoid or build up?"

He shook his head. "No. That's for me to worry over, love. You just concentrate on being beautiful and enjoying yourself. Remember that they didn't get the best of us with those pictures."

"Right," she said, looking out the window to see the crowd lining the carpet ahead of them. They were only four cars away from their entrance now. "What if they ask me about us? Or about you and Jill?"

Kline petted her hand. "Don't worry. No one's going to ask you anything. If they do it'll be who are you wearing, and that's easy enough. I'm the one they'll want to talk to. You'll just be photographed."

"Oh," Rhiannon said through a tight smile. She wasn't sure whether to be offended and he didn't seem to notice. He was too wrapped up in himself.

He let out a breath as their car crept up another spot. "This is the part I hate the most. The sitting and waiting to get out. I get claustrophobic. Is that Hanks? It is. I hate going after him! He clogs up the line, stopping to talk to everyone."

Rhiannon stared out the window, pretending to people watch, growling inside until they rolled up to their stop. Her door was opened, and flashbulbs started popping, but she knew when Kline emerged from behind her because of the suddenly deafening roar. Above the din, she could hear his name being called over and over. He stepped out, looked around and waved, then put his hand in the small of her back and ushered her forward, stopping to pose now and then. A photographer asked Rhiannon to step back so they could get some solo shots of her date and Kline winked at her before stepping a space away, waving to the crowd and blowing kisses. A PA came to move them along, so Kline reached back for Rhiannon's hand.

They did the gauntlet, and as he'd told her, no one asked her anything. The women on the media line ignored her completely, the men just leered openly. Kline fielded questions about his nerves, his tux, his upcoming film and his part in Devil's Party, and he answered them all with grace and aplomb. The only person to ask Rhiannon anything was Ashley Graham, and she just wanted to know about the dress.

Looking back, Rhiannon saw Jill a few stops down on the media line. The dress August had made was stunning, and for a moment she couldn't take her eyes away from the length of legs showing. The front of the skirt was only inches from being no skirt at all, and the black train just served as perfect backdrop for Jill's long, lean stems. Thin strapped sandals that tied around the ankle with skinny, licorice whips of laces completed that end of the look. The rest—well, she was balletic and graceful, and the cut of the fabric and slices of skin showing somehow served to make her look more delicate. She'd gone with a simple updo and massive black chandelier earrings--her only accessory. August was hanging back to let her be photographed.

"Oh, look," Kline said, "there's Jill. Let's go say hello."

"I thought once you'd gone up the red carpet you couldn't go back," Rhiannon said.

"That's a myth," Kline grinned. He let go of her hand and started down the way as Jill's cool smile broke into a matching grin. They hugged and gave a chaste, laughing kiss on the lips, then Jill leaned back, said something, and reached up to wipe Kline's mouth with her thumb. He bit at it, playing to the cameras, then slipped an arm around her waist at the suggestion of a photographer. Jill leaned in to his side, eyes on the camera managing to look both coy and devoted at the same time. One more hug, and kiss on the cheek, then Kline strode back to Rhiannon.

"You have lipstick on your face," she said, aiming toward the entrance.

He wiped it away, laughing as he caught her hand and led the way into the seating area. Rhiannon made sure she kept her head up and walked with as much grace as she could, working the dress to her full advantage. She noticed many famous faces as they moved through the crowd, but only in passing. If there had ever been a time she was starstruck by such surroundings, it was long past. Seeing the inner workings of the glamourous life had done nothing to make her want to live it herself.

Once they'd found their seats, the next fifteen minutes were spent meeting and greeting as many influential people Kline could arrange in a short span of time. She was introduced, but very few people actually spoke to her past the introduction, and she endured a few lascivious winks and backhanded compliments while Kline worked the room.

Soon, much to her relief, the orchestra cues drove the crowd back into their places. Rhiannon felt at least she'd be able to breathe, but any breath that she might have managed was stolen away when she saw Jill seated in their row right next to Kline. In fact, Kline would be sandwiched between the two of them.

Jill was laughing at something August was saying, and looked so comfortable in her skin it would have been enviable had Rhiannon not known better. Jill was one of the most insecure women she'd ever known, but she wore confidence like a costume. Likely, she was wilting on the inside. Rhiannon couldn't help feeling a twinge of bitter joy over that.

Kline hailed and hallowed them, hugging Rick Sanders, who was also their row along with Cheryl Doyle, who had also co-starred in Knight, and her date. After more introductions, the couple sat down. Jill offered Rhiannon a naked and worried smile before settling back into her game face as conversation surged around them.

Without thinking, old habit moved Kline's hand to reach over and squeeze Jill's. "You look gorgeous," he said.

"So do you. I see you took my advice." She smiled warmly, letting go of his hand to reach up and tousle his hair. She fussed with it for a few seconds, changing the part, tucking a strand behind his ear. "There. You're very messy."

"Too messy?"

"Perfectly messy. Every person in this place is going to wish they were the ones who got you that way."

"But I'm the only one who gets to," Rhiannon announced with a sharp smile.

Jill wrinkled her forehead with practiced good humor and laughed, "But of course. Anyway," she rolled her eyes, "I've been there, done that."

"And all you got was a lousy T-shirt," August quipped.

"Hey!" Kline protested.

"That's not fair, August," Jill said. "I also got years of therapy bills and psychological damage."

Those in the row who could hear them laughed and settled into conversation about who would win, what everyone was wearing, and how cold it was in the venue. It seemed forever, with false orchestra starts and mic tests, before the cue came that they were about to go live. Suddenly the lights were dimmed in the back, the kliegs groaned on over the front rows, and the stage lights blasted heat.

Keenan Thompson was hosting, and he opened the show with a monologue that was surprisingly funny. All nominees were mentioned and teased, and the audience erupted with laughter when Keenan joked, "Next year, Kline Scott's going to be nominated for Best Actor in a Drama, but this year he's been nominated for Best Actor in a Hot Tub, on a Diving Board, in the Kitchen, and Behind the Shrubbery."

Kline gave an affable little bow from his seat at the host as Thompson muttered amiably, "And I bet he'll win, too!"

Even Rhiannon laughed at the joke, equally amused at the delivery and grateful that her name had not actually been mentioned. Thompson moved on to a few other nominees and laughter filled the auditorium as the awards got underway. There were more stops and starts as commercial breaks were inserted and conversation resumed around them whenever there was a lull between sets. Kline was in his element and his mood elevated with each passing moment. He kept making little asides to Jill and then they'd both laugh at whatever it was he was saying.

For her part, Rhiannon did her best to keep a smile on her face and ignore them.

It was some salve that Jill and August held hands constantly. When they weren't, August had an arm around her shoulders, or his fingertips were grazing her knee. There was no question that August was there with Jill, although, at points it did look like Jill was there with two men.

Rhiannon watched the monitor more than the stage, seeing whom the cameras chose to focus in on, and how. Twice already they had claimed Kline and Jill in a single frame. Once while Kline was whispering something to her, and once when she was laughing. Rhiannon found herself making small talk with Rick at the first break. He'd walked over to crouch down beside her seat and speak to her while Kline gabbed with Jon Hamm a row in front of them.

Rick was trying to get Thad a reading for a film he was doing. An artsy, independent thing. He was producing it and funding it, so he had a fair amount of pull in casting, but the director and writers wanted to see a screen test first. "You see him everyday," Rick laughed, "Make him do it!"

"Is it for a lead? I can't see him doing a supporting role, not even for an indie cred," she said, seriously.

"You don't think so? It's more of an ensemble piece, but the part I'm trying to get him into is rather sizeable and vital. He just won't consider a screen test."

She nodded. "Can you blame him, though? He has his own show. What do they need to see that they can't see any given Thursday night?"

"It's a dramatic role," Rick said seriously. "No one's ever seen Thad do drama. I mean, aside from the occasional 'very special episode'. No offense. He's done comedy for all these years-- and situation comedy. They want him to read so they can see if he can pull it off. I know he can."

She laughed at the comment about the shows. "I didn't write those 'very special episodes', so no offense taken. As for Thad and drama, I'm sure he could do it. On the other hand, I'm also sure he could carry a feature. It will just take some convincing all around."

"Thad doesn't have the kind of following Kline did. I think an ensemble piece with an edgy character is the way to start." He shrugged. "But I'm glad he's got an ally."

"Quit flirting with my date, Rick," Kline grinned. "She's mine!"

"For now," Rick teased. "Go back to preening, Scott. It suits you better than thinking."

Music queued up again and Rick slipped away as the director started counting down to live. Kline laughed, and slipped an arm along the back of Rhiannon's chair as the announcement that they were back on air came and the show continued. Just before lights, Kline was pulled by a runner and a seat filler took his place. The cue for silence came before Rhiannon could even say hello.

She glanced around and noticed August whispering to Jill, the two of them huddled over his phone, and Jill gasped, her hand going up to her mouth then she leaned and whispered something to the seat filler, who rose and shifted positions with the actress.

"Rhi," Jill hissed quietly. "You need to see something."

"What? What's wrong?"

"The lights. Listen, I don't want to upset you. The dress– Your dress–it's gorgeous on you. You look smashing. Some photos from the red carpet are going up online, though, and the lights from the flash– They don't reflect on the fabric. The lights made it a bit see-through."

"What?"

"Some fabrics–the lights make them see-through. Your dress is one of them." She held August's phone with her hand covering the top of it, allowing Rhiannon a look. She may as well have been wearing nothing at all other than her thong. The dress photographed so sheer that she could clearly see the difference between the buds of her nipples and her areolas.

"Oh my god."

"Be prepared. They're going to be lined up outside to shoot you for more of that."

"You can see everything."

"It's okay. You can see that you are perfect. Just be prepared and hold your head up high when you leave."

All Rhiannon could do was stare straight ahead, and she didn't even have Kline's presence for reassurance. Jill reached for her hand and squeezed it, but she was the last person she wanted touching her, so Rhiannon shook off the grip. "I'm fine."

At the next commercial break, Jill slipped out for the ladies room and before the seat filler switched again, Rhiannon spoke to August. It was the first chance she'd had to say more than hello, and she directed her smile at him. "You two look happy," she said, "I love the dress."

"I'm very happy," August smiled back at her. "I think the dress turned out well. Plenty of media interest, and that was the idea. That and I'm trying to pull out Jill's dark side."

"Does she have a dark side? Or just dark roots?"

Before August had a chance to respond, the music swelled, and the next two presenters were introduced. The next few categories passed in a blur before Kline's name was announced and he walked out, looking as relaxed and debonair as Rhiannon had ever seen him, to take his place at the microphone at the center of the stage.

He was polished and perfect, and you could almost hear the blood rushing in the ballroom. A fan from the back screamed, "I love you, Kline!"

Kline grinned and glanced in the general direction of the voice and called back, "I love you, too!"

Without a beat he went back to reading his lines, then awarded the prize for Best Original Score, then disappeared off into the wings again. In a few minutes he was back in his seat and Rhiannon smiled at him as the seat filler slipped away.

"How was I?" he asked.

"Perfect, as usual," Rhiannon said, leaning up to kiss him.

He smiled, slipping an arm around her and settling in for the rest of the show. His category was one of the very last, and the anticipation had grown with the level of drunkenness in the room. Half the place was already well into the sixth martini of the night between breaks, but everyone seemed to be enjoying themselves. Kline started getting antsy when the Best Actress award was being presented and he held Rhiannon's hand. "I wish we could just leave now."

"So do I," Rhiannon said. When had this become her life?

When the ceremony finally ended, it was a melee of stars crowding around to congratulate one another and squeeze in some last minute schmoozing before they all retired to their corners at various after parties. Kline accepted compliments on his presentation with a saccharine humility until Jill groaned. "It's us, Kline. Just say thank you."

He feigned shocked surprise before laughing too. "Should have known better than to play up to the ones who know the real me, eh?"

"Mmm," she hummed to him. "Besides, you were the best of the lot. Next year, you'll be accepting an award instead of presenting one."

"Well, I'm really going to enjoy handing you the award the year after when you win Best Actress," he said. "Be sure you wear something like that, so I have plenty to look at."

Jill laughed again and August rolled his eyes. "That's it. I'm dressing her in flannel from chin to toenail."

"Somehow, I doubt it will matter," Rhiannon said, fairly gagging on their act. "He's seen her at her worst, remember? Hasn't changed a thing."

"Jilly doesn't have a worst, do you, darling?" Kline grinned, missing the barb. "Jilly's worst is the envy of every woman out there."

August blinked, wrinkled his nose and said, "Bugger. I agree with Kline. I hate agreeing with Kline."

"It's less painful if you don't do it often," Rhiannon said.

"We're off to the Vanity Fair party," Kline said, looking around. "Anyone for sharing a limo?"

"We're going there, too," Jill nodded. "Rick? Cheryl? Mark?"

There were nods of agreement, and Rick stood up. "Might as well share a limo, otherwise we'll be stuck in traffic for two hours as opposed to one."

"We're going to Maxim," Cheryl said, shaking her head. "I'm doing a spread for them next month."

As Cheryl was speaking, Rhiannon noticed Jill whispering to Kline, who blanched and glanced in his date's direction. He cleared his throat. "It is cold in here. Rhi? You cold? You want my jacket?"

If looks could kill, Rhiannon would have dropped Jill Parker to the floor right then and there. Had she just told Kline to cover her up to walk her out the door?

"I'm good," Rhiannon said, squaring her shoulders. "I'm feeling pretty hot, actually."

"As you should," Kline smiled, shrugging back into the garment he'd already started sliding down his arms. "You're warming up everything in sight!"

Rhiannon faced down the cameras that flashed as the group left the building, pretending to herself that it was only Kline they wanted to see, holding in her growing anger as her date completely ignored all signs of discomfort that she tried to show him. Even more irritated when they slid into the limo only to have Kline, August and Jill start laughing like hyenas, praising one another.

The three old friends were cackling. Jill threw up her hands, "Did you ever even imagine we'd be here on a night like this?"

"Remember how I used to practice my Oscars acceptance speeches in the bathroom mirror?" Kline laughed, bumping his forehead against hers, forgetting his date entirely.

"And you made me hand you the hairbrush over and over so you could practice how to take the award and make it look casual and elegant?" Jill chuckled. "Over and over." She put on a voice to imitate him, "Okay, but now like you're taller than me. Get that stepstool. What if it's someone taller than me? And I always had to tell you there was no one taller than you."

"And I made you look up how tall everyone was."

"Which was stupid because Best Actor is always presented by the Best Actress, and even in heels, who is taller than you? Maybe Gwendoline Christie, but no one else."

"You had your Tony speech prepared," Kline reminded. "And to the love of my life–"

"August," Jill interrupted, reaching across the longer bench seat to the shorter side where August sat next to Rick. "To the love of my life, August, thank you for always being there and dressing me for wherever 'there' may be."

"Aw," Kline groaned. "That's not how it used to go."

"He never dressed me back then."

August laughed and shook his head, then popped a cork from a champagne bottle stocked in the limo bar. "Let's drink to the Best Presenter. May his category be invented so he can win and use the trophy as a paperweight for his bloated ego."

Even Kline laughed at that one and tossed back his drink with glee. Rhiannon was going a little slower with her own glass, wondering how that alcohol was going to hit Kline's system after months of avoiding the stuff.

It was a long ride to the Vanity Fair party, and when they finally arrived, there was another barrage of photographers waiting, though security was much tighter. It was almost like another red carpet when Kline stepped out of the limo just behind Rhiannon, with Jill immediately after him. The paparazzi were calling his name as though he'd won something, and then Jill's as well, trying to get their attention for even the briefest moment. When Kline took a few steps forward and Jill followed, he slipped an arm around her and the two posed and smiled for the cameras.

Rhiannon rolled her eyes and, wary of more photo ops of her vanishing dress, hurried on inside the party, Rick at her heels. August hung back until Kline released his date, then he and Jill continued up to the door together. The din was nearly unbearable until they were used to it, but everyone inside was chattering happily and noisily, fawning, preening and gushing over one another.

Kline barely made it in the door before well wishes and

congratulations were being flung at him from all directions. Rhiannon had grabbed a flute of champagne from a passing tray and made her way through the crowd towards a quieter corner of the room. She didn't realize that Rick was still behind her until she turned around and nearly bumped into him, "Oh! I'm sorry," she said, catching her glass before it could spill on him. "I didn't know you were—there."

"I followed you," he said, smiling. "You cut a nice path through the chaos. It seemed like a good idea."

"Not good for business, though, is it?"

"How do you mean?"

"Well, aren't some of the biggest deals made at parties like this? You're not going to see much action on the fringe," she said, taking a sip of her drink.

Rick shrugged. "I've got plenty of deals in the works. Besides, I'm a producer. They come to me," he said, in a tone that was less cocky than self-assured.

Rhiannon decided that she liked him. He was straightforward and real, like she was. Or like she used to be. She'd become so passive-aggressive in the past few weeks it was getting on her own nerves. He was handsome, too, and had a nice smile. "I'm sure they do," she said, picking up the thread of conversation. "You seem like a man who can make things happen."

He smiled. "I am. I'm good at everything, except awards shows."

She laughed. "That makes two of us."

"Yeah, you don't seem too comfortable with all of this."

"Is it that obvious? I thought I was hiding it well."

"I don't think Kline's noticed, at any rate."

"No surprise there," she replied, taking another long drink of champagne. "He's got plenty to distract him."

"You mean Jill Parker?" Rick asked, taking her empty glass and trading it for two fresh flutes from another tray as a waiter floated past.

She looked up at him and accepted the offered glass. "I mean all of this--this insanity. He's in his element--" she trailed off and sighed, "You've read the articles, right? I mean, there aren't really any secrets here."

"True. I have read the articles," he said, with a nod. "I have to admit, most of it seems like PR spin."

Rhiannon frowned. "I don't think all of it is, but regardless, I've been given a role to play, and I don't want to perform. That's not who I am."

"Not enjoying your celebrity?"

She shook her head. "I just don't think I'm cut out to be a movie star's girlfriend. It requires too much acting, and there's a reason that I'm a writer."

He laughed. "Well, I think you're getting some well-deserved recognition for your writing abilities. Thad raves about you. He's even credited you with saving the show."

"Thad says that because he kinda likes me."

"I can see why," Rick said, taking another sip of champagne.

"Is that your champagne talking?" Rhiannon asked with a playfully arched eyebrow.

"More likely it's your dress talking," he said with an impish grin. "But aside from that, you're smart, funny, and can wear a talking dress without being shouted down."

"Well thank you."

"You're welcome."

They chatted a bit more, watching Kline work a crowd nearby. "I really hate being a mannequin," she sighed, finishing her drink and taking another from a passing tray. "He's completely forgotten I'm here."

"Likely not," Rick corrected. "He just expects that you understand and that you'll entertain yourself until he's done working. This is work for him. That's the high price of celebrity. The only time he's not working is when he's in his house."

"Oh, he's plenty acting then, too."

Rick chuckled and considered her for a moment. "So how

long before you're finished with him?"

"What?"

"Finished. Frustrated to tears. Tired of coming second to business."

Rhiannon looked shocked, and she was taken aback, but said, "He's not his job. It's the job requirements I don't like."

"He is his job. All good movie stars are. I'd say all good actors, but general actors can leave their acting on the set. Stars can't."

Rhiannon hummed, sipped her drink, but said nothing. Rick said, "He's never had much luck with normal women. They don't understand the celebrity. They don't understand how he can love the spotlight and them at the same time, when he seems to love the spotlight so much more."

"I'm sure women like Jill never have that problem."

"No, they don't. Either because they're working the same angles, or because they just understand the nature of the beast. Look around," he said, "if you want a normal relationship, normal life, whatever, don't try to be with any of these people."

"You included?" The eyebrow arch wasn't so playful anymore. She felt like she was being scolded.

"I'm a producer," he shrugged, "they come fawn on me. I don't have to work the spotlight, but it finds me. My life is far from normal, too. It's different back home. But there I was stuck directing BBC pieces and couldn't move ahead. I started the production company, did two indies, then Kline talked me into coming here for a while. The idea is to make more money than God without compromising my ideals too much, then retire and move back to England--because I want a normal life. Well, as normal as life is when you are obscenely wealthy. It's why I don't date here. These women--they couldn't survive outside the satellite of fame."

She nodded in agreement and conversation shifted to lighter things. She spotted August chatting with a trio of models. He was obviously tipsy and enjoying himself. A moment later she spotted Jill in the crowd, balanced on one foot, comparing shoes with another woman. Kline was nearby and he said something that Rhiannon could not hear over the din, but it raised Jill's head and brought a smile to her face. Rhiannon watched as Jill excused herself from the conversation and walked over to Kline. He put an arm around her and talked in her ear, making her laugh, then she patted his chest and walked away.

Sanctuary was disrupted soon after when a pair of actresses melted out of the crowd to talk to Rick. He greeted them with a smile, but the fawning Rhiannon was expecting did not follow. At least, not from him. The women were trying very hard to get close and to entice him into a quiet corner of their own. It was part seduction and part audition. He was a well-known producer after all, and producers were always looking for talent. And blowjobs. Rhiannon felt contempt and not a small amount of pity towards the women as she watched the display. She couldn't believe the lengths some felt they needed to go to in order to further their career. It was all part of the Hollywood machine, she knew, but she had made a promise to herself long ago that she wouldn't make such compromises for the sake of a job. If her script work couldn't keep her employed, then she'd find something else. Acting, saying words someone else had written, pretending to feel things someone else told her to feel had never held any allure. Watching these two women made her thankful that she would never be in their place.

To his credit, Rick handled the advances with cordial grace, but Rhiannon couldn't help wondering if he was balking because she was standing there. She decided that just because she was miserable, everyone else's night shouldn't be ruined, so she excused herself and slipped off into the crowd, leaving Rick to whatever entertainments he might actually be interested in.

She chided herself on her faithlessness as she made her way to the bathroom. It bothered her that she'd become awfully jaded in a very short period of time. It wasn't like her. She never stayed in any negative situation long enough for it to really affect her. With a sigh, she deposited the half empty champagne glass on a table and walked into the lounge of the expansive bathroom. It was definitely time to stop drinking. Three glasses of champagne was usually her limit, and she didn't like to get too tipsy and lose her edge.

She stood in front of the three-way mirror and made a few slight adjustments to her dress. The drape of the skirt was hanging so that her leg was visible all the way to the hollow of her thigh when she walked. It was a very sexy dress, and she was really glad that she'd worn it, especially after seeing what Jill had dared to bare. Not that it had made much difference, either way. Jill was still the princess of the press and Kline had been only too happy to play the charming prince for photo op after photo op. Rhiannon supposed that she wouldn't have minded that, if it had been only that, but the two of them barely spent a moment apart since the ceremony began. It was almost as if Kline had come alone—or with Jill.

Although she was glad that the press hadn't hounded her every step since she got out of the limousine, it bothered her that she was so faceless after everything that happened. She felt a twinge of anger at the thought that people were only interested in taking her picture if she was in a compromising position or talking about her if she was the woman standing in the way of the next great Hollywood Love Story.

She wanted to be proud of herself. She wanted to be proud of her work. She wanted recognition for her work, and not for the results of her workouts. She wanted people to see her as an actual talent worth merit-based notoriety, not just as some scriptwriter who happened to be screwing the King of Romcom himself.

She opened her clutch and pulled out the lipstick that the stylist had given her, slicking crushed berry velvet over her lips. The rest of her face was still flawless, even if she did look a bit tired. She glanced up at the clock. They'd been at the party for over an hour and Kline hadn't even so much as smiled at her from across the room.

Rhiannon considered going out there and seeking him out,

interrupting whatever scene was being played out by inserting herself into it, but she wasn't like that. She didn't want him that way. She was his date. His girlfriend, according to him. She shouldn't have to beg for his attention. Work was one thing. She could understand that he had obligations, but she wondered what she was doing here if all he intended to do was spend the evening schmoozing and cuddling on Jill.

Her stomach gurgled and she realized that she hadn't eaten anything since breakfast. Maybe if she ate, some of this shakiness would go away. She decided to go back out and find something to eat, then she would find Kline.

She left the lounge with a new level of resolve that quickly melted away when she saw what was going on in the midst of the crowd. Kline and Jill were dancing. A slow swaying, arms wrapped around each other, Jill's head resting on his chest. Rhiannon couldn't move. They seemed completely oblivious to everyone around them and the fact that there wasn't actually a dance floor or discernable music, lost in their own little world.

Phrases from the US article popped into Rhiannon's head, and she couldn't help but think that there was some truth to it all. Maybe Kline was just sticking with her until the lawsuit and scandal blew over. Maybe she was just some fling that was helping to keep the bittersweet drama alive until the golden couple's reunion could be arranged.

She stared. This was making her crazy and paranoid. She looked like a fool and felt worse. It was all too much. She didn't trust Kline. She couldn't trust him, and she had to get out of this before more damage could be done. There was the briefest consideration of confronting the two of them, but Rhiannon had a feeling that would only help them and hurt her more in the long run. The feeding frenzy would be legendary as soon as there was blood in the water. No, it was better not to say anything at all. Just cut the losses and go.

As casually as she could manage, she headed for the exit, skirting the crowd that had formed a small circle around the floorshow. She hit the door without so much as a sideways glance from anyone and was out in the cool night air, forcing a smile as she passed the throng of photographers. There would be no incriminating pictures of her departure in the tabs tomorrow. As far as anyone could tell, she was fine and not screaming on the inside.

The line of cars was one black limo after another, and she couldn't tell which one was hers. As she approached, a door opened and Thad climbed out, a huge grin firmly in place. Flashes filled the air and he posed, then called, "Hey, Rhi!" when he saw her. "Come pose with me! Make me look good! I'm not famous enough to get an invite to the show, but I'm here for the party!"

She walked up to him, and he slipped an arm around her waist and pulled her in close, mugging for the camera. After two rounds of flashes, they both turned their backs on the photographers and Rhiannon patted his shoulder.

"Ta', love," he said, giving her a wink. "How's the party?"

"In full swing," she said, shaking her head at him.

"What are you doing out here by yourself? Where's your date?"

She sighed, glancing around to make sure no one was close enough to hear. "Apparently, I don't have one, so I'm going home."

Thad frowned, "What? You can't leave. I've only just arrived! We need to celebrate."

"I think I've had enough to last me for one night. Enough to last me forever, really," she said, seriously. "I just want to go home."

"What happened, Rhi?"

She shook her head. "I don't want to talk about it, but if you go inside, you might be able to tell." She looked down the row of cars. "Do you mind if I borrow your car? I don't know which one I arrived in."

"Of course, love. Tell Bruce where you want to go, and he'll get you there."

"I'm not sticking you without a ride, am I?"

"No. This is my last stop before home, which I should be

heading to somewhere around dawn. Bruce will be back to pour me into the limo by then," he said, winking at her.

"Okay," Rhiannon said, obviously relieved. "Thanks, Thad."

"Anytime. I'll ring you tomorrow," he said, leaning to kiss her cheek before heading off towards the entrance.

Rhiannon slipped into the limo and Bruce closed the door. Once behind the darkened glass, she settled back in the plush leather of the seat and released a slow breath. Bruce got in and asked her where she wanted to go, and she gave him Kline's address.

Getting back onto the road was easier than she'd expected given the traffic and the time of night, and soon they were underway. When they were getting close to Kline's house, Rhiannon gave Bruce the alternate route to go in the back way so she could avoid the vultures at the front gate. He dropped her off and she went in through the hidden entrance just off the garden, following the short breezeway into the kitchen.

Seated at the island counter was a pretty young woman with medium blond hair and a golden tan, eating a bowl of ice cream. "Congrat—," she said, the word fading with surprise at seeing Rhiannon, "Oh, I'm sorry. I thought—Hi!"

"Hi. You must be Kim. I'm Rhiannon."

She nodded. "I figured. Is Kline with you?"

"No. He's still at the party. I wasn't feeling well, so I came back here. I need to get out of this dress and head home."

"Oh, okay. Well, I've just put Jack to bed a little while ago. He was trying to stay up to see his dad when he came home," Kim said, with a slight smile. "He was really tickled to see him on the television."

Rhiannon nodded. "It was a great moment. He did a good job," she agreed, heading towards the steps. The clicking of her heels sounded loud to her, and she stopped to take them off so as not to wake Jack while she changed clothes. She hurried up the stairs into the loft and grabbed her bag from behind the chair at the foot of the bed. She peeled out of the dress and pulled on jeans and a sweatshirt, plucking the antique sterling and diamond earrings out of her ears and slipping the matching bracelet from her wrist. She laid the dress on the bed and dropped the jewelry and the empty clutch onto the sheer fabric.

It took only a few minutes to collect all of the things she'd brought with her, including the toiletries in the bathroom. She didn't go near the closet. There was nothing in there that belonged to her. After one last glance around the room, she slung the bag on her shoulder and made her way downstairs.

Kim was still there, rinsing the dish she'd used. Rhiannon gave her the once over and wondered briefly if Kline was sleeping with his nanny, too. It was a passing thought and she decided she didn't really care. "I'm off," she said, "it was good to meet you."

"You, too," Kim said, looking a bit confused but not daring to question. "G'night."

"Night," Rhiannon said, before trotting back through the breezeway and into the garage where her car was parked, ready to take her home.

Rhiannon was at her computer when the phone rang, and she checked the caller ID to see that it was Kline. Reaching over, she turned the ringer off and let the voice mail pick up. She'd gone to bed angry and woken up sad and wasn't in any state to talk to him. She sipped a cup of tea and turned her attention back to the screen.

The previous night's events were splashed all over the internet. DeuxMoi was featuring the winners list and the fashion highlights. Kline's name was mentioned in several of the articles, which was to be expected. Jill's dress made headlines, as well. She was in the top ten best dressed according to Go Fug Yourself.

Rhiannon glowered at a picture for a moment, recognizing August standing patiently in the background, and wondered how he felt about everything. Surely it was even harder for a man to watch his date pretend she was on a date with someone else. And preen and pose without him.

All the major news sites had Oscars information and more than one had a picture of Kline with Jill as an attention catcher. It took several clicks before she saw anything about herself, it was not what she wanted to see. Sharon Osbourne had compared her with Jill, saying Kline was sitting between The Virgin and The Whore. Side-by-side photos of Jill working the carpet in her daring gown and Rhiannon looking startled by a flash in what looked to be the same spot. It was clear Osbourne had chosen one of the worst pictures of Rhiannon they could find, and sure enough, the dress looked like a filter over her bare body in the camera's light. "What are a couple of nipples if you've seen the whole bush?" Osbourne had written, and made another nasty remark about how no one ever saw Rhiannon in photos unless they saw *all* of her. In the last sentence she said, "It's a perfect example of the dress wearing *you*, over *you* wearing the dress."

Rhiannon finally flicked off the computer and went for her phone. She'd known Jill a long time and either something was truly up with Kline that made her lose all hope in her ability to judge people, or she was just being sucked into a vacuum of Hollywood hallucination. Either way, she was going to end it now. She dialed Jill's number.

There was fumbling on the other end of the line then a sleepy, "Hello?"

"Hello, Jill. It's Rhiannon. Did I wake you?" she asked, knowing full well that she had.

"Rhiannon," Jill repeated, then laughed a little, "I don't think you have yet, actually. But keep talking. How are you?"

"I'm--not great, actually. I think you and I should talk."

Jill hesitated, "Okay. Sure. Now?"

"How about lunch? Would you like to come here, or shall I come to you?"

"I'm at August's," Jill yawned. "I'll come to you. Oh wait—I don't have a car. Hang on." There was more rustling and some muffled conversation before Jill was back on the line, "You're welcome to come here. Is that okay?"

"That's fine. Just tell me where."

"Okay, here, I'll let August give you directions. I'm terrible at that," Jill said, followed by more rustling before August's deep, richly accented voice came on the line. He was snarky but cheerful, Rhiannon assumed because she'd woken him up, but it was more amusing than anything. He rattled off the address and quick directions. "Come round to the back, love," he said "so we don't mistake you for a reporter and shoot you."

"Sure thing. I'll be there around noon. Is that okay?"

"What time is it now?"

"Ten-thirty."

"Gods--I'm rarely up before noon. I'll kick Jill out of bed, though. Enjoy your lunch."

Jill Parker

Jill took back the phone and said goodbye, then hung up and looked at August. "She's going to be mad at me."

"Well then quit kissing her dates."

Jill smacked his arm and yelped, "Be nice! It was for work!"

"You loved it, you little minx. Don't play sweet and innocent with me."

"Hmph!" she said, rolling over in the bed. "I kissed you more."

August leaned up on his elbows and kissed her shoulder. "You did a lot more than kiss me, but I'm yours. He's not. Even if the press are having a field day by trying to make it so."

"I should take a shower," Jill sighed, snuggling back against him. "And make some juice, or something."

"Yes, you should." He nibbled her shoulder. "Go on. Out of bed."

Jill sat up smiling and ruffled his hair. "You'll make such a good father. You're so bossy!"

August gave a snort. "Not in this lifetime, darling."

"Aw. Don't you want to hear the pitter patter of little feet?"

"I have a cat. That's plenty. I don't want anything that requires that I do anything more than set out food for it."

Jill frowned a little, "I want babies. At least two. You really don't?"

"How have I known you this long and you've missed that?"

"I just thought you were grumpy because you hadn't found the right woman. How was I supposed to know you were just grumpy!"

"The vasectomy might have been a clue," August laughed.

"Oh—I'd forgotten that. Oh! I can get off these stupid pills!"

He smiled, leaning up to kiss her. "Yes, you can. I have a clean bill of health and no swimmers. No muss. No fuss. No worries," he said, reaching to pull her on top of him, "and no waiting."

Jill finally made it into the shower a little while later, leaving August snoozing happily. She had pulled on a pair of jeans and a white, gauzy shirt, fresh as a daisy, if exhausted, by the time Rhiannon arrived, and welcomed her into the house through the kitchen. "I've got some muffins in the oven," Jill told her. "You want some coffee, tea, milk, juice, or something?"

"Coffee would be good, thanks," Rhiannon said, slipping her bag from her shoulder.

"Do you still take it light and sweet?" Jill asked, reaching for a cup.

"Yes. I like a little coffee with my milk and sugar."

Jill laughed a little and poured her a cup, going for mineral water for herself before sitting down with Rhiannon at the table. "So...your dress was great last night. You looked gorgeous."

"Thanks. Yours made the top ten lists. I guess daring works for you."

"Did it? I never look at those. I'm terrified I'll end up on the wrong end of the poll. As for daring, I guess. I was afraid to sit down all night. Those shoes were not made for standing either. One of the ladies said that she got collagen injections in the balls of her feet for cushion. Another one said her husband, who is a dentist, shoots Novocain in her arches—I'm having dinner with her next week. Trying to expand my social circle beyond coworkers, you know. And maybe her husband will do my feet for the next event."

Rhiannon hummed, ignoring the meatier part of that comment. "Beauty is pain, I suppose. Still, you didn't look like you were suffering too much. The photos of you and Kline are all gorgeous."

"Oh? Are they out already?"

"As if you didn't know. It's all over the internet and the dailies. They don't waste any time around here. Red Carpet shots, ceremony shots, afterparty shots. You were the hottest couple there. August did manage a background appearance in a couple of the pictures."

Her eyes lit up at August's name, then she sighed. "I guess it was too much to hope for a good one of me and August. Maybe some fansite has one. He says those usually have the best." A timer went off and Jill got up and went for the oven, pulling out muffins. "I've got blueberry, cinnamon apple, and banana. You want one?"

Rhiannon stared at her. "You really don't think there's anything wrong, do you? Either that, or you're just playing clueless again. You're such a good actress, I can never tell."

Jill put the muffin tin down, shut the oven and turned around. "Of course, I know something is wrong. I just don't know what. You've been snippy for weeks, but haven't said why, and of course I noticed the sniping last night. Do you want to tell me what I've done?"

"Oh, I don't know, Jill. Maybe it's that you assured me that there was nothing between you and Kline when I asked you directly, and the next thing I know you're out clubbing and cuddling with him in the park in New York."

"That's what's bothering you? There isn't anything between me and Kline," she said. "Roland sent him to pick me up after the final divorce hearing. We went to dinner. I took him to a club I am part owner in. I went with him to his interviews, and we took a walk. That is the extent of my 'relationship' with Kline. That and posing for business. Better?"

Rhiannon shook her head. "No. Not better. You're supposed to be my friend, Jill. If you could have just been straight with me about him from the beginning, then none of this would have happened. You say it's just business, but it sure doesn't look like business. Not to me. Not to the entire world. I can't believe you don't read your own press. I also can't believe that you went along with all of this and didn't once think that it might upset me. You say I've been snippy for weeks, well that's because when you did call me, it was all light and breezy like everything was right in the world."

Jill looked shocked, but her eyes narrowed quickly. "Oh, are we friends? Or are we *friend adjacent* or *friend-ish*? Anyway, Rhiannon, remember what I do for a living? Acting. We're under the same management, we're doing a film together, and that requires looking cozy in public. Why do you think he was photographed all over New Zealand with Kara when they were starring together? It wasn't because they were dating. And I didn't tell you about my past with him because you seemed to like him so well. I didn't want to color that for you. 'Light and breezy' was because everything was right in the world. Nothing between Kline and me. Why would I just assume you were going to jump to conclusions?"

"I'm not even sure we're friend-ish at this point. Kline didn't have a girlfriend when he was in New Zealand. There was no one to push behind," Rhiannon said, evenly. "You could have warned me about spending time with him in New York. I had to find out about it in the papers. Right about the time all those pictures of us were being splashed all over the place. Do you have any idea what kind of a nightmare that was for me? I had mobs of reporters outside my door while you and Kline were going to his interviews together and canoodling in the park--and while you were trying to seduce him."

"I'm sorry? I didn't even know there were pictures of us!

And I did try to call you, and you blew me off—remember? I called to see how you were and ask you to lunch? I thought maybe you wouldn't want to talk about your porn spread over the phone!" Jill's eyes were angry crescents now and in the back of her head she made a note to top off her Botox, "And what the hell? When was I trying to seduce Kline?"

"He told me about it, Jill, okay? He told me that you were very aggressive with him, and he told you no more than once. I knew you were upset about the divorce, but I didn't expect you'd be so desperate."

"I'm sorry?" Jill said again, her cheeks gone red, "I was aggressive? I was desperate? Are you out of your mind?"

"I must be. I thought our friendship meant more than all of this, but I guess not."

"Who the hell do you think you are to come in here accusing me? Huh? 'Our friendship' is what kept me from sleeping with Kline twice! Yes, I was hysterical over what happened in my hearing—did you call to check on me? You knew where I was going. Did you ever once think of that? No! Because you were busy with your own issue, which was no less awful. Don't come trying to shame me for taking walks with a friend while I was being brutalized in the press by a man I thought loved me, and being photographed with one I used to love! I think it's time for you to leave."

Rhiannon stood up and grabbed her bag. "I didn't call you because I knew you were with Kline, and I was stunned by that fact after everything you told me at dinner before you left. Call it *just business* all you like, Jill. It won't make it true," she said, turning for the door. "You'll be happy to know that I won't be in your way anymore. I'm getting out of this before one of you breaks my heart."

"I wasn't *with* Kline," Jill screamed. "I didn't do anything wrong! If you're not secure enough to handle a relationship with a man who fucks women on camera for a living that's fine, but don't try to make me your excuse! I am not with Kline! I don't want to be with Kline! I am with August. I can't believe you think I would do that to you."

"And I can't believe that you don't see anything wrong with what you've been doing," Rhiannon said, with a trace of sadness. "But it's already done." With that, she pulled the door open and walked out.

Jill chased her out the door, "I didn't do anything! What do you keep thinking I did? I have been in the same places--public places--with Kline, at the same time. With," Jill shouted, "my clothes on! All of them! Now what else have I done wrong other than pose for pictures?"

"I think you and Kline should just cut out the middle man for the next awards show and actually go together. You make it seem like you're there together anyway," Rhiannon said, over her shoulder as she continued towards her car. "That romantic dance the two of you shared was a highlight of my evening."

"Romantic dance? What romantic—Oh hell! We were talking! We were talking about the movie, and I couldn't hear him, and I was swaying drunk, Rhi. It was totally innocent. Why can't you believe that?"

"Because it didn't look that way, Jill," Rhiannon said, turning around to face her, "It was like I didn't even exist last night. It was all about the two of you. You say it's just business but what kind of business is it? You're playing up to the image that the two of you are the next great Hollywood love story, giving the press and the public what they want, right? Well, where does that leave me? Humiliated. I could expect it from any other woman, really, but you are supposed to be my friend."

Jill just gaped. "Rhiannon, it is business," she said, lowering her voice. "You don't see August over at Kline's telling him off for posing with me. It's just work. And I don't know where it leaves you—that's between you and Kline. Just…don't make it my fault if things don't work for you."

"It's not your fault that things aren't working for me. I just never would have let you walk into a situation like this without some warning. But, whatever, it's just business. I'm overreacting. I shouldn't pay any attention to the fact that I'm being made to look the fool because it's just business. I get it. Thanks for clearing that up," Rhiannon said, pulling her car door open and climbing inside.

"Good god!" Jill howled. "How was I supposed to know you and Kline hadn't talked about things? You've been in this industry for how long?! You know how these things go!"

"'Bout time I learned my lesson, huh?" Rhiannon said, putting the car in gear. "Word of advice, Jill. Watch what Roland's putting in the papers about you. The man does seem to love a scandal."

Jill turned and stalked back into the house to find August munching a muffin with a quizzical expression. She sighed. "We have a problem."

"Really? I couldn't tell from all the screaming."

"How are the muffins?"

"This one's good. Lose a friend?"

"Friend lost her mind. She thinks I'm sleeping with Kline. Or something."

August sighed. "Where did she get an idea like that?"

Jill sighed back. "I don't know. From the pictures taken in New York for one. She thinks we were too cozy last night. I don't know. She wouldn't listen to me."

"I have a theory," he said, breaking off another piece of muffin. "Maybe Kline's not telling her everything. Or, he's stacking the deck in his favor when the subject comes up. That, combined with all of the press about the two of you, and the way everyone acted last night, I can see where she might be a bit upset. Especially if she wasn't prepared for it. Did you ever read that article I showed you?"

"You know I don't read my press," Jill sniffed, picking up a muffin of her own and leaning against the bar. "I always hate the pictures."

"Maybe you should start reading again, darling," he said, seriously. "You're taking big steps here and you're not on level footing like in New York. You have to keep an eye on your image."

"I have a team for that. I pay a whole media team for that. Can I hire you? Can't you do that for me? Be my complete stylist? Inside and out? Upside and down?"

"I wish I could. But you're smart, Jill. You have business savvy and you know what you want. You can't afford to have anything surprise you. That means keeping track of every aspect, including your press. Roland's good at what he does, but his ethics are questionable. He's set up this 'romance' between you and Kline without regard to anyone in your lives that might be hurt by it."

"Are you hurt by it?"

"I don't like it, but I knew it was coming last night. You still spent more close time with Kline than I would have liked, but you kept me in the loop, and you left with me," he said, honestly. "I don't think I could handle it on a regular basis, but I wasn't hurt by it."

Jill put down her muffin and gave August a one-armed hug to keep from disturbing his eating. "It won't be regular. Just at things like that. But I'll be more aware of what's being said. Will you help me?"

"Of course. You could start by reading that article."

"Okay." She went over to the drawer she'd stuffed it in and pulled the magazine out. "When do you go to Paris?" she asked. He was working on a film that would take him away for five weeks.

"In two weeks," he said. "Want to go with me?"

"Of course! But you know I can't. We go into pre-production about the same time. Oh, you'll be gone when we start filming."

"I won't miss much," he said, going back into his studio to retrieve his laptop. "I doubt they'll start with the love scenes, anyway. I don't want to miss those. Or the murder."

"They always start with the love scenes," Jill laughed. "Anyway, I don't think I could do them if you were watching. That would be creepy. Carl said that the murder scene would come toward the end of shooting because we'll be at a different lot for that. The love scenes are shot on the same set as the party scenes and the crux of the exposition."

"Hm, well, I'll just have to have a spy on the set to keep an eye on Kline and make sure he behaves. Especially now that it appears he's about to be single again."

Jill rolled her eyes at him, thumbing through the magazine. "Oh hell! They've got that picture from my birthday party. That is the worst picture of me!" She skimmed. "That's just all made up," she declared. "Anyone who knows us knows that. They didn't get our ages right, or the dates, or anything."

"It sounds pretty convincing, though, doesn't it?" August said, turning the computer towards her so she could see the screen. "Everyone's certainly buying into the mythology. Look at these pictures and notes from the Oscars."

"Oh, August," she gasped, and he smiled knowingly, "that dress is amazing! You don't notice as much when you're wearing it but, oh!"

He laughed, "Not the dress, silly! You and Kline. Look how you look."

"Posed. And damn sexy. You should dress me all the time."

August clicked through several pages of photographs and read bits of articles. With the exception of one photo of Jill alone with August cropped in half in the background, nearly every picture was of her with Kline. All the references made were about the two of them, their past romance, and the apparent rekindling of that romance. A few mentions were made about Devil's Party, but most of the press was about the two of them. "I don't see any pictures of Rhiannon at all. Not even with Kline," he said, skimming through again. "It's all about you, baby."

"That doesn't mean I'm sleeping with him," Jill defended. "It just means the press would like for us to be. So why does she believe this over me?"

"How would you feel if the roles were reversed?"

Jill sat back and tried to imagine. "I think I'd feel like you. I

know the business. It is what it is. Kline and I are about to be naked together in front of a crew of at least thirty. It's a little hard
for me to get worked up and worried over pictures of us with
clothes on."

"You didn't feel that way when he was ready to drop everything and come back here when those pictures hit the papers,
Jill, or when he chose her over you at the end of his visit to New
York. That would have hurt, regardless, but it was worse because
Rhiannon's your friend. If she was the one sharing the spotlight
with him now while you were being forced into the background,
or painted as an obstacle to true love, you would consider it a
rather big deal, wouldn't you?"

"Be quiet," Jill said, looking stricken.

August sighed and went over to slip his arms around her.
"I'm playing devil's advocate. It's just in my nature. I'm not saying
that you've done anything wrong, just that your perception and
hers are very different. I don't want to see you lose a friend over
this."

"Too late. And I think you mean you don't want to miss
a chance to vent your own spleen on the back of Rhiannon's
gripes." She shook her head. "Let's talk about something else.
Let's talk about what we're going to do when you get home from
Paris."

"We're going to buy a house and decorate it and throw fabulous parties and make love as often as physically possible."

"And have lots of babies?"

"We can get as many cats as you'd like."

"No, baby babies. I really want children, August. A lot. I
always have. I don't know if I can have them, but if not, I want
to adopt."

August sighed. "Well, it's a sure thing that we can't have
them. We just talked about that this morning. As for adopting-
-we'll see," he said, hedging slightly. "Maybe after your five-year
plan."

August wandered off upstairs, leaving Jill to peruse her

press. She moved from news page to entertainment page, then tripped through several sites that claimed to have pictures and gossip about her. This was something her NYC publicist had always done for her. Along with the divorce had come a sudden parting of ways with both her old management and publicist. They hadn't protected her from the glare of the media spotlight, and she'd intended to find people who would. Honestly, the stories she read about her and Kline didn't bother her simply for the fact that they were not true. It was when the press printed the truth about her life that she felt nervous. Still, after scouring the web for herself, she started feeling a bit more sympathy for Rhiannon and after seeing what Sharon Osbourne had said, she picked up the phone.

Of course, she got voice mail, so she tried to cram as much into sixty seconds as she could, "Okay," she said, "August just made me read all my press. I had no idea what all was out there, but having seen it, I can tell why you're upset. You have to believe that it was absolutely nothing more than what you saw with your own eyes. I couldn't warn you that I would be with Kline in New York because I didn't know he would be there. If Roland had sent Adolf Hitler to pick me up, I would have been happy to see him. It happened to be someone I knew and trusted to a degree. He stayed with me all day and most of the evening because I was a complete mess. I went with him to his Colbert taping because I didn't want to be alone, and I needed to show up in public. Then he got slammed with your pictures, so I stayed with him so he'd have some support. I didn't call you that day because he was calling you--I was there with him. He was using my phone. He was completely worried about you to the point that--" The voicemail cut her off, so she dialed again.

"Me again," she told the beep. "He was going to leave town and go straight to you. That's something he never would have done for me. We did talk about whether or not we could date again. We—*we*, the two of us—decided no. Mainly because of you, but also because he would never even think to drop everything for me. I knew all that. I assumed he would tell you that. Well, no I didn't.

I didn't even think that you might need to know it. Please try to understand that while you were being humiliated by your pictures, I was being humiliated by my husband, who had just given several interviews about our marriage, including the miscarriages I had—yes, I've had two. And he cited the miscarriages as reasons our marriage fell apart. Then he paraded his pregnant girlfriend in front of me. I wasn't thinking about you or anyone else. I think I'm justified in that." She was cut off again and dialed once more.

"I hope you're bothering to listen to these. I did try to call you twice, but you weren't willing to talk. Maybe I didn't make enough of an effort to draw you out, but I didn't know what was wrong and frankly, I was doing all I could to keep my own head above water, so I didn't think to bother with it. I'm sorry you were hurt by the press. I'm sorry that you got left out of the publicity loop. I honestly don't know why Kline would say I was trying to seduce him or being aggressive with him. That's just not true. So, whatever you think happened, here's what did: Nothing. I don't know what else to say."

This time Jill hung up before the voice mail and then opened her contacts to dial Kline's number. He answered on the third ring, and she said hello. Once they'd exchanged greetings, she asked, "Why does Rhiannon think I tried to seduce you in New York?"

"What?"

"Rhiannon came over this morning and left after a screaming fight. She's got it in her head that we're having an affair, or we have had an affair, or we want to have one. Why?"

Kline thought for a minute then said, "Oh--I might have given her that impression."

"What?!"

"Well, not that we did anything, but that you wanted to."

"Why would you do that?"

"She was upset and wasn't believing the truth. When I told her nothing was going on, she kept picture wagging. I'm sorry—I didn't think anything would come of it. I just told her how upset you were and that you were trying to get your mind off the divorce."

Jill steamed for a few seconds, then just hung up the phone. She walked upstairs, put on her swimsuit, walked back down and out the door to the pool where she laid down on a raft and stared at the willows while floating, alternately hating all men, all women, and the media. She liked puppies and children and that was it. Maybe she would move to Nebraska and start a puppy ranch. "Five years," she repeated like a mantra. "Five years then I am out of this business entirely."

Chapter 5

Rhiannon Charles

Rhiannon spent a few hours driving around and walking the strip of beach that lay behind her bungalow. The flaring anger had faded into dull numbness that she hadn't expected. She hated that she was fighting with Jill, especially over a man. This was just the scenario she'd been trying to avoid, yet she'd been drawn into it just the same. She was kicking herself for letting her frustrations and fears drive her into the passive-aggression that was Jill's hallmark, not hers.

She had ignored all of the text messages and calls coming in as she drove, tossed her bag and phone on the dining room table, and carried in the armful of things she'd taken from Kline's but left in her car. Shower first, she told herself. Then she could look and see if Kline had been one of the chimes ringing out of her phone.

Rhiannon was exhausted and started to scold herself for it but stopped short. She'd been through the wringer since she'd met the actor. She had every reason to be tired. For the moment, she concentrated on washing her hair, then her body. She threw her hair up in a towel, put on her favorite robe, made a cup of tea, then curled up on her sofa, retrieving her phone, to finally check messages.

The first voice message was from her mother, alternately congratulating and admonishing her on the awards ceremony. She loved seeing her daughter on the red carpet. Hated the dress. Big surprise. The second call was her half-sister, Derica, who was squealing like a preteen about seeing her on television with Kline.

Rhiannon had to smile at that. Derica was a 23-year-old Poly Sci major working on her master's, and she was usually so uptight that to smile might cause her to shatter into a million pieces. This was the first time she'd called since Rhiannon moved to LA.

Apparently, she hadn't seen the pictures, which really wasn't a surprise. The girl read the Wall Street Journal for fun. Rhiannon was more surprised that she even knew who Kline Scott was, let alone that she'd watched the Oscars.

The gushing ended with a "Call me, Rhi!"

She skipped the messages from Jill and went to read her texts.

Thad was most recent with, "LMK ur ok," and "you looked great last night." Then several from Kline starting with the most recent, "At least have the decency to let me know you are ok," presumably after he'd spoken to Kim. She scrolled his queries in decreasing order of upset down to the first text he'd sent about an hour after she'd left the party, "Where are you, bb?"

A few other acquaintances followed, including one of the show's producers talking about work. That was refreshing. Her phone started ringing as she eyeballed Jill's thread. It was Kline calling again. She swiped him into voice mail and opened up Jill's texts.

They were all voice, and she played each of them with a sinking feeling in her stomach. Who was she now? She'd come out to LA to make a name for herself with her work, and instead, she'd made herself notorious for who she was dating and what she was wearing, and she'd gotten drawn into Kline's narcissistic web like the outsider to fame that she was. She wasn't one of them. She didn't want to be one of them.

Now, it seemed that Kline had played both women, whether by circumstance or intention, and Rhiannon had allowed jealousy to get the best of her. One thing was certain. Kline had lied to her. He had lied about Jill and while she'd had her doubts about what he'd said, she had convinced herself that it must be true because she didn't want to think that he was purposely setting them against each other. From the sound of it, he was.

Rhiannon groaned and rolled her head back against the sofa, considering her options. She owed Jill an apology. That was evident.

Kline was another matter entirely. She was so angry at him, even more so now, knowing that he'd lied about Jill. This had all become far more than she'd ever bargained for when she agreed to go out with him in the first place. She had a life she liked before she met him, and she was going to get back to that. No more of this secret affair while he had a publicity romance for her. If she wasn't his IG official girlfriend, it was over. In fact, she decided, it was just over. The last thing she wanted was to be on Kline Scott's Instagram.

First, she texted Jill. "I got your messages. I'm sorry for the things I said and for thinking the worst. Things have just been so messed up. You were right about one thing. I can't handle it. Obviously."

She considered calling Kline, but she wasn't ready yet. It was all too raw, and she didn't want to say anything that she hadn't thought through first.

With another cup of tea in hand, she settled in front of her television with her laptop and worked for a few hours before taking a break. As soon as she flicked on the television, the familiar theme of Entertainment Tonight trumpeted through the speakers, and scenes from the Oscars started flashing. Rhiannon remembered seeing them on the red carpet and Nischelle Turner had stopped Kline halfway to ask him questions about Knight… and Jill. They showed bits of the short interview, as well as a shot of Rhiannon standing dutifully behind Kline and made mention of their relationship without adding a comment on the recent photo scandal. There was footage of Kline and Jill posing, too, and a report on the fashions. Kevin Frazier was nearly wetting himself over Jill's dark goddess, August Hall original.

They broke for a commercial with a teaser about the after-parties and Rhiannon got up to fix something to eat. She walked back in to see Erin Johnson talking about the Vanity Fair party.

"Kline Scott shined in the company of former lover and future costar, Jill Parker. He was there with a date, but he spent the whole night canoodling with Parker. The couple were inseparable at the party, including a romantic slow dance and the exclusive crowd was abuzz about their apparent closeness and their upcoming collaboration on the film adaptation of Devil's Party."

Rhiannon pressed the button on the remote, silencing the commentary. The media monster had just tripled in size.

Kline rang Rhiannon for the twentieth time on Tuesday morning, and she finally picked up.

"Are you avoiding me?" Kline asked off the bat.

"Why would I be doing that?" Rhiannon snapped. "Just because you avoided me all night Sunday? Or because you lied to me about you and Jill? Or what? Why on earth would I have reason to avoid you?"

"I did not avoid you, Rhiannon!" he snapped back. "You're the one who disappeared without so much as a word."

"You mean you noticed?"

"Of course I did! I looked all over for you. One person said you were off with Rick, another with Thad, another in some other room, someone else saw you in the powder. How the hell was I supposed to find you?"

"I got tired of standing around waiting for you to finish making headlines with Jill," she said, exasperation growing. "The thing I don't understand is, if it was such an imperative for you to spend so much time with her, why did you take me along?"

"Because I asked you," he said snippily. "If I'd known that my work was going to bother you that much, I wouldn't have. You did realize I was working, didn't you? That I was at my job? Do you think I'd be pissed for you hanging out with Thad at your work?"

"That's not even close to the same thing, Kline, and you know it. There were a lot of people 'working' at the Oscars, but they still paid attention to their dates. You were too busy creating buzz to even look at me. It was like I wasn't even there," Rhiannon replied. "The dancing was a nice touch."

"It is exactly the same thing and 'you' know it! My job is in the public. My work is to stir up interest in me as a personality and in my films. Right now that means stirring up interest in Jill as a leading lady. I would have been happy to pay attention to you, dear heart, but you jetted inside without me, and then I couldn't find you from there. If you didn't notice, I was a bit mobbed and couldn't really get away to go hunting."

Rhiannon took a deep breath and let it out slowly. "You didn't tell me that you'd signed on for Devil's Party and that you and Jill were going to have to do some press for it. I had no warning about any of that and after everything, I was really put off by the whole experience. It's also made it very clear that I'm not your type, after all. You want a woman who's willing to be an accessory or a piece of set dressing and I'm not made that way, Kline."

"The hell?" Kline snorted. "First of all, no one asked you to be an accessory. Again, I was doing my job. That is my job. I invited you to come along thinking you understood what I do for a living. Second, why would I have to tell you what film deals I have in the making? We've been seeing each other a month, Rhiannon. But I suppose I should expect that since you were digging into my scripts the first weekend."

"You were ready to introduce me to your kid, but you're too precious to tell me that you're going to be fucking your ex on screen? Your priorities are so messed up! I do understand what you do for a living, and I didn't say that you should tell me what film deals you have in the making. It would have been nice if you'd warned me that you needed to spend so much time with Jill, considering that's been an issue nearly from the start. Yes, I know that nothing's going on. I also know that she wasn't the one who did all the pursuing in New York. But you know how this is being played out in the press, and true or not, you know how upsetting it's been to me. I don't want to live my life in public and I certainly don't want to be painted a fool for the sake of box office returns. If that's the game you need to play, find another girl."

"If you know there's nothing going on between me and Jill then why are you so worried about it? You know where I sleep. I don't know what your obsession with Jill is anyway. Even if I was fucking her, it's not like we have a commitment to anything. I've been straight up with you about everything going on in my personal life. And no one's painting you the fool. The press isn't even paying attention to you anymore--or wouldn't be if you hadn't shown your tits again. If you'd worn what I suggested, they'd not even have bothered you at all. You went out of your way to get media attention in that gown. Now I'm not playing games. If you think you can handle being with me, then I want to keep seeing you but if--"

"Exactly what kind of woman do you think I am? What kind of idiot? Because you're talking to me like I don't have a brain in my head!"

"I think you're the kind of woman who'll shag a man on the first date to fulfill a fantasy, then bitch about it when it isn't the fairy tale she intended."

Rhiannon was quiet for a long moment, angry tears stinging her eyes. "I didn't go out with you because of who you are. I went out with you because you asked me, and you seemed like a nice guy. As for sleeping with you on the first date, I only did that because it seemed like there could have been a real connection between us. I didn't know that you have an act for every occasion."

"That wasn't an act, and you know that. Nothing we've had in private has been an act. I thought we could have something, too, which is exactly why I turned down Jill in the first place. I didn't realize you needed to be coddled and paraded into the spotlight—I thought you preferred it behind the scenes. I guess I was wrong."

"I don't need to be coddled and I definitely don't need to be paraded into the spotlight. When in all of our illustrious history have I sought your spotlight, Kline? Never. Early on, I thought it was just a job for you and that you preferred private time, but you really love basking in the glow, don't you? You really love being hounded by photographers and being seen and having your name in the papers, don't you?"

"What are we fighting about right now?" he demanded. "We're fighting about me not giving you enough spotlight time on Sunday and you running off like a spoiled brat! I didn't take pictures with you. I didn't work the room with you. And I love my private time, but hell yes, I love my job. I wouldn't do it otherwise. Did I ever say I didn't like the attention? No!"

"I didn't want the spotlight on Sunday, either, Kline. I wanted to be with you," she said, trying make him understand, "and instead it was like I was invisible. You can tell me I'm wrong all you like. I'm telling you how I felt. That's why I left. I was angry and embarrassed, and I didn't want to make things worse than they already are."

"Well, if you saw me, why didn't you fucking come over and talk to me? I spent three hours trying to find you when I could get away from people. If you knew where I was the whole time, why didn't you make a move?"

"I was going to, but I came out of the bathroom and saw you dancing with Jill and if I had come over then, it would have been sordid and made everything worse. She's my friend, Kline. I don't want to be in competition with her. It would have been bad with any other woman, but it's worse when it's her. Call it PR. It didn't look that way."

He sighed with frustration. "This isn't going to work. It just won't. This is my work. It's what I do. If you can't understand that, I don't know what to say. You can't be in competition because there is no competition, but you're just not getting that."

"You're right. I don't get it. I understand what your job is, I just don't understand why dating me is apparently not as good for your image as dating Jill seems to be. Maybe Roland could explain it to me."

"I could explain it," Kline said witheringly, "but not without sounding completely offensive. Look, Rhiannon, I do think you're an amazing woman. You're smart, you're funny, you're beautiful. I really enjoy spending time with you, but right now my priorities have to be Jack and work. I can't put any energy into a committed relationship with someone who doesn't understand my work and it seems you don't want anything short of exclusivity and that won't happen with the press. I can't give you that. I think it's best if we just—are we friends? Can we stay friends? Or were we just shagging?"

There was silence in response, then, "Sure. We can be friends."

"In other words, don't call me, I'll call you?" he asked.

Rhiannon sighed. "It's just going to take some time for me to get past all of this. I have trouble pretending that I'm alright when I'm not. I'm not a very good actress. I really like you, Kline," she said, sincerely. "At least, when you're being you. It's the celebrity part that I can't deal with."

"I'm sorry you feel that way," he said.

Rhiannon managed not to huff at the words. "What are you going to tell the press when they ask?"

"Nothing," Kline answered. "They won't ask. They won't care."

"I would hope that you'd be kind to me if they ask you and don't allow all of this 'love triangle' spin to go on. I could do without another scandal in my life," she said, quietly. "This is difficult enough to handle without all of that."

"They won't ask. They don't care about you. I don't expect we'll really have to worry with it at all. And again, I don't know how to say it without sounding completely offensive. If you'd been a name, then it would be hard to disentangle publicly—like Kara. I haven't seen her in months and we're still going out in the media's mind. You'll be able to just fade to black."

"So I'm learning. Take care of yourself, Kline," she said, hanging up before he could say goodbye.

Kline Scott

Kline sat on a balcony in Paris, overlooking the 8th Arrondissement. He really preferred the 3rd, but the 8th was better for being seen. He had gone to the Parisian premiere of Lone Star the night before and been feted like a conquering hero instead of an actor playing a beleaguered rancher. He'd done London two days prior. He had New York on Thursday and LA on Saturday, and then he had a week of coast to coast press, followed by engagements across Europe for a week, when finally he would get a day off.

Now, he had until ten, then his glam team would arrive, and he would be doing the rounds of the most important Parisian shows. He rang Jill.

"Not now," she answered. "I'm getting my nails done."

"Are you in the spa?"

"Yes."

"I'm coming down."

Roland had negotiated Jill's presence for the Lone Star premiers. That hadn't been easy, given how angry she'd been about Rhiannon, but Roland had managed to broker peace and Jill could never stay angry at anyone for long—too much of a people pleaser for her own good. Now, she was traveling to each opening night with him, all smiles and legs in a series of gowns made by Gus. She always looked fantastic, but Kline couldn't help feeling like the other man was right there in between them as they hugged up close for photo calls and sat side-by-side through multiple screenings of the film.

The press was eating them up, and the more they demurred about the state of their relationship, the more interest there was in why the Broadway star kept showing up on his arm. "It's just work," Jill had said truthfully, her blue eyes guileless. "And we're very old friends. Besides, Kline could have any woman in the world. Why would he tie himself down to me?"

And in another interview Kline had said, "Jill's one of the most balanced, down-to-earth women you could hope to meet in this industry. She's one of the best actors I know, and I learn something new from her every day. You've seen her! She's beautiful, she's smart, she's funny–if I could talk her into a lifetime of promises I would, but there's that smart thing. She's too smart to settle down with me!"

Reporters and bloggers, and gossips all kept asking, "Why does she keep showing up with him? It's too early for them to be promoting Devil's Party. They haven't even started shooting."

They answered themselves on a range. Some said that Kline and Jill were absolutely, truly in love. Others said that Kline needed her good publicity, and she needed his Hollywood cache. But most everyone agreed they were a gorgeous couple to look at, and wanted to believe it was a real romance. Sometimes, Kline did, too.

While the cameras were on them, Jill was a dream in his arms, allowing him chaste kisses on the photo walls, but as soon as they were in the darkened theaters, she would excuse herself to the ladies room and wouldn't return until just before credits rolled. He had a fantasy now.

He would kiss her cheek at the photo call and whisper something filthy in her ear. "I'm going to fuck you like an animal," or some such. She would blush and shiver and try to step away from him, but he would hold her wrist firmly so she couldn't get too far. He would keep that grip until the lights went down in the theater, and when she tried to excuse herself, he would hold her fast.

"No," he would say against her ear. "Spread your legs."

Because it was a fantasy, she would do it, and because it was really a fantasy, she wouldn't be wearing any knickers, and she would be drenched wanting him as badly as he wanted her. He would stroke the silken softness of her inner thighs, making her tremble, teasing at her cleft until she sighed.

Then, she would reach over and tentatively touch his erection, which would be straining against his inseam. Her delicate fingers would be like butterflies, but then she would grow brave and grip his shaft through his trousers and start to stroke him as he slid his own fingers into her waiting warmth.

He would feel her getting close and turn to kiss her mouth just as she tried to stifle a cry of pleasure. He would suffocate the sound with his lips as her thighs clenched shut on his hand, and then, before he could ruin his own pants, he would grip her wrist again and move her hand away. When they went back to the hotel, he would be ready, and he would follow her to her room. They wouldn't even get fully inside the door before she was wrapping herself around him, pulling him down to taste his mouth and dragging him to her bed.

He groaned aloud and rolled his shoulders. So far, the closest he'd gotten to that fantasy was whispering, "Want to make out?" at the premiere last night. She had broken character and burst out laughing. He could not believe all that woman was being wasted on Gus.

She was in a black turtleneck and trim black trousers, sitting at a nail table chatting easily to the tech in French when he appeared. He was hoping he looked as rakish and handsome as she did winsome and lovely. He also wondered how many hairpins held her sleek bun in place, imagining how her hair would look tumbling down.

"Jilly," he greeted.

She said something to the nail tech and both of them laughed, he felt like at his expense. "Hi, Kline."

He sat down in the chair next to her. "Are you coming with me on my circuit today?"

"No, I'm doing some shopping. Rollie and I agreed that I also need to be seen out and about alone. I'll meet you tonight to take the car to the airport, though." Her phone chimed and she laughed again. "Pick that up and look at it. August keeps sending me wardrobe cues."

Kline picked up her phone and held it to her face to unlock it, then swiped open the texts from August. Image after image of what he wanted her to be wearing. "He's so upset he couldn't come with," she said. "You know he's going to be here in two weeks. Then I'll be in LA by myself. I'm going to miss him."

"I rather prefer missing him," Kline said.

"You're just jealous."

"Maybe," he agreed.

They sat in silence for a while, Kline watching as the tech laid down acrylic on top of Jill's nails and carefully painted it into place and shape. "Are you going to stay at the Bowery with me in New York?"

"I have an apartment."

"How will that look, though?"

She fixed him with a side-eye. "Kline? Are you trying to convince me we're having an affair? Because I know better. And it will look just fine because unless you go advertising, I'm not at the hotel with you, no one will know. I'll be with you at the premiere. I'll be with you at the after party. I'll be with you in the car back to the Bowery and you'll go in the back entrance so no one will see you, and I'll go home."

"Anyway," she added. "I've got business. I'm taking a few meetings while I'm home. Clara's got a new team working for me out of the Manhattan office, and there are some brand deals to close. I can't believe how much interest I'm generating since she took over my socials! She's amazing! Now, I've just got to find my footing in LA. I still feel like I'm tripping over myself there."

"It's because you're so poised," Kline told her. "You're professional and perfect. In LA, you need to be breezy and ethereal."

"I should learn how to surf."

"Surf?" Kline laughed, thinking back to what Thad had said to him.

"Yeah. It's a good workout and it's semi-social."

"I was thinking about taking it up. Want to do it with me?"

She looked him over dubiously and he said, "Actually, a friend suggested it to me to help me get out of my own head. He said it would center me in my body and force me to ground myself, but I'm kind of afraid of looking like an arsehole. If you go with me, I may still look like an arsehole, but I'll look like an arsehole that can pull Jill Parker."

Her smile made his throat hurt sometimes. "Yeah. Let's learn to surf. Worst case scenario, you piss me off and I drown you."

"Going down with you on top of me? What better way to die?"

She swatted at him with her free hand and both of them laughed.

Jill Parker

Late on a Thursday morning Jill dressed for her lunch date with Kline wondering silently over the still sleeping August. At Roland's suggestion, she'd bought a car. "You can't walk in LA," he'd said, "And you need a way to get around that doesn't involve Herr Hall." So, she'd let him take her to a few dealerships and chosen a silver Mercedes convertible, then had nearly taken out August's gate driving it up to his place. She was going to need some practice.

He'd hated her new car and had utilized his special brand of snark regarding it, then was quiet and withdrawn most of the evening. She'd known him forever and was well aware that he was prone to moods and sulks—she'd been the cause of plenty of them—but he hadn't had one since she'd been in LA, so it was disquieting.

Her last therapist had talked with her extensively about the fight, flight, freeze, and fawn responses that came with childhood trauma like hers. Jill had learned that she was a fawn. At the slightest hint of upset in a partner, she would drop everything to try to appease. When fawning didn't work, she fled, like she was about to do. It was only to lunch, but she was still sneaking out before he woke up.

She'd been following August around like a puppy, trying to make him laugh, or at least smile since she'd come back from Kline's Lone Star tour, but ever since the talk they'd had about Rhiannon, he'd been distant. He was angrier about Kline than he had let on, and he was furious when she'd agreed to the premiere junket. She'd come too late to the realization and was in London before she could appease him. Still, she had a job to do, and it was only going to get worse when everyone had to watch Kline grinding on her up close on the big screen. She groaned aloud at that.

Devil had been hard enough to do on stage every night where every physical scene was very carefully choreographed and rehearsed to take place under a sheet, on a bed, set far enough back on the set to give the impassioned characters some privacy. This was going to be very different. Close-ups, retakes, Kline between her legs while he was kissing her. She shivered and wondered if she could wear her surfing dive skin?

She decided to ask him if he was concerned about it at all. He'd done love scenes for movies before. He knew a hell of a lot more about this than she did.

She'd spoken with Kline briefly and arranged to pick him up in her new car, which he found hilarious. "Like a giraffe on roller skates," he'd said.

Driving in through the front gate, as Kline had given her his pass code, Jill encountered a line of his fans and greeted them all with a smile and wave, then halted the car long enough to sign a few autographs before going through. Kline met her at the door with a wide, sheepish grin. "Kill anyone?"

"Not yet," Jill sniffed, rolling her eyes, "but the day is young."

"Come on in. I'll show you around before we go."

They met Kim and Jack on the tour of the living room, where Jack took up with them, giving his commentary on the house and his favorite places. He remembered Jill from the restaurant and was associating her with the memory of a day out with his father, so her presence was exciting and welcome. She seemed delighted by his attention and took his hand to follow his lead off and away from his father, whom she stuck her tongue out at.

"You just lost another girlfriend," Kim observed dryly.

"Oh, she'll be back," he said mocking her tone, "just wait until she finds out he can't pay for lunch. He may have looks and charm, but I have looks, charm, and money."

Kim laughed and shook her head, then went off to start Jack's lunch. When Jill and Kline finally left, it was after she'd had a share of goldfish crackers and some juice. Jack had insisted. "He's such a good host," she smiled, putting on her sunglasses and securing her hair clip.

Kline had settled into the passenger seat, making a great show of putting on his seatbelt. "Gets it from me."

"Certainly gets his love for shiny things from you," Jill said, as she guided the car down the drive, "and toys."

Kline laughed. "Yeah. He keeps me young."

"'Cause you're so old."

He started to wave at the girls at the gate and realized Jill was waving too. He laughed. "Attention hog."

"Famewhore," she grinned back.

"It's a living," he sighed, stretching his arms back and folding his hands behind his head.

"Thank god," Jill agreed, turning at the end of the street and heading towards the city.

He gave directions to Kato's and Jill got them there in one piece even if she was a bad driver. Kline peeled himself off the seat with a grim smile. "I'm driving home," he said.

"No, you're not. I'm just getting used to my new car."

"There's a reason you've been driven everywhere up until now," he said, with mock seriousness. "You're a terrible driver."

"I'm a terrible driver because I've always been driven everywhere. You know this is my first car?"

"I didn't even know you had a driver's license. How the hell did you pass the test?"

"I didn't take one. I think they just gave me the license."

"I believe it!"

They were ushered into the restaurant and given a prime table to see and be seen. Once they had settled in with drinks, Kline reached across the table and took Jill's hand. "So here we are at last."

"Yes, being forced to have lunch by Roland."

Kline said, giving her hand a squeeze. "Really, though, is it such an ordeal?"

"I'm kind of still mad at you. I keep thinking about how you told Rhiannon I tried to seduce you and I was all aggressive!"

"You did climb on my lap in the limo."

"Please. If I was going to seduce you, you'd get more than a lap scooch in the backseat of a car."

"I did get more than a lap scooch at the club and at the hotel," he said, giving her a wink.

"But you started it and then you turned it all down. Don't try to blame it on me."

"I'm sorry. Really. For all of it. I was faced with an uncomfortable situation with her, and I said the first thing that came to mind to get out of it."

Jill raised an eyebrow. "Oh, come on, would it be so hard to believe?" he asked. "Admit it. You want me."

"Stuffed and mounted on my wall."

"However you like it, baby."

Jill rolled her eyes, "So is that your apology for making me look like a back stabbing, desperate tramp?"

Kline straightened slightly. "I wouldn't go that far. I downplayed it as much as possible." He shrugged. "I didn't even think she believed me, but we just stopped talking about it after that. I am sorry. I've already apologized twenty times and she's out of the picture now anyway."

Jill softened then. "I know. I'm sorry. Am I sorry?"

Kline frowned slightly and shook his head. "It never would have worked. She couldn't deal with the publicity and what's required of me. It's just as well."

"Well, I am sorry. More for her. I've been dumped by Kline Scott before. It messes you up."

"And I've been dumped by Jilly Parker. Multiple times. It's just as much fuckery," he said, turning as the waiter appeared beside him. He ordered a lemon chicken salad for Jill and a Niçoise for himself. "You'll love it. Trust me," he said, after the waiter had gone.She smiled and sat through a spell of silence then said, "So, love scenes. I guess I'll be scooching around on your lap again. Are you mature enough to handle it?"

"It's a dirty job, baby, but I think I can deal with it. I'm a professional."

"I'm scared," she admitted.

"Of what?"

"High up on that list is all the critiques that will come of my body. My boobs are too small, I have no ass."

"You're fucking fantastic, Jill," he started to say.

"You, on top of me, kissing me in a room full of people."

He swallowed, then took a drink of water. "There's no such thing as anti-Viagra," he said after a moment. "It's going to be… well, I'll be acting with my whole body."

"And then they call cut."

"And then they call cut," he agreed. "And we blue ball it back to my trailer? Where we shag it out?"

"I don't want a showmance with you. I literally cannot do it again–fall in love with you."

"Jill? Can I say something serious?"

"I wish to god you would."

He reached and took her hands. "I've never not been in love with you. I've just also always been really in love with myself. I'm still really in love with myself and you scare the fuck out of me with your five-year plans and your certainty, and your confidence in me. You were always so confident in me. You were always so sure of me. You encouraged me to try things I never would have, and when I did them, it was your voice in my head that got me through the scary bits. I've never been that sure of myself.

"I think," he said, "you're always going to be at least a little in love with me. I don't think that's ever going to go away. I know it hasn't for me. I hope it doesn't for you. That's selfish. I'm okay with that."

"I always want you to be a little in love with me, too."

"I know," he said with a smile. He squeezed her fingers then let go as the waiter brought a basket of bread that Kline immediately refused. When they were alone again, he said, "It's probably going to be really awkward at first. It always is for me. You want to get into it because that's your job, but you don't want to get too into it because there's that very fine line between art and porn. It's terrifying to be that vulnerable. It's terrifying to put your flesh and your desire out there for everyone to examine, but then you realize the crew is busy. They're working.

"It'll be a closed set, so only necessary personnel will be there, and after a few minutes, you forget they are there. You get caught up in the blocking and not getting into your partner's light, and not cracking noses into each other. We'll have the intimacy coordinator there to help. But no matter what, I promise I'll take care of you during those scenes. You can trust me. I will take care of you."

Jill blew out a breath and tried to joke. "I can't wait to see you in your flesh tone thong. That's got to do wonders for your ass. Me, I'll be in my flesh tone g-string with the silicone side and back strings--which does do wonders for my ass." She dipped a finger in her water and glanced up through her lashes and said seriously, "I'm glad it's you."

"I'm glad it's me, too. I'll bet you'll be sick of me before it's all said and done. The murder scenes will probably prove quite cathartic."

"I can hardly wait. Change the subject?" She poked around in her glass more and he nodded. "So, Jack's really cute and friendly. Is he going to be on the set with you?"

Kline beamed at the mention of his son's name. "As often as I can arrange it. I hate being away from him."

"You're really lucky," she nodded. "I love kids. I always wanted a houseful."

"Well, there's still plenty of time, Jill. You're not that old."

She shrugged. "I don't want to have them by myself. August...well, you know August. He hates them. Anyway, I'm not even sure if it's a possibility for me, and maybe that's a good thing. There's the possibility that I'd be just like my mother."

Kline shook his head. "I don't think there's any danger of that. You learned what not to do by being around your mother. You're a good person, Jill. You'd be a great mother. As for August, well, he'll either come around…or you can always find someone else."

"I'm giving up on that, too. If I can't make it with August, then I can't make it with anyone. You know? Anyway." She took a drink. "Oh, I got an offer from Playboy. I didn't even know they still existed in the free-porn internet world. Does that mean I've arrived? For a cover. Me, with no tits on the cover of Playboy."

"Depends. Are you going to do it?"

She shook her head. "No. Roland thinks I should wait. I don't want to do it anyway. Besides, everyone's going to see everything in Devil's Party, so why bother?"

"And you don't really need the money, either. I guarantee they aren't offering what they will be after the movie comes out and you're the toast of Hollywood."

Their food arrived and they ate in silence for a while, then Jill looked up, "So…"

"So?"

"So, now that you're actually single, and August will be in France, I guess I'll be seeing a lot of you, huh?"

"Probably."

"Then maybe you can show me around some more? I've… you know this is the first time I've lived anywhere other than NYC?"

He smiled, "Yes, I know. I would love to show you the town. We'll be spending a lot of time together, might as well do more than sit in trendy restaurants and eat."

"Want to help me learn to drive?"

"That, my dear, is first on the list."

She laughed. "August's not happy about it. About us spending so much time together."

Kline shrugged. "Well, we're working together. There's not much to be done about it. Besides, if he would rather show you around--"

"He wouldn't. He likes to stay at home and bring the interesting things to him. When he goes out, he has his places, and he doesn't venture far off course. That was fine in New York because I knew everyone, but here? It's different." she said, with a bit of a sigh. "When he leaves, I'll have two weeks to kill before we start pre production."

"Are you in love with him?" Kline asked, taking a sip of his drink.

"No," she shook her head. "But I love him. I don't think he's really in love with me either. He's just idealized me. I'm not really his type."

"And he's the one you're pinning all your future hopes on? Do you think that's wise?"

"I don't know. But it's safe. I trust him. He'd never hurt me. And we can have--cats."

"You hate cats."

"I know," she smiled. "But their feet do patter."

"When they're not trying to sneak up on top of you and smother you while you're sleeping."

"So how about you? Rhiannon dumped you. Your old costar shagged you off. Are you sleeping with the nanny?"

"Rhiannon did not dump me. We agreed it was best to end things. Kara was--eh."

"And the nanny?"

"Lesbian."

"Ooooh," Jill laughed. "So, what are you doing for companionship?"

"Not shit," Kline said sincerely. "Nina's taking me to court for Jack as you know. I can't get mixed up in anything, and after the debacle with Rhiannon, I'm not sure I want to. Far as anyone knows, it's you, baby."

Jill frowned. "How is the court thing going?"

"She's being extraordinarily difficult. Not that it surprises me. For the moment, nothing's been changed in her favor."

"Is there anything I can do?"

He shook his head. "No. Well, unless we actually have to go to court. Then you have to come testify that we're in a solid, stable, happy relationship. And you have to say I'm a great father."

"I could go to jail for perjury," she teased. "But I'll go in character as 'Jill Parker, Broadway Star Dating Kline Scott Mega Star.' Then it will be true."

He smiled. "It would be worth it just to see your performance—and Nina's face."

Jill laughed and shook her head. "It could also backfire terribly and make you look worse for lying. I couldn't live with myself. Fooling the public is one thing."

"I hope it doesn't come to that."

She chewed thoughtfully then said, "Why don't we bring him out with us on some of our 'dates'? You'll get more time with him. I like him. And it can only improve your chances of winning since you show such complete interest."

"The paparazzi. That's why."

"Oh, honey. They're going to take pictures of him anyway. Make it controlled. We'll take him to the zoo and the aquarium. Stuff like that. There'll be too many other people around for good shots. And if they follow, we can split up, so they have to decide who to chase."

"That's just it, I don't want them to chase us down when he's with me."

"Well, if you let them take a few pictures, then they won't fight so hard to get pictures of him. It's a tradeoff. You know that."

"He's my son. Not a commodity."

"Exactly. I know. But hiding him away and only letting him out with his nanny isn't the way to deal with it. Let's try it once. I want to see the San Diego Zoo, but I need to borrow a child, so I don't feel like an idiot. Let's go down there this coming weekend."

Kline sighed, considering the suggestion for a long moment before nodding. "Alright. We'll try it. If things get too crazy, I'm taking him home."

Jill picked up his hand and leaned over to kiss his fingertips, flickering her eyes right to indicate a camera. He leaned in and smiled dreamily. "No worries. We'll have a great time. We can get him a big hat and sunglasses, or just throw a blanket over his head like Michael Jackson did with his kids."

Kline laughed. "Let's hope it doesn't come to that. Jack would never forgive me for embarrassing him that way."

"Neither would I. This place is now crawling with photogs. How long before some fan comes up and asks you to talk to her best friend on her cell phone?"

"Maybe we should go before that happens," he said, summoning the waiter to pay the check. Moments later, the two of them walked out of the restaurant hand in hand to wait for the valet to bring the car.

"I'm driving," Kline insisted. "Fork over the keys."

She did, smiling so that a single dimple showed on her right cheek and Kline bent to kiss it. "I'd forgotten how cute you are."

"I'm adorable," she said. "Don't forget again."

"No worries there, love," he said, giving her a playful slap on the bottom before she slipped into the passenger's seat.

He drove them back to his house and invited her inside. She joined him and ended up staying most of the afternoon, engrossed in a game of Chutes and Ladders with Jack. It was nearly five when her cell phone rang, August asking where she was and if she was going to be back at his house that day. "Oh," she frowned slightly. "I have to go home."

"Aw, that's too bad," Kline said.

Jill turned around to see the same pair of eyes watching her from his lap and she forced a smile. "We'll just have to continue the tournament later."

"You can come back anytime," Jack said earnestly. "The gate number is 55502."

"Jack!" Kline scolded. "What have I told you about the gate code?"

Jill watched in amusement as Jack parroted, "Do not, under any circumstances, give anyone the gate code. That gate code keeps out bad people. Jill's not bad people," he shrugged.

Kline frowned. "Well, I'd already given it to her at any rate. But never do that again. Always ask me first. Maybe I don't want her to have it."

Jack looked shocked. "No way!" He looked back at Jill and shook his head, "Don't listen to him. You can come anytime."

Jill pressed her lips together, trying not to laugh and failing miserably. "Thank you, Jack. I'll be sure to come back. Is Saturday alright with you?"

"Sure! We can play Go Fish!"

"Or we can go to the zoo," Kline suggested, leaning down to whisper the last word in his son's ear.

"The zoo! Yes!" He leaped from Kline's lap, and danced around, "I want to see the snakes and the monkeys! Yes!"

Jill giggled and grinned. "Then I'll see you Saturday and we'll go look at them. I have to run now."

"I'll see you out," Kline smiled. Jack had already torn off to find Kim and tell her his good news.

"God he's cute, Kline. Can I have him?"

"Nope. But you can come visit him anytime. Just like he said."

She gave a wistful sigh. "That's it. I'm going to go adopt a baby on my way home."

Kline chuckled, "You'll have one of your own eventually. Until then, feel free to borrow mine."

Jill leaned up to hug him. "Thanks for a great day, Kline. Really. Maybe you're a good friend after all."

"I do alright sometimes," he agreed, giving her a quick kiss before releasing her. "It was great to have you here."

"Where are my keys?" she asked, digging in her purse.

"My pocket. Why don't you let me drive you--it's rush hour

and you suck at this. I'll have a car meet me at your place and bring me home."

"Nah," she shook her head. "I have to learn sometime. Besides, I'm kind of enjoying the freedom of it."

He didn't look convinced, but he handed her the keys. "Ring me and let me know you got home okay."

"Aw. You're so sweet and worried!"

"I've got 20 million riding on a film with you! Hell yes, I'm worried!"

She rolled her eyes. "You are such the Mega Star," she said, clicking her teeth. "It's all about the money, isn't it?"

"Of course. I'm shallow."

"Well, I'm off. August is waiting."

"Tell him I said hello."

Jill snorted and then started the car, waving as she drove away, leaving Kline to wander back inside the house, looking more pensive than she would have expected after their relaxing day together.

Chapter 6

Rhiannon Charles

It was late March before the photographers stopped lying in wait for Rhiannon at the Simon Says studio, but by mid-April it was like nothing had ever happened. Nothing at all. Kline hadn't called begging her to change her mind. She hadn't called him, begging him to take her back. After she'd slept on their split for a couple of nights, it felt like something far removed.

Rick had turned up on the set looking for Thad, and Rhiannon had joined him on the soundstage to watch Thad and Kelsey ad lib into a scene the writers were workshopping.

"He's so good," Rick sighed. "He's wasted in sitcoms. He could be as revered as Ian McClellan."

"I don't know if he's that good," Rhiannon laughed.

"I do. When we were coming up, I was in a workshop with him. We did a staging of Hamlet and he played the lead role. It was a revelation. Thad as Hamlet with Kline as Laertes. It was fucking brilliant."

"I imagine so, with the trade-off between clowning and being a menace."

"I know comedy is harder. It's easier to make people cry than to make them laugh, but it's hard to make someone feel something. Thad knows how to make people feel something. It's innate with him. I've got to get him for this movie."

Rhiannon considered the man standing next to her and thought about what he'd said at the Vanity Fair party. "Have you asked Kline?"

"He's not right for the part," Rick said, never taking his

eyes from Thad. "This is business, not a charitable mission to get a friend a job. Anyway, he doesn't need help. He's got that shark working for him."

"Roland," Rhiannon drawled. "Of the publicity romance."

"Yeah! I see that's in full swing," Rick said. "He's getting papped everywhere with Jill Parker now. Maybe we could get Thad into a scandal? Get him into the press."

Rhiannon laughed. Thad's divorces never even made much of a ripple. His exes only had good things to say about him, and he was so genuinely affable that he couldn't ever think of anything bad to say about them. Even Monique was being generous about their short-lived marriage. Thad only showed up in gossip when it was a blind item about someone doing something kind anonymously. Thad was Keanu Reeves' soul in a Hemsworth's body, but with Adam Sandler's jokes. She shook her head. "He would never."

They watched him volley with his onscreen spouse until she took a long pause, closed her eyes on a beat of silence, then threw up her hands. She'd lost the thread and dropped the improv. Thad crowed, "I win! I win! Beers are on Kelsey tonight!"

"That's fine," she smirked, "Riley! Go get me Thad's wallet out of his dressing room!"

"Bah," he teased. "It's empty."

"You're useless!"

"And hungry. Is it lunch yet?"

"Oh god, it's hungry again," Kelsey feigned fear. "Someone get this thing a sandwich before his blood sugar drops and he eats one of the extras? He'll be even more useless until he's fed."

"He's useless anyway," one of Thad's sitcom teenagers rolled her eyes.

"Oi! Enough of that, young lady," Thad growled playfully. "Or no more underage drinking for you!"

The girl laughed and ran off the set.

"Looks like we're taking a break," Rhiannon said, starting to walk with Rick up to the leading man. Thad was having a discussion with one the stage managers when he noticed the two and immediately excused himself. "Well, if it isn't my two favorite people whose names start with the letter R. Ruh-ruh-Rick. Ree-ree-Rhiannon."

Rick chuckled, "I want you for a drama, not Sesame Street, mate."

"Ah, but Sesame Street wants me! I got a call yesterday."

"Seriously?"

"Yeah," Thad said with a grin. He started walking and the two Rs followed him. "I've always wanted to do Sesame Street. I asked if I could do a scene with Big Bird."

"And?" Rick asked.

"They're thinking about it."

"Well, while they are thinking, I got you a meeting with Mick Layton. He's directing that little flick I've been telling you about. Not for a read, just for a talk."

"That indie thing? I don't know, Rick. I still don't think that's something I could pull off. No one's going to buy it."

"You really need to have more faith in yourself. Besides, it's only a meeting. You aren't signing on for anything. Just talking with the guy to see what he has in mind."

"I think it's a good idea," Rhiannon said. "It'll be good for you to stretch your legs as an actor, and it will only bring more press to the show."

Thad cocked an eyebrow and tilted his head at Rick before turning to Rhiannon, "How do you know about it?"

She smiled. "Rick and I had to have something to talk about at the Vanity Fair party. We chose your career. I think it would be a good idea for you to show your chops a bit. Get some bankability outside the box and you'll be primed for lead roles in big budget pictures. It worked for Jim Carrey."

"The world hates Jim Carrey."

"Do they?" Rhiannon was genuinely confused.

"But they love George Clooney," Rick suggested.

"And we all know how talented he is," Rhiannon said, with a bit of sarcasm.

"He's more talented than Jim-bloody-Carrey," Thad argued.

"Jim Carrey has more talent in his little finger than–" Rhiannon started, but Rick was already speaking.

"Just because you don't like the man, doesn't mean he isn't a star, Thad, but that's not the point. You have talent and you should use it. You can't do sitcoms forever. Not even your own."

Thad stood stock-still for a moment, his pink cheeks turning a darker shade as a blush crawled down his neck into the collar of his shirt. His jaw twitched, then he set it. "Like hell I can't," he dismissed. "I'm going to eat."

Rhiannon made to follow, but Rick placed a gentle hand on her forearm. "Let him go. You just saw what it looks like when Thad runs out of arguments. He's going to do it."

"When is the appointment?"

"This evening. I'm going to take him."

"Good. Then he won't be able to talk himself out of it."

"Or think of another argument."

Rhiannon smiled. "Yeah, he's usually good for one a day. That was it."

Rick laughed again. "I noticed the roar has died down around the entryway. Is it good to be back at work and off the red carpet, no photographers chasing you?"

"Definitely. It was…an experience. I survived. It's done. Never again."

"Still got the Emmys yet to go. Simon Says might win there, so you're going to need another dress."

"Bite your tongue."

"Get into production. They usher you in like the king, but you don't have to stop and talk to anyone."

"Nah. I'm a writer at heart. I get to stay home in my jammies and watch it on TV."

"You're the head writer, in case you forgot. If you get that nom, they'll expect you to show up dressed to the nines. But home in the jammies? That's the way to do it! But then you don't get the goody bag. I love the goody bags."

"I'll make Thad bring me one," she said, with a shrug. "Problem solved."

He laughed again. "Good on you. You've got it all figured out then. So, how's Kline?"

"I honestly don't know," she said, tucking a lock of hair behind her ear. "I'm sure he's fine."

"Oooh. So, it's over so quickly?" Rick tilted his head. "New wore off fast on that one. He really doesn't have a good track record with women outside his branch of industry."

"Doesn't seem to me like he's got a good track record at all. Anyway, his spotlight proved too much for me. It's just as well," she said, with a shrug. "Let's just say Q1 wasn't the best time of my life. I'm glad to have moved on."

"He's a decent guy," Rick sighed. "He tries hard. He just is what he is. Better for you in the long run, though I'm sure it's uncomfortable now. Actors like him–celebrities–do exist in a vacuum. Everything flares hotter, burns brighter, burns out faster. They are emotion junkies. They get just as high on that first flash as they would on meth. They are addicted to people, and addicted to being wanted. They're hard."

"Sounds like the voice of experience."

"I've been in this industry my whole career, and I'm friends with a lot of them. They make great friends. They're just lousy partners."

"Very." Rhiannon sighed. "Well, it was nice to see you again. I better grab some lunch before I end up in meetings all afternoon. Good luck with Thad's meeting tonight."

"Ciao." Rick smiled after her. "Tell the talking dress I said hello."

She flipped him a finger and walked on to her office, where her assistant had a box lunch waiting for her. She ate quickly without even tasting the food, eyes on the production calendar on her wall.

Sweeps was coming in May, and she felt good about the episode lineup. They were running filming two weeks on, one week off until after July sweeps so the writers could keep up and respond to network requests, and she was hoping they could dovetail an Emmy nom with big summer ratings. They were doing an extended summer hiatus to accommodate network coverage of an upcoming, international sporting event, so if Thad agreed to take the indie film, he could shoot then. If he needed more time, maybe they could do a couple of *very special episodes* where Simon gets snowed in at a cabin in Anchorage or something. He could Zoom in his performances.

She tucked that into the back of her mind to start laying groundwork for just in case.

Several minutes later, she realized she'd been staring out the window, her mind a million miles away. She'd been thinking about her family and how much easier life might have been if she'd just married the Kennedy scion her grandmother had picked out for her and lived out her life on a porch in Nantucket, alternately gardening, shrieking at the nanny, doing charity work, and writing a column in the local paper.

If she'd done as her grandmother wished, she would have already completed her family by now, with at least three kids and two King Charles spaniels. Each milestone, engagement, marriage, childbirth, would unlock a new level of treasure that was laid out for her in her grandfather's will. Now, it looked like she was taking the long way around to the excessive fortune, waiting for her grandmother to die rather than accomplishing all the feats of womanhood her grandfather had thought so important.

Funny how graduating from two of the top creative writing and film school programs in the country hadn't unlocked a dime. Not that she needed her grandfather's dimes. Her mother's side of the family had plenty of those and she had been supporting herself on the interest from investments made in her name at birth since she'd left home at eighteen.

She wanted something more than the money her forebears had accumulated as her coda. She wanted to achieve something. She wanted to create something new. It was one of the reasons why she was writing. Every week, she got to contribute to a new piece of art, even if it was just a sitcom. But the sitcom was a stepping stone. She needed to prove her chops while she worked on more serious personal projects, so that when she was ready to launch a bid for her real work, she was trusted and established with a portfolio.

She wanted to get funding like any other producer, not just siphon funds out of her bank account for a vanity project. Distantly, she wondered where Rick got his funding, and then if she might want to put up capital for one of his projects. Before she could think too much on it, an alarm blipped on her laptop that she had ten minutes before she needed to be in the writers room.

As she'd predicted, Rhiannon did spend the whole of the afternoon in meetings. There was still much discussion about June sweeps and the potential guest stars, most of May was already in the can. Kline's name was mentioned again for June, with a few glances in her direction, but she simply said that he would be a good choice if they could get him. When she was finally free from the last meeting, she went to her office and gathered her things, including the latest batch of rewrites, and headed down the hall. She poked her head into Thad's dressing room and wished him luck with his dinner meeting. "Try not to talk yourself out of the part when you meet the guy, hm?"

"Right," he smiled. "I'll give it my best."

"You do that." She waved goodbye then headed out to her car. She'd just started the engine when her cell phone rang, and she dug it out and answered without looking. "Hello?"

"Hey, Rhiannon. It's Jill. Hi."

"Hi, Jill. How's it going?" she asked. They hadn't spoken since the voice mail apologies, and she wasn't sure whether this call was a continuation or another fight in the making.

"Pretty well, I guess. Uh, are we okay? I wanted to check. And warn you--there are going to be new pictures of Kline and me."

"I think we're okay," she said, with something of a sigh of relief as she pulled out of the parking space. "Thanks for the warning, but he's not my problem anymore."

"Oh. Well...I got a car," Jill offered as conversation.

"Yeah? What kind?"

"It's a Mercedes convertible. Silver. Really pretty," she said, "I feel so LA in it."

"Nice ride. Do you know how to drive?"

"Barely," she laughed. "I managed the freeway, though. I went and picked up Kline for lu— Well, August won't ride with me. He thinks it's ridiculous that I bought a car, but I'm really happy about it. He's in Paris anyway."

"As long as you're happy," Rhiannon said, seriously. "You don't need to censor yourself, Jill. I know you're spending time with him. Really, it doesn't bother me now that I know what the deal is, and I'm not part of the deal anymore, and that's fine. It was apparent that I wasn't good for him and I know that he wasn't very good for me."

"Okay," Jill said unsurely, but then added, "I was going to say I picked him up and drove him to lunch, but then he wouldn't let me drive back because I scared him so badly. Driving is so much more complicated than I thought. I never realized there was so much more than just stopping and going!"

"All those years of hired cars have spoiled you, my dear," Rhiannon said, laughing. "I'll reserve my full judgment until I've had a ride in the passenger's seat."

"You should wait. I don't want to risk killing you until I have a few more lessons under my belt, but I would love to see you. If... if we're still friend-ish?"

Rhiannon was slower to respond than she meant to be. Were they? Had they ever been friends? Could they really be friends? What did friends even mean? A little voice in the back of her head said, "We believe women and we don't fight over men." She let out a breath. At worst, she'd have an unpleasant lunch. "Yeah," she said finally. "Of course. Let's get together for lunch or something. When are you free?"

"Next Wednesday if that's good for you?"

"Sure. Do you want to come to the studio?"

"That's fine with me. Oh--right--you work! Is noon good?" Jill laughed

"More like two if that works for you. I'll have your name on the list."

"Great. See you then. Buh-bye."

Rhiannon laughed as she hung up the phone.

Jill Parker

Jill and August made it through a stilted dinner conversation in his massive dining room, the two of them seated together at the head and right hand of a table for ten. He'd been truculent and waspish since she'd picked him up at the airport, and only part of that could have been because of her driving. Finally, she leaned back in her chair with a sigh and asked, "What is wrong? What is really bothering you?"

Part of her was still stinging from the barbs he'd thrown about her convertible telegraphing her constant need for attention, and whether her reputation might suffer being seen with him instead of her *one true love*. He had barely pecked her on the cheek after the skycap put his luggage in the trunk and opened the passenger side door for him to enter, but he had looked her over disapprovingly and said, "I hope you're wearing sunscreen."

Once home, she'd given him time to decompress in the shower before joining him under the spray. Her playful attempts to seduce him with a handful of suds came up limp, and he'd just said something about not being in the mood before shutting off the water and leaving her standing in the walk-in alone.

Now, he frowned at her with a creased forehead. "Oh nothing's wrong. Just the fact that I'm going to be in Paris for another four weeks and by the time I'm back home, the press is going to have you married off to Kline--if Roland doesn't actually convince you to marry him for real. I won't be here to remind you of us. But he'll be here constantly to remind you of him."

"I'm not that forgetful," she smiled crookedly, trying to balance out the salt in his tone. "It's only a few weeks, August. And anyway, why would I give up what I have with you?"

He'd already been gone for three weeks. She'd been desperately lonely for the first few days, but then threw herself into the pre-production meetings for Devil's Party, and onto the nightlife circuit Kline was still running for Lone Star. She'd spent hours with Clara, talking about her brand and planning for partnerships, and was excited about the prospect of building up an image that would transcend her actual life story.

To that end, Clara had introduced her to a few fame-adjacent women, like a starter kit for a social group, and Jill was trying to nurture friendship to life with them in a WhatsApp group chat and a weekly Tuesday brunch. It was maddening that August suspected she was so focused on Kline. She was focused on her plan.

With branding deals, she could cut her five-year-plan down to three. She had fantasized about a cozy life with August. They would have a place in LA, probably his place, and her apartment in New York, but also a cabin in Aspen, and someplace in the south of France. Since he was so standoffish about the idea of children, she allowed herself only one in the fantasy.

They would adopt, maybe a baby from the village where they had their home in France. It would be on a vineyard, and they would entertain artists and politicians, and the most fabulous people she could think of. Everyone would praise August's taste in how he had decorated their villa, and she would–

"It's Kline." August's voice interrupted her thoughts.

"Kline?"

"Yes. You've given up what you've had with me twice. You've dumped me twice for Kline."

"I'm a whole grown-up now! I was a child then. My brain wasn't finished developing. Now that I have a whole frontal lobe to work with, I see the error of my ways." She reached to touch his hand. "Why would I waste this–what you and I have–to jump in bed with someone who is only going to decide a week later that

I cramp his style?"

August rolled his eyes and played with his food, sulking. "You're going away with him this weekend. You probably can't wait until I'm gone so you can resume your photo ops."

There were plans to take Jack back to the San Diego Zoo, but Roland and his girlfriend, and a couple of his kids, and Clara and Kim, and Delia were going too. It was more like traveling with a circus than *going away with him*. She withdrew her hand and asked, "Have I really made you feel that way? Do you really feel like I don't want to be here with you?"

"No," he said grudgingly. "But I've seen all the pictures of you out and about with him and his son. You all look very happy together."

"We are happy together. We're friends. But, Gus—August—that's all it is. When we were in New York, I think Kline really broke my heart for the last time. Well," she sipped her wine and sat back in her chair. "I think I accepted my place with him."

"You're not in love with him anymore?"

"No. And I can say that with a clear heart. I'm not in love with him. I have a whole brain I'm working with now." She grinned, hoping to cheer him along with her humor.

He sighed. "But you have loved him before."

"Come on. Be fair." He wouldn't look at her and she frowned then said, "You love me, August, but you aren't in love with me. Are you afraid you're going to meet and fall in love with someone? Or afraid that I'm going to fall in love with someone?"

His eyes came up to meet hers, full of hurt and surprise. "I am in love with you, Jill. I've always been in love with you. I'm not worried that I'll meet someone else because I have you. I am worried that you're going to fall right back into the same pattern with Kline that you did before. You seem to have forgiven him for all he's done to you, then and now. I find that worrisome, okay?"

"August," again, she reached across the table for his hand. "Don't worry. I'm happy. I'm with you because I want to be with you. Because I love you."

"Good, I want you to be happy. You've been through enough unhappiness in your life."

"Are you really in love with me, August?" she asked seriously. "I mean passionately. I know you love me, and I know it's deep and strong. But in love? Are you in love?"

"Since the first time I saw you."

Her heart sank a little, but she smiled in spite of it. Her mother had always said that in every couple, there was one partner who loved the other more, and it was better to be the partner who loved least. She could love August as much as she did and still be happy. She was sure of it. Then again, advice from her mother was seldom worth taking "So, we'll live happily ever after? Are you going to design my future wedding gown, or Vera Wang?"

"I hope we'll live happily ever after," he said, "but I wouldn't put too much planning in for a wedding, love."

She laughed, "Oh, I forgot. You hate children and you're allergic to weddings. You wouldn't even marry me, August? Not even me?"

"I would love you, tend to you, and keep you for the rest of our days, Jill. That's the same as being married."

"If it's the same, as you say, then why not add, 'I will love, honor, and cherish you, Mrs. August Hall' to that?"

"I will happily love, honor, and cherish you, dear. And if you want to change your name to Hall, you go right ahead. I wouldn't stop you."

"But you wouldn't marry me?"

"I'd think you'd have had your fill of marriage. Once wasn't enough?"

"I wasn't really married," she said with a sad smile. "We didn't live together or tell anyone. It wasn't real. So, no babies and no wedding. Would I at least get a puppy?"

August shuddered, "You want a dog? A dog?"

"Sure, they're like cats. Just a little different. Still not a baby, but you can cuddle puppies."

"You can cuddle cats, too. Furrnando adores you."

Jill cocked an eyebrow at him. "I thought you said you're in love with me and want me to be happy?"

"I am and I do."

"If only I could get you to say that last bit in front of a couple hundred of our closest friends and a priest," she sighed. "Tell me, if all of the above is true, then when do I get something I really want?"

August looked flummoxed, paling slightly, "I thought you did have what you want. We have a safe, secure relationship and I'll take care of you forever."

"I have a safe, secure relationship with Roland, too," Jill said lightly. "And he'll take care of me for as long as I want. He's just not sleeping with me. All I'm saying," she smiled when his cheeks started to pink, "is that there are some things that are really very important to me. I have wanted to be a wife and mother since I can remember. I want that more than anything else. I'm worried that you don't want to be a husband or father, because that means I can never have my dream. And Furrnando is not a compromise when it comes to children. He has fleas."

August sighed. "My cat does not have fleas. You're more likely to have fleas than he is. What if I promise to think about it? It's never really come up before, you know? Who knows how I'll feel a few years down the road? Who knows how you will?"

"I know how I am going to feel a few years down the road," Jill said. She dropped her hands into her lap. "I'm going to want a family. In a few years, I'm going to be desperate to start a family."

"We are a family. You, me, and Furrn—"

"If you say that cat's name, I will not forgive you."

He let out another big breath. "I don't want children. Period. I like my life, our life, without the shit stains and fingerprints on everything. I grew up with more siblings than anyone should ever have to have, and I did my time helping to parent them. I moved halfway across the world to get away from my family. I like peace. I like solitude. I like being able to come and go as I please, pick up and go to work on another continent without having to arrange for care. I don't want children. Never."

Jill watched his tight face and let that sink in. For a moment, she stretched her imagination into the future, a future with August, without children, without a marriage license. Their home would be impeccable. Her wardrobe would be impeccable. They would be the dinner party capital of Hollywood, a power couple. She was imagining waking up, walking downstairs to an empty house, save for the cat–which in her imagination was hairless for some reason– who hated her. He hissed as she poured her breakfast cereal.

She would drive herself to her charity work because having retired from acting with nothing else to do, she imagined herself throwing everything she was into charity. She imagined the feeling of satisfaction that came from doing a greater good, and then imagined that she might tell herself that she was able to help hundreds of children instead of just the few she might have given birth to or adopted.

Pushing further into the future, she saw them older and traveling. They could go anywhere they liked. She liked going to events like Jack's wedding and his children's christenings. Rhiannon had grandchildren she got to play with, and as honorary auntie, there were parties and graduations. August was there, standing off to the side, drinking wine.

Maybe August died first? She was alone in that big, quiet house, with nothing but that goddamned hairless cat and the help for company. She had to hope for invitations to holiday dinners or spend them alone at the country club with the other childless, elderly widows. Now she was drinking wine. Too much of it. She tripped over the cat and fell down the stairs, then bled to death while the cat looked on, waiting for her to pass so he could eat her face.

Jill shook herself. "Wow," she said aloud, blinking. "Never."

"Never," he repeated, displeasure in his voice and his eyebrows.

She started to say, "Okay." She started to apologize for bringing it up again. She started to tell him she could learn to be all right with that. Instead, she swallowed hard. "Gus– I can't do never."

"It's not really up for negotiation. I've had a vasectomy."

She shook her head, one hand coming up to her chest. "I've been pregnant. I've been so close. I wanted those babies so badly. I had names, and a nursery, and was interviewing nannies. I had all these hopes."

"And they were dashed. I'm so sorry."

"No– They weren't dashed. They were delayed. The hope just got delayed. I fully intended, I always intended to try again. To try until my doctor said we were out of options, and then I planned to adopt. I want children, Gus."

His voice was clipped as he placed his knife and fork carefully down on either side of his plate. "I don't. So? Do you want a future with me that is grounded in reality and our love? Or do you want to chase a hope that might not ever happen?"

"Oh my god," Jill breathed, hands at her heart, rising from her seat.

He rose with her. "I'm right here in front of you, Jill! I always have been! I'm right here in front of you, and I'm solid, and I'm real, and I want a life with you."

"I don't want that life," she heard herself saying. "I don't want solitude! I've had solitude! I don't want pristine furniture or cats! I want loud and messy! I don't want to be perfect and coiffed, and refined and elegant unless I'm dressed up for a party. I want milk stains and burp rags, and a messy bun, and tiny people–my tiny people–dragging on me until I'm touched out and can't stand it anymore! And I want someone who is so in love with me that he wants twelve weddings just so he can show everyone that he's mine!"

They stood there staring at each other for several long minutes until August finally cleared his throat. "Well. Then you don't want me, and that's all there is."

Again, she started to apologize. She wanted to apologize, but she was frozen in the truth. She did want loud and messy, and passionate and complicated, but it was the first time she'd ever said it out loud. Even with Gary, after the first miscarriage, they'd had a dispassionate conversation about having children, then gotten down to the business of getting her pregnant, and when she was, it was a quiet celebration that came with a conversation about how they would navigate the questions that naturally arose. No passion. No expressions of joy.

In that moment, she realized what had been missing in her life–her own ability to be passionate and express joy. Outside of her work, she held her emotions in tight check. She had never felt free to show herself to anyone, lest they reject her. Now, her world unfurled in front of her like the coastal highway, and what she wanted was the top down, the wind in her hair, with the sun making her scalp and shoulders tingle as she wound around every new curve in the road. She had shown August her deepest wants, she had shown him who she was, and he was saying no. He only wanted her if she could play the part he wrote for her.

"When I was growing up," she said, "I always had auditions. I always had to be ready for an audition or a casting call. They could come at any time, so I always had to be perfect. I couldn't go play because I might get sweaty, or scraped up and miss an opportunity because I wasn't perfect. I missed out on everything. I missed out on all that…joy. I don't want to miss out on any more joy."

He was moving. Walking out of the room.

"Maybe you should move to middle America–some flyover state," he said icily. "I hear they have joy by the barrel."

She was frozen to the spot as he disappeared into the recesses of his house, the fucking cat following him, casting a glance over his shoulder. Jill was sure he hissed. It was several minutes before she could move again. She had fully intended to follow him back to wherever it was he had gone. She had fully intended to apologize and ask him to forgive her, to tell him that she didn't need to be married, or have children, that she could be happy with just his promise of forever and pristine white furniture, but her feet started moving in a different direction and picking up her bag, she headed out to her car.

She focused her thoughts on driving long enough to get home, then talked herself into her rental like she was shepherding a lost sheep. "Go inside," she told herself softly. "Take two aspirin because you're going to want them later. Drink some water. Go get in the shower–you don't even have to undress first. Just go get under the shower and let the water run over your head."

She followed her own directions, still numb with shock, until she was soaking wet. Then, her chin began to tremble, and she let herself cry. It felt like the sequel to the outburst she'd had in New York when she realized that Kline was willing to push work aside to get back home to Rhiannon, knowing he would never put that aside for her.

Now, she cried because August kept saying he would give her the world, but he couldn't even give her a dog.

When she had cried herself out, she stripped out of her wet clothes, washed the remnants of makeup from her face, and got out of the shower. Soon, she was in her favorite robe with a towel around her hair, looking through her freezer for one of the treats the personal chef had left there.

So she wasn't enough for Kline, and she was too much for Gary and for August. They weren't only three men in the world. There were plenty more than that out there. But more than men, she just wanted friends. Maybe Gus would still be her friend?

They'd broken up before. Granted, they'd never slept together those times, but they'd broken up before and somehow stayed friends. They could get through this. She and Kline were still friends somehow. If she could forgive Kline, eventually Gus would forgive her. Maybe he would even thank her for saving him from the messy life she wanted.

Maybe, she told herself, it was time to stop worrying about whether she could maintain Gus as a friend. Maybe it was time to focus outward on a whole new social circle. She needed girlfriends. She needed to surround herself with women. She needed to make a playdate, she decided. Rather than getting over a man by getting under another one, she was going to get over a man by getting beside a girlfriend.

She scrolled through the contact list on her phone. She had Clara, but Clara worked for her. She wanted a friend who was not also an employee. So, Rhiannon. But she wanted a friend who hadn't slept with her old boyfriend. That crossed Lola off the list as well. She didn't know her new brunch club girls well enough to know if she could trust them with hot gossip.

Finally, she came to Kim's name. She was Kline's employee, but not hers. She was also a woman who hadn't slept with Kline. More, she was a lot of fun, with a great sense of humor, an enviable style, and could definitely keep a secret from the press. The handful of times Kline and Jill had taken Jack out to be seen as a happy family, Kim had been close-by, ready to swoop in and rescue the boy if the photographers got too frisky. And she'd beaten both Jack and Jill at multiple games of Chutes and Ladders.

Kim it was, she decided and sent her a text. "This is so out of pocket, but you are the only cool, young person I know in LA. Can you help me shop to be a cool, less-young person? Would Kline loan you out for the day? My entire wardrobe either screams New Yorker, or "August's Barbie." I have to assimilate. I need a costume, and I need a character study. Help? Maybe tomorrow?"

"100%," came back just a little while later. "Okay to bring Jack, or should we wait 'til my day off?"

"How bored would Jack be? I can wait."

They texted back and forth over the next few days and somehow, that was enough. It felt normal and real, and Jill found herself laughing along when Kim guffawed at Jill's idea to start on Rodeo.

"If you want to be a cool, young person, you're on the wrong street."

"It's so much easier in NY."

"You're going to be saying NY Who? When I'm done with you."

When they finally met up, Kim took Jill to several vintage shops on the famed Melrose Avenue, home to funky shops and fresh Hollywood faces alike, where they spent hours putting together different outfits. "I want to be a stylist," Kim admitted. "But it's hard to break into."

"You're so good at this, though!" Jill was modeling a pair of high waisted navy shorts with buttons down the front, that Kim had suggested might go with an elderly Beatles t-shirt and a well-worn bike jacket they'd picked up at the shop before. She'd missed out on the Grunge movement and this outfit felt like a slick throwback somehow.

"I enjoy it," Kim said. "I love vintage, and I love how you can put different things from different eras together and make something that looks like today or even tomorrow. You know?"

"I do. I get it. And I—you know what? I'm trying new things. I've always been dressed by the same people. Do you want to dress me? I've got the Tony's coming up. I'm presenting, and I kind of…fired my stylist. I'll pay you, of course. And, I'll tell everyone who dressed me. If it goes well…"

Kim laughed outright. "I would love to dress you!"

"Excellent! You saw what I wore to the Oscars?"

"Yes."

"Not that. I don't want to wear that. I want to wear something where I feel at home in my skin, not where my skin is in everyone's home."

"Let's talk more."

Jill paid for her new finds, and then offered to buy dinner. At Kim's suggestion, they ended up in a neighborhood full of food trucks where they gorged themselves on tacos and spicy salted fruits, chatting and laughing until the street lamps came on and Kim drove them back to Jill's place.

"Thank you so much, Kim. I can't thank you enough. You truly have no idea what this meant for me today."

"Happy to do it. Listen, I'll put some ideas together and I'll get you in touch with the girl I think would be a good PA for you. I know you've got a team, but out here you have to have a PA. It's going to be really important when the movie starts up. I don't think Kline could survive without his."

"Of course. Tell Kline I said hi, and I'm stealing you."

She carried her plastic bags of clothes into the house, so different from the slick bags she was used to carrying out of Chanel and Hermes, and spent the next little while rearranging her closet to give the new clothes the spotlight. She was definitely going to cry later, she could feel it coming, but for the moment, she'd had her first really good day in Los Angeles, doing exactly what she wanted to do.

Later, she called Kline and thanked him for the loan, and explained what had happened. "I realized something," she said. "You were the first time I ever did anything that I wanted to do. You were so much more alive than I was, and I wanted that. I wanted someone as alive and electric as you were to want me because that might mean that I could come alive, too. And, I think I did. I think you brought me to life back then. Wanting you made me able to get out from under *her*. Wanting you made me strike out on my own. Wanting you led me to some of the best decisions I could have made for myself. I never thanked you. Kline, thank you."

He was silent, but she could hear him breathing. "You don't have to say anything," she told him. "I'm not trying to start anything. I just finished something, you know? It's just that I realized why you've always been stuck in my craw. Why I still love you, and why I'll always love you from the bottom of my heart. It's not because I'm a masochist," she laughed. "It's because you were the first person who ever showed me who I could be."

"Wow. I– thank you. Jilly– I felt the same way about you."

"And that's why our stomachs still flip." She said with satisfaction. "Mystery solved."

"So, what do we do about it?"

"Do? Nothing. There's nothing to do. We acknowledge that we catalyzed good things in each other, that somehow even though we were stupid kids, we're still friends, and we do this movie. And we do press. And we make the jury of the readers of People Magazine see that you are the best father in the world so that Nina backs off this custody thing. And you don't mind when Kim quits being your nanny because she's gone full-time stylist."

"That last one might kill me." He laughed. "You sound different."

"I feel different. For the first time in forever, I feel like I'm going to be okay. Whatever happens, I feel like I'll be okay."

"We're not stupid kids anymore, you know? I'm single. You're single."

"No, thank you. What's the line? I choose me. I'm choosing me. No more dating people who knew me before the nose job."

"I knew it! I knew you'd had work done!"

"My mother thought I looked like a farm girl the way it used to turn up."

"Now you look like Grace Kelly."

"Oh, you haven't seen what Kim did to me. I look like… Who do I look like? I look like Jill Parker."

"I can't wait to see her."

"I can't wait to show her to the world!"

Rhiannon Charles

Thad tapped on the door and popped his head into Rhiannon's office, "Are you going to hide in here all day?"

"I'm not hiding. I'm working. Wooorrrking. Odd concept, I know, but you should try it."

"Yeah, that looks like work." He dropped into a chair and nodded at the magazine she'd put down.

"How do these get to print so fast?" she asked, pushing it over. "Look at the 'Stars Are Just Like Us' section. They were just there! Jill was texting me all day."

"Kline Scott has Jill Parker's head spinning," Thad read aloud from the caption of a photo of the two coming out of the tea cup ride, Kline carrying Jack facing away from the camera, Jill hugged up under his other arm. "The loved-up looking couple spent the day at Disneyland with Scott's young son, Jack. Parker's effortless rocker glam is a great new look—maybe to distract from a bump?"

He laughed, "Bumpwatch! I'm The Impregnator, not Kline. She hasn't even met me yet."

"Wow," Rhiannon laughed.

"That's funny. You should write that down," he said, tapping her desk. "Fancy lunch?"

She glanced at the clock on her computer. "I'm having lunch with Jill today."

"Bumpwatch?"

She looked over her glasses at him. "Want to meet her? You can tell her your joke and see if she laughs."

"I think I'm good! I thought you were mad at her, hence the joking."

"I was. Kline's a jerk. I got over it."

Thad pursed his lips, then said, "You know you'll be seeing a lot of the jerk for sweeps."

"I know. I Carl is still crying for joy over it, and he wants to scrap everything to play off the news that Kline's in the running to be Bond. What a coup."

"Are you going to be okay?"

Rhiannon turned in her chair and looked at him. "I'm perfectly fine. Thank you for asking. Honestly, my personal feelings have absolutely no bearing on the rest of the world or this show. I wrote the part for him. The two of you work well together. It's good for everyone."

He nodded. "True enough. You know you don't have to be on the set while we're shooting his bit?"

She gave him a smirk. "Yes, I do. It's my script. I need to make sure you two don't mess it up." She sighed. "I'm fine, Thad. Really. I appreciate your concern, especially since he's your friend. You've been great, but I really am dealing just fine. I'm actually relieved that it's over. I've never been a jealous, neurotic, distrustful person, especially in a romantic relationship. He managed to cultivate the worst in me in a very short time and I'm glad to be free of it all. Okay?"

"Okay," he said, smiling. "So, does that mean you're ready to get back on the horse and start dating again?"

Rhiannon stared at him. "I'm still not going to date you. I'm not going to do you, either. The pictures will have to suffice."

"I know that. I didn't mean--say, is Jill single?"

"No. Now get out," she said, picking up her stapler and flipping it open. "Don't make me use this."

"You know I like it when you get rough," he teased, standing up.

"Out!" she cried, shooting staples in his direction. They fell short and skittered in the floor as Thad backed towards the door, so she began picking up things from her desk and whipping them at him, forcing him back until he nearly fell out her door into the hallway.

He recovered quickly and poked his head back in to crow, "You missed!" and stick his tongue at her. A second later a large paper clip hit him dead center of his forehead and ricocheted off to join the other detritus on the floor. "Ow! Hey, you could have put me eye out!"

"I wasn't aiming for your eye. Go away!"

Thad ducked another clip and pulled the door closed, then turned so quickly he nearly collided with a woman in the hall.

"Hello!" she cried, backing away, hands up in the air.

Rhiannon could just see as Thad straightened immediately and looked at first like he would chide the other person for being in the way, then recognized she wasn't crew and was going to chide her for being on set, then recognized at last who she was and shifted gears entirely. She barely held back a laugh.

"The lovely Jill Parker," he smiled, offering a hand, "I just managed to miss introducing myself at the Vanity Fair party after the Oscars. Thad James. You're here for Rhiannon?"

She shook his hand, chuckling, "Yes. Nice to meet you, though."

"Lovely to meet you, finally," he said, giving her a wink and hiking a thumb over his shoulder towards the door behind him.

"Rhiannon's office is right there. Best to announce yourself, otherwise you may find yourself pelted by office supplies. She's vicious, that one."

"Only when provoked," Jill said sweetly before walking around him, calling Rhiannon's name all the same. "Hold your fire--it's just me."

Rhiannon opened the door, giving Jill a smile. "Hey! Come in," she said, swinging the door wide before narrowing her eyes at Thad, who was watching Jill walk inside. "And you stop ogling my visitor, Pervy."

"I am just admiring her ensemble."

"I have a new stylist." Jill cooed.

"You were taking measurements. Now, beat it," Rhiannon admonished. "Elsewhere."

"Really!" Thad howled, "I'm outraged that you would say such a thing in front of," he dropped his voice into a comic purr, "such a lovely guest."

"Thirty-one," Jill said mildly, "twenty-one, thirty-two. Ballet and Pilates daily. Weight training every other day. And horrible, horrible calisthenics. Now, do be a love and go away. We're going to have girl time."

Rhiannon gave him a flat smile and closed the door before he could say another word, turning to look at Jill before chuckling and shaking her head. "Now he's dumbfounded. I can't imagine what kind of damage he'll do to himself with that little bit of information you gave him."

"Aw," Jill opened the door quickly and said to Thad's retreating figure, "I also do yoga daily. I am stronger and more flexible than you can possibly imagine," then she shut the door and turned back giggling impishly.

"Oh, now he'll be impossible to live with," Rhiannon sighed dramatically. "But damn that was fun!"

"Tell him we used to have sleepovers. That'll do him in. So? Nice office." Jill was looking around at the paper strewn room. It was tidy, but very, very full. "Can you get away to eat, or are you at the mercy of Craft Services?"

"We're going out to eat. I need to get away from this office for a little while. If we stay here, we will be interrupted constantly," Rhiannon said. "There's a great Japanese place not too far from here. Quiet. You could get sushi."

"Sounds great. I'll probably just do some tuna and green tea. I have nude scenes coming up. I can't afford the slightest bump."

"Speaking of," Rhiannon tossed the magazine. "You might want to ask Roland about that one."

"Ugh. I saw it. Kline showed me."

"I can't believe you are still speaking to him outside of work. Let me grab my bag and we'll go. I'll show you around the studio when we get back, if you like."

"Great. I have so much to tell you. This past month has been messy. That's my new word. Messy. It's my life motto."

"Because it was so tidy before?"

"I'm leaning into it, now."

Jill followed Rhiannon out to her car, and they cruised down to a neighborhood Rhiannon liked. It wasn't long before they were seated and served, actually enjoying comfortable conversation. Well, Rhiannon was enjoying listening to Jill talk, the other woman rambling like someone had dropped a quarter in her, telling her everything from how she and August had broken up to having purchased her first pair of designer sneakers. Then, just as suddenly as the rush of speech had begun, it stopped. "And that's that."

Rhiannon laughed. "That's quite a lot."

"You're telling me!"

"So, what now?"

"Now? The movie and then Kline's awards season, and then movie marketing. Since I knocked out my competition–that's you–I'm Kline's official date for everything. He went with me when I did the Tonys, and we'll go to the MTV awards together."

"Lucky you."

"And then, I'm going to meet someone, fall in love, get married in a huge celebration, and have babies." She ticked off fingers.

"Are we manifesting now? Did you just read The Secret?"

"I watched the Oprah episode about it, years ago. Does that count?"

"No more five-year plan?"

She was ticking fingers again. "Well, the movie won't wrap 'til next year. I figure it might take a year to find the love of my life, a year to get engaged, a year to plan the wedding and get married, and then get to work on being pregnant. The timeline works."

"You crack me up. You and your plans."

"But for the next little while, I'm just focused on learning how to be a Californian. I joined a brunch club and Kline and I are learning to surf."

"Are you kidding me? Surfing?"

"It's a great workout for your core!"

Rhiannon laughed. "I guess it's all new to you, huh?"

"Yes. I like what I've seen of California so far, which isn't much. I was a little homesick for New York, but I needed to make a change."

Rhiannon nodded. "I know what you mean. This is a pretty big change to make. It takes some getting used to. I'm still not sure I want to stay out here."

"Right now, I'm sure I don't. But I have that plan. When that's accomplished, I'm going to Europe. Or somewhere anonymous."

"England's nice. Calm. My family has a place there. If Thad's show ends its run, I could always go to work for the BBC. I would imagine you living in France."

"I love France," Jill sighed. "I want a villa on a vineyard, with baby goats and chickens, and Kevin Kline from French Kiss? Remember that movie? Ruined me."

"You? In rural France?"

Jill considered this and her cheeks flushed. "Okay, maybe a villa in a village five minutes from Paris."

Rhiannon nodded. "It would have to be. You're too cosmopolitan for the country squire life," she said, with a laugh. "Have you ever even been in the country?"

"Ahem–I've seen movies! I watch Lifetime! I could adjust! I just hope that it all works out sooner rather than later," Jill said, with a small smile. "I'm not getting any younger."

"You've just been working away for your whole life. It feels longer than it is."

"Working away. You know, I realized the other day that I've never even had a vacation? Seriously. I have never once had a single trip that wasn't all business. It's sad. I think it's sad. It's not like I can't afford it either. But five years, and then it all stops. Then it's a lifelong vacation unless I say otherwise."

Rhiannon smiled. "You know… Thad's back on the market and he's a great guy. Loves kids. He's got six already. You could always go out with him. He's finally ready to start a relationship with someone in his age group."

Jill looked nervous. "You're not serious, are you?"

"No," Rhiannon laughed. "You might break him."

"I would not!"

"I know, but he wouldn't do well in competition with Kline. They haven't done that for quite a few years."

"Kline's not a competition for anyone," Jill said. "He's just a friend and a coworker."

"Thad is really a good guy."

Jill nodded. "But isn't he on his third divorce?"

"Yes, but he's just unfortunate. He's not really the lothario type. He falls in love rather easily and he doesn't always make the best choices in women. You know what that's like," Rhiannon reasoned. "But he loves his kids and he's a big family man. Not a slave to his management or his career. I've never seen a scandal sheet on him more caustic than the divorce settlements. Monique left him because he's too much of a homebody for her."

"Really?" Jill smiled wistfully. "Poor guy. I do know how that is."

"Well, think about it. Have lunch with him or something. It'd do you good to know some other people anyway. Can't hurt to make new friends. Or date someone you haven't known since you were in diapers."

Jill laughed. "That's true. Aside from you, August, and Kline, I don't know anyone out here, really. Kim's introducing me to her set, and I'm hopeful about the brunch ladies, but I don't know anyone well enough to trust yet. You know? I pay people to leak stories about me to the press. I don't need people pretending to be my friends doing it for free—well, I guess they'd get paid. You know what I mean."

"I do. Totally. Well, Thad's a great friend to have," Rhiannon said, flagging down the waiter. "He's the one who helped me deal with the whole photo scandal thing, and he's been great about my recent failed relationship. Oh, and he's a terrible flirt. You love that. He did ask me if you were single."

Jill laughed. "Really?"

"Really."

"I guess I could talk to him a little. It couldn't hurt."

Rhiannon smiled and paid the bill. "Let's go back to the studio and I'll give you the tour. I'll even give you proper introductions."

Jill blushed slightly. "I shouldn't have teased him so much earlier."

"Oh yes you should have! He thrives on it." Rhiannon watched Jill as they walked out. For all her professionalism when it came to her work, she was practically adolescent in her romantic life. She wondered, and then thought that maybe Thad would be actually good for her. He was used to dealing with teenage girls.

Rick's laugh caught Rhiannon by surprise when she and Jill came walking in the door, chatting on their way. "Hello," they chimed in friendly unison.

"Ladies," Thad said, hurrying to stand. He was sucking in his gut so hard, he was going to sprain something. "Have a nice lunch?"

"Yes," Rhiannon said, offering him a bag. "I brought you a salmon spring roll. Peace offering for the paper clip."

"What'd you bring me for the staples?" Thad asked, taking the bag and peering inside.

"Jill. I talked her into having lunch with you."

Rhiannon could hardly hold back her own laughter at the little shriek that came out of her friend. Jill blushed to the roots of her hair and was at a complete loss for words. Rick was laughing again at that point. "You should let Rhi pelt you more often."

"Indeed," Thad said, smiling at Jill, who had covered her face with her hands.

"Don't get too excited. It took some convincing to get her to agree to this, and you have to do the rest of the work. I'm not your pimp," Rhiannon said, taking a step away from Jill and turning her smile to Rick. "Are we interrupting anything or are you just here for the entertainment?"

"I came by to congratulate Thad on getting his part in the indie. The director loved him. I mean loved him. Thought he was brilliant."

"Great acting, Thad!" Rhiannon grinned.

"And since Thad's got a lunch date, I need one, too," Rick said. "Rhiannon, more business than pleasure, but could I borrow you tomorrow? We've had seven writers on this thing already. I'd like to talk to you about doing some work on it."

"Are you buying?" she asked.

"Of course."

"Okay. I'm dying for a pizza."

"Pizza it is," Rick grinned. "I know a great hole in the wall where no one will find us."

Thad ribbed, "Just keep her in her clothes if there are photographers nearby."

"I think I'll be okay," Rhiannon shot back. "No one seems to recognize me with my clothes on."

"Maybe if you wore them out more," He reached over and pinched her cheek.

She smirked at him and turned to Jill, "See? He's not very creative, but he looks good in a suit."

"Sounds like half of Hollywood."

Rhiannon sighed. "Yeah. Sad, really. Ah well, I'll give you the tour while I'm busy ignoring him."

"Or I could give her the tour and save you the trouble of ignoring me," Thad grinned, stepping forward to Jill, "You've already suffered through over an hour of her. I'll rescue you from boredom. Come on, I'll show you my dressing room first."

"Thad, behave yourself and stop treating her like one of your wives. She's a grown up."

"Ouch," Thad pouted. "All my wives are of age."

They started off, Jill laughing, and Rick looked confused. "I thought she was dating August Hall?"

"Long story," Rhiannon said. "But I think Thad's really more up her alley."

"He's not divorced yet, you know?"

"I know, and so does she. That's nearly cleared up. He's gotten to be an expert at handling that situation, sadly enough. Besides, it's just lunch. Who knows?"

"I like Thad," Rick said uncertainly. "I wouldn't want to see him get hurt again."

"I like him, too. I think they could be good for each other. They want the same things out of life."

"Oh really?"

"Fame, fortune, and family."

Rick nodded. "Isn't that what we all want?"

Rhiannon shrugged. "To some degree, I suppose."

"Fame and fortune is why we do what we do."

"I would modify that to success and fortune is the reason I do what I do. I can do without the fame part."

"Hm. I suppose I can too. Otherwise, I'd be doing it a bit differently."

Rhiannon smiled. "You're doing it right. All the benefits without all the hassle. You'll be able to retire to England in a few years and live a stable, quiet life. That's success."

"That's exactly right." He smiled back. "Well, I should get going. I've got another meeting in an hour, but I'll see you for lunch tomorrow."

Rhiannon nodded and smiled. "I'm looking forward to it."

"As am I," he said, his own smile lingering for a moment longer before he walked out.

Rhiannon went in the opposite direction to her office and returned to work, punching up a dialogue for one of the shows in the June sweeps story arc. An hour passed before there was a light tapping at her door and Jill walked in, a light blush still high on her cheeks and a wide grin on her face.

"Enjoy the tour?"

"I did, actually," she grinned.

"Thad ask you out?"

Jill nodded. "For Friday night. I said okay. He's married. Messy. It's perfect, huh?"

"He's separated. A few signed documents short of divorced, actually."

"Still messy. Listen, thank you. I've got to go. I need to meet Roland and find out what I'm supposed to be doing next week."

"Yeah, well, don't let him try and schedule you too much if this thing with Thad has even the slightest potential."

"We have an agreement. I have no more than four nights 'on' a week. The rest are mine. I'm not quite as good a puppet as Kline. It's funny—I'm pretty aggressive career-wise. I need to get more aggressive in my personal life. Take the bull by the horns instead of still trying to please my dead mother."

"Don't let Thad hear you say that. He'll just make horn jokes. Well, that's good. Maybe if Kline had been willing to say no and mean it, things wouldn't have gone as badly as they did," Rhiannon said, seriously. "Roland didn't approve of me, so I got shuffled out and Kline didn't do much to keep that from happening. That guy is really sneaky. Stand your ground, Jill."

Jill nodded. "I have a five-year plan. No more, but no less. I've set my terms for how to make it happen and he's willing to make it happen within my bounds because he gets a nice fee. I won't let him force me into anything uncomfortable."

Rhiannon smiled. "Good for you. Business savvy all the way."

"Always." Jill said, with a smile. "Well, I'm off. Thanks for lunch."

"Any time. You'll have to let me know how your date goes."

"I want to know about yours!"

"If it happens."

"Why shouldn't it?"

"Why should it? Listen, your motto is messy, not mine. Mine is clean and uncomplicated."

"Good luck with that out here!"

Lunch with Rick had turned into a job offer that she accepted immediately, and then into dinner as they worked through the details, and she found herself liking him more and more. She also found him in her office more and more until she felt like she had to remind him that she was at work for Simon Says, not for Circle Sky—yet. He had taken it with good humor and said, "Tell you what? Have dinner with me and I'll stay out of your office. I just keep making excuses to see you. Give me a dinner date and we'll call it even."

"A dinner *date*?"

"A date. Yes. A social engagement," he said, putting on a voice. "A date. You, me, tomorrow night and no work talk. Sound good?"

It did sound good, and she agreed just as she was being called out to the set, and she found herself laughing for no reason. A date with Rick. The most normal man she'd met in a while. That sounded really good. And maybe if he'd taken her out that night, right then, maybe it would have been good, but she had time to think about it and by the time she picked up a voice message from Rick the next morning, telling her that he'd made a reservation at a nice Italian place for dinner and he'd pick her up around seven, she knew what she had to do.

Reservations at an Italian place sounded great, but she wondered which 'nice' restaurant he'd chosen. After the initial thrill at the realization Rick had asked her on a date, Rhiannon had been analyzing the possible motives and regretting the fact that she felt the need to do that. He seemed like a nice guy, but she didn't really know him. Thad's friend, but Kline's friend, too. He was well aware of the very recent scandal and had, for all intents and purposes, seen her naked already. Plus, there was no telling what Kline might have said about her.

Part of her said that it was true that she didn't really know him, but at the same time, she'd never get to know him if she didn't take a chance. Her experience with Kline had made her gun-shy, surely, but was she really going to allow one bad relationship to put a moratorium on her social life?

Still, there was a nagging doubt. She tapped her phone against her chin, considering how to handle it. They were working together now and if things didn't go well personally, she was contractually bound to suffer through however many weeks of script development and shooting it took to complete the film. Technically, he was her boss because he was the producer who had taken her on for the project.

Rhiannon shook her head. She'd turned Thad down time and again for the very same reasons. It wasn't ever that he wasn't charming or attractive, but he was her boss, and he was still legally married, even if he and Monique were already on the outs before he started asking. Rhiannon didn't want to get into the middle of all of that, but she also didn't want to compromise her work relationships or her reputation. She didn't sleep her way to success and she didn't want anyone to believe that she had. It was that simple.

Rhiannon pulled her phone open and scrolled through the list of calls to get Rick's cell number, pressing the call button when she found it.

It rang three times and she was getting ready to leave a message when he answered, "Hello? Rhiannon?"

"Hi, Rick. Yes, it's me," she confirmed. There was music in the background and the sound of splashing water. "Did I call at a bad time?"

"No, but can you hang on for a minute? I need to go inside."

"Sure." She waited and listened to the noise fade, the sound of a door opening and closing, sealing it out completely.

"That's better. Sorry about that," he said, and she could hear the smile in his voice. "I take it you got my message?"

"Mmhm."

"And is Italian alright?"

"Yes, but-" Rhiannon started to speak, but a female voice in the background interrupted.

"Rick? You're not going to work all day, are you?" she asked, with a slightly teasing tone. "Come into the pool. The water's warm."

There was a shuffling sound and Rhiannon knew he'd covered the phone somehow, but she heard his response distantly, "I'll be there in a minute."

The woman said something else that she couldn't make out and then Rick's voice was clear on the line again, "Sorry about that."

"I guess I did call at a bad time," Rhiannon said.

"Not really. Just lunch. My assistant just jumped in the pool."

His assistant? She'd seen his assistant, Amy. Any nerves she had about canceling the date disappeared. "Ah. Well, I just wanted to tell you that I'm not going to be able to make it for dinner tonight."

"No?" He sounded disappointed. "Okay. Something come up? Some other time then?"

Rhiannon let out a breath. "Actually, no. It's- We're going to be working together and I hope you'll understand that I keep my professional relationships strictly professional. I'm just uncomfortable seeing a coworker, or in this case, a superior, socially."

Rick was silent for a moment then said, "Okay. I respect that."

"I'm sorry, I should have said so when you asked, but we've been lunching and I didn't really think of it as a date right off," she explained. "I just don't want things to get complicated."

"Right," his tone had changed completely, but he was still friendly. "I understand, and I do respect that. Then, I guess I'll see you at the next writers' meeting."

"Yes," she said, pausing briefly. "I'll see you then."

Kline Scott

Jill met Kline for coffee at one of the more popular Starbucks, where they had planned to start an afternoon of shopping. She was giddy when she arrived, chattering a mile a minute on her cell phone until she walked inside and saw him, then waved and hung up, hugging him warmly, wearing a huge grin. While they stood in line for their coffees, she burbled away about the beautiful weather, the prospect of a new house, and how wonderful her new life was.

Kline watched her with a mix of amusement and amazement, asking when he got the chance, "What's gotten into you? You're…happy."

"Oh, Kline," she sighed, "I'm figuring it all out! I'm getting my shit together! And, I had the best date I've ever had in my life last night. I mean, it was perfect. And then this morning there were roses and forget-me-nots and daisies--truckloads of them! I'm just—yeah, happy."

He cocked an eyebrow. "We had a date last night? Why don't I remember that?"

She gave a snort. "You'd remember. Trust me."

"Well, if it was the best date of your life--"

"My, when did you get so full of yourself?" she half teased, rolling her eyes. "I'm being very serious. I met someone wonderful and had the best night. Can we not make it about you, please?"

Kline frowned slightly, "What about us?"

"What about us? We're pretend, remember? You had your shot. I moved on."

"Cooold! You moved on to Gus," he shuddered. "Wait--you broke up with Gus. Who'd you go out with?"

"Technically, I think August dumped me--"

"Blah blah blah. Who?"

Jill grinned. "You're not going to believe this. Rhiannon introduced me to Thad James. He asked me out, so I went. I really didn't expect anything. It took us a while to actually meet up because of his kids' schedules, but when we did--sparks! Immediate sparks. And while we were trying to meet up, we spent hours on facetime. It was like being a teenager again," she laughed. "Or for the first time, actually, since I wasn't a normal teenager. We just talked and talked for hours. I really didn't expect to have an immediate connection, but he was just insanely perfect. It was so comfortable! We had this picnic on the beach and he brought--"

"Thad?" Kline interrupted, eyebrows nearly into his hairline. "You went out with Thad? Rhiannon hooked you up with him? He's married, Jill!"

"Shhh," she scowled at him as people looked up at them. Until then, their conversation had taken place with the two of them huddled and cuddled together in line, but Kline had just straightened and nearly shouted. They were at the register then, so he ordered for them while she smiled and hugged his waist. After picking up their drinks, they took a seat in a corner by the window where they could have some privacy, but still be visible.

"He's married," Kline hissed when he could.

"He's separated."

"That's still married."

"No, it isn't. The divorce is in the details, and it won't be long until it's finalized," she insisted, sipping her drink.

"You do realize this is his third marriage that's gone to hell, right?"

"Yes. I know all about it. He was very open and upfront

about it all," Jill sighed, coming over all dreamy again. "We just talked for hours. I fell asleep on the phone talking to him! I woke up and he was snoring!"

"Jill? Earth to Jill. Snap out of it! Thad's not right for you. Don't do this to yourself because you'll only end up hurt. I know him. I know all three of his wives!"

She tilted her head slightly, "How do you know who's right for me? You barely know me anymore. I don't try to tell you who's right for you to date."

"I'm not dating anyone."

"Who's fault is that?"

He gaped at her. "Ouch."

"Well? It's certainly not my fault," she said, with a shrug. "And you don't always know what's best for me."

"I know him. I'm telling you it's a bad idea. He's been trying to get into Rhiannon's smalls since she started working there. What does that say for him?"

"About the same thing it says for you," Jill snapped, narrowing her eyes. "Now stop it. I'm seeing him again tonight and I'm not going to let you ruin it."

"Tonight? Roland planned for us to hit the party at Westin's."

"Roland planned for *you* to hit the party at Westin's. I told him I wasn't going. I have other plans."

"You're my date, Jill," Kline said incredulously.

"No, I'm not. I told Roland last week that I wasn't going to that. I'm booked up with you next week and I wasn't going to spend one of my last free weekends watching the who's-who list snort coke at a stupid party."

"Well, that's just great. What am I supposed to do then? Go alone?"

"Or don't go, Kline," Jill sighed. "You can afford to say no once in a while. You're the celebrity, you know, not Roland. He works for you, not the other way around."

"He makes me the celebrity."

"Not true," Jill shook her head. "You're a great talent. You were blessed with perfection in the gene pool. You've got a sexy voice. Put all that together and that is why you're a celebrity. You'd be A-list if you represented yourself. You're like the genius kid in the class who hires a tutor just to get that extra tenth of a point."

"Roland's done alright for me," Kline defended. "If he wasn't so good, why did you hire him?"

"I never said he wasn't good at what he does. He is. I think he's the best at what he does, but just because he tells you to do something doesn't mean you have to jump and do it. I hired him because he's slick and he can get me what I want, but I make sure it's all on my terms. I think the problem is that you don't have terms."

Kline looked away, cheeks flushed with upset. He refused to look back even when Jill took his hands in hers. "Kline," she said softly. "Kline, look at me."

He huffed but rolled his eyes back to her. "You deserve a break, too. More than a night a week at home with Jack? Don't you want that?"

"Of course I do!"

"Well, is it really smart to be doing all the parties in your legal situation right now? Don't go tonight. Stay home and play with your kid."

"What about the publicity build for the movie?"

"There is already tons of it and we haven't even started filming. Remember bumpwatch? I'm apparently pregnant by you. The work will ultimately speak for itself. When the time comes, we'll make all the appearances and do all the interviews and collect our awards and go home, but until then, take care of real life. That's what I plan to do."

"With Thad? You think that's real life?"

Jill just looked at him, real hurt creeping into her eyes. "You know, I'm happy for you when good things happen, Kline. I didn't say I was moving in with, marrying, or falling in love with the guy. I said I had the best date of my life. I said I was happy. Can you not try to ruin that?"

"I'm not trying to ruin it. I just don't want to see you get hurt again," he said, seriously, as he gently rubbed the backs of her fingers. "You've been hurt enough."

"For once I'm not worried about getting hurt. I just want to live without worrying. If I make a mess out of it, I'll clean it up. I thought I'd die when you left, but I didn't. If that didn't kill me, I don't know what would."

Kline sighed and sat back, gently taking his hands away from her and reaching for his drink. "I'm sorry. I won't bring it up again. I'm glad you're happy."

They were silent for a few minutes then she said, "I've been working out more. For the nude scenes. I'm nervous about those."

He nodded. "I'm on two-a-days. I hired Luke Zocchi. He's killing me."

She smiled crookedly. "I can see a difference in how your shirts are fitting. You should let me do an inspection before we start shooting. Just so I'm not overwhelmed by the sight of you."

"You've seen it all before, love."

"True. Okay. Maybe I was just trying to get you naked." She winked.

"Don't tease me. It's not nice."

"Who said I was teasing? I really wanted to see you naked," Jill laughed. "I missed all your pool pictures with Rhiannon."

"Yes, one of the more stellar moments in our relationship," he sighed. "I'm sure they wouldn't be difficult to dig up. Apparently, we're still a big hit on the internet. You really haven't seen them?"

Jill shook her head, "No. I didn't look. It seemed…intrusive. Just because the pictures were out there didn't mean I needed to put my eyes on them, you know? Did you want me to see them?"

"Hell no! I never would have put all of that out there."

"I wouldn't have wanted you looking if the photos had been mine. It's like the interview Gary gave about our marriage.

I never would have given an interview like that. I'm horrified that people read those things, and so much of it was out of context or just lies… That's how I feel about the photos. I'm not going to look at something you wouldn't just show me. You know?"

He thought about that, dropping his chin into his hand. "Thank you."

"You're welcome. So? Are you going to show me?"

She was trying to tease him back into a good humor, so he gave her a smile. "No more free shows."

She rummaged around in her bag for a moment, then came up with two one-dollar bills and a cough drop, which she pushed over to him, "Really, I'd insist on paying anyway. Does this about cover it?"

"Brat," Kline snorted, rising. He didn't want to be in a good humor. He wanted to sulk. He didn't want her dating Thad. He wasn't sure he wanted her dating anyone. Gus hadn't bothered him, but what was Gus anyway? If he'd wanted to steal her from Gus, he knew exactly how to do it, and he was absolutely certain he could have stolen her from that dusty old producer. Thad was something different. That wasn't right for her.

He reached for her hand and said, "Come on. Shopping then home. You have a date."

Jill looked rebuffed but went with him. He made sure he was telegraphing waves of angst in her direction, coming on as brooding and silent the rest of the afternoon. In return, she radiated guilt and uncertainty as she tried vainly to lighten his mood. Good. She should feel guilty for dating Thad.

Before dropping her back at her car, he looked at her seriously. "I'm sorry I'm so– I'm sorry I'm so out of sorts. I really don't want you to get hurt, Jill. Be careful with Thad."

"Okay," she nodded.

"Promise?" He took her chin between his fingers, frowning a little.

"I promise."

"I couldn't stand it otherwise." He leaned over and kissed

her lips softly. "Be good."

She snorted at him, breaking the spell he was trying to cast, and opened the car door. "Really?! Really? You're going to try that on me? Save that for the cameras, Kline. And don't worry, even if I do become a notch in his belt, yours is still practically perforated with how many times you've convinced me we belonged together. We're friends," she said, slamming the door. "Act like a friend."

It was such a psychological slap, he was seeing stars. "We are friends! I just don't want you to get hurt!"

"You don't know what you want!"

"That's not true! I know exactly what I want—I just don't think it exists."

She waited, hands on her hips, looking down at him. He was half wishing he'd left the top up on the car. "Can I come inside?"

"No. I'm not taking a chance on you trying to grope me, but if you want to tell me what you want, I'm listening." Now she crossed her arms.

Kline shifted into park and turned off the ignition. Both hands on the steering wheel, he stared straight ahead into Jill's driveway. What did he want? "I want someone who knows me as Scott Kline, but treats me like Kline Scott."

"Oh." The syllable was a long time coming and he'd wondered if she'd walked away, but he was too afraid to turn his head to see. The sound of the car door opening finally made him look. Jill was sitting back down next to him. "That's heavy," she said.

"But you understand?"

"You want someone who is in as much awe of you as a fan would be, who will gas you up non-stop, but also someone who knows when to pump the brakes and remind you that your stuff does stink?"

"Yeah," he said. "I thought maybe Rhiannon would be that. You know? She's really sharp-witted and sassy, but she's had my poster on her wall so to speak."

"The thing is, though, it can't all be about you. What were

you offering her? Other than the pleasure of your company, I mean. How were you making her life better? Where were you adding value to her world?"

"What the fuck have you been reading? Adding value?"

"My nightstand is a mountain of self-help books focusing on becoming whole as a person before trying to be someone's better half."

"That's ghastly."

"And yet, you're the one crying in my driveway."

"I'm not crying!"

"You're like four seconds from it. Listen, you've got to change how you're looking at relationships. Women don't just exist to be your emotional fluffers. We don't just exist to solve the problem of your loneliness."

He hesitated then said, "I thought Rhiannon had it all together and we'd work because she was so solid. I didn't think she needed anything from me, other than just the pleasure of my company."

"You're so gross," Jill laughed. "That's so selfish."

She got out of the car again. "What you want might exist, but it shouldn't." She said, closing the door once more. "You should look for someone who loves you for Scott Kline and accepts that Kline Scott rides piggyback on that man."

"And you're sure you're out of the running?"

"I'm sure that you will never forgive me for knowing you before you got your teeth fixed."

"I do love you, you know," he called. She was walking away now, but she looked back over her shoulder and flashed him one of those smiles that sent his stomach careening.

"I know."

He sat there a moment longer, making sure she got in the door, then he started to laugh. He knew exactly who loved him for Scott Kline and accepted Kline Scott as part and parcel of the deal. All he had to do was get her to see it.

<h1 style="text-align:center">Chapter 7</h1>

Jill Parker

Jill answered the door to Thad, barefoot in a little black slip dress, a similarly small white apron tied around her waist, hair piled in a messy twist. "Hi," she smiled, "come on in. Thank you for the flowers!" He'd been sending fresh bouquets every few days since their first date–different ones every time.

"You're very welcome," he said, stepping inside and bending to kiss her cheek. "You look smashing."

"Thanks, so do you," she said, blushing slightly as he shrugged out his jacket to reveal a light blue, button front shirt that was cut to fit him perfectly. He'd chosen to wear jeans and looking at her dress, he grinned sheepishly. "I think I may be a bit underdressed."

"Not at all. I'm comfortable. Hopefully you're comfortable. No one's around to judge." She took his jacket and hung it in the front closet, then led him back to the dining nook in the kitchen. "I thought we'd eat in here," she said. "It's cozier. Is that all right?"

"Fine by me." He took the seat she indicated and smiled as she brought over a glass of wine.

"I'm off bread completely for now," Jill told him, next placing a little linen wrapped basket on the table. "But I love the smell of fresh baked bread, so there's some for you. Sweet butter is in the little blue thing there. Just help yourself. I won't be a minute with the rest."

They started with crisp salads, then moved on to broiled fish, steamed vegetables and tiny crustless quiches. For dessert she fed him a homemade cheesecake. Along with the food came another round of comfortable conversation. Neither was as nervous this time, and both were just eager to learn more about the other.

Thad cleared the table for her and then helped do the dishes before following her out into her back yard with another glass of wine. They sat on the patio sectional by the pool, taking in the night air and the sound of cicadas until their conversation drifted into a peaceful silence. Jill considered him, her feet in his lap as he lazily stroked her ankles. He'd been over several times since their first date, short visits, stealing time between obligations. Each time careful with her virtue, not wanting to start something he had to stop.

He'd said something about taking it slow, or slower than he usually did. "Trying to learn from past mistakes, you know? Maybe I'll try to get to know you before I try to marry you."

"The last thing I want to be is a mistake!" She had agreed, laughing at his self-effacing humor, but tonight felt different. His shirt sleeves were rolled up to the middle of his strong, tanned forearms. A silver Tag Heuer, the only hint of wealth about him, glinted at his wrist. She kept glancing at his broad hands and tidy fingernails, wondering how they would feel scratching down her back, and she squirmed at the thought of him gripping her thighs.

Her eyes darted back to the watch, then his sleeves, then up the line of his arm to meet his curious smile. His eyes were twinkling, a blue that matched his oxford shirt exactly, and he seemed to be waiting for something.

She cleared her throat. "Are you being a gentleman again tonight?"

"Seems that way so far," he said, but his voice was warm and husky.

She barely suppressed the nervous laugh bubbling up inside her, humming acknowledgement instead of begging him to take her, like the voice in the back of her head demanded. Biting her lips together, she wished she could just make a move, just kiss the man, but nothing in her past experience would let her move the few inches to close that gap between them.

"Is that all right?" His long fingers grazed the inside of her ankle and she gasped, electrified by the light touch. "Or?" His voice was a thrilling question as he leaned towards her, broad shoulders and biceps flexing against the seams of his shirt, his fingers still rubbing gentle circles along the hollow of her ankle, his eyes flashing with heat. "Would you rather I wasn't being such a gentleman?"

She paused again, then bit her lips together, blushing, her voice low. "You know, there's no way for me to answer that honestly without my not being ladylike. Would you rather not be such a gentleman? Because you're a guest in my home, so it's very important to me that you be comfortable." Her mouth felt dry, and blood was pounding in her ears. If he said he was playing the long game, she thought she might combust.

A smile played along the corners of his lips, and he stretched slightly to press them to hers, then gently drew her legs further across his lap so he could lean deeper into the kiss. He cradled her in his arms as she breathed into the soft pressure of his lips, matching his intensity as her skin shivered to life with gooseflesh. When his tongue parted her teeth, she allowed herself to stroke her fingers through his thick hair, gathering courage to let her fingertips slide down his throat, knowing that he was about to be her undoing.

He pulled back a little and kissed her cheek. "Is this okay?" he asked, his breath warm against her skin.

"Very much" she whispered.

He chuckled thickly and caught her mouth in another searching kiss, his hands slipping into her hair and sending shivers down her spine. Every touch seemed to stir response and soon Jill was sighing into his mouth as he wrapped his arms further around her and pulled her close.

"Do you keep overnight guests," he asked close to her ear, moments later.

"I put on fresh sheets," she heard herself answering. "I guess I was hoping I would."

Thad stood up, lifting her easily in his arms. "I'd love to see them," he said, kissing her again as he carried her to the door and into the house. With murmured direction from Jill, he soon had her in the bedroom, stretched across the cool sheets.

He leaned over her, resting his weight on one forearm as he stroked her face with his free hand. "You are the most beautiful thing I've ever seen, and I can't believe I'm here with you right now."

Delight bubbled up from her core and she let out a little laugh, she couldn't help it. He laughed back, his smile a sickle of pleasure that cut through all of her insecurities. When he ran his hand down her throat, sliding the flat of it over her sternum to fan out at the curve of her hip, Jill shivered and swallowed. When he teased his fingertips over the edge of her satin dress, then up under it to find the edge of her panties, she gasped into the kiss he laid against her lips.

"Good?" He murmured, easing the fabric aside to stroke her hidden cleft.

She could barely breathe, only managing a jagged, "Yes," in response.

"Good girl," he purred, sparking something in her soul that she had never felt before, and she yielded her body up to him like an offering to some obscure Australian god of desire, the icon of her new religion. She was too far gone to laugh at herself, so she just let Thad carry her out of her mind on waves and waves of pleasure.

When she woke later, she was still in his arms, his body curving around hers protectively and she smiled to herself. She couldn't even begin to compare what they'd just done with anything else she'd ever experienced. Not even August, who was a most effective and attentive lover. Thad had touched places in her that she hadn't even known existed, not least of all in her heart. Just the way he looked at her, seeing her as a whole, fully formed woman–it was amazing.

"Hi," he said softly, sensing her wakefulness. "How're you doing?"

"You're awake," she said.

"I never went to sleep."

"Oh!" She chuckled. "I did."

"No, babe, I think what you did was more like passing out." She could hear the grin in his voice. "I thought I'd broken you."

"Broken, fixed. Same thing." She shifted a little to face him. "Can you stay? Do you want to stay?"

"I can and I do," he said, leaning in to kiss her. "There is no place I would rather be at this moment."

"Oh good," she sighed. "I was afraid you wouldn't."

"I still respect you," he teased. "Do you still respect me?"

Jill gave a throaty laugh. "Thad, I have a whole new level of respect for you. Whole new level."

He laughed, too. "That's good to know," he said, cuddling her closer. "Just think, that was only our first time together. It gets better."

"Wow... That thought is almost frightening. Almost."

"I told you. Very big stinger." He was calling back to an earlier conversation and she loved it.

Jill burst out laughing at that, burying her face in his shoulder. They both giggled until they fell into a comfortable silence. "I've never had sex outside of a relationship before," Jill said after a while. "I'm not sure how this works. What does this mean? How does this work?"

"It works just fine from what I can tell," he teased.

"Well, yes, but this is new territory for me."

"There's nothing to worry over, love. It's an excellent beginning to what will hopefully be a long and happy relationship," he said, rubbing her arm. "When we're ready, that is."

Some of the helium eked out of her floating spirits, but Jill checked herself that he was still technically married. He technically couldn't be involved on that count alone. Besides, she'd agreed with him about taking things slowly. *'I think that word does not mean what you think it means,'* she said to herself as she settled back against his chest. "I like long and happy. And hopefully. I like hopefully."

"Hopefully is very good," he agreed. They settled for a bit before he asked, "Why did you think I wouldn't want to stay?"

"I don't know," Jill said after thinking for a moment. "Well, I did just invite you over for dinner, so I don't know what kind of timeline you had planned. I didn't know if you'd even be available to stay. Or want to."

"There is absolutely no way for me to respond to that without not being a gentleman," Thad chuckled, echoing her words from earlier. "If I say that I made certain I was free for however long 'dinner' took, does that sound presumptuous?"

"Yes," Jill laughed. "It does. But then I put fresh sheets on the bed, so there you go."

"Prepared for anything. I like that in a woman," he said, kissing the top of her head. "You needn't worry about me doing a runner on you. I'd be a fool to want to make a fast getaway."

"Kline was really upset when I told him that I was seeing you. He seemed to think you'd break my heart or something. I guess I thought doing 'a runner' might be the usual or something."

Thad was quiet for a moment. "I'm not that kind of man, Jill," he said seriously. "I could say a few things about Kline, but he's my friend so I won't. Not that it would be any news to you. You know what he's like." He sighed. "I have no intention of breaking your heart. In fact, I think I can honestly say you're going to have trouble getting rid of me."

"Really?" she said, surprise and a smile in her voice.

"Really. Don't sound so surprised."

She sighed. "I wish I weren't. You know, my husband and I didn't live together. Long story, but he didn't stay the night much and didn't like it when I stayed at his place. He thought the secret to a lasting marriage was his and her condos. Apparently, you're pretty familiar with my history with Kline, so you can imagine how that went. My only other experience has been with someone who fell immediately asleep and snored solid for at least six hours. You're a very nice surprise."

Thad chuckled. "You have no idea, Beauty," he said, shifting slightly to roll her over in one easy motion. "I'm full of surprises."

When Thad left in the mid-afternoon Sunday, Jill phoned Rhiannon again, this time from where she was floating around her swimming pool. Rhiannon answered and Jill sang a hello at her, "I owe you big time," she grinned, "name what you want, and I'll get it for you."

"Things going that well with Thad?" Rhi asked.

"Better. The best!"

Rhiannon laughed. "Good. I'm really happy for you!"

"Oh, Rhi…he is really fantastic." She lowered her voice conspiratorially, "I slept with him."

"Just now?!" Rhiannon cried. "How was he? I have to admit, I've always been curious."

"He's like a monsoon. He's a tidal wave. A tsunami. He's a force of nature. There just aren't words to describe him. I mean, he's gentle and rough, and demanding and attentive, and forceful and considerate. He's just," Jill laughed, "Okay, he's what every romance novelist has tried to write as the perfect lover. He even spent the whole night."

"Wow. Now I am duly impressed. I may have to stop picking on him."

"Don't do that. He loves being picked on. We actually talked a lot about you at dinner. He credits you with saving the show and his career. Said you were one of his best friends. He's very excited about working with you on the indie. Oh, how'd things go with Rick?"

"They, uh, didn't," Rhiannon said, clearing her throat. "So, Thad really said all those things about me? Job security is a wonderful thing."

"What happened?" Jill asked, suddenly alert.

"Nothing. He asked me to dinner and I accepted, but then I thought better of it and called it off. So, nothing happened."

"Because of work?"

"You know me too well."

"Do you want Thad back?"

"What?"

"Well, I mean, I wouldn't give him back, but I thought I'd offer."

"You really are strange, you know that? We aren't twelve, Jill. Besides, I gave him to you."

Jill laughed. "You love me because I'm strange. And you still work with him, so you wouldn't put him to proper use anyway. Is it possible to be in love with someone this soon? After just a handful of dates and phone calls? No. It is not. Forget I said that. He's a very nice boy." Rhiannon was laughing so Jill went on, "I'd better go put on some clothes. Kline's coming over with Roland and I'm floating around my pool in a serious stage of undress."

"Oh. Kline's very good at that," Rhiannon said, with a trace of snark. "Have fun. Just stay away from the diving board."

"And the lawn chair, and the shrubbery, and the hot tub, and the--"

"Enough!" Rhiannon interrupted with a shriek of laughter. "I saw the pictures, too!"

"I haven't actually seen the pictures," Jill said, still giggling.

"I think you may be the only person in the world who hasn't. They're all over the internet. Whatever lawsuit Kline claimed to have filed didn't do any good at all," Rhiannon said, an edge returning to her voice. "I swear, I almost believe that Roland orchestrated that whole thing. I wouldn't be surprised if he paid the photographer to camp out there."

"He's sneaky, but I don't think he'd stoop that low," Jill said, doubtfully.

"I'm not so sure," Rhiannon sighed. "So much for fading to black."

"What?"

"That's what Kline told me I would do when I broke up with him. Fade to black. The reporters are only interested in him. Not me. That may be true, but other people are plenty interested. I've had to change my email address at work three times and I'm looking to move out of this bungalow. Too many people know where it is. I'm getting a rottweiler."

"It's that bad?"

"Well, it's not just going away. I'm fortunate that I don't get recognized everywhere I go. Mostly. There have been a few times. I can't even consider men for anything at this point. If they look at me with anything more than passing interest, I'm sure they're just picturing me naked."

Jill was quiet for a moment, her hand trailing in the warm water. "I didn't know it was still like that. Things like this usually pass quickly in the face of a new scandal," she paused, considering. "Is that why you called off your date with Rick? You're worried about his reasoning?"

"The thought did cross my mind. I know he saw the pictures and he's one of Kline's close friends. Who knows what Kline had to say about me, especially since I slept with him on the first date," Rhiannon said, with another sigh. "Mostly it was because he's hired me to work the script for this film. I don't want to go into a production environment dating the executive producer. Then it's not about my work, it's about who I fucked to get it--even if that's not the case. Plus, if I start dating him and things don't work out, it becomes this uncomfortable, tense situation and I'm just not willing to deal with anymore of that at the moment."

"I understand," Jill said, paddling towards the steps. "He seems nice, though, and I thought you liked him?"

"I do like him, and he does seem nice, but how can I really be sure that he's not just playing me? I can't, and rather than be disappointed, I'm just not going to let it go there with him. We can be colleagues and friends. That's good enough."

"That's probably for the best," Jill agreed. "At least for now.

Caution is good, right? I mean, I'm cautiously optimistic about Thad and we're just keeping it casual for the moment."

"Well, if you get a tsunami when it's just casual, I can't imagine what you'll get when it's serious," Rhiannon said, the humor returning.

"I can't either, but I can't wait to find out!"

"I bet. Listen, thanks for the chat. I'll let you go get ready for the weasel patrol."

"Rhi!"

"What? I think I'm allowed. Anyway, congrats on your burgeoning 'casual' love affair with Thad."

At that, Jill squealed, and Rhiannon could almost hear the blush and smile on her face. "Thank you! Really. I'll call you later! Bye!"

Rhiannon said goodbye and Jill hung up, grabbing a towel to wrap around her before she bounced her way back into the house to get dressed.

Kline Scott

Kline was early to the Simon Says set for his guest starring sweeps role and was happy to be met with the excited buzzing of the crew and interns. All of them were anxious and happy, getting ready for his grand arrival. The girls on the set were in a mad frenzy, so he went to find the one he knew would be calm as the day.

"Hey," he called, poking his head in Rhiannon's office a little surprised to see Thad sitting there, "What's up?"

"You're on time!" Rhiannon gasped playfully. "Great, now I suppose the earth is going to tilt off its axis."

"No, no, no," Thad shook his head, "but one of the whores of the Apocalypse is following close behind him."

"Horses, Thad, horses of the Apocalypse."

"This is Kline we're talking about," he said grinning.

Kline asked, "Where's the script?"

Rhiannon pushed over a copy. "Kline is a former high

school friend whom you used to torment. He's become a very successful stand-up comedian, known for his sharp barbs. Since Thad has been struggling to break into stand-up, he thinks Kline is going to help him. Instead, it's a set-up for Kline to get back at Thad for all his bullying in high school. Thad and Kelsey have a very nice scene at the end with a big kiss. No garlic for the kissing this time, huh?"

"I thought I'd just be reprising my character from Knock," Kline said, flipping through the pages.

"He's too likable," Rhiannon smiled. "I didn't want you to sprain anything getting into character."

He made a sour face as Thad said, "Kline gets to abuse me? Damn. He'll enjoy that."

"People like for you to be their clown. This will go over really well," Rhiannon explained.

He frowned a little. "I was hoping I'd get to abuse him. Oh well."

"That's good because—come in?" There was a knock at the door followed by a delivery man. "I have a delivery for Rhiannon Charles."

"That's me."

The delivery man handed over a plain wrapped box and his clipboard to sign, then looked over his shoulder. "Thad James?"

"Yes."

"I've got one for you, too. Just a minute."

He disappeared while Rhiannon looked over the package finding no sign of the sender, then tore off the brown paper and lifted the lid to reveal three little boxes in Cartier red. She plucked the card from inside and opened it.

"These are rose cut amethyst set in 18k white gold," Jill's handwriting read, "These roses won't die. I saw the bracelet first, then decided you had to have the rest. And it's not just for the great introduction. It's for being a great friend. Much love, Jill."

She pulled the lid off the first box to reveal a thin and sparkling amethyst cuff bracelet, then hurried to the next to find a delicate amethyst and iolite drop pendant on an 18-inch chain. The final box was the matching ring, a smooth flat band with a perfectly round amethyst set like a belt buckle at the center.

They were checking out the jewelry when the delivery man came back in, this time bearing a wrapped tower of boxes. He handed those over to Thad and then his clipboard. "I just picked those up at Godiva," he said. "Somebody likes you."

"Everybody likes me," Thad said, grinning. He signed for the gifts and handed the clipboard back over. As the man left the room, Thad's face lit up like a schoolboy's. "Someone likes me a lot! Seven fucking pounds of chocolates"

He tore into his own card after untying the ribbon that held the boxes and passing one off the Rhiannon to open. "It's from Jill. She says that I dipped her world in chocolate, and she'd like to return the favor. Then she apologizes for being corny and says she can't wait to see me Tuesday. Aw! I like her!"

"Me too," Rhiannon said around a mouthful of truffle. "Oh my god—these are like eating heaven!"

With Kline looking on, they spent the next few minutes taking samples out of each of the boxes until they looked up at each other guiltily and started to laugh. "I'm so glad I'm not an actor who has to fit into wardrobe pants," Rhiannon giggled.

"I'm so glad I'm the star and I can tell wardrobe to toss off if they bother me."

Kline looked pained and said, "One day, I'm going to be as big as Marlon Brando, and then, I'm going to get as big as Marlon Brando. For now, I'm getting out of here before I succumb. Fucking Jill and fucking chocolate. She used to make these brownies… Fuck."

Thad laughed and Rhiannon smiled slightly. "Let's get you to the table read," she said, rising from her desk. It's that time"

It had been a long time since Kline had done a table read with a sitcom cast, and it was only a few pages before he'd caught up the rhythm again, but Thad was happy to pull him along until he did. He'd forgotten about the camaraderie of a TV cast and what it was like to laugh into a joke along with the rest of the table, and be laughed at when you fumbled your emphasis or got tangled up in a too-long sentence.

It felt good to be back in that flow, and halfway through, he found himself jealous. It was clear that everyone adored Thad, and more than once the writers waited for him to decide whether or not something would work before moving on. Kline caught himself trying to caper for the same kind of attention Thad got just by being himself, and he had to remember that he was the guest star, not the star. He wasn't sure he liked that.

Old jealousies were stirring. The kind that had sent him looking for bigger roles even back when they were getting started on Knock, and by the time the read was done and they were released for the day, Kline just wanted to get out and get going. He said his goodbyes as quickly as possible and started for the lot before the first light was out.

Thad caught up with him as he was on his way out and shouted, "Oi! Hey, you want to go for a pint?"

"Can't," Kline said, "I've got other plans. I'm taking Jill out for a late dinner, then we're going to The Frame for a while."

"More photo ops, eh?"

"That, too," Kline replied, with a shrug. Thad already had just about everything Kline thought he wanted, and now Jill, too? "Mostly we're just spending time together."

"Oh?"

Kline stopped and faced Thad. "Look...I didn't want to say anything because she and I aren't exclusive at all, but it's not all for the photogs, man. Otherwise, we'd spend all our time in public. As it is, she spent the day at my place on Sunday. Not a camera in sight. I'm not going to try to get in your way, but you should know that Jill and I are actually close."

Thad cocked an eyebrow in surprise. "Really?"

"Yeah."

"Hm. All day Sunday?"

"Yeah," Kline nodded, "There's still a spark there, you

know? Sorry, mate."

Thad hummed again. "She really must be more talented than I thought."

"How do you mean?"

"Well, not every woman can be in two places at once."

"Sorry?"

Thad shook his head. "No worries, luv. Go hop to your photo op and enjoy the spark."

Kline's brow furrowed with obvious confusion, but he didn't question it further. "Right. I'll see you tomorrow, yeah?"

"Sure," Thad replied, with a nod as he turned away laughing.

"Fucker," Kline muttered under his breath, heading for his car. It was true they spent a lot of time at his place without any cameras around. Jill and Jack had gotten to be great friends and when he was around, she always made sure the press got at least one photo of the three of them together near the house. She seemed to take that part of their PR relationship more seriously than any of the rest of it.

When he picked her up for dinner, she was waiting on her patio looking like a postcard. He couldn't help smiling at her shapely vintage sundress and burgeoning tan, "Look who's going LA," he said. "But you better hope your tan lines don't show when we start filming."

"I don't have any," she said coyly, "that's the joy of a back-yard pool."

"Just be careful that no one's watching."

"No one knows where I live yet, and I'll have moved before they figure it out," she said, cheerily.

They drove off to dinner, her chirping away happily as they went. She'd been looking at houses most of the day, but she'd also been shopping earlier. She filled Kline in on every little nuance, animated and obviously in a wonderful mood. After a moment she took a deep breath, let it out and beamed, "I can't remember when I've felt so good. And I'm so disappointed! I wanted to hate LA!"

"Why? I'm here. What more do you need?"

Jill laughed. "A lot more, darling. It's wonderful that you're here, but I can't build a life around it."

"You could," he said, seriously.

She laughed again. "Mm. Some life that would be."

"Uh! I'm crushed. You don't think we could have a good life together out here?"

"We're not together, Kline. We're friends. That's it. Anyway, I want a great life, not just a good one."

"You were open to possibilities in New York," he reminded.

"I was also out of my mind with upset," she snorted. "And still not quite over the shock of running into you. And--well, you still make my stomach flip." She said the last quietly with a little smile. "There's definitely a physical attraction. Probably always will be."

"That's as good a starting point as any, don't you think?" he said, his voice taking on a purr.

She chuckled again, "For having sex it's a good start. For having a relationship? Kline, you'd be bored of me inside a month, and you know it. You were bored with me back in the day. You're only interested right now because I'm not panting at your feet."

He shook his head. "No. Not true. That was never the case," he insisted. "I was afraid of you and how I felt about you. Boredom was never an issue."

"Yes, because I'm so scary. Grr! Are you afraid of feelings now?"

"No. Now I welcome them."

"We're talking about emotional feelings. Not tingly in-your-pants feelings."

"I know what we're talking about, Jill. We're talking about stomach-flipping- and-heart-leaping-into-your-throat feelings. I'm not a kid anymore. I know the difference."

"Stomach flipping is tingly in-your-pants when I say it. Just so we're on the same page."

"So, that's all you have for me, then?"

He could see her mind come to a screeching halt and she turned in her seat to look at him fully, "Are we really having this conversation? Why are you asking me that?"

"I'd like to know where I stand with you. If I have any standing at all?"

"Kline," she sighed. "You broke my heart twice. Twice. Not once. Then you were a bastard about it. You're lucky I let you be my friend. I don't want us to get confused about that when we're filming, because we both know how the play ends. I'd hate for any of it to carry over into real life. Okay? We're friends. We're coworkers. We share a history, and you make my pants tingle, but my pants don't rule my world."

"Are things going that well with Thad, then?"

She blinked at him. "What does that have to do with any of this? I'm telling you no because I'm not in the same place I was in New York, or even ten years ago. It took me a long time to get over you and forgive you for doing what you did to me. Let's not drag it all out again. I like you. We're great friends. Any more than that is just too volatile."

"Too volatile? Jill…Look, I think we could--"

"We could make a huge mess. I like you. I adore your son. But no. No. I need to expand my world now, not make it smaller. In my adult life I've dated one man I haven't know since childhood. One. The last thing I need to do is fall back into the pattern of dating men who are a safety blanket and throwback to my mother. Part of me will always love you. You were my first everything. But another part of me will never trust you again. I'm going with that part."

Kline looked wounded, but he didn't try to argue the point. Instead, he sighed and gave a nod. "All right. Friends it is."

"Good friends," she said, taking his hand. "Now let's eat, because I'm starving!"

They went to a cozy eatery and spent a few hours talking close and laughing together, looking for all the world like a young couple in love. There was no more talk of romance between them, but they slipped into the roles easily enough. After dinner, Kline took her to The Frame where several other notable celebrities were having drinks and looking to be seen.

After thirty minutes she was ready to leave and had to be convinced to stay a bit longer. "We should give them a good shot, though," he smiled. "We've not been seen being physical. How's about a little kiss?"

Jill arched an eyebrow and gave him a teasing smile. "I think you're just looking for an excuse."

"What's your point? A little kiss won't hurt, right?"

"Fine," she chuckled, opening her arms. Several minutes later, when he let go of the embrace, she was blushing.

"How're the pants?" he asked.

"I'm wearing a dress."

"I meant the ones underneath."

She snorted a surprised laugh. "Oh! The strings are all in the right place, thanks for asking."

"Now ask me about mine."

"What pants?" She snorted, embarrassment making her bold. "You appear to be wearing a tent."

"At the moment, yes, and it's all your doing."

"You kissed me, so technically it's your doing," she countered, grabbing her bag from the table. "Can we go now, please?"

"Guh! Fine." He scrambled out after her and nearly chased her out to the car.

"How 'bout a kiss goodnight," he asked when they reached her drive.

"How about no," she laughed. "Goodnight, Kline."

"Tease."

"I am not!" She huffed, fumbling for her phone as it began to ring. She read the display and a smile spread across her face as she hurried to answer. "Hello?"

"Hello, beauty," Thad's voice greeted. It was loud enough that Kline could hear him. How she was holding the phone to her ear was beyond him. "How are you?"

"I'm good. How are you?"

"Terrible, actually. I haven't been able to stop thinking about you all day and I've eaten nearly two boxes of chocolate."

"I'm glad you liked it. I've been out with Kline all night, being photographed kissing him. So, I've been thinking about you for inspiration." She stuck her tongue out at Kline as she said it.

"Well, I'd much rather you were kissing me, but you are an actress, so whatever work is required--am I interrupting?"

"No, we've just turned down my street. He's glaring at me."

"Hm. I can't imagine what his trouble might be, considering he's been spending time with you and kissing you all evening. Personally, I would be grinning from ear to ear."

"Aw," she purred. "You should come over. Then I'll be grinning ear to ear."

Kline called out so that Thad could hear, "She needs her rest. She's obviously overtired."

"You've got an early call tomorrow, mate. Shouldn't you be on your way home?"

"Invitation stands," Jill said.

"I was hoping you would say that. I didn't really want to wait until tomorrow to see you," Thad said, his own smile obvious. "I'll be there in half an hour."

Kline scowled as Jill got out of the car and waved goodbye as she practically ran into the house.

Next morning on set, Thad was grinning, giving Kline a slap on the rear as he passed by. "'Lo," he cheered. "D'you have a nice date last night?"

"Very," Kline replied, with a tight smile.

"Good. Let's get to work, hm?" Thad replied, whistling as he continued down the corridor to his dressing room.

The set lit up with excitement around two, just before they broke for lunch. An intern came running in, whispering to an aide off sides, then pretty soon the set was buzzing that Kline Scott's girlfriend, Jill Parker had just driven onto the lot and creamed another car. Apparently, she'd swerved to miss a courier and had hit a studio boss's Porsche instead. No one was hurt, but the Porsche was totaled, and Jill had ended up with an offer to star in an action comedy.

She was escorted inside shortly after, rubbing her forehead and Rhiannon welcomed her with a sardonic smile. "Hey, Crash, are you alright?"

"Yeah, I just bumped my head," she said, with a pout. "My car got hurt, though."

"You can afford to get it fixed. And hire a driver."

"I don't want a driver. Then I have to wait for them to go where I want to go. And I know I can get it fixed. But the studio is fixing it."

"What?"

"Apparently, I'm charming and adorable. And they're afraid I'll sue."

Rhiannon laughed, shaking her head. "Charmed life. That's all I can say."

Thad appeared behind her, worry evident on his face, "Jill? Are you okay? You weren't hurt, were you?"

"Hi!" She spun to greet him. "I was coming to see you. I'm fine."

He took both of her hands and looked her over. "You have a bump," he frowned, brushing her bangs with his finger. "You're sure you're alright?"

"Absolutely," she said, grinning and slipping her arms around him. "I'm great now."

He hugged her and kissed the top of her head and Kline, without thinking, put a hand down on her shoulder. "She's obviously delirious. She's forgotten who she's dating."

"Oh, Kline," she said, surprised. "I didn't know you were here."

"Obviously," he said, with a smile. "But I'm here! And so are photographers, so…"

"They're everywhere," Jill said, looking up at Thad apologetically as they separated.

"You can talk in my office if you're just talking." Rhiannon shook a finger at Thad.

Kline looked back at Rhiannon with a grim statement as Thad led Jill off. "If she's photographed with him while I'm around--"

"Then you'll get even more publicity out of the scandal. Just shut it, Kline. You'll have her to yourself soon enough. Thad leaves for Prague next week--as soon as we wrap for the summer hiatus."

"Prague?"

"He took a role in Rick's latest production and he's going over there to film his bit."

"Really? How long's he going to be gone?"

Rhiannon narrowed her eyes. "Too long if you're thinking what I think you are. Leave them alone. They're both happy."

"I have nothing but their best interest at heart," Kline said icily as he turned to walk away.

Rhiannon Charles

Rhiannon didn't respond to Kline, seeing that he was waiting for it, and turned off to the Craft Services table before she could change her mind and throttle him. The rest of the week was dark, and she was glad it was the finale. Hiatus was sorely needed. After Jill's visit, Kline seemed to take so much pleasure in slinging the barbs that had been written for him at Thad's expense, Rhiannon was wishing she hadn't written them. It was to the point that the rest of the cast was starting to show discomfort. The usually happy group was startlingly silent between takes, and his sitcom kids stayed huddled close to Thad--like they felt the need to protect him.

For his part, Thad was a trooper with a smile and seemed not to notice. He took his verbal falls with practiced grace and was rewarded with delight from the studio audience when the afternoon came. Rhiannon had sussed out that he was spending most of his free time with Jill, which in turn seemed to solidify his ability to roll with Kline's punches. It was all water off a very happy duck's back.

The photos of Jill and Kline clenched up in a club surfaced quickly, and rumors spread that they were moving in together. Candids of Jill leaving his drive were offered as proof. "These don't bother you?" Rhiannon asked him when a second round of make out pictures, these taken from Kline's well-known backyard, showing the two of them in bathing suits and each other's arms appeared alongside photos of them surfing together.

She and Thad were in the VIP Lounge at the airport waiting for their flight out to Prague, and he was texting back and forth with Jill.

Thad shrugged a bit. "Is that the worst they've got? It's acting. I figure the people who are important know who you're seeing. Even the media really knows. The press knew when you were on the red carpet with Kline, remember? They set up the story to get clicks and sales. They aren't actual journalists trying to find and report a truth. It's just work. It's like the golf game that seals the big deal you sign in the office or something. How the fuck do I know? I've never had a real job."

"It would bother me," Rhiannon grumbled.

"It did bother you. I remember. Nobody likes to see someone they care about tangled up with someone else, but that's that, you know? It's this business." A new text chimed, and he chuckled at something on his phone.

"I just think if you care about someone--"

"Hey, we haven't gotten that far," Thad interrupted gently. "We're not to a point in this where I can start huffing about how she spends her time. I'm trying to take things slow. Jill agreed she wanted to take things slow, so that's what we're doing. I care. I feel a really strong connection. I think she does too. But right now, we haven't made any promises, and she was straight up from the beginning that she had this publicity to do and didn't feel right getting exclusive while that was on. I respect that."

"I don't like it."

"You don't like Kline," he said blandly as he typed in a text.

"Guilty as charged. I just think—I don't understand why. I don't understand it. I will never understand what's wrong with her that she's willing to let publicity drive her to this when she could be with you?"

Thad laughed and gave Rhiannon a one-armed hug. "Okay, two things. One, don't worry about it. I'm not worried about it. When the time is right everything will fall into place. Two, maybe it's good for me to not be trying to marry someone else for a while? Maybe it's good for me to get to enjoy a woman and her company casually? Maybe it's good for me to just hang out on the phone with a woman, or text a woman and get to know her before I propose? I've married the last three women I've dated."

"Still. He's going to make a play for her while you're gone. You watch."

"I'd rather not. Look, Rhi, I've been at bat a few times now. I know sometimes you win, sometimes you don't. I also know that you can't quit just because the game looks bad. Do I like seeing his tongue rammed down her throat? No. Am I going to like seeing it rammed down her throat at the movie premier, when his tongue is the size of my whole body up on that screen? No. But I do know that's all he's got rammed anywhere, and he won't have it there as soon as her film is over. It's work."

"I want you two to make it."

"You are weirdly invested in this." He shook his head and looked back down at his phone.

Rhiannon sighed. "I am. I can't make my own love life work, so I want to fix yours. I want to write you the happily ever after."

"You're a writer, Rhi. You know that happy endings don't always happen. But I guess I do too. I can admit that. And I can see the writing on the wall with Kline, too. What I'm going to do is be me. I'm going to make things as easy on her as possible so that when everything comes down, the comfort level she has with me is freedom and trust. Not business. She and I talked—we talk all the time now. She's comfortable and she feels good about me and what I'm going to be doing off in another country on my own. I feel good about her. No worries. There's our flight being called."

Rhiannon looked up and stood, and laughed when he grabbed his and her carry-ons. "Gentleman until the end."

"Or maybe I want your snacks. I saw what you bought at the kiosk."

It was a ten-hour flight into London Heathrow where they had a layover, and Rhiannon spent most of the time on her laptop, typing up production notes and ideas for the next season of Simon Says. She'd finished her script doctoring for *Circle Sky* in less than ten days, after two production meetings and extensive conversations with the director and the original screenwriter. The 'finished' product was something that everyone involved was very pleased with and she'd received kudos for her talent and her expediency in bringing the project to the table a week ahead of schedule.

Now it was the script supervision that needed done, and honestly, she felt like that was going to be a walk in the park. Basically, it felt like she was getting an all-expense paid vacation in Prague, and she couldn't say she minded. Every mile away from LA seemed to bring a new level of calm. Things had just been too tense and too crazy lately.

She'd been feeling restless. Life was good…at least, her career was good. Life could use a little help. Her search for a new house had been placed on hold due to the overload of script work she'd had to complete, and now that she was going to be in the Czech Republic for at least six weeks, it would be that much longer before she managed to find a suitable place and move.

The problems that had arisen with her overexposure in the tabloids had lessened slightly as the days passed, but she was still being recognized, propositioned, and stared at lasciviously. She'd been forced to change her email address for a fourth time when she started receiving nude pictures of a man in Idaho who wanted her to come play in his 'kiddie pool'. Needless to say, she was hoping for some peace and anonymity in Prague.

In the Heathrow VIP lounge, she plugged in once more. Thad was taking the four hours to do a dine-and-dash lunch with half of his daughters, whose mother was keeping them in London while he was in Prague, so that gave Rhiannon some time alone to think. While she was busy typing up an email reminder to herself, her instant messenger dinged, and she clicked on the window to see who was contacting her. She didn't recognize the ID, but she opened the message anyway.

Grnlite1: Hard at work?

Sighing, she punched up a swift response:

ScrptDr: I don't have time or interest, pervert. Move on.

There was a pause, and she was about to close the window when another message appeared:

Grnlite1: Sorry. Should have mentioned. This is Rick.

Rhiannon's eyes went wide. "Shit."

ScrptDr: Oh. Sorry! I wasn't expecting--how did you find me?

Grnlite1: Thad gave me your ID. I just wanted to see how the flight was going?

ScrptDr: It's fine. Very long. I'll be glad when it's over.

Grnlite1: Are you relaxing or are you working?

She smiled.

ScrptDr: Working, of course.

Grnlite1: That's me, as well. Listen, I wanted to tell you that I'm already in London. We're taking the same flight to Prague from Heathrow. Meet you in the lounge?

ScrptDr: I'll be the woman sunbathing in the light of her laptop.

Grnlite1: Radiation tan! Love it. See you in a few hours.

They said goodbye and Rhiannon closed the window and logged off, a small smile on her face. She knew she was blushing, and she was glad no one was there to see it. Rick had continued to seem interested, even after she gave him her reasons for refusing to date him, but he had maintained a comfortable distance.

For her part, Rhiannon was still very attracted to him, even though she had only seen him a handful of times over the previous weeks. There was still the concern that his interest was more to do with her notoriety and possibly Kline's assessment of her, but that worry had become less as they got to know one another a little better. Caution had prevailed, however, and she hadn't allowed herself to veer off course and give in to the urge to ask him out. How could she really, without coming across as someone who was playing games? Not only the worry of looking like a player, they had a good working relationship and she didn't want to mess that up.

She mused on that while she picked at the plate of lounge food she'd brought back to her seat with her and sighed. Maybe when all this was over?

Two hours into her wait, she saw Rick's dark head appear and she waved. He was up at the counter checking into the VIP lounge and waved back when he saw her, pausing to fumble in his satchel and then hold up a slip of paper with "ScrptDr" written on it in black marker. She laughed and waved again, feeling foolish even as she did so.

"Hello, hello," he said, rolling his carryon bag over to where she sat. For a moment she thought he would hug her, but he seemed to think better of it. "What you got there?" He looked at the crumbs on her plate.

"I've had cheese, salami, and tiny pickles. I probably smell like an antipasto salad."

"Oh, I like those! Watch my stuff while I go graze? I'm starved."

"Of course."

She watched him go up and down the buffet line picking and choosing, and asking for and receiving a glass of red wine. "I'm not sure about this pairing," he lifted his plate and his glass then sat down beside her. "But beggars can't be choosers."

They chatted about the difference in qualities of lounge between LAX and Heathrow, and Rick told her his favorite and least favorite airports. She shared the same with him and found herself explaining that her family traveled regularly with her father's business, so she'd been all over the world with them before she'd started going off on her own. Airports were old hat, almost second homes.

"So, how're things back home? I've been gone a week and feel like it's been months. How did the finale shoot go?" He asked when there was a lull in the conversation.

Rhiannon shrugged. "It's over. That's about the best thing I can say for it. Thad did well and the audience laughed in the right places, so I guess that's a good sign."

"That's the best you can say? What went wrong? I thought it was the grand reunion of everyone's favorite sitcom hunks."

She took a sip of coffee and sighed. "Well, Kline was kind of a shit. Actually, he was a huge asshole, And Thad is Thad. Thad's life philosophy when it comes to assholes is give them enough rope and they hang themselves. I'd rather him just beat the loving hell out of them once in a while."

"You know," Rick took a sip of his drink, "I've actually

known Kline longer. I've watched him grow from a really inse-cure, posing tosser into an older, insecure, posing tosser. I know," he held up a hand. "I told you he was a good guy who was just unlucky in love. And in a lot of ways, he is that. But he's terri-fied of not being in the public eye, and that brings out the worst in him. So does that Roland thing he's got lurking around with him like some Renfield all the time. Or is Kline the Renfield? It's frightening the amount of control that man exerts."

"It's hard to tell who's who when it comes to those two. I thought that Kline did only as much publicity as he needed to and preferred more private time, but he doesn't. Not really. He gets antsy if he has to stay home and nothing is going on. Of course, even when he's convinced himself that he wants to stay home, Roland calls him and orders him out. He grumbles and goes and has Roland to lay blame on for it, but if he didn't really want to go, he wouldn't. He allows himself to be puppeteered so he doesn't come across as a glamor junkie."

"I think you've hit it on the head with that last bit. How 'bout your friend? Jill? I've seen some new pictures of those two looking mighty cozy. I had a long talk with Thad before I left and suggested cutting that loose until filming is over."

Rhiannon frowned. "I don't know what she's doing. She says the whole thing with Kline is just for show, for publicity, and I believe that because she's positively giddy about Thad. He says he's alright about it and knows that it's just business, but it would drive me crazy to see that everywhere," she said, then considered for a moment. "Like he pointed out, it did drive me crazy. Thad's taking it in stride."

Rick sighed. "Is she safe for him? I mean really? Thad's like a brother to me, and no offense because I don't know her well, she just comes off as flighty, fickle, and fame-centric."

"She's been acting since childhood. It's just work for her."

"I think the child stars are the worst. Their growth is stunt-ed. It's not just work for them, it's life. It's how they were social-ized."

"Thad was a child star," Rhiannon reminded. "And Jill's not stunted. She's actually really very sweet and she could be grounded and centered with the right man."

"Thad is the exception to the rule. Anyway, I'd rather see him date someone who is grounded and centered–someone outside the industry before he gets attached to her," Rick said pointedly. "If he hadn't already had his heart broken so many times, I–"

"I care about what happens to Thad, too. If I thought she was a pump-and-dump, I wouldn't have suggested it. I think Thad's the right man, but she's in the middle of this circus with Kline and doesn't really see what kind of damage it could do. She's a little naive when it comes to love. Her experiences haven't been good ones," Rhiannon explained, detailing some of Jill's history to illustrate her point. "The other part of this that's a problem is that Kline is playing on the forced closeness and their friendship to try and get over on Thad. He really is unbelievable."

"Frankly, I'm fed up with him. He called me a couple of times to see about getting a role in Circle Sky. He wanted the part I'd slated for Thad. Mentioned how much more experience he has, and how Thad really needs to be available for his girls."

Rhiannon felt her eyes widen. "He didn't!"

"He did. It's exactly like the first couple of seasons of Knock. He's in full competition mode."

"What set that off?"

"I'm not sure. Probably your little friend. It was always Kline competing with Thad, though. Not the other way around. Thad doesn't need to compete. It didn't stop until Kline started getting the offers for the movies. Thad was getting them, too, but he turned them down. Mainly because of his family. He had three little girls, nearly by himself when we first started, then three more and a new wife halfway through, then six girls in and out without any help before it was all over. And happy as a pig in mud with it. Kline was getting all the attention by default. Thad gets enough attention at home, I suppose."

"I'm glad he's doing this."

"Me too."

Rhiannon took one of the cornichon from Rick's plate and bit into it, "Why are we even talking about this like it matters what we think?"

That made Rick laugh and he shrugged amiably. "I'm just glad you're talking to me. You've been avoiding me."

"Ouch."

"What should we talk about?"

"Tell me about Prague."

Chapter 8

Jill Parker

Pre-production wheels had begun to turn on Devil's Party and Jill was happy to have Kline there as they started to rehearse and move through the late stages of costuming. She hadn't done a feature before and the pacing was wildly different from the stage. It seemed like every time something started to move forward, something else halted the momentum and it took an hour to fix to move on again.

Even the blocking was stop-and-start for the lighting and the angles. She was exhausted by the end of every day, even though she felt like she was doing nothing. Getting in and out of the character of Devon at the drop of a hat was as challenging as she had feared it would be, but she was a professional and she was going to make it work.

She was equally glad that August hadn't signed on for costuming. There'd been some drama just before he left, and the lead designer was fired. She and August had shared happy pillow talk of how much fun it might be for him to have that job, if only the timelines with his other projects had worked out. Fun. Sure. That would have been mortifying.

While they waited on set for something that was supposed to take five minutes and not fifty, meaning they didn't have time to drift away elsewhere, Jill sighed to Kline from beside him on a sofa, "Wardrobe! They are so mean!"

"Mean?"

"What's a breakfast body?"

Kline started laughing. "Where did you hear that?"

"Two of the girls were talking about how hard it is to fit me. They said I had a breakfast body."

"Fried egg tits and a pancake ass," Kline said, still laughing. "They're calling you skinny."

"I'm supposed to be skinny! This character is a dancer!"

"Have you seen the dancers out here? The Laker Girls?"

Jill glowered at him. "A ballet dancer."

"It's not bad. It just means they're having to do their jobs. I'm sure Mel's creaming over you. She hates thick actresses."

"Devon is a fragile, overworked dancer. She's not supposed to inhabit a cheerleader's body."

"Babe, I know."

"No one's ever complained about my body before," she said sulkily.

"Welcome to Hollywood."

"What are they saying about you?"

"Behind my back? No idea. But to my face they all appreciate the work I've been doing. Mel says I've never looked better."

"I've never looked better!"

"You want me to take a look?"

She considered the offer and was about to answer when everything buzzed back to life around them. "Mic's hot," came a voice. "Lights. Good. Set that a little left, Joe. Good. Good. Okay. Camera ready. Ready on set." The AD picked up the slate. "In three, two, one…" And the voice trailed off as the director pointed.

Kline had his hands on her shoulders, gripping them hard. No, not Kline. Andrew. Andrew had his hands on Devon's shoulders, gripping them hard. He was angry because she'd embarrassed him in front of his friends. She was afraid he was going to hurt her and was cringing away from his snarling words. He lifted his hand and the director called cut.

"Great! Good! Mark that. This is one. Let's get set up for beauty one and beauty two, then long one and long two. I like it. This is going to be beautiful."

Jill tried to shake off the fear she'd channeled between the set ups, but with each repeat, it was that much harder, until at the end of the day, she was a shivering mess. "Kline," she said, taking a seat next to him in the golf cart that would drive them to their cars. "This is hard!"

"No shit! You've been up there on the boards looking down on all of us movie actors, and now you know."

"It's entirely different muscles!"

"Entirely. But you can do this, Babe. You did great today. When we actually get filming, it'll be better. The studio will be quieter and not as insane in the background, and you can just kind of roll better. You don't have to get in and out of the body, you know? You can just kind of stay in it between setups. Just go to your trailer and rest, or whatever."

"What do you do?"

"Whatever," he grinned. He fixed a lock of hair that had come loose from her bun, tilting his head at her. "You want to come over tonight and decompress? I've got Indie on contract until we're finished filming, so I know we've got great food. Has the studio set you up with a chef?"

"Yeah. Chef, housekeepers, and Kim's friend, Jennifer, for my PA. Also different from New York, these people want to talk to me. My staff in New York was invisible! Everyone here is all, 'Hey Girl!' But at the same time, I feel so exposed in my house! I know I've got security and gates, and more security, but it's so different from my place at home. I miss Bernie."

"I know what you mean. Being in a place in the city—there's always someone around to ignore you when you scream. Here, they just can't hear you."

Jill laughed. "Exactly. I feel like someone else could be living in my house with me, and I'd never even know it."

"Come over to my place. Play some Chutes and Ladders with Jack. Drink some wine. Don't be alone. Especially not after a day like today. Alone is when it's bad."

"Honestly, that sounds good."

"Just stay the night," he urged. "Not in my bed. I promise not to make a move. But come over and stay the night, and I'll bring you back to the studio tomorrow morning. I promise it makes a difference just being around people. Okay?"

It fed into what Roland wanted anyway. She had balked at his firm suggestion that she start spending nights at Kline's place and be photographed leaving in the mornings, mainly because she was trying to fall in love with a life of her own making, not one that had been orchestrated for her. Then, Roland would repeat her five-year plan to her, and she would sigh. But this was her idea, not his, and really, she didn't want to be alone.

She considered calling Thad, but she had no idea what time it was in Prague. Part of her felt like she needed to tell him what she was doing, but another part said, "No. You're not exclusive. He knows your job. Leave it. Stop trying to get everyone's approval."

"Okay?" Kline asked again. The golf cart had stopped beside her car.

"I can call and have my PA bring a change of clothes over," she mused aloud. "And my toiletries."

"Have her bring a couple of changes over. Just hang out all week. Jack will love it."

"Okay," Jill said, feeling a smile.

He slapped the top of the golf cart. "My car, please."

In under an hour, Jill and Jack were in Kline's game room playing cards, while Kline poured wine for the grown-up's dinner. Kim had fed Jack before they'd gotten home and he was, as Kline had expected, thrilled to have Jill's company until his own bedtime. Kline seemed genuinely pleased to have her company as well.

It was the old comfort, they decided together. They weren't having to be on their best behavior, or sucking in their stomachs to impress someone new, or deciding which bits of information to share or hide from a burgeoning romantic partner.

While Kline's PA and Jill's unpacked a few things in the

guest bedroom, the two of them took glasses of wine onto the sprawling patio and sat down in the swinging chair. "When did your mom die?" Kline asked out of nowhere.

"Jesus. Eight years ago. Just before Gary. You know what's funny?" She sat up from where she'd slouched. "Everyone expected me to be so sad. I wasn't. I was relieved, but who can admit that? So, I pretended to be sad, and Gary was pretending to care, and I got pregnant. Oh!" She covered her mouth and cringed at Kline's expression, then sat back again. "I've had three miscarriages. Gary married me because he knocked me up. I was twenty-two and he was fifty, and I wasn't going to get rid of it, and my mother had just died, and he'd just gotten caught cheating on his childhood sweetheart a year before, and it would have been really bad for business. And, I think he was at least a little in love with me. The new hadn't worn off anyway.

"But he'd just gotten divorced from Irina–there may have been a little overlap, if you know what I mean–and he had a daughter my age, so he asked if we could keep it quiet until the baby started to show and I needed to take hiatus. Then the baby never started to show, and he loved me a little and he didn't mind staying married as long as he could do his own thing. I acted myself into believing I was madly in love with him, and we were a modern, elegant, forward-thinking couple, but looking back, I just didn't want to be alone."

"I think I fucked my way through half of Hollywood before I got Nina pregnant. I didn't want to be alone either."

"Think it's just part of the acting gene?"

"It might be. Who are we without an audience?"

She raised her glass to his. "No one."

"Who did you date between me and Gary?"

"Gus and I went out a few times, but I didn't date anyone, really. I'm so bad at it. I'm so bad at letting people get to know me. I didn't sleep with anyone until Gary. Oh! Let's count them up. I slept with you," she raised a finger. "And then Gary. And then Gus. And then Thad. I need one more to make a fist."

"You could sleep with me again," he offered.

"Doesn't count. Has to be someone new."

"Fuck my luck."

They stayed out talking a while, watching the valley sparkle down below, then Jill made her excuses and went to shower. She was looking herself over in the wall-length mirror, muttering about eggs and pancakes when Kline knocked, then opened the door to the bedroom without waiting. "I brought you a couple of aspirin and some water," he called.

She could hear him crossing the room and he paused by the open door to the en suite. "Are you on a flaw-finding mission?" he asked.

"I'm–yes. Yeah," she had to laugh. He'd seen it all before, so she just reached for the robe she'd slung over the back of the vanity chair rather than scrambling for it.

"There's only one."

"Which is?"

"You covered it up," he said with a grin. "Aspirin and water. Bedside table. See you in the morning."

"Goodnight, Kline. And thank you."

"Thank *you*," he said, and walked out of the room.

When he'd left, she stretched out on the guest bed after popping the aspirin. She let her mind wander to what life might be like with Kline, but it was a dead-end road that just ended up with her being a lifelong crutch for an ego that needed to be in traction. Hoping to drift off to happier thoughts, she called up the memory of the last date she'd had with Thad.

It had been another wrangling of schedules to get the times to line up and she was buzzing with nerves by the time he got to her door.

He had driven her out to another beach spot he loved, a quiet cove that appeared out of low tide, and he'd put down a tarp and then a massive beach towel he'd pulled from an equally massive tote bag. "That'll keep our bums dry," he had said. "It's pungent tonight."

"It's no worse than the Hudson."

That had made him laugh. "You know, I've only been to New York a couple of times, and always just in and out for press. Is there a big difference?"

"Huge," Jill had told him, and given him her impressions while he poured Solo cups of wine he produced from a chilly-bag inside the tote. "I never thought I'd leave. I was very snobby about it! I'm a native New Yorker and proud of it, but here I am, and I'm kind of falling in love with this weird place."

They'd already had the conversations about acting and she'd given him the mini-version of her rise to stardom, then asked the same of him. They discovered they'd both suffered from overbearing stage-mothers, though his dropped out of sight as he got older. They both had similar mindsets about their work, as well.

Thad loved his job, but it was a job. He shrugged off the idea that he could do any other kind of work that would pay him so much to do something that came so easily to him. He seemed to like her five-year plan; he asked her a lot of questions about where she saw herself in six or seven years, delighted by her semi-urban goat villa idea, and told her where he wanted to be. Married for the last time! Jill found herself just smiling at him while he talked about his past relationships. She couldn't imagine ever not smiling at him.

"I married my first wife because I was madly in love. I was nineteen when we got married, but we were both in school when we met. We had our first daughter when we were twenty. She was with me through all the struggling child-to-adult actor days, and I'd just started work on Knock when we found out she was pregnant again. The twins came just after the first season wrapped.

"My schedule and the sudden US fame were really hard on her. The transition to LA was hard on her. I wasn't ever home, she was away from family with tiny babies, and she didn't have any friends here. I'll admit, I could have–should have done more to help, but I was in my head a bit. She was exhausted and I was just another mess for her to clean up, so she left, and left me with the girls. I was bloody lucky my parents could help. My stepmum and dad moved over here to help with them until I remarried.

"The second time I married I was madly in love again and I'd known her all of two weeks. I was much more successful at that point, though, so I figured I wouldn't have the same problems as before. But, looking back I see that I was as in love with the idea of having a mum for the girls as I was with Jessica herself.

"We had twins first, then we had a single--all within three years. I didn't have the same problems as before, but my work schedule hadn't changed, and it left her alone with six kids all the time. She ran off with her personal trainer. So, then my first wife realized she'd missed out on a helluva lot with the girls, and she asked to have them live with her. So, she's got them seventy-five percent of the time.

"We're friends now. She's remarried and very happy. The girls have a more stable existence with her, and I get them all the time. That's Emily, by the way. Jessica, wife two, has primary custody but we have a fifty-fifty living arrangement. She married the personal trainer, and they are living happily ever after. Monique," He shrugged. "I married Monique because she was gorgeous, and I was lonely. I think she thought life with me would be much more exciting than it was. That was really over before it began. She hates children.

"But that's enough about me, huh? You're never supposed to talk exes on a date."

"I don't see why not," Jill smiled. "I mean, now I know you aren't some lothario who just enjoys walking the aisle and then casts aside his latest for the newer model."

He shook his head, "Nah. I do like being married, though. I'll get it right eventually. Wife and kids in the same house at the same time. One big happy family. I don't think that's too much to hope for."

"I've always wanted a houseful of kids. I'm an only. My mother was an only. My father disappeared before I was old enough to know anything about him. I grew up among adults and the only kids I knew were the ones in my dance classes or who were in shows with me."

"What about school chums?"

"I had a private tutor. I didn't go to school."

Thad gaped at the revelation, "You're kidding me."

"Nope. I had to be free for auditions and available to work. My mother hired a woman with a degree in elementary education, and off we would go to the kitchen of our apartment and study. But I learned Latin, French, and Italian, studied all the classics, and she beat me to death with mathematics. Admittedly, my knowledge of science is a bit lacking, but I know more history than most historians and--and I'm just babbling now. But I don't actually have a high school degree. Diploma? I never graduated from anything or took the equivalency test. Babbling. Stop me before I end up telling you about how I ran away to a school once."

"Ran away to a school?"

"Yes. I nearly managed to fake it until lunch time but one of the teachers decided to take roll and figured me out. My mother was livid," Jill sighed. "I just wanted to see what it was like to be normal for a change."

Thad nodded. "I went to school when I wasn't being trotted off to auditions. I did pretty well, even as a boy, and ended up in commercials and adverts pretty regularly. Of course, the backlash at school was horrendous. There were days I'd much rather had a private tutor. Nothing normal about growing up that way."

She bit her lip in sympathy. "Yeah, I know what you mean. Even in dance and acting classes, other little girls could be brutal. I was lucky. I was doing well enough that their mothers were afraid to let them torture me, but there were other little girls who just didn't make it out intact. How old were you when you started?"

"Just a wee bairn," he grinned at her. "I was three months old, and I got a nappy commercial. You?"

"In the womb. Literally. My mother's belly was featured in a cocoa butter ad. That was my first gig. Then as soon as I was out,

I was doing diapers, wipes and the like. On the plus side, I have a lot of baby pictures."

Thad laughed. "So how many kids makes a houseful in Jill-land?"

"How many rooms in my house? I don't know. I just know I want more than three. I want a huge family. Even if I have to go buy them."

"I have six I can lend you. You'd love them."

"I'm sure I would. Kline's son is fabulous."

"He truly is. I love that kid. I'm his godfather, you know?"

The conversation trailed off and they sat just listening to the waves for a while, sipping wine and just sharing the night. After a little while Jill sighed. "Thad? I have to admit, I don't really trust my own judgment with men right now. As my few friends are quick to point out, I'm a horrible judge of character–in fact most of my friends are more like frenemies, or at least started that way. Rhiannon promises that you're different than the rest of the actors out here."

"I try to be," he said, giving her a sheepish grin. "While we're confessing, I should tell you that I'm mad jealous of the time Kline gets to spend with you. I know it's work–I'm not worried about that, and I trust what you've told me. I just wish it was me. Maybe you can come work on Simon Says and I can PR date you to promote that."

She laughed until she coughed. "Kline is my last PR relationship. When this one's over, it's only real ones from then on."

"Well, normally I would warn against listening to anything Rhi has to say about me, but in this case, believe every word."

That was when she had put down her Solo cup and reached for him, pulling him in for a kiss, then she'd shifted up to her knees beside him, wrapping her arms around his shoulders to put all of her body behind the next kiss, easing back with him so that he held her down against his chest. It was just the sound of the ocean and the blood pounding in her ears as she slid her hands up under his navy polo shirt, scratching lightly at his chest.

She felt like she was eighteen again, not quite sure if what she was doing was right, but sure she wanted this man by the handfuls.

She crept down his torso, kissing his chest through his shirt, until she came to the waistband of his jeans, grinning when he gasped. She stroked his rising erection as she unfasted his button-fly, and then took him in her mouth before she could think twice about them being out in the open night.

He moaned softly and stroked her hair as she sucked and licked him to his full length and girth, then she made quick work of her underwear and climbed up to mount him. Their bodies covered by the broomstick skirt she wore, with Thad clutching her thighs, Jill rode him until he exploded with orgasm, coming quickly behind him as he throbbed inside her.

They had both cracked up laughing as they tried to right themselves minutes later. Thad had knocked over the last of his wine, and Jill had gotten tangled trying to get her underwear back on under her skirt. It was fun and funny, and she hadn't wanted the night to end. But, schedules as they were, it had to.

He had driven her home, face still glazed with sex, and kissed her so hard at her door she thought it might bruise. In fact, she'd hoped it would—a souvenir.

"Prague is too fucking far," he had said, hugging her fiercely.

"I'll still be here when you get back, though."

"You'd better!"

That night was the best sleep she'd had since she'd gotten to LA, and now, she was hugging a pillow in Kline's guest room trying to relive all the feelings she'd felt. Prague was too far, she decided, half wondering what it would be like to do a love scene with Thad. Trying to imagine that wasn't getting her any closer to dreams, so she shook herself and started counting sheep.

Kline Scott

Kline stayed true to his word to help Jill over the rough

spots. Through rehearsals into production, she stayed at his place most nights. They'd talked over the sex scenes a few times. Both of them were nervous for various reasons.

When the day arrived, he drove them to their four-a.m. call and dropped Jill off at her trailer with a kiss on the forehead. "It'll be fine. It'll be over before you know it." And then he'd gone off to his own.

They were doing body makeup and it would take a while to get him contoured and glowing. He had to look sexy and sweaty rather than greasy and gross, and as much as possible, they had to blend his flesh-colored thong to his body. He snapped the waistband, hoping the garment would stretch to accommodate an erection. They didn't always.

When his hair was styled and his lips were blotted, he was helped into a velvety robe that would cut down on his makeup rub-off, then escorted to the closed set.

A stunning bedroom straight out of an upper West Side, New York penthouse sat up on a three-foot rise, the bed against a backdrop of the midnight skyline. An AD flipped back the top sheet and showed Kline his mark, indicating the tiny dot stitched onto the pillow that was sewn down to the bed.

He took his direction and got in, shivering a little as a PA walked away with his robe. It was freezing on set. He always figured they did that for the nipples, and maybe to keep the leading men from getting so hard they couldn't act anymore. It didn't matter. Once all the lights were on, it would be blazing hot.

As he thought that, a lighting guy came and got to work, and Jill's stand-in sat in Jill's spot until she arrived a few minutes later. After the same instruction, Kline had gotten, the same PA took off with Jill's robe, and she hurried into the bed, one hand over her bare breasts. "Hi," she breathed at him, shivering.

"Hi. You look gorgeous." She did. Chronologically, this was the first of the two big sex scenes, when her character was still flush with love, and the makeup team had lit up her face and skin with soft pinks and golds, with her hair in rivers of soft waves.

They would shoot the scene leading into the bed later, likely with body doubles for the closeup ass shots, but this was all them. "Ready to sell it?" he asked.

She laughed, "No, but I'm ready to get paid for it, so that's the same thing, I guess."

He laughed too and whispered away from the boom mic in case it was hot, "If I get hard, I'm sorry. If I don't get hard, I'm sorry. It's not you. It's the room temp."

"Just don't get me dirty."

"Fuck, if it gets that far, Mitch hasn't called cut fast enough. You know how to get out of here when they release us?"

"PA comes back with my robe? That's what the intimacy coordinator said."

"Yeah. They'll come for you first and get you out as fast as they can," he repeated what the director had already told them. "And then me. Then dinner?"

"Can we see how weird it gets first?"

"You mean you might need a little alone time?" He wagged his eyebrows and she laughed again.

"Sure. I might need some alone time."

"Yeah, we'll play it by ear."

A member of the makeup crew came and blotted Jill and powdered Kline, their director walked up to offer last-minute instructions and give a little pep talk, then it was lights, camera, action.

For this take, they started sitting upright, Jill straddling Kline's lap. He needed to run his hand up her back and into her hair, then cradle her body in both arms while he kissed her, and roll her under him. It was harder than it sounded, and even though they had worked with the choreographer, now that they were nearly naked, it was different.

It was the first time he'd had his hands on her skin since that junket in New York.

On action, he started with the kiss. She melted forward against him like she was supposed to, and he worked his hand up her back into her hair. An AD stood just off camera doing a count, and when it came time for the turn, he wrapped his other arm around her waist.

To accomplish the move, he had to lean back, engaging his core, while she leaned forward and to the right, giving the camera her left side, so that Kline could roll up on his left shoulder to press her beneath him, still engaged in the kiss. It didn't go well.

Jill burst out laughing as Kline grunted, stuck partway in the roll. "No one does it like this," she said to him, patting his head. At least he wasn't hard, he thought. For a second there, he thought he was going to be.

They reset and got it right on that take. Two more in the can, and then a reset for different angles, and a handful more for insurance. Kline lost count as both he and Jill warmed up to the work. Between powdering, blotting, and hair brushing at every re-set, nearly all the sexiness was sucked right out of their clenches, but they got through the morning without incident.

When they broke for lunch, Jill went to her trailer alone, and Kline went to his, where he briefly considered jerking off in the shower, but didn't because that would mean another full hour in makeup. Instead, he drank a protein shake and took a nap until he was called back to set.

That time, Jill was already on her mark. This would be the long shots of them making love and meant the makeup team was even powdering the bottoms of his feet. They would kiss while he mimed fucking her, then he would kiss down her throat while she arched up into him. She would wrap her legs around his waist and fake an orgasm, then he would, then they would collapse together in afterglow.

Five takes, Kline counted. And this time, the friction and the touching, and the scent of her skin, and how she knew just where to kiss him meant a raging boner. He was sucking air be-tween his teeth and letting it hiss out between takes, sitting with his knees up to his chest under the sheet to hide it. Every time, just as the blood flow started to recirculate in his body, he was back on top of her, rubbing his cock against her G-string, fighting every urge to just reach down and make fantasy reality.

It seemed to be getting to her, too. She was keeping it cool, but the last take they did, when she faked the orgasm, it came with a little something extra and he silently congratulated himself on a job well done.

A PA came for Jill, who went arms first into her robe, and scuttled away from the set, and then Kline's came. Both of the PAs did their best to shield the actors' bodies from view between bed and robe, and Kline thanked his quietly as they walked to his trailer. They had one more shot for the day, this one the afterglow pillow talk, with their bodies mostly under cover, so Kline had his shower and wank, then returned to the makeup chair to get his nipples bronzed one more time.

Again, Jill was on set before him. They were arranging her blonde hair against the navy blue pillows and making sure her lighting was right so Kline waited a moment before taking his mark, this time getting to wear flesh-toned bike shorts. Flicking the covers back enough to get in, he grinned at Jill's granny pants and pasties. "Killer," he growled playfully.

"Yeah, loving those," she pointed at his shorts.

"I feel like a Ken doll."

"You look like a Ken doll! Those abs! My god!"

"Literally painted on." It was the most they'd talked all day.

She was still topless, and when he settled into his mark half holding her against him, he couldn't help licking his lips. Quietly he said, "You really do look good, Jill." Adding, hoping to make her laugh, "Good enough to eat. I have syrup in my trailer."

She just groaned and rolled her eyes at him. Then said, "Three days of this, and I might let you."

But the next two days were the distressing ones and she'd gone home to her own house to decompress from the first big day. Now, it was carefully choreographed, angry sex, and then a hate fuck for the books. By the end of the third day, she couldn't even look him in the eye. Granted, he could barely look himself in the mirror. He'd never played a character like this before, and it scared him a little how easily he'd slipped into the anger and abuse, how cathartic it had felt to call her those names and make all those threats. He wanted to talk to her, but she was clearly avoiding him after they'd been released, so he let her escape to her trailer, and he went to his.

He was just collecting his things to go home after a shower, when he heard a knock. "It's open," he called, and Jill popped her head in the door. She was squeaky clean, her hair still damp as she clambered up inside. "Hi," he said.

"Hi. I wanted to check on you. Those scenes were always really hard on Doyle, but he got to die every night, so he could be reborn after the curtain. You okay?"

"Fuck," he sat down hard, overwhelmed with a sudden gratitude and relief. He realized he'd been afraid she would never look at him again. "That was–that was hard."

She nodded, shutting the door behind her and sitting down next to him on the little couch. "You're not a mean man. You're not a bad man." He felt his eyes welling up with tears and she grabbed his hands and squeezed them. "That character is not who you are, and I know it was really hard for you to be him. I know you would never hurt me like that. Okay?"

He took in a deep, shuddering breath, trying to get hold of himself. "Yeah. Thank you."

"Really, it was really hard for Doyle, too. As a play, you get to do it in chronological order and it's a full ride. There's a beginning, middle, end, and curtain. You get the scene done and roll to the next until it's done. This is so different. I was worried about you."

"I was worried about you. I should have come and–"

"No, you did right. You let me get out of the character, remember who I am, remember who you are, and clean up." Her eyes searched his face until she found whatever it was she was looking for. "Want to go grab dinner? Do you want to come back to my place? Do you need some space before you have to go be

'Dad' again?"

Another sucker punch of relief nearly took his breath away. "Yeah. I think that would be good."

"Call Delia. I'll drive."

"Oh hell no. I'll call Delia, but I'm driving."

"Fine," she laughed, wiping a stray tear from his cheek. "By the by, your American accent is really good."

"Yeah?"

"Yeah. I'm impressed."

She chatted him back down to earth like he was a stray dog, he thought, but he didn't mind. Her stream of consciousness kept him focused through the drive, and helped ground him back in reality as she went about pouring wine and putting the personal-chef-prepped meals on plates.

"I should be taking care of you," he finally said, watching her clean up their dessert dishes. Dessert was a clever take on berries in cream that wouldn't go straight to his waist.

"I've done this hundreds of times. Been Devon, I mean. I've been through those moments with her before. You've never been Andrew before. Honestly, I'll let you take care of me after Devon murders him. That's the hardest part for me. It's such an abrupt ending. Besides, you already took care of helping me make it through that first day. That was so much more vulnerable for me! More wine?"

"Thanks. How many carbs are in this?"

"Too many." She refilled his glass and then hers, leaning against the kitchen island, watching him. "This is nice. Just sitting here talking about the craft."

"It is," he agreed. "It really is."

"Remember when you went on that Chekov kick? And how we spent so much time trying to dissemble The Seagull so you could give it something new?"

He laughed outright. "I was so young!"

"And so serious about giving them something they hadn't seen before. If anyone could do it, though, it was you."

"I'm not sure I like who Hollywood has made me," he said after a beat, swirling his wine.

"What do you mean?"

"I've done some shitty things to get ahead."

"So, stop." She shrugged. "You can't change what you've already done, but you don't have to do those things again."

"I've done some shitty things recently."

"Then apologize and fix it."

"I'm sorry I've been such a dick. I'll quit trying to talk Thad out of seeing you. I'll tell him you have my blessing."

Jill smiled at him. "That would be nice. I like him."

"But you love me?"

"Always and forever, no matter who I am dating."

Kline swallowed hard. "Can I spend the night? I won't try anything. I just…"

"Don't want to be alone? Of course you can. I'll be the big spoon."

Rhiannon Charles

Filming in Prague had been riddled with issues and the small cast and crew were starting to joke that it was a cursed set. Thad kept reminding people that no one had died, but Rick just kept grumbling, "Yet."

It was a hard time on the calendar to be working, and the little delays were stacking up until they were bumping up on their planned two-day break, making even the affable Australian tense and waspish. No one went into an indie like this thinking they'd be getting a great vacation, but when a summer storm came down like Thor's wrath, flights were grounded, stranding the whole team. Given his plans to jet to London to see his kids for a few days, it was the last straw for his morale.

Rhiannon spent most of the stormy Saturday in her hotel room going over her notes and checking various inputs from the director and the continuity team, only looking up when Rick had knocked to see if she wanted to join him to walk down to a local pub for dinner.

The work she was doing had been much more intense than she'd expected, and in ways, Rhiannon felt like she was just keeping her head above water, though she'd rather chew razor blades than admit to that. Now, with production shut down by rain and one of their sets literally stuck in the muck until Tuesday, she'd gotten caught up on her work and decided she could put the laptop and binders down.

Working with Rick was easy, if unusual. She considered him as they walked down the hotel stairs together. This movie had become a money pit for him, and even if he was richer than God, he had to be feeling a pinch. But he'd kept production from stalling twice, with quick thinking and an open mind to alternatives, and he hadn't let what was clear stress and agitation affect how he treated the people around him. Simply put, he was just a nice man.

The more she saw him in action, working with the crew—because he was actually picking up slack all over the set—the more she liked him. Unlike most of the money guys on a set, he didn't just stand around watching over his investment. He was in the thick of it, always looking for a way to help and be useful.

Now, as they raced to the corner pub under twin umbrellas, she found herself laughing. "I don't know what I was thinking when I said Prague in rainy season," Rick laughed. "Wait, yes I do. Sixteen-hour days that would let us shoot a movie set in the wet outdoors in half the recommended time. I got exactly what I asked for. Rain."

"How bad is it—production-wise?"

"Honestly, not too bad. It feels bad. It looks bad. But I planned for contingencies, so we'll be okay on the timeline. What I'm worried about is morale. Everyone's been working hard, nearly twenty-hour days for weeks, and I know they were all looking forward to getting out for the weekend, no matter how briefly. I don't want this to be the worst experience these people have ever had. I'm afraid it's putting Thad off film forever."

All she could do was hum at him as he was echoing Thad's sentiments exactly. "You can't control the weather."

"I keep trying! I can't find any virgins for the ritual sacrifices."

They both laughed. He seemed to be waiting for something as they sat down in a booth and ordered. Finally, when drinks had been served, he shrugged. "So, I don't know how to ask you this, so I'm just going to do it. Did you know your friend Jill Parker had gotten married to Kline Scott?"

The words were so foreign that they passed right over Rhiannon's head for a moment. "What?"

"This came across yesterday." Rick pulled a few folded pages from the interior pocket of his leather bomber jacked and pushed a fax of a trade publication across the table. "Did They or Didn't They?" Was the headline above a grainy picture of a grinning Kline and Jill huddled together and running out of what appeared to be a wedding chapel, Jill with an armful of flowers. A smaller picture inset showed them leaning over a desk, apparently signing a document, the wobbly caption reading, "Did all those days steaming up the set on Devil's Party send the hot, hot, hot couple down the aisle? Studio insiders say the two didn't seem like they were acting while filming the big love scenes last week, and we know we've all been following Bumpwatch!"

The story below detailed the couple's wild romp in Vegas, following up with the speculation that they'd tied the knot at the same chapel as several other hot Hollywood names. Camp flacks for Kline were refusing to comment on his private life. Camp flacks for Jill weren't returning calls.

Rhiannon read over it twice, her eyes narrowing in disbelief. "This can't be true."

"It certainly looks that way to me," Rick said, seriously.

She shook her head. "It's probably just some press setup and speculation."

"In a wedding chapel in Las Vegas?"

Rhiannon bit her lips together. "Shit."

"Yeah. So, I showed Thad, wait–" He put a hand down on hers as she started to protest. "He's one of my best friends. I know they've been talking a lot, but I also know they left it as 'we'll see what happens' and he needed to know. She didn't even drop him a courtesy call. It was all over the internet fifteen minutes after I got that fax, and I didn't want him to run across it accidentally."

Rhiannon felt herself deflating. "There has to be some misunderstanding."

"It's the business, though. Couples get into character in these roles, fake fucking for a week, then convince themselves they are in love. Those two have a history, and Kline's in full competition mode with Thad. It writes itself as they say."

She let out a long breath. "I'm going to call her and ask."

"Did you read the last? She's gone on a mini-break with him and his kid in the Maldives. That's a dead zone for Wi-Fi."

"I told Thad to just make a clean cut. Even if it isn't what it appears to be, that's shit. If they did set that up for the photo op--" Rick made a disgusted noise. "That's sick, especially if she hadn't warned him."

"She wouldn't have married him," Rhiannon insisted.

"You don't know that, Rhi. It's Hollywood. People do stranger things."

"Is Thad okay?"

"He was when I left him down here last night. He said he just wanted to be alone and think."

"I'll check on him in a little while."

"Probably good. I'm sorry to spring this on you."

"At least you got to tell Thad and he didn't just find out."

"At the very least. I hate the fucking PR machine. I wish we could just make good movies and let people watch them, but the only way to get attention seems to be scandal or something so big people can't ignore the film."

"Do you just hate the business entirely?" Their food had come, but Rhiannon was feeling sick. All she wanted to do was clear out of the booth and try to call Jill, with whom she'd been playing phone tag for days.

"Honestly? Yeah. If I had my life to do over, I'd be a farmer."

They both laughed, "No you wouldn't!"

"No, I wouldn't. But maybe investment banking or something. Not this weird shit. How about you?"

Rhiannon pushed her hair behind her ears and let out a breath. There wasn't anything she could do about Jill or Thad in the moment, so she tried to shake that off. "I don't know. I don't really have to work–trust fund baby–and I've never wanted to do anything other than write. I can't say that writing has turned out to be what I thought it would, but it's not terrible. I was supposed to go to college and get my MRS, and I mortified my family by getting an MA instead. I've been trying to make my own name, outside the family. I'd still want to do that. Maybe I'd study psychology along with the writing so I could understand people better, though."

"Yeah. It's people that are the problem. Not the industry," he said with a laugh.

"People are the worst."

"The worst."

They sat in silence for a little while, each eating slowly and mulling over their own thoughts until Rick cleared his throat. "So, when this ends, if it ever ends, you going to let me take you out?"

She could feel herself smiling. "I think I might."

"Good. Then my evil plan to get you close to me long enough to realize I'm not a terrible guy worked."

"Good plan! Yeah, it didn't hurt watching you help put up rigging. Who knew you worked out?"

"My trainer. Jesus. He's killing me."

They finished out the rest of their meal in amiable conversation until Rick walked Rhiannon back to her hotel room door. "Thanks for the company," he said, and for a moment, she thought he would kiss her, but he pulled back.

"Yeah. You too."

When he had gone, she hugged herself for a second, surprised to realize that the crush she'd started nursing on him months prior had escalated into full-on desire. She didn't think she could concentrate on work, didn't want to read, and didn't want to watch another rerun of the A-Team on Prague's TV channel, so she decided to go check on Thad.

She went up a floor and down the hall to the last room on the corner and knocked. It was several seconds before a rumpled, beautiful woman answered in heavily accented English. "Yes?"

"Uh—is Thad here?"

The woman turned and called over her shoulder. She was wearing the bed sheet. "Thad! Is a woman?"

There was grumbling from within the suite and then Thad appeared, buttoning up his blue jeans. When he saw Rhiannon, he blushed to the roots of his hair and looked crestfallen. "Come on in," he said. "Ah—fuck—um, hey, sweetheart?" He addressed the sheet-clad woman, "This is business. I'm going to have to ask you to leave, okay?"

"Sure, sure. I leave you my number."

"And your name," Rhiannon suggested. "Write that down, too."

Thad gave her a look of horror and she mouthed, "What?"

"You want some coffee?"

"It's nearly seven, Thad, no, I don't want coffee. Do you need some coffee?"

"Yes, probably." He moved into the kitchenette and started the Keurig. "Piss poor excuse for coffee, but it'll do."

They made small talk until Thad's date was dressed, thanked, hugged, assured she was fantastic, and shuttled out the door, and then Rhiannon raised an eyebrow at him. "What was that?"

"That was me getting over one of my best friends stealing the girl right out from under my nose."

"Thad!"

"What?"

"Have you talked to her?"

"No. I tried to call, but just got voice mail. And before you say anything, I cut the ties with her before I brought my new friend back here."

"On voice mail?" Rhiannon felt her eyebrows fly up into her hairline.

"What else was I supposed to do? It makes sense. They've got the rest of this movie to go, then Kline's award season for Knight, then promos, then their award season for this movie. That's almost two years of publicity romance. Does that sound fake to you? This is all just a game to them."

"To him," Rhiannon corrected. "Him. Jill wouldn't have done this without telling you. She really likes you."

"She tried to call a few times, but we just played phone tag. She texted that she was going to be out of pocket and wanted to talk before she went off the grid. She probably did try to tell me." He had his hands around a strong-smelling cup of coffee by that point, bare-chested and unshaven, Rhiannon thought he ought to look like shit, but he actually just looked like an adorably rumpled lumberjack. "Anyway. I need to keep my head on until this shit with Monique is over. I don't need the distraction of a relationship. Anyway," he repeated, letting out a huge breath. "The thing with Jill is done. I never could compete with Kline."

"I'm sorry, Thad," Rhiannon said finally. "I know you liked her."

"Yeah," Thad said, weaving a little on his feet. He was tired "I really liked her."

"I know. Maybe quit dating actresses. They all suck."

"Isn't that one of the things I like about them?"

Rhiannon patted him. "Probably. Now go find yourself a nice quiet girl."

"She was a nice quiet girl."

"One that doesn't act."

"I don't know any."

"We'll find you one. Better yet, lay off women for a while. Can't hurt you."

Thad tried to give her a hard look and failed miserably. "I guess it can't."

"Just focus on the work for a while. Yeah?"

"Yeah. No, yeah, you're right. I'll focus on the work. Maybe I'll make a five-year plan."

"Even better."

Thunder boomed and rain poured that night to match Thad's mood when she passed him in the hall on Sunday, and Rhiannon found herself wishing she was anywhere else. Where else would she be, though? She spent the early hours of the morning trying to call anyone who might confirm that Jill was still Parker and not Parker-Scott, but it seemed like everyone was on hiatus and half-way across the world reading the same tabloids and wondering. August just hung up on her when she got him.

Rhiannon felt bad for Thad, but she refused to believe that Jill willingly did something so stupid as to marry Kline. Even for a publicity stunt.

Rick rang her hotel room phone and let her know that all the assembled, stranded crew was going to go down to the corner pub for lunch. He had bought the place out for the day, all drinks and pub food on his tab. "I'm a great producer," he bragged when she laughed. "Besides, the Emmy nominations are coming out and I think you'll be getting a phone call. Let's all be in one place, so we can celebrate"

The calls came before they could make it past the lobby. Simon Says was up for Outstanding Comedy Series, with both Thad and Kelsey getting nods for leading roles, and Rhiannon had scored a nomination for writing on a comedy series. It was the first bit of good news they'd had since arriving in Prague, and she felt lighter than air until she processed Thad trying to enjoy his nomination in spite of his heartbreak.

She pushed that aside. Kline and his PR machine had already stolen too much joy from her life, and she was not going to miss out on this moment because of him. She gave Thad a shove and said as much.

She, Thad, and Rick walked down together, huddled close under their umbrellas. "This is bullshit," Thad grimaced. "I'm an Emmy-nominated actor and I'm growing webs between my toes."

"When this is done, no more Prague," Rick growled, laughing.

"This weather is worse than England, mate," Thad said, slipping an arm around Rhiannon, "Poor Rhi looks like a drowned rat."

"An Emmy-nominated drowned rat," she corrected.

They hurried down to the corner, happy to find that most of the cast and crew were already packed inside, along with a smattering of locals the cast and crew had picked up along the way. The place was already loud with laughter and drunken merriment, and they had to swim through the moving tide to get to the bar. Thad repeated his drink preference to the bartender and soon the three of them were cradling steins of beer. "Oh good, the last thing dry on me was my throat!" Rhiannon said, taking a sip.

"Yep, definitely damp," Thad said, patting her rear.

She cocked an eyebrow at him over the rim of her glass as she took another drink, "You're awfully bold for someone who said I looked like a drowned rat."

"I've got bollocks of steel dear lady," He grinned. "Or glass. Whichever."

"Right. Be careful where you put your hands, or we might just find out which it is."

He chuckled and patted her back as Rick looked on with a slight frown, glancing away when he caught Thad looking. "You two?"

Rhiannon rolled her eyes to glance at Rick, then put her nearly empty glass on the bar. "Not while I'm working for him. I'm going to the ladies and then I'm going to see if there's any music to be had in this place," she said to Thad. "Order me another one, will you?"

She used the tiny toilet and washed her hands. There were

worse places to be than with people you actually liked, she decided. And she did really like Rick, and she adored Thad. She walked back into the pub to find the two of them stood sipping their drinks at the bar and laughing together, Thad's head popping up when music erupted from the corner of the room where an old jukebox had been tucked away. 'Stuck in the Middle' by Steeler's Wheel began thrumming through the not quite as ancient speaker system and Rhiannon soon grooved back up to the bar, a huge grin on her face. "I love this song! The whole juke is full of 70's music!"

"Ooh, 70s!" Thad crowed. "Great music!" He wriggled around in his seat.

Rick rolled his eyes and looked the other way. So Thad spooned up behind him and shimmied. "Cut it out, you big oaf!" Rick laughed. "Go dance with someone who fancies you."

"Fine, I will!" Thad sassed, sticking out his tongue before grabbing Rhiannon's hand and nearly pulling her off her stool. "C'mon, baby, let's dance!"

She went along without a complaint, laughing merrily as they made their way to a clear space in the floor near the jukebox and soon they were moving together to the disco backbeat from the speakers.

Some of the assembled crew started snapping pictures, and as soon as they did, Thad grabbed Rhiannon, dipped her back and kissed her dramatically before pulling her back up and spinning her out. "Love it, baby! Work it!"

She was laughing, slightly tipsy and enjoying herself for the first time in weeks, and she kept pace with him with little effort. All of the showing off that Kline had done on their first two dates faded in comparison to the natural responsiveness that Thad was capable of. He was a hell of a dancer. There was a grace, an awareness of the body and how it moves that couldn't be taught by even the best instructor. Rhiannon was dizzy when they finally stopped. "Wow, you're good!" she said, sweeping her hair back from her face. "That was fun!"

"Dancing. The vertical expression of a horizontal desire,"

he grinned. "You think I'm good on the floor you should have me in the--"

"Oh no I shouldn't."

"Rhiannon! I'm crushed," he exclaimed, looking wounded.

"No, you're not. You're just persistent."

Rick was smiling, watching them. "You are a great dancer, Rhi. Got good rhythm."

"Thanks. One of my dad's girlfriends was a dancer. I learned a few things," she said, smiling. "Quite an education growing up in the Charles household."

Dinner was lively and the morale that had been missing from the shoot seemed to appear from nowhere. "It's a Christmas miracle in July!" Rhiannon crowed, taking the floor again with Thad, dancing until they were both sweaty.

"What do you say we head back to the hotel?" Thad suggested, his cheeks red with exertion. "I've got plenty of mixers there and we can drink free. Or have coffee."

"Sounds good to me," Rhiannon said, draining the rest of her rum. "This glass is empty."

Rick looked between them and shook his head. "I'm going to stay here a while and mingle with the crew."

"Suit yourself, mate," Thad said, offering an arm to Rhiannon. "Shall we?"

"Yes," she said, nodding, taking his arm, and giving Rick a small wave.

"Night, Rickers."

Back at Thad's room he poured her a drink, handed it over and asked, "So what's the deal? I know you fancy him. Why the wait?"

Rhiannon's smile faded. "Aside from the fact I'm working for him and I'm really trying to develop a reputation as someone who doesn't sleep her way to the top?"

"Yeah, aside from that?"

She sighed, thinking about what had really bothered her in their most recent conversations. "Well, according to his philosophy, a picture's worth a thousand words, right? There must be some truth to what's being printed all the time?"

Thad sighed. "You're upset about what he had to say about Jill."

"Yes, but it's not just that. If he's so quick to believe the worst of her, Thad, based solely on what he sees and reads in the papers, what must he really think of me? That I'm some starfucker who couldn't wait to take Kline Scott for a ride and grab my fifteen minutes?"

"Rhiannon," Thad scolded gently, "He's gotten to know you. He knows you're not like that. He doesn't know her. Okay?"

"No, it's not okay. He doesn't know her. That's the whole point. He believed the worst and was awful about it, and I know I was getting some of the blame for setting you up with her," she said, seriously. "I know he's your friend, but she's my friend and if he thought so highly of me why would he doubt my judgment so sharply?"

"He's got his reasons."

"I'm sure he does. Everyone has their reasons. We all know what mine are," she said, sarcastically. "I just didn't think he judged people by their press."

"Rick was married, did you know that?"

Rhiannon looked surprised. "No."

"Yeah. He married this little girl from Iowa or somewhere. Really cute girl. Seemed to be a decent actress. They dated about six months, he got her into a film, then things started getting really serious. He proposed, she said yes. Blah blah. Right before the wedding, photos start coming out of her and another up and coming actor. She tells Rick that it's all made up press.

"She doesn't know why the media is picking on her. They get married, more photos crop up. More blah blah it's just the media. Turns out, she was a really good actress! She'd been having an affair the whole time. She even talked Rick into giving her lover a slot in a movie. He found out, realized she was using him to further her career and divorced her so fast she didn't have time to change her name on her driver's license."

"God, that's awful."

"Yeah. It was really hard on him. He was gutted," Thad said, taking another swig of his drink. "He swore off women in the industry, actresses especially. Of course, he doesn't date much as a result."

She nodded. "I guess not. I'm leery of actors, myself."

"Hey!"

"Well, you're different. I know you. And I'm not looking to date you."

"I'd date you in a heartbeat," he smiled.

"Why ruin a good thing?"

He shrugged. "I think you're still stuck on Rick anyway."

Rhiannon sighed and emptied her glass. "I am attracted to him." She shrugged helplessly.

"So, talk to him."

"Are you going to talk to her?"

"Rick didn't fuck your friend."

"That's very grown up of you."

His jaw tightened. "I don't know what I'm going to do. Maybe it's just better that it's finished. I really don't want the ghost of lovers past haunting my steps."

"Maybe it is best, but Thad, she did genuinely care about you. I can't believe she would marry Kline, or pretend to, without talking to you. Well…maybe the timing was just wrong."

"I would say that's true. The timing was very wrong," he sighed, swirling the dregs of his drink in his glass. "I'm just going to give it some space for the time being. I can't do anything while I'm here, anyway. You really should talk to Rick, though. It seems a shame that the two of you aren't even going to give it a go."

Rhiannon shrugged. "I'll think about it."

"You do that."

Rhiannon stood up, petted Thad's head and walked out of his room. Rick was coming up the stairs as she walked down the hall to her own room, and she offered him a small smile. "Tired of the crew?"

"They were tired of me. I'm the boss. They can't play with me there."

"They like you," she said, "you just need to loosen up a little bit. You have something of a reputation for a being a workaholic."

"That's because I am a workaholic," he said, chuckling. "You know that."

She nodded. "Yeah, I know that. I also know that you can be a little laid back and fun. Maybe you should let that side out a bit more."

He half smiled. "Maybe. We'll see."

"I guess we will," she agreed, opening her door. "G'night, Rick."

"Goodnight."

"Rhi?"

"Yeah?"

"Mistletoe," he said, pointing up at the sprig someone had taped above her door and everyone else's. "It's a Christmas miracle." He stepped forward and kissed her lips in one motion. When he drew back, his eyes were questions, so she stepped forward to answer, pulling him back into her room with her. They did not speak again, they didn't breathe another word until Rick was in her bed, asking, "Like this?" as he stroked his fingers inside of her.

"Yes," was the first syllable she'd managed to exhale. This was man. Not a boy. Not some actor who was worried about how he looked in the reflection of the mirror beside his bed. Not a fumbling date who'd had too much to drink. This was a solid man who knew exactly what he was doing and was taking his time to do it well.

When he had worn her out with sensation, he lay down beside her, stroking her hair, letting her spoon back against his chest. "I've been thinking," he said quietly. "I said a lot of things I didn't mean about your friend, mainly because I'd been jealous of Kline. Jealous he got to you first. And you being friends with Jill means Kline coming around, and I just made me see green. If Thad was dating Jill, more Kline. More Kline meant more opportunity for you to realize he was what you wanted. Not some stodgy producer who can't put the phone down for five minutes."

"Strange pillow talk," she said dreamily. "But go on."

"I've wanted to take you out since the Vanity Fair Party."

"I think if you'd asked me that night, I would have gone with you."

"That dress…"

She let out a throaty laugh. "Now you've seen the rest."

"I'd like to keep looking, if you don't mind."

"Mind? I'll be offended if you don't."

He laughed and kissed the back of her head.

"You can keep apologizing, too."

"Mea culpa, mea culpa, mea culpa."

They lay quietly then she said, "Jill said her attitude was that she couldn't control what was printed, so whatever came out, she just lived her life around it. She said the media makes its own character of her, and at some point, you can't control the narrative. All you can do is make an audience laugh or cry with you, and when you do that, you've won. She said people believe what they want, whether it's the kids in school passing rumors, or the gossip columns. She said if you know the person, the print shouldn't matter."

"I suppose."

"Thad told me about your ex."

"I guess I didn't know that person well enough to read between the lines of the print."

"It happens." She turned in his arms to face him.

"I think I've gotten to know you pretty well."

"I hope so." Rhiannon grinned. "You should see if Thad is willing to do a PR showmance to overshadow all the issues we've been having. Get the crew's mind off the 'curse' and onto something else."

He laughed. "And see if I can sell some nudes of him? Can you sneak into his room with a camera?"

"Why me? I don't want to see that!"

"Me either. I guess I'll have to think of something else."

Rhiannon woke to the sound of Rick's voice, soft and deep from the next room. She rolled over and snuggled into her pillow, taking a deep breath of the scent of him and sighing contentedly. She stretched, her body feeling comfortably achy after the evening's ministrations. He had proven an amazing lover, both passionate and thorough, alternately insistent and tender.

She couldn't remember when she'd experienced such deliberate attention or felt such a strong emotional response to the simple proximity of his body to hers. It had all been unexpectedly delightful and she was glad that they waited until the attraction was something more than physical before sharing that closeness. She finally felt as though she was getting it right.

She smiled and sat up, stretching again before slipping from the bed to wrap a robe around her and pad into the living room where Rick stood near the windows, pacing a slow space between them with the phone pressed to his ear. "Yes, Kyle. Just check your email. It might take a while to load. I really need you to make sure this is managed. We're already too far behind," he said, looking up and smiling at Rhiannon when she appeared. He held a hand up to indicate that he'd only be five more minutes. He mouthed, "I need to tell you something."

She nodded, knowing full well that five minutes never meant only that, especially when he was talking to his assistants, and she had other plans than talking. There were always fires to put out, and from the things he was saying, she gathered that Kyle was in a panic. She watched him for a few moments more, admiring the muscles of his back as he moved. He was wearing only his trousers from the night before and she felt her stomach do a tiny flip as she remembered what he looked like without them.

With a sly smile, she crossed the room to stand in front of him and when he gave her an apologetic look, she raised an eyebrow and sank to her knees, leaning forward to graze the muscles of his stomach with her lips as she moved steadily lower.

"I-uh-know, Kyle," he said, his breath catching slightly as her fingers slipped beneath the waistband of his pants and began to tug them down. She was planting small kisses and licks along his abdomen when he covered the phone and whispered, "Rhi, baby, what are you doing?"

"Nothing," she said, looking up at him from beneath her lashes with a bitten-lip smile.

"Heh," he managed as watched her move lower, then he uncovered the phone, "Kyle? Kyle. Listen to me. Things are--" He gasped a breath, one hand immediately reaching down to tangle in her hair when he felt the moist heat of her mouth surrounding him. "Great. Things are fine. I-I have to go. I'll check in later. Bye." He pressed the button on the phone as a moan escaped him, then threw it at the couch, for the moment completely unconcerned if it hit the floor and shattered into a million pieces.

Jill Parker

Jill stood on her patio, drinking coffee, looking out over the palm trees and rooftops that made up her view. They had a day off, and now that the sex scenes were behind them and they were into the meat of the dialog and action, she was a very different kind of tired. That tired was exacerbated by the turmoil she felt personally. Like some kind of masochist, she'd kept replaying the voice mail Thad had left for her while she'd been snorkeling in the Maldives. She hadn't heard it until the middle of the next week, given the cell phone service, but in a way, she was glad for that. If she'd gotten it before, she wouldn't have been able to enjoy a moment of the trip. She'd had trouble relaxing at it was, worried about not hearing from him.

After Thad's last voice message, she was a different kind of disheartened. "Hey, it's me," he said, sounding sloshed. "Listen. I think while I'm away, we should just cool it. Less than no strings. Just over. You're a great girl. I'm really glad we connected. You've got to go do your thing with Kline, so I'll just be here doing my thing with... whoever. But that's that. So that's that. Yeah. Um... Good luck. Right. That's that. Bye." Then, before he hung up, she could hear him calling out to someone, "Oh, hey, Beauty. Want to dance with a movie star?"

She'd just been able to pick up her messages once they were in the airport, waiting in the VIP lounge to go home, and it was all she could do not to cry when Roland, white-faced, had pulled her aside with Kline and presented a People magazine. "I didn't do this," he said. "This wasn't my plant. I'll get this sorted out as soon as we land, and I swear to God I'm never leaving the country for a wireless vacation again."

She, Kline, Roland and his new wife Shanna, Jack, Kim and Delia had come back to the States to a media frenzy that was just dying down as city offices and official documents were coming to light to lend a new narrative to the photos that were splashed across every tabloid.

Jill had thumbed through the pages of several magazines on their flight home and felt her heart sinking further with every caption that mistook her for a bride, wearing a light blue slip dress and carrying a bouquet that she'd caught when Shanna threw it backwards with glee. Even photos of Kline and her signing Roland and Shanna's wedding license as witnesses had been reported as the two of them making their own relationship legal.

The two of them had gone on a morning show to laugh about the debacle and also celebrate Kline's record-breaking box office, with Lone Star still playing hot in multiplexes across the country.

"I'm not saying it will never happen," Kline had beamed for the camera, taking Jill's hand and raising it to his lips. "But is this the kind of girl you take to Vegas for a quickie wedding?"

"Roland's going to murder you for that line," Jill teased when they were leaving.

"Then maybe don't marry the kind of girl you take to Vegas for a quickie wedding."

If he'd been interested in how the news and the retraction

of the news had affected her, he hadn't said, but he was caught up in his custody battle with Nina, and had said more than once that if he could get Jill to just marry him for a little while, he could have that sorted out in a week.

"Smashing proposal," she'd told him the last time he'd mentioned it. "I'm going to give it exactly the amount of consideration it deserves."

By the end of the first week back at work, Jill had managed to pull herself through the worst of what she recognized as heartbreak. Heartbreak and disappointment, she corrected herself. She had thought better of Thad. Still, better to find out now, she told herself.

Her therapist had congratulated her on dating someone she hadn't known since she was in leading strings, and suggested that on her next at-bat, she try dating someone even further outside of her inner circle, but Jill thought that had to wait until after the Oscars, when she could stop being so visible with Kline.

"Five-year plan," Kim had reminded her, as they talked through what she'd be wearing for the next couple of paparazzi strolls.

Somehow, Jack's nanny had become a dear friend. She hadn't wanted to tell Kline about the voice mail, and she wasn't going to call Rhiannon about it while she was away at work. So, she'd told Kim and let the other woman be the voice of reason. "Keep your eye on the prize. Five years and you're out, and then you can find a nice construction worker, or coal miner, or oil baron. But you stick to your plan, and you won't need an oil baron."

"They're all the same though, aren't they?"

"I'm a lesbian. If I weren't a lesbian, I'd be alone forever because, yes, they are all the same."

"Did Cooper call you? About the job?" Jill changed the subject before she could start to cry again. "I want our conversations to pass the Bechdel test."

Kim laughed, "Yeah. I've got kind of a styling audition next week."

"Oh good! I'm so glad."

"Thanks for doing that. I really appreciate it."

"My pleasure. It's all about who you know, right? It's only half talent. The rest is just getting to meet the right people. But I have dibs on you because you have one hundred percent talent that I need desperately."

After Jill had approved the rack of outfits, Kim had gone on her way. Jill had turned off her phones, landline ringer and mobile, and tried to read for a while. Unable to focus, she'd gotten in her car and driven to Kline's for dinner, rejecting another of his silly advances before going home to sleep in her own bed.

Now, mid-morning and mostly alone, save for the house-keeper and the PA, who had actual work to do, she took a deep breath and wondered what it was going to take for her to feel true fulfillment. She called up her therapist's office in New York and asked for an additional appointment.

In the past, she'd spent all her time with him talking about her mother, or why she wasn't enough to hold a man. Maybe she'd been asking all the wrong questions, though. Maybe, instead of how to hold a man, she needed to work on why she felt like she needed one.

She could have held Gus, she realized. He and the life he offered just hadn't been enough for her. So, as he'd said, she was giving up a solid reality to chase a fantasy.

What if she never met anyone? What if she never had any children? What if her life didn't make it possible to adopt and parent the way she wanted?

What if, she asked herself, this is all there is. What if it's just work, simple friendships, and a view from Beverly Hills?

"I have to be happy in the here and now," she said aloud. "I have to find a way to be satisfied in the present, so I've got a hope in hell of enjoying the future. And it can't be because I'm pinning my hopes on a man. Oh—that's healthy. I need to write that down."

Healthy carried her into the next day and through the next week. Healthy carried her all the way into the makeup chair on

Tuesday, where it promptly abandoned her with a lapful of mag-azines that the hair girl had brought in.

Thad and Rhiannon, together at last, her brain captioned the photos of the two of them dirty dancing in some kind of bar. The two of them looked more comfortable together than she'd ever felt with anyone in her life.

The story that accompanied the exclusive photos was a nas-ty little piece about how Kline Scott's former flame had started a fire with his best friend only weeks after Scott had set her aside for the love of his life. Eyewitnesses to the kiss captioned with, "Simon Says kiss me, kiss me, kiss me, said that the two had been inseparable on the set of Circle Sky in Prague, and wondered what the future held for the writer and sitcom star.

While she worked that day, all she could hear was the last line of Thad's voice mail ringing in her ears. "Oh, hey, Beauty. Want to dance with a movie star?" He'd been talking to Rhiannon, she supposed. At least she didn't have to draw on old wounds to bring up the tears Devon needed to cry as she decided to murder her lover. The fresh ones would do just fine.

When they were released, she found herself walking toward Kline's trailer instead of her own and swallowed hard. She knew what she was going to do, and if he rejected her, it was going to be brutal. Hell, if he accepted her invitation, it would be brutal in an entirely different way. But, at least it would hurt less than this.

She knocked and felt her stomach flip when he opened the door smiling quizzically. It wasn't too late. She could just ask him to dinner and see what happened. She could just tell him how much she had appreciated his friendship through the shoot so far. What she did was walk up the steep steps, close the door behind her and ask, "Do you want to have sex?"

And then it was Ugg boots, and sneakers, and hoodies and shirts, and jeans, and underwear flying like a tornado had explod-ed in the small space, and lips, and teeth, and hands, and nails, climbing each other until he was finally inside of her. It was fast and filthy, and then the next time was slower–almost like both of them were making sure they had actually just survived the last bout, until they were recovering on their backs, holding hands in the middle of his trailer's bed.

"You've learned some things," he finally said appreciatively.

"You have too."

"That was amazing."

"Yes." She was nodding.

"Come home with me?"

"Oh, yes."

When the next week's magazines came out, there weren't any new photographs of them to run, but one of the internet sites ran a blind item about a fake couple that had gone real, asking if that's why no one had seen the two lately. They worked, they went back to his place, they ate, they played with Jack, then they fucked like rabbits until they had to go back to work the next day until several days later when they woke up, looked at each other, tried to kiss, then both started laughing.

"You're done?" Kline asked. "You get that out of your system?"

Jill considered his face a long time, then shrugged. "Yeah. I think I'm good."

"Me too."

"Friends?" She asked, knowing the answer.

"Always and forever."

She sat up and went toward the shower. "I'm just gonna— And then I'm going home."

"Sure." He was grinning. "Hate when you leave, but I love to watch you go. Use me to burn out your heartbreak anytime."

"What?"

"I read the tabs," he shrugged, sitting up in bed. "I figured you'd talk if you wanted to talk. I kinda like the way you decided to deal with it, though. Worked out for me."

Jill groaned and threw one of his shoes at him, "You've heard the saying about getting over someone by getting under someone else."

"I'm just glad I could be of service."

Once she was home, she sorted through a pile of messages her PA had transcribed from the answering machine for her. Several were from Rhiannon, who was worried that Jill hadn't returned any of her earlier calls. Without bothering to check the time or even think about what she wanted to say, she dialed her friend's number.

"I'm fine," she said to Rhiannon's voice mail. "It's just been an intense schedule with some pretty dramatic days. The worst is over until I have to kill Kline on camera. Hope you're staying dry. Kiss, kiss."

In another couple of hours her phone rang and she answered. Caller ID said it was Rhiannon, and Jill wondered what her friend would have to say, or if she was even still her friend. "Hello?" She let *Jill Parker Tony Award-Winning Actress* answer the phone. *Jill Parker Jilted Lover* would have to wait her turn.

"Jill! I've been so worried!"

"I'm so sorry. I wasn't prepared for how hard shooting a movie was going to be. I've been exhausted. How are you?"

"And you haven't answered your phone at all?"

"I haven't. Anything work-related has been going through Jennifer or Roland, and I honestly just turned off real life. Jennifer's my new PA. She's the best! I'm so sorry I haven't called. I didn't think you'd be worried. It didn't occur to me."

"And you didn't marry Kline."

"No! Ha! No. That was... Roland and his girlfriend got married. It was a quickie thing in Vegas, and he invited Kline and me along. I caught the bouquet." Jill explained with a little more detail, hoping that might encourage Rhiannon to offer her own.

"And signed as witnesses," Rhiannon sighed.

"Yes. The press had a field day until the forms went public and everyone could see it wasn't us."

"It made it all the way to Prague."

"What?"

"Yeah. That's why– Thad thought–"

"Oh," Jill said, clucking her tongue. "Oh. That makes sense."

"He was gutted."

Jill felt her eyebrow arch involuntarily. "Yeah, he was really broken up."

"What?"

Laughing, she imitated the Aussie's last words before he'd managed to hang up. "He was so sad. Clearly."

"He really was!"

"How about you? Were you gutted?" She hadn't meant to say it. She hadn't meant to break character. At least, if she did, she had meant to just come out and ask about the photos. Of all people, Jill understood the havoc a well-timed shutter click could wreak. But something in her heart had wrenched at the thought of Thad's hands-on Rhiannon's hips, his face buried in the curve of her neck as he danced up behind her. One more man who preferred that woman to her.

"What?"

"Oh, maybe your own affair hasn't made it all the way back to Prague yet."

"What?"

"I have to go, Rhiannon, but it's rich coming from you. Really, really rich." It was unfair, and Jill knew it, but it was also beyond her to be reasonable right then.

As Rhiannon parroted her question again, Jill hung up. "I need new friends," she said to the telephone. "A whole new list of friends. And I want a dog."

Chapter 9

Rhiannon Charles

Rhiannon hung up the phone and turned to Rick, who was just entering the room with a towel wrapped around his waist. They had four days left in Prague, then it was back to LA where she and Thad would immediately start work on the sitcom, and start campaigning for the Emmys.

The news of the nominations seemed to have broken the curse the production struggled under, and brought its own miracle. The last two weeks of work had been seamless and even a little magical, as cast and crew threw in together, working their asses off to make up for lost time. It was exhausting and amazing, and she couldn't remember working on anything that gave her such a sense of fulfillment. Granted, Rhiannon was looking at everything through the rose-colored glasses of a blossoming relationship, but everything did seem like it was finally making sense. Now this phone call?

"That was Jill," Rhiannon explained. "She was… 'upset' seems like an understatement. She was saying something about my affair?"

Rick frowned. "About us?"

"I don't know. I don't think so."

He hummed and went to his laptop. He pecked around on the keyboard for a few seconds, then let out a long breath. "Fuck," he said.

Rhiannon grabbed her robe and hurried around behind him, feeling her eyes bulge a little as she looked over his shoulder. He had opened up on a gossip blog, one of the nastier ones as she recalled, and there were photos of her with Thad from the night they had danced in the pub. The night she'd gone back to the hotel and gone to bed with Rick.

The captions were awful, calling her a starfucker and a slag, showing censored versions of the photos with Kline, and some of the photos from the damned Vanity Fair party with her dress gone sheer in the lights. Rhiannon was shocked, her mood deflating almost as quickly as it had the first time she'd seen herself naked on the cover of a tabloid. "What? We're--"

"What's next for the star of Simon Says?" Rick read aloud, switching tabs to People Magazine online. "Thad James split with his third wife, supermodel Monique Pelletier, only weeks ago. Now he's in Prague filming Circle Sky. Love life? Hot! He's been heating up the scene with a familiar face. They got rude for a sec, I'll skip that." He continued with, "Kissing, clowning, and carrying on, is this the next future ex-Mrs. James?"

"Oh god," Rhiannon groaned. "And there are all the pictures! Oh my god."

Rick clicked through a few more links, all more of the same, until he came to one where Kline was quoted as saying, "Good for them! Thad's one of my best friends, and Rhiannon's a great catch." He clucked his tongue. "At least he got that bit right."

"Not funny, Rick. Jill believes this. How could she believe this?"

"The photos do match the captions," Rick said carefully. "If I hadn't been standing there myself…"

"Don't say that."

"Don't say what? That a picture is worth a thousand words?"

Rhiannon covered her mouth and started to cry. It was just a stream of tears at first, but then a sob broke through and her whole body was shaking. Rick shoved the laptop aside and stood, spinning around to grab her up in his arms. "No, no, baby, don't cry. It's okay. This is okay. It's just a misunderstanding."

"It's my life!" she sobbed. "It's my career and my friendships, and my family will see that! My writing staff will see that!

Everyone's going to think my entire success is because of who I am fucking!" She pushed back from him.

"No! They won't, they'll–"

"It's like the 'wedding photos' Rick!" She recounted what Jill had told her, watching his face change as he realized what he had done in encouraging Thad to cut ties over a gossip story.

"Okay," he said softly, and she watched him shift gears again into solution mode. "Okay. You're right. Listen… Why don't you stay here today. I'll tell everyone you're sick. I'll talk to Thad and I'll call Kyle. We'll get this figured out. Don't worry. We're going to get this figured out."

"I just don't understand how it happened. It means that someone on our team sold the pictures and the story."

"Or a local. It could have been a local."

"How would they have contacts at US? For an indie film?"

"Well, we have been here a while. Maybe a local outlet is connected?"

"This is… It's mortifying, honestly." Rhiannon wiped her face and took a shuddering breath. "At least with the nudes–at least that was the truth. But this? You were there! You saw what it was."

"With my own two eyes," Rick said. He shook his head. "I'm so sorry this happened. This fucking film–it's cursed. I'm so sorry."

"You didn't do it," Rhiannon said.

"No, but it happened on my watch. On my film. Jesus."

"They just make up the stories they want to tell to sell the magazines. You can't even live a life without someone there to take a picture if you're halfway famous."

"Are you going to be okay?" He looked stricken.

Rhiannon sat down on the edge of the bed. "I honestly don't know." She threw up her hands. "I went to LA to take the Simon Says job because it would look good on my resume. I knew it was a setup. Everyone said it was a setup because they were trying to cancel the show, so if they brought in an inexperienced head writer it would be easier to blame me when ratings dropped. I took it on as a challenge and I got them nominated for an Emmy. I went to LA to prove myself, and just when I thought I had, just when we got the nomination–this. I just look like I sleep with everyone. Now? This is going to overshadow everything I've worked for.

"I took this job thinking I could prove myself in a different way, and now it's going to look like I only got the job because I was sleeping with Thad. And god forbid anyone finds out I'm actually sleeping with you."

He said nothing, just let her continue. "I hate how it is for women in this industry. In my internships, in my first few real writing jobs, they all came with a certain amount of getting my ass slapped. I took it like everyone else does. I laughed at the jokes like everyone else does. I tried to be above the constant harassment– even Thad's teasing, you know? But I never slept with anyone for a job. No matter how hard I work, though, there's always something that brings it back down to who I might or might not be fucking."

"I didn't give you this job because I wanted to sleep with you," Rick said in a strangled voice.

"I should hope not!"

"I gave you this job because I was impressed with your work. I know you never slept with anyone for a job."

"Well, the rest of Hollyweird seems to think that since I slutted it up with Kline, I'm just willing to slut it up with anyone. Now with this, it's going to be even worse."

"I'll make a statement on behalf of you both," Rick said. He was looking for his pants. "I'll make it a priority."

"I don't want any statements made. The pictures show exactly what the captions describe. There isn't a statement that can be made that changes that. People are going to look at those pictures and see what they want to see. I just don't know if this is the life I want to have. As long as I'm working in this industry, being in the same room with famous people, I run the risk of more of this."

"Please don't let this stop you from your career! You're good at your job!"

"If it affects my career, it's only going to be from the perspective of where I'm sitting. I'm not going to let those bastards keep me from doing what I love. I'll just find a different way to do it."

Jill Parker

The trailer was still and quiet, nothing but the constant hum of the air conditioning unit stirring the air as Jill sat staring at the clock. Now and then, a voice or laughter from outside would turn her head, but for the past eleven minutes she'd been daring the digital numbers to flash forward to 10:27. She had four more minutes to go before she could walk back into the bathroom and check the results on the pregnancy tests she'd taken. Technically, she told herself, she could have just stood over the tests in the bathroom for fifteen minutes to watch them develop, but that had never helped before.

It was the last week of filming, and she was realizing that what she thought was stress, or a bug simply wasn't. She had felt this way before, with a constantly sour stomach and sore boobs, and even though she wasn't truly late for her period yet, it also hadn't started when she'd expected. So, she had asked her PA to discreetly pick up a few home tests. Now, watching the clock, she couldn't decide how she wanted the tests to read.

If it was negative, she told herself, no worries. Negative was good. Negative meant the five-year plan was on track and she just needed the warning to be more careful about birth control. If it was positive? She couldn't even let herself think about that because if it was negative, she was going to be so disappointed. Just the thought of being pregnant made her heart leap and she couldn't let herself even go down the path of all the cons of an unplanned baby without that little voice in her head echoing the word, "baby!" Anyway, if it was positive, she was sure her entire team would be there to outline every wrinkle it would cause.

In a show of self-discipline second only to how long it had been since she'd tasted ice cream, Jill waited six minutes before steeling herself. The four steps from where she sat on the bed of her trailer to the closed door of the bathroom stretched out like a mile until she could put her hand on the doorknob and give herself the big reveal.

She had three different tests lined up in row, and every single one of them was a full on, no-mistaking-it positive. Staring, smiling, she picked each one up and inspected it carefully before quickly hiding the three tests in a zippered pouch she used to carry tampons. She washed her hands, the sink counter, then took all the detritus from the test boxes and crushed it all up together, tying the trash tightly in the drugstore bag it had all come in. That went into the bottom of her tote bag.

She would tell her PA that the results had been "nothing to worry about," she decided. The next step was going to be seeing an actual physician so she could be sure about the timing, but she had a very strong feeling that this was just the beginning of an entirely new drama. Suddenly, all the cons started rolling in.

If this was Kline's baby, she was tied to him for life. At least she knew him. If it was Thad's baby, all she really knew about him was three women had divorced him, and now he was sleeping with Rhiannon. He had tried to call a few times since her brief conversation with Rhiannon, but she blocked his number. Same with Rhiannon. She didn't want to deal with either one of them—the film was taking all her energy—and she certainly didn't want to deal with them over the phone.

Before she could start to spiral, she quashed the thoughts like she'd done the boxes the tests came in.

She'd lost three pregnancies before. There was no reason this one should be different. She could lose this one just as easily, and given the schedule she was keeping and the work she was doing, and given that she couldn't exactly call a halt to the work or the schedule to announce she was knocked up, she needed to take a breath, relax, and not get too attached, at least not until she had passed the three-month mark. In fact, she decided, she wasn't going to tell anyone until she'd passed that mark.

When her assistant came to call her to set, she walked out with an air of relief. "Nothing to worry about," she told her, fanning herself.

"Oh good!"

"But would you do me a favor and get me scheduled to see a doctor? A scare like that—I want to make sure I'm all loaded up on the right prescriptions. You know?"

"Of course! I know just the right practice. I'm sure they'll get you in."

"Thank you." Jill dimpled, then spoke to crew as she passed by each one. That was something Kline was good at that she'd stolen from him. He talked to everyone. He was surface friendly, and he glad-handed like a politician, but he learned every name on the set and then used everyone's name when he said hello to them each day.

She was less flirty about it than he was, but after the first week, they'd started competing to see who could assemble the most information about crew members' lives in their short conversations between takes. Jill was in nearly every scene shot, so she had one up on him when it came to exposure to the crew, but his Hollywood charm was much more well-developed, so they were neck-and-neck as they were coming to the last few days of principal photography.

Two days prior they had completed the murder scenes, and now it was just dialog to close out the unfinished pages, and Jill found herself wistful about the shoot coming to an end. Something she'd been terrified of doing, and then exhausted by doing, had become a little family of actors and technicians she looked forward to seeing every day.

The Devil's Party set had begun to feel like a home, much like the Broadway theater had. In ways, it was more like a home because of the way people took care of her there. On the stage, she moved through her role nightly with a cast that felt equally balanced. Maybe she had the lion's share of the dialog, but it took every actor being in place to make the stage show run. It was more equitable, and while she may have closed the curtain with her bow, they all shared the final spotlight. She had even done her own makeup for the stage show.

On the film set, she and Kline were obviously the stars, and they were pampered and coddled, set apart and treated like they'd come down from Mount Olympus when they stopped to say hello, not to mention the girl whose job it was to just blot Jill's nose and chin between takes, and smooth down her hair with a rattail comb and spritz.

She had told Kline, "I understand how people get addicted to the attention. I always thought nothing could compare to the ovation at the bow, you know? But now I've had people telling me how amazing I am all day, every day. Even when Mitch has notes, there's someone there to pump up my ego after he's deflated it. That's someone's job. Someone gets paid just to tell me I'm pretty and I say things out loud well."

"You are pretty, and you do say things out loud well."

She laughed. "If you ever decide to get out of acting, I have a job for you!"

"It is addictive," he agreed. "When I did Knock, you know, I went from underwear modeling to that. Just boom, I was on a sitcom. And for most of us, it was our first big job. We all kind of fell in love with each other and the crew, and whenever we went on hiatus, it felt like getting kicked out into the cold. We'd been in this cocoon for months, all warm and happy, and then we were just on our own. It can do your head in."

"I'm afraid this is going to do my head in, when we wrap."

"That's why you always have to know your next step. What's yours?"

"Roland's negotiating into that action comedy I crashed my-self into. Clara thinks we'll see things heat up after Devil's Party gets released, but for now, I guess I'm doing the rounds to meet the right people, shake the right hands, and avoid the wrong couches."

"I'll help you do that."

"You are a wrong couch!"

He laughed and patted her on the head.

Jill had walked in and out of rooms in her house until her own wee hours. She'd picked the one she wanted for the nursery, she thought. It was bright and full of natural light. This time, she told herself, as soon as she thought it was safe to do it, she was buying the tacky green and purple frog decor she had always secretly wanted. It was cute and friendly, and if there was going to be a small person in her home, that's what she wanted the space to reflect.

That's what she was thinking about when she left the physician's office with a bag full of pre-natal vitamins and ultrasound scans. Well, and that she had to make it through the wrap party without anyone noticing she wasn't drinking, and wondering how she was going to tell Kline. Roland was going to kill her, she thought.

But when the time came, Roland had surprised her with calm, clear-eyed support. When she'd questioned him, he said, "You're an investment, sweetheart. What's my ROI if run you off? Anyway, if the kid's cute, we can put him to work. Here's what we're going to do: We're going to get you cast as the voice of a Disney princess, or a Pixar monster or something. We're going to get you the highest paying, behind the scenes job we can find you. You're going to do the makeup thing your guy at Gersh got you, you're going to do the bit in the that Thanksgiving movie, and then you're going to have this baby and get back to fighting weight before anyone even knows what's happened."

"I'm not sure how that's going to work," she'd said.

Clara gave her a smile. "You can trust us. We're your team and we're going to get you through with your plan intact. Maybe slightly delayed, but intact."

"Your five-year plan is my kid's Harvard tuition," Roland teased. "I'm not giving up on it. She graduates in four years."

"So," Jennifer said, "we just need to get you through the

wrap of Devil, and then your biggest public facing events would just be as Kline's date to the Globes, the SAGs and Oscars. Easy enough. With any luck, you won't even be showing until after the Globes and do you know how much mileage we can get out of one babydoll dress on the red carpet? It's perfect. Devil won't start promotion until next October and you won't premier until December. We'll blast you everywhere until you start to show, then we'll send you underground, but we'll have so much saturation it won't even matter. Trust me. I'm an expert."

"Or," Roland said, "you could use this to build a new narrative and—"

"I think I'll go with Clara's idea on this!"

"When are you going to talk to the father? Is he going to be a problem? Is it Kline?"

"Uh… we had to rehearse?"

Roland snorted out a laugh. "You have the worst luck in love, kid."

"Tell me about it."

Clara made some notes. "Make sure you let Kline know. Your stylist and your PA will have to know—all your staff, but we've got them under NDAs and they're well vetted, so I think you're safe. When you talk to Kline, just let me know how you guys want to play it out."

"And if he doesn't want to play it out," Roland said, "you send him to me."

Kline Scott

"You sure you're up to this?" Kline asked Jill as Kim zipped her into a silver gown with a deep, plunging V-neck, sure to pop on the red carpet at the Golden Globes, where he was nominated for actor in a drama motion picture.

"I'm fine," she laughed over her shoulder.

He considered her. The gown was a shimmering, body-skimming sheath and if he hadn't known what was going on under the paillettes, he never would have guessed. She'd been sheepish and afraid when she'd told him, defensive and hopeful, then defensive again. She'd rejected his proposal and insisted she would only ever marry someone because they loved her, not because her birth control had failed. "Anyway," she had sniffed at him. "You'd just cheat on me."

"Open marriages are a thing," he had reminded, and she'd swatted him.

"No. I don't want to marry you, and you don't want to marry me. We'll just…we'll co-parent."

"And in five years when you want to move away?" He had felt his stomach start to turn as he said the words. Jack was in Florida with Nina and her parents until March, Nina deciding–and Kline being unable to disagree–that it would be better for Jack to be with her during awards season, while Kline would be off campaigning for his Oscar non-stop.

"In five years, you're still this baby's father," Jill had promised him. "If you want to be part of its life, I won't move off or shut you out. I missed so much not having a father. I wouldn't do that to this baby. Anyway, I've seen you in action. You're pretty good at the dad thing."

Now, Kim was applying double-sided tape to the daring neckline of the gown, and the makeup artist was dusting a fine silver powder across Jill's shoulders, arms, and decolletage while Kline tied his own tie. Jill had talked him into a man-bun that she had done up herself, and two days of stubble. Looking in the mirror, he had to smile at himself. "I'm really fucking hot," he said to no one in particular.

"You're gorgeous. You look like an angel gone bad," Jill agreed.

Her own hair had been carefully styled into a mess of pre-Raphaelite curls, done up in a halo of silver ribbon. "You just look like an angel. Next year, when Devil's Party is up for all the awards, you need to do this exact look in black."

"This time next year…oof. Life is going to be very different."

"Yeah, you're going to have a Golden Globe and be an Oscar and a Grammy away from being the first EGOT in the family."

"I need to get to work on that album, don't I?"

Dressed, Kline handed Jill her little bag and they headed out to the car while Kim and her assistant took care of the mess that had been made. Once they were in the limo, Kline said, "You know Thad and Rhiannon are going to be there?"

"I know. And hopefully they win all their categories."

"Have you talked to either of them?"

Something like shame crept up over her face and she shook her head. "No."

"Jill! I told you! It was all a big misunderstanding!"

"I saw Thad's statement."

"But you still haven't returned any of his calls?"

"Kline, he dumped me via voice mail. Regardless of what all went down between Rhiannon and him, he dumped me by voice mail, and then he didn't return my calls when I wanted to explain. I really liked him, but that's not going to work for me."

"What about Rhiannon? She's your friend."

"Yeah, I'm sure she wants to talk to me after I took her head off over a gossip story that wasn't even true. Pot calling the kettle black and all. Anyway, I wasn't a great friend to her when I was in New York with you. I can admit that. She's so close with Thad that I think it's just better to just leave it alone. He's her friend and her coworker. I need to just let it be."

They rode in silence for a little bit and then Kline scooted sideways to wrap an arm around her shoulders, kissing the top of her head when she leaned into him. They were friends, he thought. Actual, real friends. Somehow, in the past several months, she'd become one of his best friends. There were worse things than having a baby with a friend.

"You know, we could buy a bigger place," he mused aloud. "Like a split property. We could live on it together and still have separate lives."

"Your house is already that big," Jill teased him. "It's just not baby-proofed at all."

"Well, let's look for something? It can't hurt to look. And Roland will love it if we get papped looking at homes together."

"I just moved into my house! I don't want to move again! I'm right down the street from you anyway. When," she lowered her voice, "when the baby gets here, I'll give you a key and you can come and go as you please."

"But–"

"Eventually you're going to start dating someone again. I really don't want to walk out into my backyard and find you nailing some girl over the diving board when I just want to tan."

He considered that a moment, then shrugged and chuckled. "Fair enough. But how about for now? For tonight? You are looking very nice in that dress. I could help you out of it later."

"Is there such a thing as an anti-roofie? Can I slip it in your drink? What happened to Jerri?"

"She got a job on the Brad Pitt thriller. I think she's sleeping with him now," he nuzzled her neck, smiling when she let him and even tilted her head a little. He kissed her ear. "We want to hit the carpet looking loved up, right? So, let's make out a little?"

That was how they had tumbled out of the limo, laughing and mussed, to walk up the red carpet looking like the happiest couple in the world. At each press station, they repeated their answers. He was in Tom Ford, hair and glow by Jill. She was in vintage Halston, wearing Cartier jewels and was delighted to be the new face of the brand. They were both so happy to have finished Devil's Party and so proud of the work, and Jill was thrilled to be there for what she was sure would be Kline's big win for Knight.

Their table was up close to the stage, where they sat with other Knight attendees. Kara Viceroy was there with her date, some no-name from some tech company, and the director and screenwriter and their dates. He and Jill separated to work the room, and he found himself over with the cast of Simon Says, hugging Thad and Rhiannon in turn. "How's it going, movie star?" he asked Thad.

"Fuck off! I'm never doing that again. Sitcoms for me only."

"That bad?"

Rick appeared from out of the crowd and said, "Everyone was joking that the movie was cursed, only I don't think it was a joke."

"We were filming over an ancient burial ground," Rhiannon said seriously, making him laugh.

"Jill here with you?" Thad asked, eyes scanning the crowd.

"Yeah. I think she's over talking to Chenowith."

Without another word, the tall Aussie walked away, and Kline said to Rhiannon, "She's embarrassed. She feels terrible about the whole you-and-Thad picture thing."

"I think we've all got plenty of embarrassment to go around," Rhiannon sighed as Rick slid an arm around her waist. "Plenty. I just don't want it to ruin our friendship."

"If it's an actual friendship, it won't," Rick said.

"She's had a lot going on," Kline said. "The end of the shoot came with some surprises that have pretty much taken up all the space in her world, you know?"

"Is she okay?" Rhiannon asked.

"Yeah, yeah. I've been there for her. Oh, don't look so shocked. Now and then I can do something for someone else. I can be a good friend."

"He can," Rick said with a weary sigh. "But it'll cost you. You have to keep that ego fed."

"What can I say? Big talent, big ego." Kline grinned at both of them. "What's your next move, Big Man?"

"Development deal with the Beeb to turn the Dove of Dreams book series into a serial drama. I'll probably be here a few more weeks, until that's done, then I'm back off. I'm trying to convince this one to come with me if I do." He gave Rhiannon a squeeze and she smiled like a teenager in love.

"I'm thinking about it." She looked back to Kline. "I've got this season to finish, though, and I don't want to leave the team in the lurch. Honestly, that whole group has been fantastic with me through my own drama, you know? Two photo scandals in under a year?"

"Proves you're a hot commodity on the wrong side of the camera," Kline said. "The camera loves you, baby."

They stood chatting amiably until the orchestra started, and then Kline shook hands and hugged his way around their table, offering luck until Thad reappeared and they shared their own man-hug. "Break a leg," Thad told him. "I'm rooting for you." He sat down, dateless Kline noticed, with Rhiannon and Rick beside him.

Striding back to his own table, he found Jill already seated, chatting casually with Kara's date. Kara was on the other side, so the directors had decided to focus on Kline and Jill, not on trying to make a threesome happen. "Hey, babe," he greeted, sitting down next to her and reaching across to introduce himself to the date. He kissed Jill's cheek and murmured, "Did Thad find you?"

She nodded and leaned into his side as a camera panned and said back through a painted-on dreamy smile. "Mm hmm. I just got a nice little ass-chewing about how much I'd hurt Rhiannon."

"What?"

"Mm hmm. But he did say I looked nice."

"You look better than nice. You okay?"

The orchestra swell was rising, and she shrugged slightly. "I really liked him, and I thought that he really liked me, but you know what they say. Fast fires flame out fast. Not that it matters, Daddy."

He felt himself actually blush and gave her another squeeze. It was a long night, and he was antsy, waiting for his category, which came late in the show. He watched Jill pick her way across the room to lean down and speak to Rhiannon at a break, and then he made small talk with the seat filler who took her place. When Jill hadn't returned after the next break, he started to worry, but she reappeared looking only a little pink around the edges just before he had to take the stage to present an award, so her seat filler just moved on over.

From his vantage point onstage, he flirted with the crowd and acted out his banter with Kara Viceroy, his co-presenter, and after they'd announced the winner, he stepped back to wait for the speech. He caught sight of Thad and his table. Rhiannon was back, too, under Rick's arm. She looked the same as always, caught somewhere between a wry smile and boredom, he thought, and he wondered what had gone on between the two women.

He was back in his seat by the middle of the next break and asked Jill what had happened. She shrugged and said, "Thad gave me hell for hurting Rhiannon, then Rhiannon gave me hell for hurting Thad. I've taken my lumps, now I get on with it. Granted, it was a cowardly move to try to talk to her during a break, but it's done. I've done it. I've apologized to both of them in person."

"It'll be okay," Kline promised, hoping it would, since Thad was one of his oldest friends.

"If it isn't, I'll pretend it is, and so will they. So, in a way, it will be. What's the next category?"

"Thad's and then the show."

"If he wins, I'm not clapping."

"You could just go to the loo."

"Oh! I could. You're a genius!" She kissed his cheek and disappeared without another word, returning only after Thad and the cast and writing team for Simon Says had both collected their awards. Then, she was in adoring girlfriend mode through the last segment of the evening, kissing Kline with a happy passion when his name was announced as the winner for his category.

He took the stage steps by twos and held his award high over his head, pumping it in the air. "I know it's uncool to be this excited," he said, leaning into the microphone, "but I am this excited! It's amazing to win this award." He took a moment to gaze at the little statue in disbelief. Acting. He'd earned that paperweight! "I cannot thank you enough for recognizing this movie and my work in this movie." He rattled off the list of names he needed to thank, then paused just long enough for the camera to pick up the look of love he had called up around his eyes. "Jilly? Babe… Thank you!"

The orchestra swelled, the crowd cheered, out of the corner of his eye he saw that the monitor had picked up Jill blowing him a kiss with both hands, and he walked into the wings, still holding his award high over his head, before having to hand it to the PA, who would run it back to another presenter to reuse. His real award would come in the mail.

The Knight team was right back up after sweeping their big categories, Kara winning for her role, and the movie winning as well. By the time he finally made it back out to Jill, his whole face hurt from smiling. She met him with genuine happiness and played her part as his adoring partner through the night into morning as they made the rounds to various parties, then crashed out in his bed without even taking off her dress.

But, by the time he woke midday, she had already gotten up and gone back to her own house, leaving him a note that said, "Have a great day, Winner." Winner. He liked the sound of that.

Chapter 10

Jill Parker

ill left Kline sleeping and drove the half block back to her own home, surprised to find paparazzi at her gate. She rolled down her window, waved at them and yelled, "Don't you guys ever sleep? That was a long night!"

One called back, "Where's Kline?"

"He's snuggling his trophy. There isn't room in bed for me with all the trophies!"

"Picture?" Another one called.

"Give me thirty minutes to wash my face and I'll come give you something if you'll leave me alone. My head is splitting!"

They agreed, so she drove into her garage, making sure the gate shut behind her and only her, and then went into the house. She felt like garbage, but she washed her face, piled her hair up in a messy bun that was actually kind of cute given how all the curl had held, then put on her tiniest satin robe and prepared to walk down to the gate. First, she hit the intercom. "I'm going to come out and go to my mailbox," she told the photographers. "You're getting me without makeup, so be nice!"

They were as nice as paparazzi ever are, snapping pictures like their lives depended on it as she strolled down to her empty mailbox, and then hurried back up to her gate as though she'd been caught out unawares and was horrified. As soon as she was back through the wrought iron, the cameras stopped and one guy called, "Thanks, Jill!"

"Anytime." A no-makeup photo of any actress was worth big bucks. A no-makeup photo of an actress in a short robe that barely covered her ass and showed off her nipples? Someone was putting a kid through at least a semester at college. She was going to have to figure out the short robe equivalent of a baby bump.

Back inside, she started retching as if on cue, and spent the next ten minutes alternating between telling herself that morning sickness was a good sign and wishing she'd never heard the word 'sex.' She brushed her teeth and got a ginger ice pop from the freezer and sucked on that until her stomach started to feel right again. Then she blended one of the smoothie mixes the chef had left for her and drank that with her vitamins.

Finally, she stripped to the skin and waded into her swimming pool to lie on her back and float. She was turning into a prune when the intercom buzzed her up and back into her robe to take a delivery of flowers. "I was incredibly rude last night," the card on the bouquet of white roses read. "Start fresh? Thad."

In turn, that made her call up a florist and send an apology arrangement to Rhiannon. "Sorry for ambushing you. I'm the worst. Mea culpa. JP."

Then, chewing her bottom lip, she unblocked both of them on her contact list. No sooner had she finished, but her phone was ringing, showing Thad's number. She hesitated, but answered. "Hello?"

"I got a delivery notification, and I was hoping you'd read the card?" he said without preamble.

"You were pretty rude."

"I'm sorry. I'm so sorry. I've been a great arse about this whole thing and when I saw you, I lost my head a little. A lot. It was easier to get mad than to get honest."

"Well, you were certainly angry."

"I'm sorry. Jill, I'm sorry. I can make all kinds of excuses about how I was out of my element in Prague, and I was feeling insecure and having all the imposter syndrome, and missing my kids, and drowning in mud, and how it affected my judgment, but the bottom line is that I didn't give you benefit of the doubt when you'd already told me all the truth about what was going on and what would continue to go on with you and Kline. I fucked up."

"I was in the Maldives when the story came out. We went on a little holiday with Roland and Shanna. We didn't even know about it until we got to the airport, so I couldn't warn you. With everything–when those photos of you and Rhiannon came out, well. I thought you were moving on."

"No. I mean, I didn't spend my time alone over there, to be perfectly honest. But I also didn't spend my time with Rhi outside of the time the whole cast and crew were together, and you saw all those pictures. It was bad timing."

"I didn't spend my time alone here either, if we're talking about that."

"Kline?"

"Yes."

"Are you two an actual couple now?" She thought she heard him swallow hard.

"No. In a funny way, it was just good closure. Got him out of my system, so to speak." She almost laughed at her own words. No one had ever been more completely tied to her system.

"Do you want to have lunch? Start over? My divorce is final and I'm actually single."

"Thad–"

"If you don't want to, that's okay, but I really felt like we had a connection, and I don't want to lose that because I was so fucking stupid. At least would you give me the chance to run you off with my boring, mundane, never at home because I'm always working life like the rest of them?"

"I don't think you're boring or mundane."

"I am always working."

"So am I."

"So, lunch?"

"I like lunch."

It took a while to find time in their calendars, and honestly, that was fine with Jill. They had made and rescheduled two dates since their call, but he'd sent flowers and chocolates, and called every day, texting her jokes as he thought of them, so she felt like she'd spent a lot of time with him. It was a soft launch back into friendship–that was the most she was letting herself hope for at the moment.

In another attempt to regain ground, August had been over to see her. "I promised you we'd always be friends," he had said, kissing both her cheeks. "I keep my promises. Are you back on carbs? You look bloated." He walked through her new home scrutinizing it in a way that made her very glad she hadn't tried to shoehorn herself into his very clear aesthetic for the rest of her life, and it felt very naughty and good to be sitting across from him with a human baby cooking inside her, and her new puppy scampering around at her feet.

It felt less good and was very difficult to not tell Thad about the baby each time they talked, but she was still afraid that things might fall apart and she didn't want to have to go through the sympathetic smiles and well-wishes if she lost this pregnancy like she had the others. She could wait a minute more.

When he arrived for a late lunch on a Sunday, she met him at the door with a chaste side-hug and showed him around most of the new place before walking him out to the patio where her part-time chef had laid out a wonderful spread for them. "I saw your Lancôme campaign at the mall," Thad said, digging into the salad. "It's stunning."

"Thank you! I had so much fun doing that. My agent at Gersh and Roland have been talking to see where they can work other brand ambassadorships in. There's a tentative thing with Saint John–I love Saint John–that we'll know more for sure about in a few months. If all goes well, I'll be doing a special campaign with them. It never even occurred to me that working with brands could cut time off the five-year plan."

"The plan!" He cried throwing up his hands, making her laugh. "How's that going?"

"I think well. Lots of things in the works, but it seems like everything hinges on one thing or another. You know."

"And then you're out of LA for good."

She made a sound against her teeth. "Actually, I've kind of fallen in love with LA. Well, with the surrounding areas. Not LA itself. But I love this house. I love the view. I love that I'm not far from the beach. I'll probably stay here a while."

"Really?"

"Yeah. How about you? Headed back to Prague anytime soon?"

"Fuck no! No, if I could, I'd be back in Queensland in a heartbeat, but I can't uproot the girls at this point. I guess I've got a fifteen-year plan? I'll stay out here and work until the kids are grown, then maybe go back home? It's hard enough as it is. For now, I've got a beach in my backyard, so I can't complain too much."

He talked about surfing while she listened, half wondering if she would ever learn to cook as well as this chef she'd hired. Everything he put together was amazing, and she was starving all the time now. She briefly considered just pulling the roasted vegetable and goat cheese with pine nuts serving dish right in front of her and eating directly out of it, but served herself another helping onto her one plate instead.

She asked about the sitcom and Thad explained that the network was looking at going a different direction with the line-up, and he thought they would get canceled when their two-season extension was up. He was already in talks for a lead role in a medical drama and he thought he might like that as a change. "Still regular hours," he said. "But at a different pace."

"You'd be great as a doctor. You have caring eyes," Jill told him, watching him take the last of the vegetables. She was going to ask the chef to make a lot more of that. "You come across on screen as very warm."

"It'd be a nice change." He was watching her like she'd watched the last squash land in his plate. "You alright?"

"Perfect! Never better."

He tilted his head. "Are you seeing anyone?"

That made her laugh, somewhat ruefully. "No. Just that little last hurrah with Kline. I was trying to, oh, I don't know what I was trying to do. Focus on work."

"Oh," he said, quickly taking a drink of the mint water Jill had served along with the chardonnay.

"I blame you. You broke my heart a little." She chided him gently, but patted his hand before reaching for the breadbasket. "But honestly, it was for the best–him and me. I got to end things on my terms finally. Closure and all that." She pulled out a breadstick and broke it in half, taking a bite and swallowing it before going on. "So, I'm just focused on me for the next little while. You?"

"Divorce is final, as I told you," he said, taking a breadstick for himself. He joked, "So, I guess I'm ready to get married again."

"Ha! Well, I know a great place in Vegas."

"I'm never going to live that down, am I?"

"No. Never."

They chatted amiably for a while, but he was watching her in a way that was starting to make her feel self-conscious, so she got up and went for the crème brûlée the chef had left for them in the sub-zero. "Dessert?" She asked him, brandishing the bowl topped with fresh raspberries.

"Definitely."

Rather than bother with new dishes, she simply brought two spoons to the table and they went to work sharing, until both of them were chasing around the dregs. "I need his name," Thad groaned with his last bite.

"I'll get you all his information. He's amazing."

"How about you? Hm?"

"Me?"

"Is there anything you want to tell me?"

"I– No?"

"You know, I've had this conversation before. I've been told this same thing before. I'm not going to freak out."

Jill said haltingly, "That a chef is fantastic?"

"That I've gotten someone pregnant."

She felt her mouth drop open. "What? No!" She'd dressed so carefully in flared jeans and an off-the-shoulder peasant blouse that Kim and all the pictures they took of every outfit assured her that her just-noticeable bump was well hidden. She'd avoided the nursery area on their tour, and she'd even pretended to sip at her wine so he wouldn't suspect.

"I have six kids. Six. Am I having seven? Or eight? I make twins, apparently. I know what pregnant looks like."

"I–" she faltered. "I'm not–"

"Aren't you? The glow? The appetite? The–sorry to say, but I certainly couldn't help but notice–the boobs?"

That made her laugh, and then she sat back into her chair and sighed. "It's not yours. You didn't get me pregnant. Closure with Kline got me pregnant. And please don't say anything. I'm still not sure I'm past the safety point with the baby, so I'm not telling anyone who doesn't need to know."

"Kline?" His face was doing something confusing.

"Yes. I'm positive. It was– It's not the ideal situation, but we're friends and he's okay with it, and I'm actually very happy about it. I've always wanted kids, you know? And maybe this isn't how I thought I'd have one, but there are worse things than getting knocked up by someone you like, and someone you know is a good parent to his other child." She was talking fast. "I haven't even told Rhiannon. I'm not sure how I'm going to tell Rhiannon. August doesn't know. Only Kline and my management. And my stylist. And my chef. Oh, and I guess the doctor. And now you. Just people I trust."

Thad had gone still, and Jill's heart started pounding in her ears. It was suddenly very important that he know she hadn't chosen Kline over him. "Thad," she said, leaning forward and grabbing one of his hands in both of hers. "Thad, it was after the voicemail. I swear. I didn't have any plans to see anyone but maybe you when you got home, and if the voicemail hadn't happened, neither would Kline. I swear. You never called back even after the press cleared it all up and I'd talked to Rhi. I found out before we got it all worked out, and…" Her voice trailed off. "I just hoped we could be friends at least. I really enjoyed your company so much, and I just hoped…does this change things?"

She hadn't planned on this conversation. She'd just wanted to see him. She had missed him and his happy presence, and now she was stricken by the thought that this might be more than he would be up to. She swallowed hard and slowly withdrew her hands back into her lap, the lizard part of her brain wondering if he was going to finish the half of the breadstick he'd put down and never picked back up.

"I think," he started to say, pulling his own hands into his lap. "You know, this is the first time someone's told me that I didn't knock them up. When I got over here and I saw you, sorry Beauty, I knew as soon as I saw you. I thought you were gearing up to tell me. I was gearing up to be ready to do the right thing."

"What's that mean?"

"Propose. Make an honest woman of you."

Jill frowned, heat creeping into her face. "I'll tell you the same thing I told Kline. I don't want someone to marry me because they feel like they have to, and I'm not marrying someone just because my birth control failed." She crossed her arms. "I'm not some broke teenager who can't afford a baby. I'm plenty well-positioned to give this baby a very good life completely by myself."

"I didn't mean to insult you! I mean, I wasn't going to be upset if it was me. This whole time we've been sitting here, I've been thinking what it would be like. I've been picturing it."

"Well, you don't have to. It isn't yours." She was worried she might cry, so she snatched up his breadstick and stuffed a quarter of it into her mouth. God, it was good.

Half his mouth quirked up. "I'm kind of sad it's not. I wouldn't mind being stuck with you. Fuck Kline's luck."

Jill chewed and swallowed, then stuffed the rest of the

bread in her mouth to keep from speaking, so he went on, reaching over for her glass of wine and taking a deep drink of it. "On the way here, I was trying to figure out how to ask if you wanted to start things up again. Date. See each other. See where it went because I really think it was headed in the right direction before Prague drowned my brain. I've had time to sort myself out now and I wanted to take you out properly.

"So, when I saw you're up the stick, I thought I had my way in. Now, I see I don't have my foot in the door like I thought I did."

"If it weren't for this, I would absolutely start things up again," Jill finally said, patting her stomach.

"But this stops you?"

"Doesn't it stop you? I'm pregnant with someone else's baby. With Kline's baby."

"I've got six kids by two different women," Thad said with a shrug. "It's not like I'm coming into this with a clean slate. Besides, I've been doing my own head in trying to figure out how to get you back. I'm not going to miss a shot just because, as you say, your birth control failed. If you start things up with me, I come with six children and two very involved ex-wives. I can't hardly mind if you come with a baby and one of my friends. Anyway, I like babies. I'm a pro at nappies!"

She started to smile, and he asked, "How far along?"

"Just barely five months. If I can make it to six, I think everything will be okay."

"Morning sickness?"

"Just getting better now."

"Starving all the time?"

"All the time. All the damned time."

"Em and Jess were always hungry."

"I am always hungry. I was so mad when you got the last of the squash."

"I saw it on your face! Always hungry." He nodded, then grinned impishly. "And horny?"

She laughed outright and he did, too. Then she made a face.

"All the time."

"I could help with that."

"Could you?"

"If you'd like."

She laughed again, but then stood up and tossed her napkin aside. "Yes, please. Come on. I'll show you the bedroom."

The lead-up to the Oscars was a non-stop parade of fashion, with Jill's waistlines expanding as her necklines dipped lower and lower. The media speculation was frenzied every time she took the red carpet with Kline. Along with presenting at the Grammys, Jill was Kline's arm candy for his win at the BAFTAs, and then she was a one-woman cheering section for two men as Knight and Simon Says swept their categories at the SAG Awards. At each event, Jill stood more self-assured and delighted as she shared the secret to her glow.

"I have the most fabulous stylist, Kim Sinclair. I stole her from Kline, and he hasn't quite forgiven me, but whenever he grumbles about it, I just do a spin for him. He can't argue with these results."

When they hit the carpet for the Academy Awards, she and her style team shifted gears, and she walked the photo line in a daring, backless, skin-tight sheath of black jersey that left no doubt about their future as a family. With Kline's protective arm around her as the photographers went wild trying to capture her bump, Jill beamed into the flashbulbs. They posed together, him with one arm around her shoulders, and one hand splayed wide over her belly, kissing for the cameras, then waved off all interviews until after Kline had taken possession of his Best Actor award.

They had made a triumphant pass through the after parties together, each accepting congratulations and well wishes until they finally pulled themselves away in the wee hours of the morning, Kline drunk and happy, and Jill just happy.

The limo dropped her home first, and she went inside to

find Thad waiting up for her with green tea and ice cream, her current favorite combination.

"Hi," she cooed. "He won."

"I saw," Thad smiled, pulling out a chair at the dining table for her. "You looked amazing in every shot they caught of you."

"You're sweet," she said, tilting her head up for a kiss.

"I am," he agreed.

When she was halfway through her second scoop of vanilla bean, Thad tapped his finger on a blue folder she'd overlooked, and he slid it across the table to her. "I have something for you."

"What is it?"

"It's not the south of France," Thad said as she flipped open the folder. "And it's not Queensland. But it is a working vineyard, and it comes with multiple properties and goats. You said you liked goats. It's in Santa Barbara, and when I showed it to Kline, he fell in love with it."

"Kline?"

Thad shrugged. "I had to ask for his blessing, and I knew you wouldn't make any moves that would separate him from his baby."

"What?"

"I have something else."

Jill dropped the spoon she was holding as Thad slid out of his chair and onto one knee. "I love you, Jill," he said. "I want to marry you. I want to be your family and I want you to be mine. I want to fill up an estate on a vineyard with you and watch you smash grapes and dress goats in pajamas and have dogs and dinner parties with friends who can come and hide out from the spotlight with us.

"I want to have a big, loud, messy life with you, and me, and my girls, and yours and Kline's baby, and Jack, and Kline and whoever he ends up with—because I know you promised him all the access he wants to his kid, so he's our family forever, too. I want this chaos with you because it sounds like heaven to me.

"Will you marry me?"

Her eyes were brimming, and her heart was overflowing. "Are you proposing to me with real estate?"

"Oh! And a ring! I have a ring!" He fumbled slightly before producing a ring box from Cartier, opening it to reveal a blood-red ruby in a vintage setting. "Will you marry me?"

"Yes," she breathed, then said again firmly, "Yes! Yes!" And she held out her hand, watching as he slid the ring onto her finger.

Kline Scott

Kline sat with Roland at his kitchen island, flipping through pages in a magazine. French doors were open wide, and a sweet-scented breeze wafted through the massive kitchen overlooking the southern half of the Santa Barbara vineyard he was recently calling home. "I can't believe they paid us for this," he said, looking down at the headline. "Devil's Family."

"After a whirlwind romance on the set of their blockbuster film, Devil's Party, Oscar winner, Kline Scott and Tony winner Jill Parker welcomed a son together. Though the couple are no longer romantically involved, (Parker is currently romancing lucky Simon Says star, Thad James) they plan to co-parent. Rounding out the unusual family unit are Rhiannon Charles, Scott's former flame, and August Hall who was previously linked to Parker, as godparents to the new baby.

"I've loved Kline my whole life," Parker told People in an exclusive interview. "And I feel so fortunate that I get to share our son with him. It's not your typical arrangement, but I feel so blessed to be on this journey with someone who is truly one of my best friends. We don't have to be together romantically to raise our son with love and devotion. Kline's an amazing father to Jack (Scott's son from his first marriage) and he'll be an amazing father to Parker."

The baby boy, named Parker Davis Scott, arrived just in time to help his parents celebrate the box office success of Devil's Party, which enjoyed a record-breaking first weekend and steamed up the movie screens at number one for two months.

Kline Scott said, "Parker's the perfect souvenir from our time on this film. I'm so proud of the work Jilly and I did, and very proud of us as people and parents to this wonderful little guy. However we do this awards season, I feel like I've won the biggest honor already."

Older pictures of Kline and Jill with Jack from Disneyland were inset on the exclusive photos of them holding the new baby together. More gushy drivel filled the space around four other exclusive photos on two more pages, and Kline scanned them, before pushing the magazine aside. "Well, that's his college paid for anyway," he said.

"And then some! Hell," Roland laughed. "That commission is my kid's college paid for."

"Glad to know you're overpaid," Kline grunted, waving Jill and Thad and the stroller they pushed inside through a pair of doors. "Let's talk about my next project. Diapers aren't cheap."

"Your next job is to win back-to-back awards for Knight and Lone Star."

"And then for Devil's Party," Jill said, kissing him on the cheek when he moved to give her a hug.

"And then I'll be tied with Hanks. What are the odds I can pull out four in a row?"

"Honestly? If anyone can, it's you."

Roland laughed, "You've got the work ethic for it."

Kline was lifting the baby from stroller, after greeting Thad, who had gone to help himself to the fridge when Clara, Kim, and Delia arrived from another direction. Jack was riding piggyback on Delia, and he gave a happy shout when he saw his little brother. "Parkour! Parkour!"

"I told you," Thad said over his shoulder.

"Someone was going to make fun of his name no matter what we called him," Jill huffed. "Parker is a fine name."

"And Parkour is a fine nickname. Isn't it?" Kline gave the baby's cheeks loud, smacking kisses. "It sounds athletic."

"It sounds like–"

"Your name is Thaddaeus," Kline reminded. "You have a child named Carraway."

"It's a family name!"

"So is Parker!" Jill was laughing. "Or have you forgotten?"

"I'm working on changing that. Or have you forgotten?"

Roland interrupted the good-natured ribbing. "No one's forgotten anything. We're just trying to line it all up for maximum press potential. Anyway, a long engagement's not going to hurt your reputation one bit."

Kline looked around smiling. It wasn't your typical arrangement. It looked nothing like a normal family, and that was something a judge was about to take a long, hard look at in the next few weeks as his long-dragged-out custody case with Nina came to a close, but he had a good feeling about it.

Jack had monkeyed himself over to Thad's broad shoulders and was already talking his ear off about a video game. Jill and Clara were crowded around Kim's laptop, talking about how the stylist was going to create a Scott-Parker-James branded look for the set of them. Delia was setting out lunch for Jack. Roland had answered a phone call and was waving them all off as he walked into the next room for quiet. It wasn't an average family, but it was his family, and in that moment, he realized it was the happiest he'd ever been, living what amounted to a sitcom life.

"You," he said to the baby in his arms, "are one lucky little devil."

He realized Jill was smiling over her shoulder at him, and his stomach flipped, but this time it was because he couldn't believe his own luck.

The End

About the Author

Nicole Lane has loved romance novels since she was old enough to sneak them from her grandmother's well stocked shelves. She grew up reading the soaring sagas of Judith Krantz, Danielle Steel, and Jackie Collins, sharing dog-eared paperbacks and giggling with girlfriends over all the more instructional passages. She is living her very own, uneventful, happily-ever-after in a sea of sweat socks and Matchbox cars in Dallas, Texas.